STRANDS OF GOLD is an unforgettable
treasure...one for the keeper shelf!"

—*Literary Times*

A DANGEROUS EMBRACE

A growl rumbling deep in his chest, he pulled her closer,
pressing her young, yielding form tightly to his. And, as she
shifted position slightly, her flat belly brushed innocently
over his groin. In the reflexive response of a passionately
virile man, Dane's sex hardened, thrusting tautly against his
breeches.

Arien must have felt the sudden change in him. She went
very still, then placed her hands on his chest and began to
push him away.

"Please, m'lord," she cried softly, desperation in her voice.
"Pray, let me go."

Though he heard her words and knew it was the right and
honorable thing to do, something in Dane rebelled against
releasing Arien. It was almost as if he feared that to free her
now was to lose her forever. He dared not sever the fragile
bonds that had begun to spin between them. Strands of gold
they were, precious and rare, to be carefully guarded lest
they fray and then disintegrate.

Strands of Gold

KATHLEEN MORGAN

LOVE SPELL BOOKS ◆ NEW YORK CITY

150101 ①

LOVE SPELL®

December 1997

Published by

Dorchester Publishing Co., Inc.
276 Fifth Avenue
New York, NY 10001

Copyright © 1997 by Kathleen Morgan

ISBN 0-505-52239-X

Printed in the United States of America.

To Sean, my dragon heart, my sweet boy, my son.
I promise I won't forget about you ever.
Not even when I'm a hundred.

We are not permitted to choose the frame of our destiny.
But what we put into it is ours.
—Dag Hammarskjold, *Markings*

Strands of Gold

Chapter One

"By all that is holy! I don't have a good feeling about this, Phelan. Not a good feeling at all."

Dane Haversin shot his cousin, Lord Phelan Guilford, an exasperated look as they rode along, a small entourage of attendants trailing in their wake. "With every triennial gathering, the king's devious machinations and divisive plottings increase. Each time, it becomes more difficult to regroup the nobles and regain the union we so desperately need."

With a leather-gauntleted hand, he paused to brush aside a recalcitrant lock of hair from his forehead. "I swear, Phelan. If the other lords succumb to Cronan's self-serving schemes just one more time . . ."

" 'Tis most disheartening," his cousin agreed, his pale blond hair fluttering gently in the late-afternoon breeze. "You've striven mightily to unite the nobles all these years. Yet, though much good has been accomplished in the process, the king appears equally intent on ensuring you'll never acquire lasting power or success in Greystone. You've been wise to block his efforts to annex your lands. If not, he'd have already swallowed up Haversin along with all the rest."

At the reminder of the king's last attempt to gain control of his lands, memories clutched at Dane, twisting his heart. He fought to regain control, but, for a long moment, myriad emotions—from gut-wrenching pain to white-hot anger—held him in thrall. Then, with a wild, fierce effort, Dane swept them all aside. He turned, retreating to the present—the only reality he could bear.

"Naught will stop Cronan Talamontes in his quest for total power," Dane said with a growl. " 'Tis the hard fact of the matter, and the true motive for his triennial gatherings. The old goat but uses them as pretense to reevaluate his nobles' loyalty. Mark my words, Phelan. This Triennial will be no different from the rest."

Aye, Dane thought bitterly, at the king's instigation old friends would betray each other, new alliances would be formed, and fortunes would be made and lost. Then, after a week of meetings interspersed with banquets frequently ending in drunken brawls, the nobles would depart to their holdings, once more at odds, once more suspicious of each other, all coalitions the king deemed threatening weakened, if not destroyed.

"He's naught but a viperous worm, an inhuman wretch," his cousin muttered. "Indeed, if not for your generosity since he raised all our taxes, I'd have long ago surrendered Guilford holdings along with Dunbarton Castle in payment."

"Aye." Dane cast a quick look over his shoulder. Their retainers rode along, out of earshot of their conversation. "Cronan would be livid if he knew

I was secretly subsidizing your taxes. And the sad truth of the matter is, I don't know how much longer Haversin's mines can support both of us. If another rich vein of ore isn't found soon . . ."

"You've done more than most men ever would. Though the rest of us may fall, the king will never bring *you* to your knees."

" 'Tisn't just for myself that I attempt to block the king at every turn," Dane protested, uncomfortable with his cousin's undisguised admiration, "though I know Cronan has always viewed me as the greatest threat to his throne. I but wish to unite the realm in peace and prosperity, to permit all to live how and where they may. Simple desires, to be sure, yet desires," he added caustically, "the king appears determined to oppose."

"He rules most effectively in animosity and strife. A weak ruler is always best served when his nobles cannot unite against him. 'Tis also why I caution you to play the loyal subject this next week. Assuage his concerns with a ready smile and a mild reply. You're in his territory now."

"Come now, cousin," Dane chided with a sardonic arch of his brow. "Are you implying the other lords wouldn't stand with me, if it came to a confrontation with the king?"

Phelan gave a hoot of laughter. "You know that answer as well as I. Committed as many of them are to improving the plight of our people, something happens each Triennial to change them. 'Tis almost as if . . . as if they've fallen under some strange, debilitating spell."

"Your suspicions aren't as far-fetched as you might imagine." Anger filled Dane anew. "The king's two daughters are members of those vile Moondancers." He grimaced and shook his head.

" 'Tis said they dance naked beneath the light of the full moon, using their evil magic to capture the energy of that orb's light, spinning spells to ensorcel the hearts and minds of the people. 'Tis also said those two witch princesses use the king to their own purposes. 'Tisn't too hard to imagine them bespelling us into renewed complacency each Triennial."

Overhead, a raven cawed, then dipped low and disappeared behind a thick stand of birch and alder. "By the Mother!" Phelan blanched and made a quick, furtive warding sign. "It sickens me even to consider such a possibility."

"Aye, but it must be considered nonetheless." At seventeen, Dane thought grimly, Phelan was still young, but it was past time he faced what lay ahead. "Though I've little stomach for overthrowing the king, he must be made to rule Greystone with a more generous and benevolent hand. If that fails, he must be toppled from power. We've no other choice, Phelan, and little time left, either."

"But how can we fight the powers of magic?" The younger man sighed. " 'Tis impossible!"

"Impossible?" Dane gave a scornful laugh. "Naught is impossible. And I've yet a score to settle with those demon's spawn at any rate. I've not forgotten that it was a Moondancer who placed the curse that killed my wife and unborn child."

Phelan cast Dane a worried glance. "Pray, have a care, cousin. That wound of yours has festered these three years since the last Triennial. And a man in such unremitting pain risks making foolhardy, if not fatal, decisions."

And don't you think I know that? Dane silently raged, tears unexpectedly clouding his eyes. To

14

spare himself the humiliation of his cousin seeing his uncharacteristic display of weakness, Dane pretended sudden interest in the fields of oats and wheat glimmering like burnished gold in the late-summer sun.

'Tis why I've bided my time, he thought, while seeking the perfect solution to my dilemma—a dilemma forced on me by the king when he endeavored to bring me to heel after the last Triennial. Yet, though I've considered and cast aside myriad plans, one rises repeatedly to the forefront. And that plan is to strike at the heart of the Talamontes—at the king's two daughters.

But to see that vile deed through to completion . . . Dane shuddered at the consideration. No matter how the deaths of his wife and child cried out for retribution, Dane didn't know if he'd the heart to cold-bloodedly kill other human beings.

His anguished gaze lifted to the distant hills. There, stroked with gold fire in the light of the setting sun, perched a magnificent, multiturreted castle. Constructed from the famed gray stone mined in the surrounding hills, Castle Talamontes loomed over the surrounding farms and villages like some beast of prey, ever vigilant, eternally ravenous, awaiting the first opportunity to strike. And strike it did, often enough to wound and debilitate, but never kill, until the weakened, demoralized land and people cried out for surcease—or death.

That was why, in the end, Dane had come to view the destruction of the king through his daughters as the only solution to Greystone's travails. Even if the king was yet his own man, Dane doubted he'd ever change. While his daughters remained members of that evil sisterhood, Cronan

15

possessed access to unearthly powers that common men had no hope of besting. Even worse, if his two Moondancer daughters truly sought to augment their powers through him, the situation was more dire still. Yet to fight evil with evil, to usurp the rightful ruler and murder his only children . . .

Such an act would destroy him, Dane knew, if not in body then most certainly in soul. It was a price, though, he was willing to pay. There was naught left of happiness in this life, at any rate. The Moondancer witch had cursed him and his legitimate heirs until the end of time. The Haversin line was doomed to extinction.

"I-I didn't mean to cause you further distress, cousin."

From somewhere far away Dane heard Phelan's words, heard his sincere concern and regret, and knew that before he could heal the ills of a kingdom gone awry, he must first confront and overcome his own demons. With a mighty effort, Dane turned, forcing a taut smile. "You but spoke the truth, and your words bear serious consideration." He swung back to the road ahead, his gaze riveting on the castle growing ever nearer.

Viewing it, a searing anguish engulfed him. By the Mother, Dane thought, I cannot bear to enter that place just now. In this state, I'll indeed make foolhardy, if not fatal, decisions. Decisions that will affect more than just myself.

Abruptly, he reined in his horse. The entourage immediately halted behind him.

Phelan pulled up, too. Turning in his saddle, he glanced back at Dane, a quizzical expression lifting his finely molded lips. "What ails you, cousin? Even now the sun dips toward the mountains.

'Twill be nightfall in another few hours. We must gain the castle, or risk losing our way in the dark."

"Go on without me." Dane motioned toward the stone-shrouded fortress. "I'll join you later."

"And what shall I tell the king, when I arrive without you?"

A hard, implacable resolve filled Dane. From the startled look in his cousin's eyes, he knew his barely contained rage had been apparent in his expression. Regret filled him, then died in the renewed need to find the answers he so desperately sought. Answers that would ease, at last, the sordid, shameful conundrum that had become his existence.

"Tell him," Dane said between clenched teeth, sensing in some ineffable way that he was indeed being called to the solitude of the ancient hills, "I but go to unravel the twisted strands of my destiny. And that, when all is set aright, I'll again seek out the company of men."

From the carved stone balcony overlooking the castle's huge reception area, Princess Arien Talamontes gazed briefly down at the frenzied chaos of servants milling below, then heaved a great sigh and shook her head.

"Weary of it all, are you?" the ebony-haired woman standing beside her asked with a low, throaty chuckle. "And these years past I imagined that you reveled in the power you gained by overseeing the triennial gathering. 'Twas the reason you so abruptly assumed the position when you were but fifteen, was it not?"

Well aware her older sister was baiting her, Arien clamped down on an irritated retort. "Nay, Edana. I saw how great an undertaking the Triennial was and but wished to help you," she said instead, forcing herself to modulate her tones in a manner befitting a woman of breeding.

"As well you should," Edana purred, lowering her arms to lean languidly on the marble banister. "The demands of my office leave me little time to carry such additional burdens."

"Aye, 'tis well understood. 'Tis just that all this pomp and circumstance seems but a thin screen for . . ." With yet another sigh, Arien let the words die. As much as she might wish it otherwise, her sister would never understand her misgivings, much less sympathize with them.

Edana, after all, was crown princess and heir to the throne. She was twelve years older than Arien, and it seemed as if a lifetime of experience and differing expectations already separated them.

Below them, serving maids, dressed in snowy white caps and billowing aprons tied over their simple, homespun gowns, bustled to and fro. Some were laden with linen to make up the myriad beds in the guest bedchambers. Others carried baskets overflowing with long, thick carrots, plump turnips, fat heads of cabbage, and dirt-encrusted potatoes all freshly gathered from the castle gardens—and all intended for the cook pots simmering in the cavernous underground kitchen.

"I must get down to confer with Cook." Reminded of yet another area of the castle requiring her supervision, Arien rehooked the silk braid knot fastening the high-necked, shimmering purple-and-black gown she'd temporarily loosened in the late-afternoon heat. "Our remaining guests

18

will be arriving soon. I'd wager they'll be ravenous and expecting a hearty supper."

"Aye, get along with you then. 'Tis a sad waste of your magical powers, though," Edana offered in snide response. "You could have set the entire castle aright with but a few spells, if you'd had a mind to do it."

Arien smiled good-humoredly. "Aye, if I'd had a mind to do it." She'd heard that statement many times before. Malicious words and cutting comments were as far as Edana ever went, though. The full burden of responsibility for the triennial preparations always fell on Arien's shoulders. Yet, as with the day-to-day household duties she also oversaw, it was Edana, the favorite, who seemed to garner all the credit.

"Well, you know I cannot squander my special talents on trivial pursuits such as banquets and other household preparations." Haughtily, Edana gestured to the servants scurrying below. "Besides, your gentler form of magic is far more suited to such things than mine will ever be."

You mean, rather, Arien thought, that your magic has become all but ineffective in the cause of good. That you chose the easier course years ago in turning to the dark side, and now 'tis too late to regain what you so recklessly forswore.

"There's truth in your words," Arien said instead. "But, I, too, choose not to squander my magic whenever normal ways will suffice instead. Father doesn't seem to mind how the preparations are accomplished, just as long as they're accomplished."

Edana smiled secretively and nodded in agreement. "Indeed, Father has far more important issues at hand than how and when you choose to

19

use your pitiful form of magic." She leaned toward Arien, a conspiratorial smile on her scarlet-stained lips. "I'll share a little secret with you. Even now, he's busy arranging to wed me to a very powerful nobleman. An arrangement that should assure, once and for all, the future of our royal house and the kingdom."

Eyes wide, Arien turned to her sister. As darkly beautiful and seductive as Edana was, as politically advantageous as her eventual assumption of the throne might be, no Moondancer was permitted to lie with a man. Forever vowed to remain chaste in service to the people and the land, Moondancers lived among others, yet were never truly a part of them. But now Edana and her followers had turned to a darker kind of magic, creating an illegal sect called the Ravens. . . .

Revulsion rippled through Arien. If the horrible rumors were true, there was great danger for any man who married Edana. And mayhap great danger for the Moondancers, who, at long last, ruled as the supreme sorcerers in the land.

"I understand Father's need to assure our succession to the throne," Arien began carefully, seeking to further draw out her sister. "But, considering our sacred vows as Moondancers—"

"Dispensations can be made, our high priestess has assured me, in special cases such as mine." With a dismissive wave of her hand, Edana brushed aside the protest. "One of us, sooner or later, would have been expected to produce an heir to the throne. As crown princess, I feel that duty is rightfully mine.

"Besides, the union will serve many purposes, as political marriages always do. This man's wealth and stature among the other nobles will strengthen our position immeasurably. His joining with the royal house will also force him, by law, to swear complete fealty to us. And, after he impregnates me and I safely deliver an heir, well," she added with a careless shrug, "he'll then be my plaything to use as I deem fit, until I need him no more."

Somehow, rather than reassuring her, Edana's words confirmed Arien's growing fears: fears the tales were indeed true, that Ravens secretly bedded men to enhance their already dark sorcery, tapping into the masculine side of magic otherwise denied them. Bedded them until they'd taken all they needed—and then sacrificed their lovers in a bloody, brutal ceremony to honor the moon goddess.

"Does this mysterious nobleman have a name?" Arien forced herself to ask casually, knowing it was the best tack to take if she hoped to learn the truth. Edana gloried in tantalizing her with interesting bits of information, and then, when Arien rose to the bait, quickly tired of the game without revealing aught. This was one time, however, when the information could have shattering consequences, and not just for the hapless man in question.

Edana's dark brown eyes sparkled with triumph. "Ah, I see I've finally snared your interest with something other than insipid good deeds and futile self-sacrifice in the service of others. Why is that, sister dear?"

At Edana's mocking tone, Arien's face flushed with anger. Once again, she means to provoke me, she thought. This time, though, I dare not give her the satisfaction, nor reveal my suspicions.

She turned to gaze down into the reception area. "No particular reason," Arien said with an offhand shrug. "I but wished to know which lucky man will soon be my brother-in-law."

"Do you now?" Edana chuckled softly. "Well, you'll learn his name soon enough. In the meanwhile, watch the nobles closely in this next week, and see if you can fathom the man's identity. No fair, though, using one of your tedious little spells to discern the truth. You wouldn't want to squander your talent, after all, when normal ways would suffice."

"Nay, I wouldn't." Arien gripped the balcony railing until her knuckles turned white. "Besides, 'twill not be so difficult. A woman in love is hard to miss."

"Did I say I was in love?"

Twirling a lustrous lock around a slender finger, Edana smirked. Though, for a change, she was wearing the Moondancer *luna* and was garbed in the same floor-length, modest robes as her sister, Edana's vanity precluded covering her glorious mane with the traditional long, gauzy veil. Arien wondered why Dorianne, their high priestess, hadn't taken her to task long ago.

"Nay, sister dear, 'tis as I said before. I but take a man who will best serve both Father's and my purposes. Ultimately," Edana added with a brittle, knowing smile, "I intend to be both queen of Greystone *and* the entire assembly of Moondancers, you know?"

" 'Twill take more than a noble marriage to gain you supremacy over the Assembly," Arien said. By the Mother, it was as she suspected. Edana must be very sure of herself to reveal such a secret. "Especially," she added, "if you persist in dabbling with the Ravens."

Edana stopped fiddling with her hair, and wheeled to confront her sister. A cold, hard light gleamed in her eyes. "Though the Ravens are yet a small, handpicked band, they're growing in size and strength with each passing day. 'Twould be the wisest course for you to face the truth and join us while you may."

"The Ravens are renegades, committed to the foulest form of dark magic!" After multiple attempts to convince Edana otherwise in the past years, Arien knew her words would most likely fall on deaf ears. Still, for the sake of the common blood they shared, she would never give up trying. "They care for naught but power, even if it requires selling their souls to the demon. Have a care, sister. The wisest course for you is to face that truth, and leave them while you may."

Rage flashed in Edana's eyes. "You'd like that, wouldn't you?" she snarled. "Then you'd have it all. 'Twould assure your rise to the Moondancer supremacy, once old Dorianne passes. 'Twould give you a power barely less than mine, when I become queen. You, who've never once had to struggle or strain for any magical ability you wished to acquire."

"Mayhap my admitted ease has more to do with the kind of magic I use—and my respect for it—than with any special talent. Doing good *should* come more readily than causing harm."

The succession of the Moondancer supremacy was a touchy subject with Edana. It was well known that Arien was Dorianne's choice, and the high priestess almost always designated her own successor. Still, it was a dubious victory over her sister, especially since Arien wasn't all that certain she wished to be high priestess. Her only hope was that her succession would counter Edana's future and potentially despotic reign as Queen of Greystone.

Arien laid a hand on her sister's arm. " 'Tisn't too late to change, Edana. Come back to the Assembly and make atonement. Then I and the others will gladly teach you the better way."

"The better way? And what purpose would that serve?" Edana threw off Arien's hand as if it were some foul, contemptible thing. "All 'twould do would be to enable you to lord it over me at last, as you lead your poor, misguided sister back down the path of righteousness. Well, I won't have it. *I* am the eldest and heir, not you. And I will have it all. Do you hear me, Arien? All!"

In a swirl of lustrous black-and-purple robes, Edana stalked away, leaving Arien to stand there staring after her.

"She's a twisted, bitter woman," said a soft voice behind Arien, "and beyond any hope o' redemption."

Arien wheeled. Onora, her lady-in-waiting and trusted friend, stood there. Quashing a savage sense of frustration over Edana's stubborn refusal to turn from evil, Arien focused her attention instead on the pleasingly plump young woman who was barely two years older than she. "And, pray, how long have you been eavesdropping on us?"

Onora smiled and shook her head. "Have no fear, m'lady. I just now walked up. I cannot tolerate that woman's presence any longer than I must."

At her servant's caustic remark, the tension ebbed from Arien. "You really should have a care, Onora, in what you say about Edana," she cautioned with a giggle. "If the wrong person should ever overhear—"

"And to whom else would I say such things but to ye, m'lady?" Onora grinned unrepentantly, the expression on her plain, freckled face endearing and sincere. "I'm no fool. Though I cannot help thinking yer father has been sadly misled where his eldest is concerned, I know the situation here for what 'tis."

Arien smiled sadly. "Aye, and a dismal one it has become, ever since Edana made her choice for the Ravens. Sometimes I wonder if she hasn't woven one of her dark spells to compel Father into the course he has taken of late."

"Mayhap," Onora agreed grudgingly. "But then again, I think the king lost his way long ago, when yer mother died."

At the mention of her beloved mother, now dead these past eighteen years, sadness swamped Arien. She knew the rumors surrounding her mother's strange death as well as Onora did. The queen had just given birth to her second daughter, and appeared to be doing well. Then, unexpectedly, she'd died. Some said the king had killed her in a fit of rage over her bearing him yet another girl child. Some said it was the result of witchcraft. Whatever the cause, to this day, the truth had yet to be discovered.

"You came here for a purpose, did you not?" Arien prompted. "Speak it now. I must be off to see what further help Cook needs in the kitchen."

At the blunt demand, Onora's smile faded. "Aye, that I did. 'Tis a boon I must ask o' ye."

"And that boon is?"

As if finding sudden interest in the intricate pattern created by the undulating, vermilion swirls in the dove gray slabs of marble, the lady-in-waiting's glance dropped to the floor. "I ask permission to leave the castle this eve just before sunset." Onora lifted her gaze back to Arien's. " 'Twill not take more than an hour's time. I swear it, m'lady."

"But sunset is when I'll need you to assist me in dressing for the banquet. Can't this little excursion wait until the morrow?"

"Nay, m'lady, it cannot." A decidedly uncomfortable expression settled over the red-haired woman's face. "Ye see, Tomas and I visited the Stone o' the Little Men yestereve to leave a gold coin and a drawing o' the wedding rings we wished the dwarf to make for us, and I dare not risk someone else coming by this eve and stealing our rings." She managed a wan smile. " 'Tis said wedding rings made by a dwarf confer the promise o' a happy, fruitful marriage to the rings' owners. And Tomas and I . . . well, we want to begin our wedded life with all chance o' happiness and success."

Arien frowned. Though she'd never met one herself, she'd heard all the legends about dwarves. They were said to be the masters of certain magical artifices, especially the working of stone and metal to fashion magical weapons, tools, jewels, and ornaments. The elusive, rather shy creatures—who dared not come out above ground during the day for fear of being turned to stone by the sunlight—were also purported to possess unusual knowledge and foresight.

But those powerful attributes, in combination with their dark, earth magic, had also set the misshapen little creatures frequently at odds with their closest human counterparts—the Moondancers. Only in this past century had the sister-hood finally managed to assert their higher, purer power over the dwarves.

" 'Tis dangerous," Arien murmured, "venturing out at night to visit a dwarf's dwelling place. If you must go, take Tomas. I give him leave to be gone for an hour as well."

"He cannot, m'lady. The head stablemaster is ill, and three o' yer father's prize mares are due to foal at any time. After the headmaster, Tomas is the next most experienced stable man."

With a wry grimace, Arien digested that unexpected bit of information, then expelled a long, weary breath. "Well, we both know how dearly my father values his horses. 'Twould indeed be foolhardy to risk even one of his prize mares." Quickly, she considered several other options, discarding all but the final one. " 'Twould be equally foolhardy, however, for you to seek out the rings on your own. I could mayhap send one of the castle guards with you, but I must confess to a certain curiosity about encountering a dwarf."

Onora's eyes widened. "But surely, m'lady, ye don't mean—" In her apparent shock, further words momentarily escaped the maidservant. "Surely," she said finally, recovering command of herself, "ye don't mean to accompany me?"

"Indeed, and why not?" Arien cocked her head, her long, fat braid of ebony hair tumbling from beneath her gauzy veil onto her chest. Her fists came to rest on her hips in a teasing expression of mock indignation. "Am I not, with my magical powers, sufficient to protect you from some dwarf?"

27

"Oh, 'tisn't that, m'lady." Onora blushed furiously, deepening the color of her already pink, freckled face to a mottled crimson. "Yer powers are renowned in Greystone and beyond. 'Tis just that . . . well, I never presumed to impose on ye in such a manner. Especially not with all the dignitaries out and about."

Arien grinned and stepped closer. "Well, if you promise not to tell anyone, I'll share a secret with you. Already I'm heartily sick of the preparations and pomp and circumstance of this Triennial. I feel stifled in this dreary castle, and would love a short excursion outside. Especially," she added with an impish twinkle, "one promising an occasion for adventure."

"Well, I don't know, m'lady," her servant hedged, not looking at all convinced. "What will yer father say, if he discovers ye're gone? He's placed the responsibility for overseeing all these preparations in yer hands. He'll not be pleased if something goes awry, and ye're not present to set it aright."

"Aye, 'tis true enough." Arien paused. "On the other hand, what could go wrong? Everything's in readiness. All the servants know their jobs and how to carry them out." She took Onora by the hand. "Oh, let's do it. I so love a good adventure, and it has been weeks since I've attempted aught more exciting than planning menus and assigning bedchambers to all the guests. And 'tis for a good cause, is it not? The future happiness of two lovers."

Tentatively, a smile found its way across the lady-in-waiting's face. "Aye, 'tis indeed for a good cause, m'lady. I'll set out yer banquet gown and put a kettle o' water on the hearth before we leave.

That way, just as soon as we return, ye can complete yer personal preparations for the banquet."

"Then 'tis settled," Arien proclaimed. " 'Twill be sunset in another hour. Join me at the gatehouse and wear a hooded cloak to hide your identity." She released Onora's hand. "In the meanwhile, I've a long-overdue meeting with Cook awaiting me."

Not pausing for a reply, Arien turned and hurried across the balcony to the wide expanse of curving, marble stairs. For the first time today, she actually looked forward to completing her tasks. And for the first time in a long while, Arien realized with a small start of surprise, she experienced a joyous certainty that a great adventure indeed lay just ahead.

Aye, a great adventure, the young sorceress assured herself, and she'd no intention of missing it for the world.

Chapter Two

As the sun set behind the western mountains, waves of scarlet and purple rolled across the land, drenching the hills and valleys in deepest shadow—shadow that effectively masked the surreptitious escape from Castle Talamontes of two cloaked and hooded women. Taking the summer-dry drainage ditch that siphoned off the moat's excess during heavy spring rains, Arien led Onora far from sight of the castle before finally climbing out. Then, after brushing the dust from the hems of their cloaks, they continued on.

In the distance, a faint shimmer of white towered above a grassy hillock. Encompassed by a stand of oaks, the rock stood there, gleaming like some lonely sentinel set to guard the land. It was the Stone of the Little Men, Arien realized with a delicious shiver of anticipation. The dwarf was said to live beneath it, awaiting only the coming of dusk to venture outside.

He was said to be the last of his kind in Greystone, the rest driven out when the Moondancers came to total power. No one had actually seen this particular dwarf, though, in many years. Yet tales continued that payment and a drawing of some tool, or weapon, or piece of jewelry such as Onora and Tomas had commissioned were always honored promptly with the item requested. The dwarf's willingness to make human contact, however, remained to be seen.

"We must use all stealth in approaching the stone," Arien whispered to her companion. "If the dwarf has yet to leave his cave, we just might be able to spy on him as he climbs out."

"To what purpose?" Onora whispered back. "All I want is our rings. I've no wish to visit with a dwarf." She shuddered. "They're said to be old and ugly and deformed. 'Tisn't a sight I'd care to encounter after dark."

"They cannot help the form or appearance they were given. It doesn't mean they're evil, just because they're ugly."

"I know that." Onora sighed in exasperation. "I just don't want to see—"

Arien drew to an abrupt halt. They'd entered the circle of trees, and were but ten feet from the jagged finger of luminescent stone thrusting from the little hill. Using her magic to enhance her vision in the gathering gloom, Arien studied the slender pillar. There was no sign of any package in the hollowed-out rock set at the base of the standing stone, the traditional spot where the dwarf's customers were said to find their completed items.

Excitement thrummed through Arien. The package's absence meant the dwarf had yet to leave his secret cave. She glanced around, searching for a place where she and Onora could hide, and found it in a nearby fallen tree. It faced the stone, and they'd be able to see him as he climbed up the hill to reach it, Arien decided.

"I hope he doesn't take his sweet time with our rings," Onora muttered softly as she took her spot alongside Arien, crouching behind the dead tree. "We daren't stay away too long, or someone is certain to note yer absence."

"Aye, 'tis true," Arien muttered back. "But I won't leave you here alone, either. Besides, 'tis said dwarves leave their caves as soon as they can after sunset. I'd imagine they're eager to breathe the fresh air, and experience something other than damp earth and—"

A sound, like rock grating on rock, caught Arien's attention. She clasped Onora's arm, raising a finger to her lips in warning. Onora's eyes grew wide. She swallowed convulsively, then ducked behind the comforting bulk of the fallen tree. Beside her, Arien sank down as far as she could and still see over the top of the tree, and waited in breathless anticipation.

Rock scraped on rock again. Then came the tread of heavy footsteps, and the sound of a low, gravelly voice humming a tune. The simple melody rose on the gentle breeze, bittersweet, haunting, yet strangely compelling. A short but powerfully built gray-bearded dwarf, dressed in a ragged brown homespun tunic tied at the waist with a stout rope, darned hose, and threadbare, misshapen boots, appeared around the far side of the hillock. A moment later he broke into song.

"Mage-fire courses through her,
Gifting her wi' wondrous powers,

Yet she doesna heed it,
She isna ready.

"Faery light surrounds her,
The goddess moon above her guide,
Yet still she's lost her way,
She isna ready."

As he staggered awkwardly up the hill to the
hollowed-out rock and the standing stone, a small
packet wrapped in a tattered rag in his hands, he
sang on, his voice assuming a curious, heartrending intensity.

"Too late, too late,
Fer her, fer us all,
Unless she names the secret
o' her shame—and her glory.

"Love at long last beckons,
Ripe wi' goldspun promise,
Yet still her eyes are closed.
Will she e'er be ready?

"Too late, too late
Fer her, fer us all,
Unless she names the secret
o' her shame—and her glory."

Once more, as he drew up before the standing
stone, he hummed the melody. Then, bending,
the little creature placed the cloth-wrapped parcel in the depression of the rock. He took his time,
his knobby knees creaking like rusted iron hinges
with each movement he made. At last, though, he

stood and gazed out with eyes glowing suddenly bright.

Gazed straight at them.

Ever so softly Arien sucked in a breath, but moved not a muscle that might betray them. Onora, however, her curiosity stirred by the dwarf's song, had just then lifted her head to peer over the log. At sight of the gnarled little creature's glowing eyes, she gasped.

"Holy Mother, save us!" Frantically, she made a warding sign.

The dwarf froze, his demeanor now rigid and watchful. "Who's out there, I say? I dinna like nosy folk coming to titter and gawk. Show yerselves now, or risk a taste o' my magic."

"A-Arien." The serving maid scooted close and grabbed her mistress's arm. "Wh-what shall we do?"

"Why, do as he asks," Arien replied with more bravado than she felt. Climbing to her feet, she faced the dwarf. " 'Tis evident he knows we're here, so why pretend otherwise?"

Boldly, she locked gazes with the little creature, and managed an unsteady smile. "There's no need for magic-wielding this night, kind sir. Mayhap my friend and I were wrong to spy on you, but we did so out of curiosity, not malice." As she spoke, Arien reached down and tugged on Onora's arm. Slowly, reluctantly, the maidservant rose to stand beside her.

"Ye came here out o' more than simple curiosity, young princess." The dwarf smiled. "Didna ye?"

Arien frowned, puzzled. "I don't know what you mean."

34

"Dinna ye?" He shrugged. "Then no matter." Stooping, the dwarf scooped up the parcel from the stone. "Here." He tossed the small bundle down to Arien.

She caught it and handed the parcel to Onora. "Open it and see if 'tis the rings."

The other woman nodded mutely and, with trembling fingers, unwrapped the little package. A pair of gold rings, beautifully etched with ancient symbols, lay in the center of the cloth. She lifted her gaze to the dwarf.

"I—we . . . we never paid ye for such fine rings, kind sir," the maidservant stammered. "We but wished for a pair o' brass rings. 'Twas all we could afford." She rewrapped the rings and made a motion to return them.

He halted her with an upraised hand. "And do ye now reject my gift to ye?" The dwarf sighed and shook his head. "Truly, ye humans are an ungrateful, insulting lot."

"Nay, 'tisn't that at all," Onora cried. "The rings are exquisite. But we cannot pay ye any more than what we first left ye. I'm sorry for that, but my Tomas is but a stable man."

"And did I not say 'twas my gift to ye?" The dwarf gave a disgusted snort and shook his head. "Ye owe me naught more, woman. Is that plain enough fer ye?"

Onora turned to her mistress. "Take them," Arien urged. "Dwarves aren't known to be overly generous. If this one wishes to be tonight, then I say make the most of it."

With a joyous smile, Onora glanced back at the dwarf. "My thanks, kind sir. 'Tis the grandest gift I've ever received."

"Harumph," he grumbled. "Well, dinna go on so about it, or I'll be tempted to take back the rings. I do what I do 'cause it suits me, and fer no other reason."

Onora gave a start, then nodded quickly in agreement. "Ah, well, aye . . . o' course."

An uncomfortable silence settled over the little glen, and, in that deepening quiet, Arien decided they'd passed enough time talking with the unsettling little creature. "Come, 'tis time we were heading back to the castle." She took Onora by the arm and began to lead her away.

"A moment more, fair princess." The dwarf scrambled down the hill until he stood before the two women. "The song. The one I sang but a few minutes ago."

Unnerved by the dwarf's temerity in drawing so near, Arien decided it was time to exert her royal authority. She met his gaze, staring down the dainty length of her nose. This close, he barely came to her waist. A faint, musty odor of old clothes and earth rose from him.

"Aye?" She arched a regal brow.

"The song," the little creature persisted, looking up at her with a curious intensity. " 'Twas about ye, fair princess. Ye, and no other."

"Me?" Before Arien could shake off the uneasy premonition, a chill rippled through her. The dwarf wanted something, she tried to assure herself, and was but playing some game.

Arien forced a lighthearted laugh. "And, pray, exactly when did you compose that charming little song? Just a few minutes ago, when you realized who had come to spy on you?"

The dwarf rolled his eyes and shook his head. "Think what ye will, young princess. The song, though, is an ancient one, passed down from my father and his father afore him."

"Well, be that as it may, that doesn't mean it applies to me. The song could be about any sorceress."

" 'The goddess moon above her guide'?" The dwarf smiled grimly. "Nay, I think not. 'Tis a Moondancer the song speaks o'. And 'love at long last beckons.' " He paused to cock his head speculatively. "Have ye yet to find yer true love, fair princess?"

"She's vowed to the chaste life," Onora intruded hotly. "If ye know her to be a Moondancer, ye know that."

"And do all Moondancers live as their vows bid?" The dwarf locked gazes with Arien, and a knowing light gleamed in his eyes. "Does yer sister, fer one, plan to do so much longer?"

At the veiled implication that he knew more than he'd any right to, Arien's heart began a violent pounding. She needed to hear what he had to say, to discern what he was about and why. She didn't, however, dare allow Onora to be privy to the encounter.

"Return to the castle," Arien abruptly commanded her maid. "There are things I must discuss with this dwarf that aren't suitable for your ears."

"But, mistress, I cannot leave ye here alone with him, nor permit ye to journey back without escort."

"My magic is sufficient to protect me, both against this dwarf and anything else I might encounter on my return." Arien took Onora's hand and gave it a reassuring squeeze. "You know that."

37

"Aye," the red-haired woman agreed slowly. "But—"

"No more of it, Onora." Arien released her hand and stepped back, forcing a stern expression. "I'll return soon enough, and will expect everything in readiness to prepare me for the banquet. Now, begone with you."

"As ye wish, mistress." Doubt still in her eyes, Onora backed away. Clutching her precious package to her, she turned then and hurried off into the night.

"I didna think ye'd have the courage to face me alone."

Arien spun about to confront the dwarf. "Indeed? And since when does a Moondancer, especially one as gifted as I, have aught to fear from a dwarf?"

He grinned, revealing several rotting teeth. "Never, it seems." His squat body swinging to and fro, the dwarf waddled over to a pile of rocks. Jumping up onto one of the lower, flatter ones, he indicated another rock nearby. "Come, sit and ease yerself. We've much to discuss."

Grudgingly, Arien followed him, but refused to sit. "I'll stand, if you don't mind."

"Ye dinna like getting too close to me, do ye?"

She flushed. " 'Tisn't that. I simply cannot linger here too long. My father's nobles are even now arriving at the castle. And my father is depending on me to be there to help welcome them at tonight's banquet."

He grinned wryly. "So, like lambs to the slaughter, the nobles, at the king's bidding, return again and again. He'll destroy them—and the kingdom—in the end, ye know?"

Though he ventured where others would never dare to go, there was still something about the dark little creature that engendered trust and a curious camaraderie. Arien opened her mouth to agree with him, then clamped it quickly shut. No matter his honest demeanor, no matter the light of concern she imagined she saw burning in his shiny black eyes, he was a stranger. And family problems must always remain in the family.

"I didn't stay to speak of my father or his problems with his nobles," Arien snapped instead. "You mentioned my sister, Edana, earlier, implying she's been unfaithful to her vows. How dare you speak such vile lies about her? Not only is she a Moondancer, but also the crown princess!"

"Ye dinna see what ye dinna wish to see, fair princess." The dwarf peered up at her, undaunted. "E'en now, yer sister plots wi' yer father to force the love o' yer heart to wed her. 'Twill undoubtedly be the death o' him *and* yer precious Moondancers if she does."

Arien lurched back, stunned. "The love of my heart? Truly, little man, you see things where naught exists. I'm chaste, and plan to remain that way."

"Yet ye dinna deny yer sister and father plot to win her an unwilling bridegroom, do ye?" The dwarf chuckled softly. "Ye're a shrewd one, sharing naught ye dinna wish to share. Yet ye canna succeed in undermining their plans wi'out my help."

At last, Arien thought triumphantly, he begins to reveal his true purpose. She went rigid, her hands fisting at her sides. "And I say you presume far too much. I don't know how you gained your knowledge of what my father and sister plan, but 'tisn't any of your concern. Furthermore, I don't wish to undermine them, or need your help in doing so." She took a few more steps backward. "This conversation is at an end. I bid you good night."

As Arien turned to leave, however, the dwarf's low, gravelly voice halted her. " 'Tis strange that a young woman o' such fine intelligence and endless concern fer others isna interested in learning more o' the man fate has chosen fer her. Will ye, then, give him o'er to yer sister wi'out e'en knowing who he is, or what ye could've shared wi' him?"

She shouldn't weaken. She shouldn't succumb to the questions plucking at her heart. *The man fate has chosen for her.* But how could that be? Her destiny was already determined, ever since that moonlight-drenched night she'd made her sacred vows.

"Yer first and highest vow," the dwarf murmured, "is to serve the land and people. To my way o' thinking, 'tis a higher calling than some paltry vow o' chastity." The dwarf paused, eyeing her closely. "Now, I ask ye once again. Do ye wish to know the man o' yer heart and what ye could've shared wi' him, or not?"

Aye, Arien thought, her heart suddenly thudding painfully beneath her breast. *Just once, I'd like to know what 'tis like to fall in love, and how 'twould feel. Just once, before I put aside such desires forever.*

"I don't trust you," she said instead.

"Think I'll ensorcel ye, do ye?" The dwarf jumped down from the rock, straightened his shabby tunic, then looked up at her. "What if I gave ye something with power o'er me, to even things 'atween us, as 'twere? Something no one save my father and mither e'er knew?"

Arien's eyes narrowed. "And, pray, what would that mysterious power be?"

"My name."

"Your name?"

"Aye." The little creature looked quite miffed. "Have ye no' heard the tales o' the secret power contained in a dwarf's name? Why, the hold ye then have o'er him is jest as strong as ye'd have o'er a dragon, if ye knew *his* name."

"And exactly what power is that?" Arien demanded, not at all convinced.

"Why, 'tis the power to subdue, if not totally destroy, a dwarf's magical abilities. 'Tis a terrible power to hold o'er any magic-wielder, and one not lightly given."

"Then why give it to me? I'm a Moondancer, after all, and you know as well as I that dwarves and Moondancers ceased to be friends long ago."

"True enough," the dwarf admitted, "but there are dire things afoot in Greystone and action must be taken, and soon, or 'twill not matter who are or aren't friends anymore. If the truth be told, I dinna much care to share my name wi' ye, but if ye dinna soon open yer eyes and take the first step on yer life's greatest journey, 'twill be too late fer us all."

His words sounded suspiciously like those of that strange little song he'd sung, Arien realized. The song he claimed had always been about her. Suddenly indecision overwhelmed her. Dared she believe him? And, even more important, did she dare risk learning what it might be best she never knew?

She'd thought encountering a dwarf would be an exciting adventure. Now Arien was no longer so sure. Something had drawn her here this night. Something more powerful than herself. But was it the result of the dwarf's magic, or did it arise from a force even stronger and greater than either of them? And was that mysterious force good—or evil?

One way or another, Arien resolved, she must know. And really, there was naught to worry about. Her magic was good, strong, and few were more adept than she. Certainly not this nondescript little dwarf, she thought, eyeing him critically.

"Tell me your name then." Arien stooped to bring her face close to his. "What you ask requires the yielding of my mind—and, if only temporarily, my magic—to you. I'll not do so without some advantage over you in return."

"Fair enough. The risk should be equal. And, since the welfare o' Greystone hangs in the balance, I'd say 'tis a risk well taken."

The dwarf lifted on tiptoe. His musty scent wafted over Arien; then his breath brushed against her ear. " 'Tis Garth. Garth Dorwen," she heard him say.

Arien straightened. "You give your word that's your name?"

"On the honor o' my mither and father, and the great Mither Earth, who protects and nourishes me."

It was the most solemn vow a dwarf could make. Arien nodded her acquiescence. "What would you have me do?"

" 'Tis quite simple, really. Ye must sit, as I must put ye in a trance to weave my magic more easily." Garth grinned. "Have no fear, though, fair princess. 'Tis a willing trance. Ye can leave it anytime ye wish."

"That certainly puts my mind at ease." Arien glanced around for a comfortable spot, and decided the fallen tree was as good as any. She walked over to it, sat, and, after rearranging her skirts, leaned back against the trunk.

"I'm ready."

Garth Dorwen ambled over and squatted beside her. "Close yer eyes, young princess. I canna work my magic wi' ye staring up at me wi' those big green eyes o' yers."

Arien stared at him for a moment more, then closed her eyes. "Don't think I'm not watching you, Garth Dorwen," she warned, "even with my eyes closed."

He chuckled softly. "Oh, there was ne'er a doubt o' that, fair princess. Nay, ne'er a doubt."

A hand touched her head, the pressure light but comforting. "Now, take yer ease and let me work my spell. Take yer ease and look inward. Inward," the dwarf intoned, his voice gone unexpectedly low and compelling, "to where he's always been, in yer mind and in yer heart, since that day, now three years past, when ye first met him."

Soothing warmth flooded Arien. Before her closed lids, she saw gossamer, golden strands burst suddenly into view. Arising seemingly from out of nowhere, the gilt threads furled upward, spiraling into the air as if they were being spun from some invisible spinning wheel. Glinting brightly, the strands merged into a whirling, resplendent ball, turning faster and faster until a vortex formed.

Yet even when that powerful, golden maelstrom began to draw Arien inexorably into it, she
didn't resist. It was but the dwarf's own unique
form of spell-casting, she realized, all her magical
senses acutely attuned to his quite foreign but re-
markably pleasant form of enchantment. At the
same time, however, Arien recognized it was like
no other she'd ever experienced.

The golden maelstrom reached for her, the
strands unfurling to wrap about Arien and pull
her in. And, as they touched and twined, memories beckoned with an irresistible, heartfelt call.

Gradually a scene took shape, a scene of a
sunny summer's day when she'd been but fifteen.
In the throes of final, frantic preparations for the
Triennial, Arien had rushed down the steps of the
keep and across the inner bailey, slamming into
a tall, dark-haired nobleman—a tall, dark-haired
nobleman who had been none other than the
Lord Dane Haversin.

After regaining his balance, he spun about and
immediately took her by the arms to steady her.
At first, Arien hadn't had the courage to meet his
gaze. But when he laughed, saying that beautiful
girls were now finding the most inventive ways to
meet him—an over-the-hill married man, no
less—Arien couldn't help laughing, too, and finally looked up at him.

His eyes were a deep, indigo blue, dancing with
a merry amusement that was overlaid with
warmth and kindness. Though his features
weren't what could be called classically handsome, Dane Haversin was still ruggedly attractive,
from his straight, dark brows and strong blade of
a nose, to the proud jut of his chin and jaw. His
mouth was well shaped and sensual. His slightly

wavy, dark brown hair dipped from a center part onto a wide, intelligent forehead, falling nearly to his shoulders. In the late-afternoon sun, his hair glinted with rich chestnut highlights.

Gazing up at him, Arien found herself mesmerized, and surprisingly smitten in the bargain. Awkwardly, she apologized for running into him, then introduced herself as the king's younger daughter. In response, Dane Haversin took her hand and gallantly kissed it, assuring Arien in a voice deep, rich, and, oh, so stirring, that he was honored yet again to make her acquaintance.

At Arien's puzzled expression, Dane explained he'd last met her at the previous Triennial, when she was but twelve. She blushed again, this time at not having remembered him from before. Dane merely chuckled, claiming she'd not forget him henceforth, after this last and most memorable of meetings.

His pronouncement had been eerily prophetic. Not only did Arien seek out every excuse to linger in his vicinity throughout that next week, but also filled the remaining hours dreamily reliving their meeting. The feel of his hands on her arms . . . the heady pleasure of standing so close . . . and the excitement of having his complete attention, if only for a few, wondrous moments.

It hadn't mattered that he was happily married at the time, or that his wife was due to deliver their first child in but a few months. Dane Haversin was Arien's first and only romantic infatuation. She reveled in it with the natural exuberance of a girl just becoming aware of the thrilling differences between men and women. Then, two months later, she became a Moondancer. After that, Arien thought of Dane Haversin no more.

"Ye must leave the past now, fair princess." The dwarf's low, soothing voice intruded into Arien's dreaming. "Journey forward to what is to come, if ye've the courage to face it. Forward . . . to yer wedding day."

Immediately, another scene filled Arien's mind, of the castle chapel, festooned with colorful banners, of every nook and cranny overflowing with tall vases of flowers, and myriad fine beeswax candles burning brightly. She saw herself standing before the priest at the foot of the altar, Dane Haversin at her side.

A tense, angry, unsettled feeling emanated from the church's occupants, radiating not only from Dane—whose expression was as grim and foreboding as a thundercloud—but also from her father, sister, and all the nobles in attendance. Dane gripped her hand in an icy, impersonal clasp, all but ignoring Arien save for the required ceremonial actions forcing him periodically to repeat his vows directly to her, and finally to slide the wedding band onto the third finger of her left hand. Yet, paradoxically, his kiss, when the ceremony was completed and the priest urged him to seal his vows in the traditional manner, was anything but icy and impersonal.

With rage smoldering in his eyes, he pulled Arien close. Before she had a chance to react, Dane slammed his mouth down on hers. At the sudden, unexpected brutality of his kiss, panic swamped Arien. For a fleeting moment she tried to pull back, and failed. The iron clasp of his hand on the back of her head effectively squelched any consideration of escape.

There was naught to be done but submit. With a low moan, Arien pressed into his hard, unyielding body. And, at her gentle acquiescence, something changed between them.

Dane's hold on her eased, became almost caressing. His mouth softened, gliding warm and hungry over hers. A shudder vibrated through him. Deep in his throat, he groaned.

At the heart-wrenching sound, compassion flared in Arien. An ache rose from deep within and she wanted, ah, how she wanted, to ease Dane's pain and fury. How she wanted to lie in his arms and assuage the anger and frustration still hovering, like some cruel, unfriendly specter, between them. Assuage it with her heart and soul and body . . . until there remained naught between them and they were truly joined as man and wife.

"Ye see how 'tis 'atween ye?" the dwarf whispered. "E'en when ye hurt him sorely, and his passion fer ye is equally one o' anger as o' need? But in time ye can heal that wound 'atween ye, and then the loving . . . ah, then 'twill be all ye could e'er hope fer."

Riding the wave of intense emotion her wedding kiss with Dane had stirred, Arien slid immediately into the next dream—a dream of them lying naked in bed. This time, however, there was no anger, only a deep, overwhelming sense of despair—a despair entwined with an equally overwhelming passion. This time their mutual need rose like some thick, warm mist, enveloping them in a torrid embrace.

It was a madness such as Arien had never experienced, threatening to blot out all reason, thought, and sanity. Even as she watched her and

Dane entwine in passionate embrace, apprehension filled her, burgeoning rapidly to outright fear. That fear was finally enough to call Arien from the dwarf's magical, goldspun dream.

"N-nay," she whispered, horror-struck at what she'd just seen and experienced. "It cannot be. I cannot bear it!" She shook her head to clear the unsettling yet still strangely exciting images. She forced open her eyes. For a moment, gilt threads whirled crazily before her. Then Arien's vision cleared.

She sat in the glen enclosed by the mighty oaks, the tall standing stone thrusting from the hillock before her. A gentle breeze scampered through the trees, setting leaves to rustling and branches to clacking. Far overhead, stars flickered brightly in the ebony vault of the sky.

"Ye say it canna be, that ye canna bear it," the dwarf declared beside her. "Yet 'tis yer destiny, fair princess. A destiny o' great import not only fer yerself, but fer the young lord and yer people. Can ye, wi' good conscience, turn from it, now that ye've been gifted wi' the foreknowledge o' what must be?"

With a gasp, Arien jerked her gaze to him. He knelt there, his position exactly as she remembered it. Only now a strange, intent light burned in his eyes.

"Foreknowledge, you say?" She gave a strangled laugh. "Mayhap, but then again, mayhap not. You're skilled in your magic, dwarf. Mayhap, in some mysterious way, you sensed my former attraction for Dane Haversin, and utilized it to construct a romantic fantasy to suit your own purposes."

"Aye, 'tis indeed possible," the dwarf admitted gravely. "In the wrong hands, the ancient magic could indeed do jest what ye suggest. Naught I can say this night, though, will convince ye o' my true intent. Ye must first find the answers in yer heart."

Arien rose to her feet. "Aye, that I must. But I won't find them here this night." Suddenly, inexplicably, the image of herself lying naked in Dane's arms flashed again through her mind. Intensely ardent emotions flared anew, setting Arien's heart to pounding. An unnerving warmth, a throbbing, insistent ache, settled deep within her woman's core.

By the Mother, Arien thought, panic filling her. With only the slightest effort, the dwarf manipulates my memory and emotions again and again. I must be gone. Now, before I'm lost!

"I-I must leave," she stammered, stepping back from him. "The banquet . . . my father—"

"Aye, yer father awaits ye." The dwarf rose. "And ye've important matters aplenty in the coming days. But ye'll be back, mark my words. Ye'll be back when ye finally face the truth o' what was revealed this night—and ye find I'm the only one wi' the power to aid ye."

She'd no intention of ever returning to this oak grove, or encountering the strange little dwarf again, Arien thought. She certainly had no further need of his aid. Yet, unaccountably, the images of her and Dane flashed through her mind once more. A mindless terror—that she'd no power to control these unnerving visions—swelled to uncontrollable proportions.

Begone from here, a voice screamed within her head. *Now, before 'tis too late!*

"F-farewell." Arien managed to choke out the word, before she turned and fled.

Into the quiet, comforting darkness of the night she ran. Ran toward the warm haven of glowing candles in distant castle windows. Ran toward safety, toward the only life she'd ever known. Ran on, heedless of the rocks she stumbled over, the branches and brambles that caught and tore at her cloak like grasping talons.

Ran on, for once oblivious to the night—and its inherent dangers.

From out of nowhere, a huge shape loomed from the blackness. With a startled snort, the fearsome apparition reared before her, teetered for a long, sickening moment, then toppled over backward. In the depths of that horror-stricken instant Arien heard a man's voice, shouting a warning. Then something massive and heavy struck the ground, and the voice came no more.

Chapter Three

With a startled squeak Arien leaped back, tripped over the hem of her cloak, and fell, sprawling on the ground. Silence, for a brief moment, encompassed her, and Arien wondered if she'd but imagined the fearsome beast and the man's voice. Then, with an exasperated snort, the animal heaved itself to its feet.

Using her magic-aided night vision—vision that would have prevented such an unfortunate mishap if she'd been clearheaded enough to use it—Arien saw that the fearsome beast was naught more than a huge warhorse. She glanced around, searching for the man she was now certain had been riding him, and found him crumpled in a heap, facedown, several feet away. Even from the distance separating them, however, she could tell by his fine apparel that he was a nobleman.

" 'Tis a fine muddle you've stumbled into," Arien muttered in disgust as she hurried to the man's side. "Not only will you now be late for the banquet, but, in the doing, you may well have killed one of your father's noblemen." Kneeling beside the unfortunate man, she ever so carefully turned him over and cradled his head in her lap.

He was dressed in a fine, open-necked white linen shirt, equally fine, lightweight woolen breeches of some dark color, and knee-high leather boots. Save for the dirt and bits of grass now clinging to his clothing, and the oozing gash on his forehead, he appeared unharmed. A few tentative pokes to his shoulder and firmly spoken words, however, confirmed he was quite unconscious.

As she held him, a curious conviction grew within her. There was something strangely familiar and compelling about the nobleman. Concentrating all her powers in order to intensify her night vision, Arien carefully scanned his face. Though his features were a bit more careworn, and a copious amount of blood from his wounded forehead flowed down his face, there was no mistaking the man's identity. It was Lord Dane Haversin.

At the revelation, the world spun dizzily before her. How could it be? Arien thought in rising horror. Not fifteen minutes ago she'd been having a magic-induced dream about this very man. Then, as she'd fled in panic, the dwarf had called after her, taunting her with assurances that Dane was her destiny, and that she'd be back sooner or later to seek his own help in fulfilling that destiny.

Gazing now at the nobleman's ruggedly handsome features, so peaceful in repose, Arien finally allowed herself to wonder if it was truly her destiny to link her life with his. It was strange enough to encounter him this very night in such an unusual manner. Coupled with the dwarf's bizarre predictions, the coincidence defied any other rational explanation.

Ridiculous coincidence or not, Arien firmly roused herself from her troubled musing. Contemplating this night's meeting with the dwarf was doing nothing to waken the Lord Dane Haversin. She glanced to where his big warhorse stood, now placidly grazing on a succulent patch of grass. A leathern water flask hung from the saddle horn. Perhaps if she washed his face with cool water . . .

Ever so gently, Arien laid Dane on the grass and rose. At her approach, the horse snorted nervously and took a few prancing side steps. Finally, though, he calmed enough for Arien to remove the water flask.

She hurried back to Dane's side. After unstoppering the flask, Arien lifted his head and poured some of the water carefully over his gash. The fluid sluiced down to his eye, pooled for an instant, then spilled across his cheek.

Dane didn't respond. Once more, Arien poured water over his gash and down the side of his face. This time most of the blood rinsed away.

Pulling a fine lawn handkerchief from her bodice, Arien dabbed at Dane's face, finally working her way up to the gash. Gently she patted the wound dry, then laid the folded handkerchief over it. A few moments more and Arien had a long strip torn from the edge of her undershift. Using the finely woven cloth, she wrapped it about Dane's head to bind the handkerchief in place.

Just as she finished tying off the bandage, he groaned and moved slightly. Arien froze.

"M-my lord? Can you hear me?" In spite of her best efforts, a tremor vibrated in her voice. "If you can, tell me if you've any injuries besides this wound on your head."

His eyes fluttered open. For a long moment he stared up at her, his expression dazed. Then, slowly, comprehension appeared to dawn. "M-my head?" he mumbled. He lifted a hand to his gash, touched the bandage-covered wound gingerly, and grimaced. "By all that is holy! What happened?"

Arien flushed. Dane Haversin was sure to be angry when he discovered she'd been the one responsible for his accident. Yet she couldn't lie. Moondancers were also sworn to tell the truth.

"I didn't see or hear your horse's approach, and frightened the animal when I ran before it. The beast toppled over and you were thrown from the saddle, striking your head. I cleansed your wound as best I could, then used my handkerchief and a strip of my undershift to bind it." Arien inhaled a shuddering breath and forged on. "I beg pardon for my carelessness, m'lord, and hope someday you'll find it in your heart to forgive me."

Moved by her evident concern and efforts to care for him—and the growing conviction he'd seen her somewhere before—Dane eyed her with curiosity. " 'Tis already forgiven, lass." He smiled up at her. "I'm only glad you weren't trampled. If you had been, your injury would have been far worse than mine."

Rising on one elbow, Dane narrowed his gaze. "Your face, your voice. They seem familiar, yet, try as I might, I cannot quite place them."

" 'Tis understandable, m'lord. We met three years ago." She smiled wanly. "I'm the king's daughter, Princess Arien."

Dane gave a jerk of surprise. Though it was hard, in the dim light of stars and crescent moon, to discern much detail, a closer inspection of the young woman's face did indeed confirm the truth of her words. Excitement quickened his pulse. Fate was indeed with him this night. But must he so soon repay kindness with evil?

Savagely, Dane tamped down his burgeoning sense of regret and gratitude. Her apparent goodness in caring for him could be—and most likely was—some ruse. All that truly mattered was the reality that the Princess Arien was here, alone, and at his mercy. Indeed, could destiny have delivered her any more conveniently or expeditiously into his hands?

But how should he kill her? he wondered, forcing his thoughts down a more violent but necessary path. He could easily, at this close distance, take the princess by the throat and strangle the life from her. Yet such an act might also provide sufficient time for her to use her magic on him. Then his one opportunity, as well as his life, might well be lost.

Nay, Dane decided, a quick slit of her throat when she least expected it would be best. Unfortunately, his knife still hung from its saddle scabbard.

"If you will, your grace, help me sit up." The sooner he reached his horse, he decided, the sooner this onerous task would be over. "No purpose is served by lingering here. 'Tis best we return to the castle."

"Aye." Arien struggled to assist him to a sitting position. "Your wound can be better cared for once we're back at the castle."

Once he was upright Dane cradled his head in his hands, waiting for the spinning lights to abate. Then he looked up. "If I can impose on your generosity one time more, your grace, I'll need assistance standing as well."

" 'Tis the least of the debt I owe you, m'lord." She lowered her glance until her thick fan of ebony lashes fluttered against her cheek. "Tell me how I can aid you, and I'll strive to do my best."

She has matured well in the past three years, Dane thought, momentarily distracted as he gazed up at her. She's as beautiful, in a softer, more delicate sort of way, as is her elder sister. Edana's was a ripely sensuous beauty. Dane sourly recalled Edana's multiple attempts at the last Triennial to seduce him.

At the unpleasant memory, Dane fleetingly wondered if it was Edana's anger at his repeated rejections that had resulted in the severity of the curse laid on him and his family by the Moondancer witch. He swiftly shook that question aside. It didn't matter who had prompted the arrival of the witch at Castle Haversin. In the end, the Moondancers and all their kind were equally responsible.

Tonight, though, opportunity was with him— an opportunity to embark on his plan to rid Greystone of the onerous burden of evil magic. Aye, Dane thought, it was an unparalleled opportunity . . . if only he'd the courage to see it through.

Noting Arien's quizzical look, Dane forced himself to return to the immediate present. "Help me get my legs under me. Then get a good grip on my arm and begin pulling me up. I think I can manage the rest."

"As you wish, m'lord." Arien assisted him as instructed. Several seconds later, Dane stood upright on surprisingly wobbly legs.

"Can you walk, m'lord?"

To stay further questions, he held up a hand, all the while staring intently at the ground to maintain his sense of equilibrium. "Give me a moment, your grace. My head feels suddenly as if 'twill explode."

"Do you need to sit back down then?" There was an edge of worry in her voice. When Dane felt enough in control to meet her gaze, he found that same worry burning in her eyes. What shade *were* her eyes? he wondered, distracted yet again by the princess's startling beauty. Though the darkness muted all color, it failed to hide the glorious luminosity of the orbs lifted to him in what seemed to be genuine concern.

By the Mother, Dane cursed silently. He must not succumb to that niggling temptation to spare her life. His strange and most precipitous attraction to her could well be the working of some spell. In her own way, the Princess Arien was surely as evil and perverted as her sister and all their fellow Moondancers.

He must never forget that. Never!

"M'lord?" Arien persisted. "Are you all right? Do you need to sit back down?"

"Nay." Dane shook his head vehemently. The action set his skull to pounding, but he hid his misery, refusing to reveal further weakness she might seize to her advantage. "Just hold tight to my arm and permit me to lean on you as we walk to the horse, your grace," he said. "I'll be fine in but a short while. Truly, I will."

Kathleen Morgan

"As you wish, m'lord," Arien muttered in reply, the disbelieving look she sent him ample evidence she wasn't at all convinced. She held tightly to his arm, nonetheless, and set out toward his big war-horse.

Though the journey was short and not overly strenuous, Dane still felt light-headed by the time they drew up beside his horse. It would take all the power left in him to mount the beast, he realized in rising despair. How could he ever hope, in such a debilitated state, to muster the presence of mind, much less the strength, necessary to kill her? Unless . . . unless, he thought with a sudden surge of elation, she rode before him and he took her unawares.

"Once I'm mounted, you must . . . you must climb up and ride before me," Dane said, panting, his stomach gone queasy. "I fear I cannot find my way to the castle without your assistance."

"Mayhap 'twould be better, then, if I walked before your horse and led it back?"

She was reluctant to get close to him. Whether the cause was an unlikely modesty or some presentiment of danger, Dane knew he couldn't allow her to refuse. "I'm loath to presume such liberties with your royal personage, your grace," he ventured carefully, "but I fear if I don't have someone to hold on to, I'll surely lose my balance and tumble from my horse."

"Oh, I hadn't thought of that." Arien hesitated a moment, then nodded her acquiescence. "If you need me to ride before you, m'lord, I'll do so and gladly. 'Tis the very least I owe you, after having been the cause of your distress."

At her sweet words, anger surged through him, briefly clearing Dane's mind of the persistent diz-

ziness and lending renewed strength to his limbs.
"And I told you before, your grace, 'tis already forgiven." He turned toward his horse, grasped the
saddle horn and pommel, and heaved himself up.
The attempt to mount, however, failed miserably.

When he was finally able to catch his breath,
Dane turned to glare at her. Vainly, he tried summoning additional anger to fuel his resolve and
bolster his rapidly fading strength. As he gazed at
Arien, however, that futile endeavor died a quick
death, extinguished like some hapless spark falling into a pool of water—a pool as deep and fathomless and beguiling as Arien's glorious eyes.

With a silent, frustrated moan, Dane wrenched
his wandering attention back to the issue at
hand—the problem of mounting his horse. He
turned to the saddle, tried to pull himself up, and
failed yet again. His chest heaving, Dane leaned
his head against his mount's belly, fighting to
deny the truth of the situation—and failed ignominiously at that, too.

"I-I'm sorry, your grace." In his shame and frustration, Dane gripped the saddle leather tightly.
"I fear I must also ask you to help me mount."

Arien stepped close and laid a hand consolingly
on his back. "What would you have me do?"

At her touch, Dane couldn't help an involuntary
shudder, but whether it was one of revulsion or
pleasure, he didn't know. Already, his logical, dispassionate plans to rid the realm of the Talamontes were rapidly deteriorating.

Self-disgust filled him. Was he so morally weak,
so cowardly, that he couldn't bear a few pangs of
conscience, or control his more primal urges?
Both Talamontes princesses were beautiful, yet
Dane knew their beauty was superficial, hiding

souls rotted by evil magic. He must not—he *could* not—allow himself to fall under their spell.

He swung around to face Arien. "Forgive me if this seems ill-mannered, but, as I attempt to leap onto my horse, could you give me a boost?"

She frowned in puzzlement. "A boost? How? Where?"

"Where else? On my buttocks." In spite of himself, Dane's face warmed with embarrassment. "As crude as 'tis, 'tis the most effective place from which to push."

"Er, if you wish." Arien averted her gaze. "I confess to having never laid hands on that particular portion of a man's anatomy, but if you think 'twill work, I'll do what I can."

" 'Twill work, your grace," Dane muttered, hating to ask even such a small favor of her. If the truth be told, the last thing he wanted right now was her hands on him. Dane turned to his horse and grasped the saddle firmly. "On the count of three then," he said, shooting her a quick look over his shoulder.

Arien nodded, her little chin set resolutely. "On three."

Dane counted to three, then heaved himself upward. Instantly, two small hands cupped his behind and pushed hard. Her strength was surprising. Dane almost sailed over his horse's back.

"E-enough!" He gasped, struggling to regain his balance. To her credit, Arien complied immediately.

Though she stopped pushing, however, she didn't let go. For a heart-stopping instant, it seemed as if the imprint of her hands seared clear to the core of Dane's being. By the Mother, he thought in an agony of acute and most pleasurable awareness, *her touch feels so right, so good, planted as firmly as 'tis against that intimate part of me.*

"Are you able to swing your leg over, m'lord?"

"Wh-what?" Blushing furiously, Dane wrenched himself from his increasingly heated thoughts. "Aye." He threw his leg over his mount. A few seconds more, and Dane glanced down at Arien from the considerable height of his big warhorse. "My thanks for your help, your grace."

Once more, she averted her glance. " 'Twas my pleasure, m'lord." Then, as if realizing the double meaning of what she'd said, Arien gasped in horror and met his gaze. "Truly, I didn't intend that the way it sounded. I-I just meant—"

Though he tried to hide it, a tiny smile lifted one corner of Dane's mouth. "I knew what you meant, your grace." He leaned down and offered his hand. " 'Tis best, though, if we don't linger here overlong. Surely the king will be wondering where you've gone off to by now?"

At mention of her father, Arien's eyes grew wide. "Oh, aye. In all the excitement, I'd forgotten." She took his hand and swung lithely up to sit before him. "I suppose he'll be angry with me," she added shyly, half turning to look back at Dane. "I was expected to join him at this eve's banquet to help open the Triennial."

As Arien glanced back, the scent of her hair, hair redolent of summer roses and sunshine, wafted up to him. Dane encircled her with his arms, gathered up the reins, and urged his horse forward. "Well, I wouldn't worry overmuch." Fiercely, he quashed yet another swell of physical attraction. "I doubt even a king can do much to punish a Moondancer."

She shot him an exasperated look. "Do you imagine Moondancers are above filial respect? My father has many cares. I don't wish unnecessarily to add to them."

"Indeed?" Once more anger rose within him. He didn't like knowing that even black-hearted witches loved and respected their parents. Somehow, such devotion made them seem more vulnerable, human. "Your paternal loyalty is commendable," Dane forced himself to reply. "Commendable and most surprising. I hadn't thought Moondancers answered to anyone but their supreme priestess."

"You've some strange impressions of the sisterhood." Arien gazed pensively out into the night. "Though we're bound by all natural laws, in the end, the rule of conscience overrides even that of our high priestess."

"A dangerous prerogative," Dane muttered, intent just then on guiding his horse down the road leading to the royal castle.

"How so, m'lord?"

"No two consciences are alike. No two people view the same situation in exactly the same way. Where one might see the good in doing evil, if the many are well served, another might say naught good can ever arise from an evil deed."

"And what would *you* say to that dilemma, m'lord?"

Her question drew Dane up short. For an instant, memories swamped him in wave after wave of pounding agony. "More important, your grace," he rasped thickly, "what would *you* say?"

" 'Tis a difficult predicament." Arien paused, cocked her head in thought, then sighed. "For a Moondancer, though, the choice is simple. Our form of magic won't permit us to do evil, even if we see it ultimately as a greater good."

He knew he shouldn't venture into such murky and potentially dangerous waters, but he was tired, bruised, and his emotional control had been sorely tested this day. And now to listen to her sanctimonious pronouncements when it was well known that she, along with her sister, willingly chose to do evil . . .

"That's not at all what one hears these days about your sisterhood, your grace," Dane gritted out. "The Moondancer name is repeatedly besmirched, and the rumors of your sisterhood's evil deeds abound."

"Aye, 'tis true enough," Arien agreed with a thoughtful frown. She was silent for a long moment. "I'm not certain I should be speaking of this to you," she continued at last, "but you seem a good, moral man, and 'tis past time the truth came out. There is indeed evil in the Moondancers, an evil arising from a sect called the Ravens. They've found ways to pervert our sacred powers, and now grow and thrive on the darker forms of magic."

"How can that be? A moment before, you said your Moondancer magic wouldn't permit you to do evil." Dane's gaze narrowed. This was an interesting and heretofore unexpected development. What was the princess's game?

"There are ways to circumvent any law, even if that law is based on the soundest and most pure of intentions. And, sadly, oftentimes those of the greatest ability fall the farthest when corrupted by pride or a lust for power." Arien gave a bitter laugh. "You know the saying usually applied to the nobility, don't you? 'Where much is granted, much is expected, lest they drag down us all'? Well, that old saying pertains just as fully to the Moondancers."

There was something in the princess's words and manner that prompted Dane to risk her anger in speaking what many dared not even consider. "Then you've a sacred responsibility to discipline these Ravens," he offered carefully, "and, if that fails, you must destroy them! There can be no middle road in this."

"Aye." Arien nodded slowly. " 'Twould seem so. But you forget. Moondancers who adhere to the ancient ways are forbidden to do evil. And Dorianne, our high priestess, has tried repeatedly to discipline the Ravens. She is old, however, and I fear the spirit to fight fled her long ago. Not that the Ravens," she added, "have ever respected her or her sacred authority."

"Then choose another to rule in her place. Choose one with the strength and courage to control these Ravens."

"That cannot be. Dorianne leads us until the day she dies."

Frustration flooded Dane. "By all that is holy! Your own laws, then, will destroy you. The tragedy will not be just the end of the Moondancers, though. 'Twill be the end of Greystone, too."

"Aye," Arien whispered in a tearful voice. " 'Twill indeed be the end of us. To my mind, though, the greatest tragedy is that evil will have finally found the secret to overcoming good."

"And that secret is?" Dane prompted, suddenly convinced he must spare this princess's life until he had the time and opportunity to delve deeper into her shocking claims. As much as he hated the Moondancers, he refused to kill if there were yet questions unanswered, and less violent solutions to be found.

The fact that he was also moved by Arien's unexpected insight and concern was of no import. The time for heeding his gut instincts was past. Cold, hard logic was all he had left. He must use it with ruthless determination.

Her face profiled by the moonlight, a single tear, glinting like some precious jewel, trickled down Arien's cheek. "The secret is to turn good against itself by hampering it with well-intentioned but inflexible laws," she said softly. "Naught more is needed. The monster is set free. The destruction wrought will all come from within. As a fortress built on an unstable foundation finally will topple, so shall the Moondancers."

A wild hope flared in Dane's breast. Mayhap, just mayhap, she might yet serve as an ally, rather than as the enemy he'd originally imagined her to be. Mayhap there was yet some way to use her against her own kind.

"Then do something about it, your grace," he urged. "You, of all people, have the authority."

"Nay, I cannot, m'lord."

Once more, Arien looked back at him, and the haunted, bittersweet light burning in her eyes touched Dane to the depths of his soul. "You cannot?" he repeated softly, his mouth but a hungry, heated breath from hers. "Pray, why not, your grace?"

"In turning from the ancient ways of the sisterhood," she said, "I'd become no better than the Ravens. And that alternative, for a true Moondancer, is worse than death itself."

Chapter Four

Dane and Arien's arrival at Castle Talamontes created quite a stir. As they rode into the inner bailey and dismounted, Onora, who must have been anxiously on the lookout for Arien, ran from the great stone keep and down the steps.

"M-m' lady!" Breathlessly, she hurried to her mistress. "Where have ye been? 'Tis over an hour since I returned to the castle, and ye just now arrive? The banquet has begun. Yer father wasn't too pleased when ye weren't available for the opening ceremonies."

Arien sighed. "I know, Onora, but it couldn't be helped." She indicated Dane Haversin, who, after handing his warhorse off to a groom, had come up to stand beside her. "Lord Haversin and I, er, accidentally met on the road. After caring for his wound, we came here posthaste. My father will have to content himself with the fact that I didn't leave one of his nobles lying unconscious in the dirt."

"He'll not find your charity to me as admirable as you might imagine," Dane said with a chuckle.

"He and I haven't seen eye to eye on things for many years."

The sound of his voice, so close, so rich and deep, sent a curious little shiver down Arien's spine. She knew if she turned their bodies would be mere inches from touching, knew if she stood on tiptoe her mouth could easily brush his.

Troubled by the realization, Arien moved a step away. That she even considered such an act, much less found it so exciting to contemplate, was most discomfiting. Most discomfiting, after this night's encounter with the dwarf, Garth Dorwen.

"It doesn't matter!" Casting Dane Haversin a quick glance, Arien replied with a fierceness she knew was quite inappropriate for the mildness of his statement. "As a Moondancer, I couldn't have left you lying there, either."

"Well, whether the king approves or not," Onora interrupted with an impatient, dismissive wave of her hand, " 'tis best ye hurry to yer room and prepare yerself for the banquet. Then, once ye're—"

"Nay, Onora." Arien silenced her with a shake of the head. "First I must see Lord Haversin to his room, where I intend more thoroughly to treat his wound. While I'm doing that, fetch the basket of ointments and simples. Then hie yourself to the kitchen, have Cook prepare a tray of food, and, when 'tis ready, bring it to Lord Haversin's room."

"Your grace, there's no need—"

"And I say there is, m'lord." Arien turned back to him. "While you remain at Castle Talamontes, your health and welfare are my concern, as well as my responsibility." She moved nearer to prevent Onora from hearing her next, softly spoken words. "Besides," Arien whispered conspiratorially, "from the beginning, I've had little interest in attending the banquet. Your care but gives me an excuse to miss it."

Dane lifted a dark brow. "Indeed? Earlier I was under the impression you were the king's most devoted daughter."

"I planned and saw to all the details of the banquet, as well as to most of the other preparations. 'Twill run smoothly enough. Henceforth, my sister can see to the more public aspects of playing lady of the manor."

"Are you saying you're no longer needed, then, your grace?"

She shouldn't reveal so much, she well knew. No good would be served by sharing the sad details of her low favor with her father. But that intent look he'd sent her just now, a look of concern and caring, undid Arien. As much as she hated to admit it, she greatly craved Dane Haversin's interest.

"Aye, for all practical purposes, 'tis true enough," was her honest rejoinder. "I'm no longer really needed."

"I don't know what ye two are mumbling about over there," Onora cut in, her eyes narrowing in suspicion, "but one way or another, 'tis best ye not linger overlong in the courtyard. If some servant should inform yer father . . ."

Arien took Dane by the arm. "Come, m'lord. My maidservant speaks true. 'Tis best I escort you to your room with all discretion and haste."

"Ah, so now we must skulk into the castle, must we?" He smiled, but the smile faded quickly with Arien's sudden look of distress. "As you wish, your grace," Dane hastened to reply.

While Onora hurried to the kitchen, Arien led Dane into the keep, across the two-story reception area, and up the curving expanse of marble stairs. As they passed, servants shot them curious glances, whispered behind their hands, then scurried away. From the great hall that lay off to the right of the reception area, the sounds of laughter and boisterous toasts mingled with the sweet music of lute, mandolin, harp, and flute. Mouthwatering scents of roast boar, stag, and various game birds wafted upward on the night air.

Schooling her mind to the matter at hand, Arien blocked out all sounds and smells, and forged doggedly on. Since she'd supervised the assignment of the guest chambers and their preparation, she knew exactly which of the rooms in the upstairs corridor was Dane's. Tallow candles impaled on iron-spiked wall sconces lit the way, their wavering light illuminating the myriad small tapestries and weapons collections displayed on the walls. They passed five oaken doors before finally reaching Dane's—doors all cleverly carved with individual faerie-folk themes.

Arien paused before the door decorated with an intricate motif of dwarves plying their magic in underground mines. For a long moment she stared at it. The disconcerting coincidence of assigning Dane to this particular room stirred anew the memory of this eve's visit with the dwarf. Was the door yet another uncanny reminder, she wondered, that destiny had linked both Dane Haversin's and Garth Dorwen's fates with hers?

Coincidence though the room assignment might be, Arien still didn't like dealing with such eerie events. There would soon be an end of them, though, she told herself firmly, grasping the door

handle to Dane Haversin's room. Once she'd settled this disturbingly handsome lord for the
night, she meant to avoid him for the rest of the
Triennial. And, once he was gone, she would not
see him again for another three years. The dwarf's
prediction would fail to occur—if it had truly
been meant to happen this Triennial—and she
could go back to her life as it had always been.

Arien smiled grimly, then shoved open the door
and entered the bedchamber. She'd show that arrogant little dwarf. No one determined her fate
but her. No one!

As befitted Dane's high rank, the room was one
of the finest in the castle. A huge four-poster oak
bed, draped with emerald green velvet curtains,
adorned a broad, wooden dais. The mattress was
stuffed with goose down, as were the green satin
pillows and satin-covered comforter. A carved
chest sat at the foot of the bed, and another chest,
twice as large and high, stood against a nearby
tapestry-covered wall. Rushes mixed with sweet
herbs had been freshly laid on the floor.

The hearth fire burned brightly, as much to il-
luminate as to help dissipate the ever-present
chill from the thick stone walls. A pleasant tang
of woodsmoke mingled with the summer-sweet
scent of the rushes. Two high-backed wooden
chairs, comfortably padded with cushions, stood
before the fire, a small table between them. On
the table sat a crystal carafe of wine and two silver
goblets.

Stepping aside, Arien allowed Dane to enter,
then shut the door behind them. He walked to the
fire, bent, and extended his hands to the flames.

" 'Tis a fine room," he said finally, glancing
around. "And I see my belongings have already
been delivered."

Arien's gaze swung to the leather packs stacked neatly against the far wall beneath the iron-grilled window. Though of moderate size, there were only two. She frowned. "Are you certain they delivered all your belongings? Surely you brought more than two packs for a week's royal visit?"

"I brought what I needed, your grace, and no more." Dane turned from the fire. "When home, I'm a man of simple tastes. One pack is full of court finery, and the other holds the clothes I'll wear when not required to be in the king's presence."

"Ah, well . . ." Arien flushed, embarrassed she might have inadvertently implied he didn't know proper court dress. "I-I beg pardon, m'lord. I didn't mean to insinuate—"

" 'Tis of no import." Dane left the fire and walked over to stand before her, a chuckle rumbling in the depths of his broad chest. "And you really don't have to stay with me, you know. Your maid spoke wisely, suggesting 'twould be best if you attended the banquet. 'Tisn't proper for you, a princess and maiden," he added with a wry twist of his mouth, "to keep company alone with a man."

"And who here imagines I can be ravished against my will, m'lord? Indeed, what man aware of my magical abilities would dare try?"

There was something in the princess's voice, even as she stated the obvious, that snared Dane's attention. She sounded, he thought, almost wistful, as if she knew few men would ever want her for a lover, much less a wife. Yet, as a Moondancer, the princess was vowed to a celibate life. She shouldn't desire, much less regret renouncing, a man's touch.

He started to question Arien further, then thought better of it. Though he hoped to gain her trust and discover the truth behind her claims about the Ravens, Dane also knew he didn't dare risk becoming emotionally involved with her. Yet, as he stared down at Arien, the flickering fire bathing her intermittently in red-gold light then shadow, once again Dane found himself drowning in the turbulent, sea green pools that were her eyes.

Longing welled within him, a heart-deep pull as ancient and primal as the feelings he'd once had for his beloved Katrine. The realization startled him. Feelings for a soul-rotted Moondancer witch? Truly, the stress of his difficult circumstances must have finally tipped him over the edge of sanity!

Yet, try as he might to regain his usually clearheaded, pragmatic outlook, Dane couldn't shake the notion that he and Arien shared a common bond, were somehow linked by destiny. But how, and why?

Anger flooded him. Anger at his rising confusion. Anger at the loss of emotional control whenever he contemplated Arien's beguiling face or gazed into her luminous eyes. It was far past infuriating; it was unnerving, and more than a bit frightening.

The longer he was with the sprightly princess, Dane admitted, the less he believed she was the evil sorceress the tales made her out to be. But therein lay the rub. He'd come to Castle Talamontes determined to set aright the problems facing Greystone. And one of the biggest problems was the issue of the Moondancers, and the effects the two Moondancer princesses were said to have upon their father.

It would be difficult to ascertain in the course of a week whether the king's youngest daughter truly was as innocent as she seemed. However, the alternative—cold-bloodedly killing her along with her sister—was equally troublesome. Dane inwardly cursed. If only things had gone as he'd first planned . . .

"Your magic, be it truly of good origins," Dane forced himself to reply, "shouldn't deter most men, your grace. You're of royal blood, and most comely in the bargain. Many men would desire such a pleasant, as well as advantageous, union."

And what of you, Lord Haversin? Could you ever desire such a union? Silently, Arien asked what she knew she dared not say out loud. Then, realizing belatedly that he'd rendered her a compliment, she flushed. "I thank you, m'lord."

Dane frowned, puzzled. "For what?"

"You said I was comely. I rarely hear such words from men's lips." She smiled with wry self-disparagement. "Well, mayhap 'tis for the best. Though vowed to lifelong celibacy as a Moondancer, I'm still a woman and find my head easily turned by such flattery."

"So 'tis best you not hear any, is that it?"

At the tone of gentle compassion in his voice, Arien's head jerked up. "You must think me a fool."

"Nay, never that." He moved yet closer and took her by the arms. "In truth, I find you most disconcerting, and naught like the woman I thought to discover."

Gazing up at him, Arien found she could hardly breathe. He stood so close that the scents of man and leather and horse engulfed her. Ah, how she wanted him to take her into his arms and hold her tight.

There was strength and sanctuary within the span of those powerful arms. Yet there was something else, too. Something compelling and mysterious. Something that whispered ever so softly of yet another way, a way of peace, happiness, and fulfillment such as she'd never known before—never . . . not even in her most sublime moments of magic, when she danced and sang and spun her spells beneath the light of the full moon.

A knock sounded at the door. Arien staggered backward, wrenching herself free of Dane's light clasp. "The . . . the door," she gasped inanely. "Someone's at the door."

"Enter," he called over his shoulder. Then, as if realizing how close they were standing and how that intimate stance might appear to their unknown visitor, Dane also took a few quick steps backward.

The door swung open and Onora walked in, the basket of ointments and simples hanging from one arm, and a cloth-covered tray in her hands. "Yer supper, m'lord," she announced rather loudly, shooting Arien a quelling look. The maidservant made a beeline to the fireside table, shoved aside the wine carafe and silver cups, and laid down the covered food tray.

"There's a slab o' roast boar; two pigeons stuffed with bread, raisins, and almonds; a mess o' fresh greens from the garden, a small round o' good yellow cheese; and, for dessert, fresh plums and a mincemeat pastry. Ye've already got wine, but I also brought a tankard o' dark ale, in case ye've a taste for a more hearty sort o' drink."

"I'm sure 'twill all be quite tasty." Dane walked over and took a seat before the table.

Onora glanced at Arien. "Well, there's no point in ye lingering here, m'lady. Lord Dane is quite capable o' feeding himself, and yer father—"

Reminded her father was still expecting her at the banquet, Arien immediately cut off her servant's less than subtle hint that it was inappropriate to remain here with Dane Haversin. "Aye, m'lord's indeed capable of feeding himself," she stated firmly, "but he still needs assistance in tending his head wound. You may go, Onora. When I'm finished"—Arien slipped the basket of ointments and simples from the other woman's arm—"I'll meet you in my bedchamber."

"But, m'lady, if yer father were to find ye alone here with the Lord Dane—"

"He'd find naught amiss, Onora." Arien leveled a stern stare at her maid. "Now, no more of it. I'll see you shortly."

The servant bowed and backed away. "As ye wish, m'lady."

Once Onora had shut the door behind her, Dane finally spoke. "Your grace, my supper grows cold. If you're still of a mind to treat my head wound, then pray, let's be about it."

Arien whirled around from her frowning contemplation of the closed door. "Oh, aye, I suppose you're right." She pulled over a padded footstool, took her seat before him, then placed the basket upon her lap. After sorting through its contents, Arien extracted a small, covered pottery jar, clean bandages, and a flask of watered-down wine. She carefully untied the makeshift bandage from Dane's head, removed it, and set it aside. Taking up the flask, she next poured some of the watered wine onto a clean cloth.

"This may sting a bit,"—Arien dabbed the cloth lightly over the gash on Dane's forehead—"but 'twill cleanse and disinfect the wound."

As the cloth touched his head, Dane winced but said nothing. Arien quickly cleansed the gash, then scooped a small dollop of a bright yellow ointment from the pottery jar.

Dane eyed it suspiciously. "What's that?"

"Naught but a simple marigold salve to hasten your healing." She arched a brow. "Have you never used such a salve on your wounds before?"

"Aye." His mouth tightened. " 'Tisn't that. I but wished to ascertain if the salve was made solely by man, or had some magical spell woven into it."

"Why would you fear a spell, even if 'twas in the ointment?" Arien leaned back and studied him intently. "After all I've told you of the Moondancers, do you still think me capable of using my magic to harm you?"

"There's great evil afoot," Dane muttered, averting his gaze. "And 'twas you who admitted that not all Moondancers are good."

She sat there, myriad emotions churning within her. "You don't trust me, do you, m'lord?"

He met her gaze unflinchingly. "Nay, your grace. I cannot say I do."

"Well, I suppose there's no reason for you to trust me." Arien toyed with the thick, gooey ointment to avoid looking at him. "You hardly know me, and the tales flying around Greystone about some of the Moondancers are fearsome indeed." She forced herself to look up. "But I tell you true: if I wished to place a harmful spell on you, I wouldn't need to hide it within some ointment.

Indeed, my magic is of the highest kind. You'd never know you were bespelled."

Dane's mouth twisted wryly. "You've a high opinion of yourself."

"I only speak the truth. I've been gifted with a unique ability to acquire magical powers with the greatest of ease. 'Tis the result of no special skill on my part, mind you, but only a natural propensity I've had since I was a wee one."

"So you're the most powerful sorceress among all the Moondancers, are you?"

Arien sighed. "There are none more skilled than I, save our high priestess, Dorianne."

"Yet you seem distressed by this. Why is that, your grace?"

" 'Tis a heavy burden, m'lord, carrying with it a large responsibility." She glanced down at the glob of ointment still glistening on her fingertips, then back up at him. "Now, no more of this. Will you permit me to finish caring for your wound or not?"

His gaze bored into hers. Then he nodded. "Aye, finish what you started. I beg pardon for my tactless words earlier."

"No apology is necessary, m'lord." Arien dabbed the ointment on Dane's wound. "You were honest. That in itself is a mark of confidence. If you thought me evil, you'd never have dared broach such a subject."

"And you're far too naive if you think me that transparent." His gaze became hard, ruthless. "Have a care, princess. Most men aren't what they seem, and a good, trusting heart is more easily manipulated than a corrupt one."

She applied a clean, folded cloth to his forehead, then began wrapping a fresh bandage about

78

it. "Is that, then, what you plan to do, m'lord? Manipulate me to serve your needs?"

Dane went tense, still, beneath her hands. "I've no heart for the manipulation or destruction of others," he said at last. "But I tell you true: I also cannot stomach watching Greystone's slow and inevitable decay."

"I'd never wish such a tragedy on Greystone, either, m'lord." Arien tied off the bandage and leaned back. "But you never answered my question. Do you wish me harm?"

He was quiet for a long moment, and then said softly, "Nay, your grace. I cannot say I wish you harm."

Gazing into Dane's eyes, Arien saw the truth of his words, and saw, as well, an equally anguished turmoil. He's in sore conflict, she realized, battling opposing needs that are slowly tearing him apart. Harking back to the dwarf's disturbing visions earlier this eve, she felt a lancing pain shoot through her. So, Arien thought, it begins.

An impulse to reach out to Dane, to take him into her arms and soothe away his torment, filled her. But it was also an impulse, Arien reminded herself sadly, that would neither be appreciated nor welcomed. She was naught to him, naught save the second daughter of a sovereign he neither respected nor wished to serve. And, despite the dwarf's strange mutterings this night, that was all it must ever be.

Dane turned, twisting to take up a cup and fill it with ale. As he did, the light caught on his white linen shirt, exposing a long rent in the cloth over his left shoulder and back. The fabric's edges were stained with blood. Deep within the tear, the flesh appeared reddened and lacerated.

"M'lord," Arien cried out, reaching out to him. "You've yet another wound on your back."

As if realizing too late he'd revealed more than he wished her to know, Dane jerked around, the cup clenched in his hand. From his guilty expression, it was evident he hadn't meant for her to see his other injury. " 'Tis of no concern. I've suffered far worse than this wee scratch."

"Mayhap so, but 'tis foolish to ignore what I can easily care for as well." She stood and held out her hand.

Warily, he stared up at her.

"Give me your cup. Then I'll help you remove your shirt so I can better cleanse that wound on your back. Though you call it a scratch, I see it far more clearly than you. 'Tis deep and angry."

"And you, your grace, are long overdue at your father's banquet. You need to return posthaste to your maid and bedchamber."

Arien smiled down at him. "Aye, that I do. Needless argument, however, only delays my departure." Again, she extended her hand. "Your shirt, m'lord."

"Stubborn little wench, aren't you?" Without further protest, Dane handed her the cup, then unfastened the front of his shirt and attempted to slip out of it. The effort, however, appeared to set his back to throbbing. He grimaced, clenching his teeth.

"Here, let me help." Arien leaned down and began tugging at his shirt. His sudden nearness set her head to whirling. By the Mother, she thought, why did he stir such a fluttering in her chest and rouse such longings with just the closeness of his presence? True, he was a handsome, strapping man, but she'd seen many fine specimens such as he every day in her father's guard. It was beyond comprehension that a man should suddenly and inexplicably affect her so.

She shoved Dane's shirt open and off his shoulders, exposing his broad, powerful chest. Staring down at it, Arien felt the breath squeeze from her lungs. His firmly muscled pectorals, covered by a light sprinkling of dark brown body hair, jutted above a tautly undulating, hair-roughened abdomen. As his chest was exposed to the stone-cooled bedchamber, a shiver rippled over his skin and his flat male nipples hardened into taut little peaks.

Arien couldn't tear her gaze from Dane's chest. With all her might, she battled a compelling but equally shocking desire to lower her head and gently lave his nipples with her tongue. The need was surprisingly painful, an ardent lance that pierced straight through to her woman's core. Yet Arien also knew she dared not surrender to such carnal impulses. Nay, not even though an answering light of desire gleamed just as brightly in the depths of Dane's striking blue eyes.

Her heart thundering, Arien tugged the shirt down Dane's arms and pulled it away. "There," she said, her voice little more than a dry croak, "if you will, turn and I'll see to your back."

Almost as if he hadn't heard, Dane sat there for a long moment, staring up at her, his hands clenched at his sides. His big chest rose and fell erratically.

"Arien . . . I . . . ." His voice faded. He inhaled a ragged breath. Then, without another word, Dane leaped to his feet and turned away.

Presented with the muscled, masculine expanse of smooth, broad shoulders tapering to a trim waist, Arien had all she could do to maintain her rapidly waning composure. With trembling hands, she poured more watered-down wine on the cloth and began dabbing at the long, shallow slash angling from Dane's left shoulder blade to his backbone. A few minutes more, and the marigold ointment was slathered generously over the wound, and another folded cloth covered it.

Binding the bandage snugly in place, however, was more difficult than Arien had expected. Dane Haversin was a tall, strongly built man. Even with his assistance in anchoring the bandage in place while she moved about him unrolling the cloth strip, Arien still found it necessary to lean against him to reach around and grasp the end. Inadvertently, her cheek brushed his chest. Coarse body hair stroked her face. His musky male scent filled her nostrils.

Arien froze, swallowing hard. *Holy Mother* . . .

"You make it hard for a man to respect your royal position, much less your Moondancer vows of chastity,"—Dane's deep voice rumbled against her ear—"when you press your soft, sweet body so close to his."

With a gasp, Arien leaped back. She lost her grip on the cloth she'd just managed to grasp behind his back. In a languorous flutter of white, it fell to the floor.

"I-I'm sorry." Twinkling blue eyes met hers. A hot rush of blood flooded her face. "I-I meant naught by it," she stammered. "You're just so big, and the cloth so hard to—"

"Step away from him, daughter. Now. I command it!"

At the angry demand, Arien turned toward the door. King Cronan Talamontes and Edana stood in the open doorway, fury emanating from their every pore. Arien shot Dane an anguished glance.

"Do you wish for me to explain," he asked her quietly, pointedly ignoring their unexpected visitors, "or do you think 'twould come better from you?"

Another quick look at her father's face convinced her that Dane would have a difficult time extricating himself from what appeared to be a most compromising situation. A compromising situation, she admitted, which her stubbornness had unintentionally mired him in.

"Nay," Arien whispered with a quick shake of her head, " 'twould be best if the explanation came from me." She managed a wan smile. "Stay here. Let me deal with my father."

For a long moment Dane studied her gravely, then nodded. "As you wish, your grace."

Arien squared her slender shoulders, lifted her chin, and turned. As she strode across the bedchamber to stand before her father and sister, two hostile pairs of eyes followed her every movement. "Your majesty," Arien murmured, rendering the king the customary deep curtsy, " 'tisn't at all what it seems. I-I found Lord Haversin unconscious on the road leading to the castle and brought him here. I was but seeing to his injuries and assuring his comfort—as any good hostess would do—before hurrying to join you at the banquet."

"Indeed?" King Cronan glared down at her. Bushy, iron-gray brows met and melded. Dark green eyes glittered with disbelief. "I'll expect an explanation later as to why you were roaming in the dark this night of all nights, rather than sitting at table with me, as well as why I now find you unchaperoned in the room of a half-clothed man. For the present, however, go with your sister and await me in the Great Hall. Lord Haversin and I," he added, his mouth hardening into a thin, white line, "have a few things to discuss in private."

Arien opened her mouth to protest. "In *private*, daughter," her father silenced her savagely. "Now, go!" With an imperious finger, he indicated Edana.

"As you wish." Not daring another glance at Dane, Arien turned on her heel and joined her sister.

Edana graced her with a disdainful look, but her high color and the angry flash in her eyes belied her attempt at contemptuous indifference. "Come, sister," she said, and stalked from the room.

However, just as soon as they were out in the corridor and the door was closed behind them, Edana's cool demeanor was immediately snuffed out in the renewed conflagration of her rage. She grabbed Arien by the arm, her long nails gouging painfully into soft flesh. "How did you discover my secret with such speed and ease?" Edana hissed. "Did you at long last use that simple-minded magic of yours? 'Twould be so like you, Arien, to thwart the most important scheme of my life."

"I-I don't know what you're talking about." Unsuccessfully, Arien tried twisting free of her sister's bruising clasp. "I used no magic. 'Tis as I told Father. I but wished to help Lord Haversin."

"Did you now?" Edana pulled her close, her eyes smoldering pits of hatred. "And to what end, sister dear? To steal the man I intend to wed right from beneath my nose?"

Arien stared at her, dumbfounded. "The man you intend to wed?"

Her sister's lips curved in a cold, triumphant smile. "Aye. The man I *will* wed. The Lord Dane Haversin. The man who'll assure, once and for all, the future of our house and kingdom—until I need him no more."

Chapter Five

"In preparation for the monthly feast of the full moon, our high priestess is in seclusion and cannot be disturbed," Ursla said with a distasteful little pout. "You know that, your grace, as well as I."

Frustration filled Arien. By the Mother, she thought, this wasn't the time or place to insist upon ceremonial niceties. At the very least, a man's freedom could hang in the balance. And, at the worst . . .

Arien shivered. At the worst, her father and sister could be plotting some heinous crime against Dane Haversin. A crime of forced marriage that might ultimately strip him of his ancestral lands and power. Such a plan would suit their father well, she knew. But what did Edana stand to gain? Would she truly use Dane to strengthen her Raven's powers, draining him of his life essence before finally killing him?

The thought sickened Arien. She could not, would not, allow such a terrible injustice to occur. Dane was a fine, honorable man. It wasn't right that he should be batted about like some pawn in her father and sister's self-serving games. And Greystone . . . already Greystone had suffered far too much.

Yet Arien's powers—strong as they were—were bound by Moondancer strictures and limited to nonharmful, noncoercive purposes. There seemed nothing she could do to stop her sister. Only Dorianne might still bear enough influence over Edana. And Dorianne had to be informed immediately.

"Aye, I know 'tis time for our high priestess's seclusion, dear sister," Arien gritted sweetly at the short, pinch-faced older woman. "But I've information that cannot wait until the full moon rises in another two days. By then, it may well be too late."

"If you interrupt her," Ursla grumbled, "she'll be displeased, and I'll be to blame."

Good, Arien thought, she was finally making some headway. "Nay, sister. I'll tell her I insisted, that I all but pushed you aside in my determination to see her. Besides, Dorianne knows no Moondancer save she can withstand me."

Ursla scowled. "True enough. Not that you must constantly puff yourself up boasting of your superior powers. It doesn't endear you to any of us, you can be sure."

Arien flushed. "I beg pardon, sister. Truly, no offense was intended. 'Twas thoughtless of me."

" 'Twas indeed." The other priestess motioned toward the stone building set on the hill. "Have at it, then. You'd get your way sooner or later at any rate, wouldn't you?"

"My thanks for your understanding," Arien murmured, gathering her long skirts and sweeping past Ursla. Though it was most disturbing that some of the Moondancers, like Sister Ursla, seemed to resent her, there was no time to spare just now worrying over it. Matters of potentially far greater import to a great many more people drove her on.

Without even a backward glance, Arien hurried on, her attention already focused on the long building up ahead. Gleaming milk white in the midmorning sun, the marble-faced structure with its pillared porches formed a three-sided framework for the lush garden and small stone hut in its center. There, Arien knew, their high priestess had taken her monthly retreat from the rest of the community.

In the rising warmth of the summer morn, the drooping willows and flowers blooming everywhere imparted an impression of coolness to the garden. As she passed the small fountain fashioned of moss-covered boulders with a simple jet of water spurting from its center, a refreshing moisture misted Arien's face. She brushed aside the damp hair clinging to her forehead, then, as she drew up before the hermitage's polished ebony wood doors, made one last check to assure her *luna* was properly fastened and hung in modest folds from her neck to her fingertips and toes.

"Enter, child," came the soft command before Arien could even lift her hand to knock. She smiled. At least that aspect of Dorianne's powers was undiminished by age. Lifting the carved, crescent-shaped door handle, Arien opened the door and entered.

The high priestess sat across the expanse of the whitewashed hut, gazing out the room's single window onto the back side of the garden. The one-room dwelling was simply furnished with a neatly made bed; a small table set with a pottery pitcher and cups; two chairs; and an altar covered with a white cloth, several unlit candles, a bowl of water, and a ceremonial knife. At Arien's entrance, Dorianne turned and held out her hand.

Hurrying over, in a gesture of loving respect Arien knelt and kissed the outstretched hand. Royal princess though she was, in the presence of the Moondancer high priestess, Arien was of no more consequence than any other sister.

Dorianne cupped Arien's chin, lifting her gaze to meet hers. Kind gray eyes, rheumy with age, studied her slowly, thoughtfully. Though the old woman's face was furrowed, the skin was still soft and becomingly washed with shades of rose and cream. She wore her long, white hair bound beneath the traditional gauzy veil and white gold circlet of her office, from which dangled an oval moonstone at the center. Her elegant *luna* encompassed all the varying hues, from onyx to silver, of moonlight.

"Rise, child."

"My lady," Arien made haste to say as she climbed to her feet. "Forgive my impertinence in coming to you at such a time, but I—"

" 'Tis forgiven, child." Dorianne motioned to the other chair. "Sit and take your ease. You would never have dared interrupt my seclusion save for the most urgent of reasons. Sit."

Arien sighed, then did as requested.

Dorianne waited until she was settled, and then smiled benignly. "Now, what is it, child? What has happened to cause you such distress?"

She squared her shoulders and inhaled a steadying breath. " 'Tis Edana, my lady. She plots with my father to wed the Lord Dane Haversin."

"Indeed? And, aside from violating her vows of chastity—vows easily dispensed with as a royal princess—what is so terrible about that? Her marriage would serve us well."

"How so, my lady?" Arien asked, puzzled.

"Though marriage is severely frowned upon, Edana could remain a Moondancer if she weds. She could never, however, become high priestess. Moondancer law forbids it." The old woman smiled thinly. "With Edana's marriage, the greatest threat to your own ascendancy would finally be eliminated."

Arien clamped down on a bitter retort. Why did everyone assume she wanted to be the next high priestess?

To hide the rebellious fires she knew must be burning in her eyes, Arien lowered her gaze. "Aye, 'twould seem so, my lady."

Dorianne cocked her head. The moonstone on her forehead angled sideways. "Is this Lord Haversin truly as good and kind as the tales would have him?"

"From what I know of him, aye, my lady."

"Then, mayhap, if Edana comes to love him and he, her, 'twill turn her at last from the Ravens' evil ways." A hopeful, dreamy light flared in the old woman's eyes. "Love has been known to work miracles."

The possibility of Dane falling in love with Edana sent a strange little pain twisting through Arien. Dane deserved a far, far better woman and wife than Edana could ever be. That such a woman might possibly be herself, though, was a notion from which Arien immediately recoiled.

" 'Twould be a wondrous thing—Edana rejecting the Ravens—but one I fear will never come to pass." Arien leaned forward, resting her forearms on her legs, and clasped her hands before her. "I fear Edana and my father plan to use Dane for their own ends and, when he's served his purpose, discard him."

Dorianne's white brows slanted into a frown. "Kill him, you mean?"

"Aye. Father hates Dane and, after Edana and myself, views him as someone who might claim the throne. He also covets Dane's rich mountain lands. And Edana . . ." Arien paused and stared down at her hands, unsure how to phrase her next words. Finally, she decided that to spare the high priestess the truth would only minimize a very real threat. Besides, it was past time Dorianne confronted the true gravity of the situation with Edana and the Ravens.

"Go on, child," the older woman prodded gently. "I cannot be of assistance unless I know it all."

"And know it all you shall, my lady." Arien looked up. "I fear Edana thinks to further her Raven powers by taking Dane as lover and drawing on his masculine strength. Then, when he's no longer of use, she'll sacrifice him." She paused, a sudden, troubling thought assailing her. "I've a question, my lady."

"Aye, child?"

"This law you spoke of, the one forbidding a wedded woman from ever becoming high priestess. Is Moondancer magic strong enough to enforce it? Against Raven power enhanced by bedding one of the finest, bravest men in Greystone?"

The high priestess blanched. For a long moment, Arien thought she might faint or fall into another one of her apoplectic seizures. Rising, Arien hurried to the table holding the pitcher and cups, and poured out some water. "Here, my lady," she urged, returning to Dorianne's side. "Drink. 'Twill help you compose yourself."

"Will it now?" Her look haunted, the old woman accepted the cup and quickly downed its contents. "You utter terrible accusations against your sister," she said finally, handing the cup back to Arien. "What proof have you to support these suspicions?"

"Only what Edana has told me, and—" Arien hesitated, unsure if she should risk upsetting Dorianne further by mentioning the dwarf. She'd already decided it wasn't the time to press her about the adequacy of her abilities, as high priestess, to control Edana if she grew much stronger.

"Go on, child."

Arien wavered but an instant longer. It was worth the risk, she decided. Dorianne must know it all. She forced out the words. "What Edana told me of her plans for Dane Haversin, a dwarf only just recently confirmed."

"A d-dwarf?"

For an instant, Arien feared the high priestess might yet swoon. Then Dorianne recovered and, leaning forward, eyed her narrowly.

"Whatever possessed you to speak with a dwarf?" she demanded. "They are tainted souls. Their motives, as well as their magic, are suspect."

"I met the dwarf two nights past, my lady, when I accompanied my maidservant to retrieve a pair of wedding rings she'd hired him to make. He told me many things"—slowly, Arien wet her lips—"things that disturbed me greatly."

"The dwarf who lives beneath the Stone of the Little Men?" Rising horror edged Dorianne's voice. "You met and talked with *that* dwarf?"

"Aye," Arien replied carefully. "I know of no other."

"There is no other, and I'd have done well not to have allowed that one back in Greystone. But he seemed half-mad, and without the support of his brothers. . . . Well, obviously he cannot be trusted." To add emphasis to that pronouncement, the old woman gave a vehement shake of her head. "His powers are of the old kind. One can never be certain which master he truly follows. 'Twas that way with all dwarves. That was why, in the end, we Moondancers were forced to assert our power over them."

"Are you implying, my lady, that this dwarf might have told me what he did to manipulate me to his own purposes?"

"Aye, that I am. Indeed, 'tis even conceivable he's somehow in league with Edana, and they plot to ruin the Moondancers through you."

She'd considered just such a possibility, Arien thought, that night Garth Dorwen had reminded her that her duty to the land and people was a higher calling than any Moondancer vow of chastity. Yet what evil purpose was served in trying to get her, instead of Edana, to wed Dane Haversin? Dorianne had assured her that legitimate dispensations could be made from Moondancer vows, enabling her and Edana to wed and further the royal line.

Then, in a sickening rush of insight, the answer came. If she wed Dane Haversin, Arien realized, she could never be high priestess. But whose purpose did the dwarf serve in preventing her from becoming Moondancer high priestess? Edana's, his own, or someone else's altogether?

The consideration angered Arien. It was one thing for her to bemoan her destiny as Moondancer high priestess. It was another entirely for some churlish, conniving rogue of a dwarf to interfere in matters of the gravest import both to the sisterhood and Greystone alike.

"We cannot know what the dwarf truly plans," Dorianne muttered to herself. " 'Tis evil, whatever 'tis. Therefore, 'tis best to take the middle road, allowing fate to journey where 'twill. Aye, the middle road," she said, brightening with resolve. " 'Tis the wisest course in difficult times such as these. Too much meddling can only cause unforeseeable and irreparable complications."

The middle road . . .

The words made her recall Dane Haversin, passionately arguing that Arien had a sacred responsibility to take control, to do something about the Ravens before it was too late. That there could be no middle road . . .

Yet the Moondancer high priestess was now advising just such a plan, and Arien was sworn to obey her in all things. The thought of abandoning Dane Haversin to the evil magic and machinations of her sister, however, was painful to contemplate. He'd surely be destroyed if nothing was done to save him. Indeed, what other fate could possibly be his, when dark magic desired him, body and soul, and white magic hesitated to help him?

Despite Dorianne's pronouncement, where was the justice—or wisdom—in that?

"You must do naught, child." Dorianne's thin, wavering voice intruded on Arien's anguished considerations. "When I am gone, you are the Moondancers' only hope. The time, though, is not yet right for you to confront the Ravens. As powerful as your magic is, you are not ready. And, until you *are* ready, you must not risk your precious gifts scrabbling with your sister over some man. Edana would be the only winner, I assure you."

She isna ready.

Why now, Arien thought in an agony of seething frustration, must those words of the dwarf's strange little song return to haunt her? If they truly did speak of her, what did the words mean? And did she dare heed them?

" 'Tis true enough we cannot allow Edana to win, my lady," Arien forced herself to reply. "But 'twould also be wrong to allow Lord Haversin to suffer."

" 'Twould indeed be a tragedy, if such a thing were to come to pass." The moonstone bobbed up and down as Dorianne nodded her agreement. "We cannot be certain, however, that 'twill come to pass. In the meanwhile, I forbid you to interfere in Edana's wedding. Do you hear me, child? Do you understand?"

Aye, she understood quite well, Arien thought. Yet why, when all was said and done, did the understanding bring no peace or acceptance? Never had she felt such pain, such unrest, such . . . such outright resentment.

The greatest torment of all, though, was that shattering sense of being torn asunder, of suddenly finding herself straddling two worlds.

"Tell me true, cousin," Phelan demanded the next day as he and Dane returned to Castle Talamontes after a brisk morning ride. "I've held my curiosity back as long as I could, hoping you'd share the news with me. But now, since 'tis apparent you're determined to be singularly closemouthed . . . well, you've forced me to ask outright."

Amused, Dane glanced at the younger man. "Then, pray, ask away. I haven't any idea what you're talking about."

"Haven't a-any idea!" Phelan sputtered indignantly. "You're to wed the Princess Edana and wear the crown matrimonial, and you've no idea what I'm talking about? Pfffff," he snorted in disgust. "If I didn't know better, I'd wager a month of Guilford's taxes that you're the only person in Castle Talamontes who isn't in on this."

"Wed Princess Edana? Be granted equal right to rule upon the king's death?" Dane gaped at his cousin in disbelief. "And when did *this* outrageous tale arise? Last night in the midst of your cups?"

"I wasn't drunk," Phelan protested stoutly. "I was but pleasantly inebriated, as were all the other nobles who remained behind in the Great Hall after you left for bed. 'Twas then that I heard the tale, straight from Duke Nevyn Crowell, the king's closest adviser. He spoke as if 'twas already settled, so I thought you must already have offered for the princess's hand."

By the Mother, what more could happen to befoul his plans? Dane wondered. "Naught has been settled," he snapped. "Indeed, the Princess Edana is the last woman I'd conceive of taking to wife."

Just then, the pennant-topped turrets of Castle Talamontes came into view. With a savage snarl, Dane urged his warhorse into a fast gallop.

Phelan, left suddenly behind, gave an outraged shout and spurred his mount after him. "Cousin, have a care! Wh-what do you mean to do?" he cried when he finally drew alongside Dane's horse.

"What do you think?" Dane shot him a furious, frustrated look. "Seek out Duke Crowell and get to the bottom of this, before the ridiculous rumor spreads!"

"Duke Crowell is in conference with the king, who has expressly stated that they cannot be disturbed for the next several hours," the royal seneschal proclaimed imperiously. "I can, however, convey your desire to speak with the duke. Mayhap, when the king no longer requires his presence, 'twill be possible to gain audience with him later this afternoon, before he retires to dress for this eve's banquet. And, if not," the gaudily dressed man added with a careless shrug, "there's always the morrow."

"Indeed?" Dane turned to Phelan. "Obviously there's at least one other person in the castle besides me," he muttered softly, "who doesn't know of my recently elevated status as the king's future son-in-law. 'Twould place me well above a duke, would it not?"

Phelan grinned. "Aye, 'twould seem so. Mayhap 'tis why Crowell is even now conferring with the king, in hopes of filching the fair Edana for himself. But if such were the case, why would he have shared the news of your and Edana's upcoming marriage with us last night?" The blond nobleman shook his head in puzzlement. "Truly, this gets stranger and stranger with each passing moment."

"Aye, does it not?" Dane swung back to the seneschal. "Tell me, then, where might I find the Princess Edana? For what I need to say, she'll do equally as well."

"The princess is in seclusion in preparation for the morrow's feast of the full moon. She has asked not to be disturbed."

Dane inhaled a shuddering breath. "One would almost think the king, princess, and duke intend purposely to avoid me. I must insist—"

Just then, Princess Arien's maidservant hurried by. Dane promptly forgot the seneschal and raced after the woman. "Lady . . . er, Onora . . . pray, stop. I must speak with you."

The red-haired woman slid to a halt. "What is it now? I'm a busy woman and haven't the—" As she realized who'd called out to her, the indignant expression faded from Onora's face. She flushed crimson to the tip of her nose. "Ah, I beg yer pardon, m'lord. I thought ye some other servant and—"

"It doesn't matter." Dane drew up before her and forced a smile. "Your mistress, the Princess Arien. Where may I find her at this time of day?"

Onora scrunched her brow in thought. "Well, I haven't seen her since she rose at dawn to supervise today's preparations. I wouldn't be surprised, though, if she isn't somewhere in the vicinity o' the kitchen, or else overseeing the picking o' the vegetables in the garden. These nightly banquets have kept the poor dear running nearly from dawn to dusk, and wi' no help whatsoever from her lazy sister, either." As if realizing she'd said too much, the maidservant looked horrified and covered her mouth with her hand. "Oh, I beg pardon, m'lord, for speaking ill o' the Princess Edana. Ye willna tell her, will ye, m'lord?"

"Nay, I'll not tell her if, in return, you'll do me a small favor."

"A favor, m'lord?" Onora's eyes brightened with interest.

"Find the Princess Arien for me, and ask if she'd be so kind as to meet me in the castle garden beside the dragon fountain. I promise not to squander too much of her precious time, but 'tis most urgent I speak with her."

"She's very busy just now, m'lord," the red-haired woman said, eyeing him doubtfully. "Mayhap this afternoon—"

"Ask her, if you please. 'Twill not hurt at least to ask." Uncertainty filled Dane. Was Arien, then, also involved with this strange plot, and attempting to avoid him? After their encounter two days ago, he hadn't imagined her capable of such deception or dissembling. But then, it was also strange he'd not had opportunity to speak with her in the past two days. Nay, not even during last night's banquet.

"If she cannot come, you can deliver her message to me and spare her further inconvenience," he urged. "But tell her 'tis most important I speak with her. I wouldn't importune the princess otherwise."

Onora hesitated, then nodded her acquiescence. "I'll find m'lady and deliver yer message, m'lord. Ye can count on it."

"Good." Dane grinned in relief. "Tell her I'll await her in the garden for the next hour—in the event she can spare a few minutes from her other duties."

"I'll seek her now, m'lord." The maid curtsied and bustled away.

"And what do you hope to accomplish by speaking with the Princess Arien?" Phelan asked, coming up behind him. "From what I hear, she has little influence with the king. I'd wager she won't be able to extricate you from any royal machinations, be they the king's or her sister's."

"Mayhap not," Dane said with a sigh. "I hope, though, at least to hear the truth from her lips. Though the truth is a rare commodity these days in Castle Talamontes."

Cursing her ill fortune, Arien paused at the head of the stairs leading from the sprawling stone balcony down into the large flower and shrub garden. Until this moment, she'd been inordinately successful in avoiding Dane Haversin. If only she could have managed to continue to do so for the next four days!

His request to meet him in the garden had surprised her. Until now, he hadn't evidenced any desire to speak with her, which both relieved and unsettled Arien. She should have been glad for his lack of interest, but she wasn't. Nay, if the truth be told, she wished greatly to be with him.

Gathering her skirts, Arien made her way down the stairs and along the flagstone path bordered by neatly trimmed box hedges and raised beds crowded with creamy white lilies, regal irises, brilliant orange poppies, fragrant lavender, and her beloved rosebushes. Normally, Arien immersed herself in the unrivaled beauty and rich scents of the huge, circular garden. Today, though, more pressing matters dampened her enjoyment.

Surrounded by elm and sycamore trees, the dragon fountain could be heard before it was visible. The huge stone beast, its massive wings spread, reared on hind legs, its front feet clawing the air. From its fanged, open mouth, water spewed in a stylistic imitation of fire, then plummeted into a stone basin carved as an enormous treasure chest.

Nearby, beneath the sheltering span of leafy branches, Dane quietly awaited her. Arien forced a tremulous smile, then settled herself on the herb seat planted with sweet-smelling thyme. Unable to meet his steady gaze, she stalled for time by busily arranging and rearranging the shimmering folds of her *luna*.

"Forgive my boldness in requesting a private moment with you, your grace." Dane's deep voice, suddenly close by, startled Arien from her anxious preoccupation with her robe. "I know 'tis an imposition, but I had to speak with you."

Wide eyed, her heart racing, Arien glanced up. He'd moved nearer, and now stood directly before her. Words died in her throat.

" 'T-tis never an imposition to share a few moments with you, m'lord," she stammered finally. "Unfortunately, 'tis truly but a few moments. The dessert for this eve's banquet failed to rise— thanks to an inattentive new assistant—and Cook is beside herself. I promised I'd return shortly and help her choose another recipe."

" 'Twill not take long, I assure you." Dane hesitated, then gestured to the empty seat beside her.

101

"Would you mind if I sat next to you? My words are for your ears alone. If we're close, 'twill lessen the likelihood of our being overheard."

There were spies aplenty in Castle Talamontes, Arien well knew, some serving her father and others her sister. Knowing now what lay in store for Dane, she was loath to add to his misfortunes in any way. She patted the thick mass of tiny green leaves beside her. "I don't mind at all, m'lord. Come, sit and tell me what 'tis you want."

Dane lowered himself to the herb seat. As he did, the rich, tangy aroma of thyme rose to fill the air. Arien inhaled deeply, willing the scent to soothe her jangled nerves.

Whatever effect the thyme would have had, however, was lost in the immediate and overwhelming awareness of Dane Haversin's imposingly virile presence. Each time she was near him, Arien was struck anew by how big and powerful he was, by how blue his eyes were in contrast to his tanned skin, by how his shoulder-length chestnut brown hair so softly and naturally feathered back from his square-jawed, ruggedly handsome face, by how good he smelled.

A faint whiff of leather and horse wafted up to her. He'd only recently returned from riding, Arien realized, caught up in a sudden vision of Dane's long, strong legs expertly gripping his big warhorse. One vision swiftly led to another, until she saw that same strong body unclothed as he held her in his arms.

Ah, curse that wretched dwarf for showing me such images, Arien silently wailed. She feared she'd never be totally free of them again. In truth, she didn't want to be free of them, either.

"Your grace? Are you feeling well?"

With a painful effort, Arien wrenched her attention back to the moment. "What?" She flushed. "Aye, all is well. I was but momentarily distracted."

A fleeting look of confusion clouded his expression, then was gone. "Ah, the problems in the kitchen. I understand." Dane turned more fully to face her. "I'll not keep you any longer than I must. I but need confirmation of something recently shared with me. If 'tis true, 'tis most unsettling and places me in a very difficult position."

"And what would you have me do, m'lord?"

"Answer me honestly, then assist me, if need be, in extricating myself."

Arien frowned. Whatever was Dane about? "I'll be as truthful as I can, m'lord." She took his hand in hers. "Tell me what distresses you, m'lord. I can be of little use until I know the problem."

"Aye, 'tis true enough." Dane sighed and stared down at her hands. Then, dragging in an unsteady breath, he forced his gaze back to hers. "It has come to my attention that tales are being spread about me and your sister, the Princess Edana. I wish to know if they are true."

"And what are the tales, m'lord?" she made herself ask, all the while dreading the inevitable answer.

Dane's eyes darkened. " 'Tis said I'm to wed your sister, your grace. Tell me true. What do you know of this?"

Chapter Six

For a fleeting moment, Arien wished fervently for the ground to open and swallow her. One look at Dane, however, and she knew she couldn't run from the situation, even if the opportunity had been offered her. Was that how fate would entwine their hearts and lives then? Arien wondered. By forcing them together in a common cause?

"My sister mentioned her intent to wed a nobleman who'd attend this Triennial," she responded. "She didn't reveal 'twas you, however, until we left you and Father that night of your arrival."

"Then 'tis true." He eyed her narrowly. "Yet you said not a word of it to me in the past two days."

" 'Twas not any of my business who you chose to wed, m'lord."

"Chose to wed!" Rage flashed in Dane's eyes, but was quickly masked as he struggled visibly to control himself. "On my honor, your grace," he continued finally in a calmer voice, "I was never consulted about taking your sister as wife. I was only told of this a short while ago, by my cousin, no less."

"Then mayhap I was premature in corroborating your cousin's tale. Mayhap my sister may yet change her mind, and doesn't wish you to know until she's certain."

"Mayhap," Dane agreed grudgingly, "but I don't think so. At the last Triennial, your sister made her interest in me quite clear. Forgive my bluntness, but many were the times that she, in subtle and then not-so-subtle ways, offered to bed me. And many were the times since my wife's death that your father has sent envoys offering me your sister's hand in marriage. Nay,"—he shook his head—"I fear some new plot is afoot to ensure I will not escape a free man again."

"And is it such a terrible fate, m'lord? Wedding the crown princess?" Though it was obvious Dane seemed unwilling to marry Edana, Arien wanted to know why.

Dane subjected Arien to a cool, appraising look. "And what would you have me say? However I answer, I'm damned."

"Answer from your heart, m'lord." In spite of her efforts to control the response his piercing regard always had upon her, Arien's face flushed with rising excitement. "Whatever 'tis, I swear I'll find no offense in your reply."

His glance lowered to his hands. "Nay," Dane said softly, "I don't believe you would." He lifted his head and met her gaze. "Even as I lay there on that road in your arms, Moondancer though you are, I was swiftly and strongly convinced you were a good, honest woman." Dane chuckled wryly. "Yet when I rode out from Castle Haversin to attend this Triennial, I rode out with hatred in my heart for all Moondancers, and you and your sister in particular."

"Why, m'lord? What have we ever done to you?"

"What has your kind ever done to me?" His smile faded and his features contorted into a mask of impotent fury. "Naught," Dane ground out, "save place a lifelong curse on me and mine, forcing me to choose between my wife and unborn child, and my people. A choice condemning the Haversin line to extinction."

He shot her a sharp look. " 'Twas a Moondancer witch named Reyene. In the guise of providing a special adviser, your father sent her to spy on me. And I, not trusting anything or anyone who bore the king's mark of approval, soon turned Reyene out, ordering her to return to her master. 'Twas then she laid the curse upon me—a curse I could lift only by surrendering my will, and the control of Haversin and its lands, to the king. 'Twas too much for a man of pride and honor to bear. I, of course, refused. Two months later, my wife died in childbirth, unable to deliver our son."

Arien's eyes shut in horror. "So," she whispered half to herself, "Reyene must also be a Raven. No other kind of Moondancer would have possessed the dark powers necessary to cast such a spell." Her lids lifted and a single tear trickled down her cheek. "In the name of all my sisters, I am deeply ashamed and sorry. In her cruelty to you, Reyene has tainted us all."

"The blame isn't yours, your grace." Dane leaned over and, with a callused thumb, wiped her tear away. "I've finally realized that. But I cannot help suspecting Edana is somehow involved, as well as your father." His mouth twisted derisively. "Hence my lack of enthusiasm for wedding your sister."

So, Arien thought, her heart sinking, she had her answer. Dane loathed sorceresses. It was surprising he could even tolerate her.

"Edana has lost her way," she said by way of reply, wondering, even as she did, why she continued to justify her sister's actions. "I was too young to note it, but 'twas said it began when our mother died. Edana was at a very sensitive age then, just entering womanhood, and turned to the wrong people for guidance and support."

"The Ravens?"

Arien nodded. "Aye. By the time I was old enough to recognize their hold upon her, 'twas too late. And our high priestess . . . well, suffice it to say she is weary of life. Increasingly, she prefers compromise and avoids conflict whenever she can. Unfortunately, 'tisn't the time for such tactics, especially not with a sect as aggressive and determined as the Ravens. Yet without Dorianne's help, I fear Edana is forever lost."

"And you can do naught to change what is to come."

Stung by his gentle but unmistakable reproof, Arien bit back a sharp retort. "I am neither queen nor high priestess."

"Yet as royal princess, and an avowed Moondancer, isn't your first and highest calling to serve the land and people?"

At his words, something plucked at her memory. Arien's head jerked up. By the Mother, first the dwarf and now him! But they didn't— couldn't—understand.

Hands clenched at her sides, Arien stood. "Do you think I don't know my vows? Do you imagine me so selfish, so uncaring that I can turn my back on what is happening around me? I try to compensate for the evil, the injustice, in any way I can, but I'm only one person. Ah, by the Mother!" Arien squeezed shut her eyes and lifted her face to the heavens. "I try, truly I do, but I don't know what else to do!"

Rising, Dane took her by the arms. "Look at me, Arien."

Startled by his touch and the use of her name, Arien's eyes snapped open. "Wh-what do you want?" she choked out, knowing she teetered on the brink of bursting into tears and throwing herself into Dane's arms. But the comfort Arien sensed she'd find there would be fleeting; it would only deepen her agony when she must watch him go to her sister.

"I want to help you fight this Raven sect," Dane said with a fierce resolve. "Two people are better odds than one. Besides," he added with a lopsided grin, "warrior and leader that I am, my magical skills are sadly deficient. That's where you, fair lady, come in."

"You would join with me against my father and sister?"

"Aye, if 'twas necessary. 'Tisn't my desire, however, to turn you against your family." His expression darkened. "Once begun, though, there'd be no turning back. And the outcome could be bloody and brutal."

He speaks of overthrowing my father, Arien realized, mayhap even killing him. Yet if the king were threatened in any way, Edana would throw her support with him and be drawn into the carnage as well. And if the Ravens then cast their lot with Edana . . .

A fierce shudder racked Arien. "Nay," she whispered, her head drooping like some flower wilting on its stem, "there must be some other way. There must."

"If there is, sweet lady"—Dane's grip tightened on her arms—"I'll find it. You've my solemn vow on that. But you must also be fully aware of all possible consequences."

" 'Tis easy for you to say!" Arien wrenched herself free and staggered backward. " 'Tisn't your family who'll suffer. 'Tisn't your family who might well be destroyed."

"Nay, my family is already destroyed," he rasped thickly. A savage, scorching fury built and began to emanate from him. "But I still said and did what I had to, when I banished that Moondancer witch to protect my lands and people. And, to my eternal agony and regret, my family did suffer, and they were destroyed. So speak to me not of your fears, lady. We all may suffer the torments of the damned before this festering evil is cleansed from the land."

Arien stared at him aghast, conflicting emotions of shame and anger churning within. Then, as Dane's expression of righteous anger faded to haunted anguish, Arien's heart swelled in compassion. Holy Mother, how could she have been so tactless, so callous? Already he'd suffered so much! Yet if Edana took him to husband, his suffering would have just begun. . . .

She extended a hand. "Dane . . . I'm sorry."

"Nay. Don't." He took a step back, shaking his head, his expression ravaged, confused. "I don't need . . . don't want . . . your pity."

She turned away, overwhelmed by conflicting emotions. "I-I'm sorry." Her voice faltered. "I-I must go."

"Nay, Arien. Wait."

Dane moved toward her. It was, however, the worst thing he could have done. With a choking cry, Arien turned and fled, racing through a garden that had suddenly become a place of fearful destinies—and guilt-ridden, unspeakable possibilities.

"Shall I wash yer hair for the banquet, m'lady?" Onora asked late that afternoon as she emptied the last, steaming bucket of water into the big wooden tub. " 'Twill dress much more easily then," she added, sprinkling dried rose petals into the water, "and I've an exquisite new style I've been meaning to try on ye."

Arien turned from her bedchamber window. "Aye, if you wish."

The banquet would begin in another two hours. She had resolved numerous crises throughout the remainder of the day, and now all was finally in readiness. Ironically, for a change she'd almost been grateful for the frenetic pace and minor calamities. They'd kept her mind off the morning's disturbing visit with Dane.

But now . . . now when all the work was done, there was nothing left to distract Arien. She wondered anew how to extricate herself from this fearsome muddle. There had to be some other way. There just had to.

"Yer bath, m'lady," Onora said, interrupting Arien's morose thoughts. " 'Tis ready."

Schooling her features to hide her inner turmoil from her perceptive maid, Arien turned. Not surprisingly, Onora's eyes, as they scanned her face, were clouded with worry. "Come. I haven't a moment to spare." Arien began to unfasten the ties at the neck of her green silk dressing gown. "I must speak with the king before this night's banquet."

The maidservant cocked her head. "Ye must, must ye?"

She expected further explanation, Arien well knew. In the past, they'd always been more like close friends and confidantes, sisters even. But not this time. This time it was far too dangerous to involve anyone not already embroiled in Edana's horrific scheme.

"Aye, I must," Arien replied, her lips set in unswerving resolve. "And one thing more, Onora. 'Tis best you forestall washing my hair."

"And why is that, m'lady?"

"If the truth be told, after a day such as I've already had, I've neither the time nor patience for such an indulgence."

The king was in his massive library, taking his leisure in a great leather chair set before a roaring hearth fire. Garbed already in his banquet finery of a floor-length, purple silk tunic covered with a cloak of gold cloth overlaid by appliquéd gold-work embroidery that he'd then artfully arranged to hang over one shoulder, her father presented an imposingly regal picture.

A nearly empty crystal ewer of rich, red wine sat beside him on a brass table. A silver goblet filled to the brim dangled indolently from his pale, corpulent fingers, and an inebriated but decidedly predatory smile danced about his lips.

Arien quietly closed the secret door whose hallway linked the royal bedchambers and library to an escape tunnel leading far from the castle, then turned back to study her father. He was plotting something. Was it Dane Haversin's downfall? Was her father even now celebrating his imminent victory, counting the untold riches he'd acquire when he was at last legally united not only with the Haversin family, but its rich lands?

The skirts of her scarlet silk undergown rustled as she made her way to her father's side. At the sound, the king's head turned. Ever so slowly, a wide grin lifted his lips.

"Ah, Arien," he said, his deep, if somewhat slurred, voice muted in the huge room. "Come to usurp your sister's prerogative this night and escort us to the banquet?"

"If 'twould please you, sire, 'twould please me as well." She halted before him and curtsied. "But first, if you will, I've a need to speak to you of more serious matters."

Cronan frowned, then leaned back in his chair and took a sip of his wine. "A serious matter, is it? And has old Dorianne sent you on yet another errand for the Moondancers, then?"

"Nay, Father." Arien sank to her knees before him, and placed a hand on his silk-covered leg. " 'Tisn't for Dorianne I come here this night. 'Tis for the sake of a man, and mayhap, as well, for the sake of the kingdom."

A steel gray brow lifted. "Indeed? 'Tis as serious as all that?" He covered her hand with a short, broad one, the jewels of his myriad rings flashing brilliantly in the firelight. "You haven't gone and found yourself a man to wed, have you? 'Tis our right, and ours alone, to choose your husband."

For an irrational moment, Arien had to lower her head and choke back a laugh. Found herself a man to wed? Were her father and the dwarf in some strange sort of partnership, then, that both believed she should forsake her Moondancer vows? Yet, as unsettling as that question was, it was not nearly as unsettling as the realization that the dwarf envisioned a far different sort of mate than her father ever would.

But the king need never know what the dwarf desired. Indeed, if she could convince her father to order Edana to abandon her cruel plan, there'd never be any need to think of it again. If only she could convince him . . .

"Nay, sire." Arien gazed up at her father. "I've no wish to wed. I'm content to live out my life in chastity as a Moondancer. 'Tis of Edana I speak. Edana and her wish to wed Lord Haversin."

For a moment, the mention of his enemy's name must have swept aside the drunken mists. King Cronan's hand clenched about his goblet. His mouth hardened into a thin line and his shoulders stiffened. "Are we to assume, then, you don't approve of her wedding Haversin?"

The king was her last hope. She swallowed hard. "Nay, sire, I don't approve."

"And why is that, daughter? What could possibly disturb you about your sister wedding Lord Haversin?" the king inquired softly, the glint in his eyes belying his gentler tones. "Do you mayhap desire the man for your own, or are your motives more devious and petty?"

Arien frowned, puzzled. "Devious? Petty? Truly, sire, I don't understand."

"Don't you?" The king paused to take another deep, greedy swallow of his wine. In his carelessness, some of the dark red fluid trickled down his chin and pooled briefly on his tunic, before soaking into the expensive cloth. Heedless of the mess he was making, Cronan glared at Arien. "Edana warned us of your growing jealousy," he growled, "as she has gained increasing mastery of her Moondancer powers. In an attempt to foil your sister's success as our rightful heir, do you now seek to undermine her alliance with one of the realm's most powerful and wealthy nobles?"

"Nay, sire," Arien replied hoarsely, barely containing her impulse to hurl far more damning accusations back at her father. "I but fear for Lord Haversin's life. Though you may imagine her the obedient daughter in acquiescing to your long-standing wish to join with House Haversin, Edana does naught unless it wins her personal gain."

Ever so slowly, Cronan set down his silver goblet and leaned forward until he was but a wine-saturated breath from Arien's face. "Have a care, daughter. You come perilously close to maligning the crown princess."

"She's a Raven, Father! A Raven who dabbles in dark magic. And the only way a Raven attains power beyond that of the normal Moondancer is to draw it from a male during the act of mating."

Each word was wrenched from her with agonizing effort as Arien blurted out the painful secret she'd long withheld from the king.

"Do you think we care how your sister gains her powers?" Cronan hissed, his face now a livid mask. "What matters is that she uses those powers to serve us, rendering us a service you've always felt was beneath you to offer."

The blood drained from Arien's face. "Nay, Father," she whispered achingly. " 'Tisn't true. I've always been willing, tried to serve you, but there are limits, Moondancer limits, to—"

"The Talamontes accept no limits but those they choose to place upon themselves!" The king jerked away from Arien and slammed back into his chair. He gazed down at her with a furiously regal glare. "We are besieged on all sides, from peasants and nobles alike. And the Lord Haversin, above all the rest, threatens us most sorely. But once he is wed to Edana, he'll be forced to pledge total allegiance to the Talamontes. He'll be brought to heel at long last, and, with his submission, the nobility at last will be subdued."

"He'll never willingly wed Edana," Arien cried. "He despises all Moondancers after what Reyene did to him."

"Reyene, eh?" Once more, the king took up his goblet and drank from it, a slyly triumphant smile playing about his mouth. "A pity about his wife and unborn child," he observed when he'd finally had his fill. "But Haversin brought that tragedy down on himself. 'Twas his unyielding pride, in the end, that destroyed his wife and child. All we asked of him was a simple compromise, but he refused even to consider it. And then, while his wife writhed in her childbed pains, we tried once again, offering the services of one of our Moondancers to aid her. Yet still Haversin refused, preferring to see his wife die than choke down even the smallest bit of his monumental pride.

"Nay," Cronan said, "We pity the Lady Haversin, but never her husband. And as far as Dane Haversin's willingness to wed Edana, well, 'twas never of the slightest concern to either ourself or your sister. We want Haversin brought to heel; we want access to his lands, and we care not a whit how your sister gains his consent. One way or another, that man *will* wed Edana."

"All vows made under the auspices of dark magic are invalid."

"Did we say Haversin's vows would be made under the coercion of a spell?" The king shook his head, a pitying light in his eyes. "Ah, my poor, naive child. Think on it. We've but to use that noble's overweening pride against him yet again. If we and several other nobles—nobles handpicked for their unimpeachable honor yet also known for their loyalty to Haversin—find him coupling with Edana, who could doubt the truth of the discovery? And you know the law as well as we, daughter. If the deflowering of a noblewoman by a nobleman is observed by noble witnesses, there's no other option left for a man of honor. He must wed the woman."

"But Edana's no maiden," Arien protested, knowing, even as she did, there was no way of proving such a fact without shaming not only the Talamontes but the Moondancers as well.

"And who would dare accuse her? You?"

Arien closed her eyes, shutting out the horrible consequences of such an act. Once again, she was trapped. To publicly speak out against her father and sister was as unthinkable as to defy Dorianne. Yet therein lay the choice, if Dane Haversin was to be saved.

Once again, a pain like none she'd ever experienced lanced through Arien. A sense of being torn asunder, of straddling two worlds. Her father's face blurred; the room began to whirl before her. A rushing noise filled her mind, harsh, garbled sounds that gradually coalesced into a voice, then actual sentences.

Ye'll be back, mark my words. Garth Dorwen's rusty tones echoed in Arien's head, just as they'd echoed after her in the suddenly foreboding darkness as she'd fled him and the disturbing visions he'd spun for her. *Ye'll be back when ye finally face the truth o' what was revealed this night—and ye find I'm the only one with the power to aid ye.*

Had his parting taunt alluded to this exact situation? He'd admitted he knew of the plot to force Dane—"the love o' yer heart" had been his exact words—to wed Edana.

Once more, the panic rose to seize her. Had her carefree, girlish plan to spy on a dwarf at last come full circle? Arien asked herself. Dorianne had failed her when she'd needed her most. Her father's greed and her sister's lust for power had become a force carrying them all headlong to destruction. And Dane . . . Dane was helpless, doomed, unless she did what was forbidden.

From somewhere far away, hands closed cruelly on her shoulders and a voice, thick with drink, beckoned to her.

"Arien? Arien? Are you ill? Should we call your maidservant to fetch you?"

With a soft moan, she forced open her eyes and gazed up into her father's face. Somehow, he seemed different. Though his features were familiar, the king looked strange, indeed a stranger. She blinked, hoping to clear the disquieting impression. It didn't help.

"Nay." Arien shook her head. "I beg pardon if I alarmed you."

"What has alarmed us is that you'd even contemplate maligning your sister in such a way. To announce to the world that Edana's no maiden . . . For shame, daughter."

"Indeed, 'twould shame us all." Arien rose to her feet. "I couldn't do such a thing, even for Lord Haversin's sake."

117

Cronan grinned in relief, lifting his goblet to her in salute. "A true Talamontes, to think first and foremost of the family honor. We're proud of you, daughter."

"My thanks, sire." She took a step back and curtsied. "The time for the banquet draws near. By your leave, I'll depart now to ascertain if all is in readiness."

"And what of your earlier offer to escort us to the banquet?" The king paused to take another draft of his wine. As he did, the library door opened.

Edana swept in, magnificently attired in an amethyst silk gown encrusted with jewels. Her long, ebony hair was contained in a matching amethyst and silver-colored caul topped by a silver coronet. Striding over imperiously to Arien and the king, she graced her sister with a brief, disdainful glance, then curtsied to their father. " 'Tis nearly time for supper, sire."

"Ah, so 'tis." Cronan eyed Arien. "If there's naught else, daughter, you've our leave to depart."

Arien curtsied once more, then turned and all but fled the library. With her emotions lying so close to the surface just now, it was foolhardy to risk saying something that might betray her. Arien could only hope her father's wine-besotted memory would fail him when it came to the sharing of their earlier conversation with her sister.

'Twas a chance, however, she must take. There was scant time left to squander in impotent quaking. Scant time, as well, to bemoan the cruel fate now compelling her to such a desperate act.

No matter the risk, she must confront Garth Dorwen one more time. If there was any way to learn what the dwarf knew and planned, she must hear it. As it now was, she was trapped between loyalty to her father and the Moondancer high priestess, and her outrage at their indifference to what was soon to happen to Dane Haversin.

Mayhap the dwarf knew more of Edana's plans than he was willing to share. Arien meant to find out. Garth Dorwen would tell her this night, or she'd threaten to use the knowledge of his secret name to destroy him. She didn't know what she'd do, though, if Garth Dorwen called her bluff.

Now that Dorianne, however, knew of her first visit to the dwarf, she was sure to have set watchers over him. There was only one way to prevent the high priestess from discovering her disobedience. Tomorrow night, on the feast of the full moon, all Moondancers were called to the great stone circle in the Glen of Women to celebrate the moon's rising. All Moondancers save her and Edana, who, because this month's full moon coincided with the Triennial, had been temporarily excused.

As loath as Arien was to debase that sacred eve in seeking out a user of dark magic, there was no other choice. It was most likely her one and only opportunity to meet with the dwarf undetected, and time for Dane Haversin was most definitely running out. Somehow, Arien knew Edana and their father meant to take Dane before the Triennial ended. And the Triennial ended in but another four days.

The exact details of when the plot would be carried out still remained to be discovered, however. It was but another mystery she must soon solve.

At the thought of the enormity of the task that lay before her, a dispiriting weariness encompassed Arien. The Mother save her! There was so much yet to be done, and so little time left in which to do it.

Chapter Seven

Thunder rumbled in the distance. High above, the blustering wind drove moisture-weighted clouds before it. Though a perfect sphere of silver moon gleamed overhead, its brilliance was erratic, marred by the wildly tossing limbs of ancient trees and wispy smudges of vapor racing across the storm-blackened night. A mournfully eerie wail swooped down from the mountains, filling the air with unholy sound.

It was a night best spent curled before a warm hearth fire, with a soft down coverlet tucked snugly about one's legs and a cup of mulled cider in one's hands, Arien mused wistfully, gazing out her bedchamber window at the turbulent night. It was a night best suited for undead creatures and corrupt spellcasters, for those of evil skills and equally evil intent. It was a perfect night indeed, she added with glum foreboding, for the work she planned.

Still, Arien hesitated. Was she but a naive fool? she asked herself for the hundredth time. But a pawn in some gamester's hand, her destiny manipulated by others to some sinister purpose?

There was no way of knowing, at least not until she braved the uncertain terrors of this night.

She must confront her destiny and discover what it truly was. Only then would the questions be answered; only then could she make the right decisions. Only then could she finally and truly follow the voice of her conscience—wherever it led.

Squaring her shoulders, Arien turned from the window. She walked over to a tall, oaken wardrobe, took out a dark mantle, and flung it over her shoulders. Then, clutching the cloak to her, she made her way to the opposite wall and a floor-to-ceiling framed tapestry depicting a unicorn in a sunlit, verdant meadow. As she reached for the spot on the tapestry that freed the hidden door leading to the secret corridor, a surreptitious knock sounded behind her.

With a startled gasp, Arien wheeled, her gaze riveting on her bedchamber door. Who could it be at this hour when all were abed? Surely not Onora. She was to wed Tomas the day after the morrow, and was exhausted from days of working past midnight on her wedding dress.

An impulse to ignore the knock was quickly squelched when a voice—Dane's voice—came through the door. "Your grace," he whispered tautly. "Please, I beg of you. Let me in."

Panic filled her. By the Mother, what was she to do? Dane Haversin was the last person she wished to speak with this night.

That was the reason she'd so assiduously avoided him since their meeting yesterday morning in the garden. Even at the banquets since then, Arien had taken great pains to seat Dane to the right of the king and Edana, while she took the lesser place of honor on her father's left—well out of easy conversational distance with the disturbingly handsome lord. And with Edana's increasing possessiveness of Dane, it had been surprisingly easy to stay out of his way.

But now . . . now he tapped on her door. Somehow, Arien knew he'd awaken the entire castle, if need be, in order to gain admittance. There was naught to be done but confront him, and hope to satisfy his foolhardy need to speak with her.

She pulled off the mantle, flung it onto a nearby chair, and donned her silk bed gown over the simple peasant's kirtle of drab russet. The plain clothes had been intended to disguise her identity as she journeyed to visit the dwarf. She clutched her bed gown closed and hurried to the door to unlatch it and open it a crack.

He stood there, his mouth tight, his eyes dark with worry.

"Aye, m'lord?" The sight of the tall, strapping nobleman made Arien's voice go husky and her heart commence a wild pounding. " 'Tis late. Couldn't this wait till the morrow?"

"Nay, your grace," he rasped. "I must talk with you now. Pray, let me in."

Arien shook her head. " 'Twouldn't be proper. I'm sorry." She made a move to close the door, but Dane was quicker. He shoved his booted foot between the door and its frame.

"Forgive my impertinence, your grace," he said, "but I don't think you understand. I'm in dire straits, and you're the only one who can help me. I'd never have troubled you otherwise. Besides, how different is this from that first night when you entered my bedchamber to tend my wounds?" He lifted his right hand, a crooked smile on his lips. "On my honor, I swear even to keep my shirt on this time."

Ah, curse him, Arien thought, stifling a giggle. Did he know how hard it was to refuse him when he looked at her like that? And then to have the audacity to mention that last time, when he'd stood so close, smelling of horse and man and leather, his powerful upper torso bare . . .

At the memory Arien choked back a despairing groan. The Mother forgive her, but she couldn't deny Dane Haversin. She sighed and, most reluctantly, opened the door wider.

"Have it your way, m'lord." Arien stepped aside and motioned him in. "This clandestine meeting, however, shirt or no, cannot persist overlong. You know as well as I, the circumstances this night are far different."

"Aye, your grace"—Dane slipped past and into her bedchamber—"that they are. Indeed, the circumstances have far worsened."

She closed the door and slid the bolt shut, then turned to face him. "And pray, m'lord, how have they . . . ?" Noting the direction of Dane Haversin's gaze, riveted now on the gaping bed gown that revealed her peasant dress beneath it, Arien's voice faded. She grabbed the silken fabric and snatched it closed, knowing even as she did that it was too late.

"Strange sleeping apparel, wouldn't you say?" he inquired with an arch of dark brows. "Did I interrupt something? A lover's assignation, mayhap?"

Arien's cheeks flushed fiery hot. "Nay, far from it," she mumbled with an embarrassed shake of her head. "My personal plans for this night, however, are hardly the issue. You said you were in dire straits and needed my assistance. Pray, tell me what that might be, and then be done with it."

Dane scowled. "Your sister. She tightens the web she weaves about me. I find I can no longer leave the castle."

"My father has put you under guard?"

"Nay," he muttered disgustedly, not quite meeting Arien's gaze. "Naught so obvious or sure to rile the other nobles. 'Tis far more subtle than that. Your sister has fashioned some sort of spell preventing me from departing the castle. Try as I might, every time I attempt to leave, my limbs fail me. 'Tis as if . . . as if I'm slamming into some invisible barrier."

Already Edana begins to use her Raven's powers against him, Arien thought. To keep a person somewhere against his will was magical coercion, and forbidden a Moondancer.

"And why would you wish to leave, m'lord?" she asked, deciding it was wiser to divert Dane from the subject of Edana's spells. "The Triennial isn't over, and the king has yet to give his leave. Once he has, though, my sister will be compelled to let you go. To fail to do so would, as you say, 'rile the other nobles,' something I doubt my father would ever countenance."

"Your father would countenance far worse than your sister's attempts at keeping me here," Dane retorted with a disdainful laugh. "Even you must admit I take a grave risk each time I ride into this castle. Indeed, until three days ago, I never expected to find any friend at all within these grim walls."

He paused, his mouth tightening and his expression going bleak. "Yet now 'tis evident even you've no desire to help me avoid wedding your sister. Your deliberate avoidance of me since my arrival here has been duly noted. Especially," he added bitterly, "after you ran from the garden two days ago."

" 'Twasn't you I was running from," Arien was quick to explain. " 'Twas the situation, and my failure to aid you."

Dane stepped close, staring down at her from his considerable height. "Then you now regret that failure, and agree to aid me?"

Suddenly Arien couldn't bear to meet his gaze. It was too piercing, too intense—too hopeful and trusting.

By the Mother, she thought with a bittersweet pang, how she wanted—needed—his trust! How she desired really to matter to him. In the past days of her self-imposed exile from Dane Haversin, Arien had missed him and dreamed of being with him and hearing sweet words fall from his lips.

That was more, though, than she deserved or dared hope for, Arien thought sadly. She lowered her head. " 'Twas cowardly, I know, m'lord, running from you and your problems like that. 'Tis just that so much has happened, so much has changed, since that night I met you on the road."

Strong, long-fingered hands clasped Arien by the arms, drawing her up against a hard-muscled body. "As it has for me, sweet lady," she heard Dane say, a catch in his deep voice. "Ah, if only you knew . . ."

Arien looked up, and was ensnared in the turbulent depths of his deep blue eyes. As his hands stroked up and down her arms, the fragile control Arien had held over her emotions shredded. A hot, wanting heat filled her.

"Tell me," she whispered, lifting herself on tip-toe, straining toward what she knew not, but knowing that she needed it as desperately as he. "How *has* it been for you?"

"As it has been for you, I'd wager," Dane rasped thickly, leaning down until his lips were but a warm breath from hers. "As 'twill always be for us, sweet lass."

With that, he covered her mouth with his, devouring her soft, full lips before gently forcing them apart. He knew he shouldn't rush her—it was evident from her hesitant, uncertain response that she'd never kissed a man before—but he was suddenly so eager to taste her, to savor her sweetness and warmth in the only way his rigid code of honor would permit. And, untutored as the lovely princess was to the ways of a man, Arien never once protested or pulled away. She wanted him, Dane realized with a savage triumph. Wanted him as much as he wanted her.

A growl rumbling deep in his chest, he pulled her closer, pressing her young, yielding form tightly to his. And, as she shifted position slightly, her flat belly brushed innocently over his groin. In the reflexive response of a passionately virile man, Dane's sex hardened, thrusting tautly against his breeches.

Arien must have felt the sudden change in him. She went very still, then placed her hands on his chest and began to push him away.

"Please, m'lord," she cried softly, desperation in her voice. "Pray, let me go."

127

Though he heard her words and knew it was the right and honorable thing to do, something in Dane rebelled against releasing Arien. It was almost as if he feared that to free her now was to lose her forever. He dared not sever the fragile bonds that had begun to spin between them. Strands of gold, they were, precious and rare, to be carefully guarded lest they fray and then disintegrate.

Aye, fray and disintegrate, Dane thought as unbidden memories flooded his mind. He'd let the bonds of his first marriage unravel, then sever. He had no right to expect a second chance.

. . . naught good can ever arise from an evil deed.

He bit back a bitter, strangled laugh. The self-righteous words were his, first spoken to censure Arien for being a Moondancer. Yet, though he'd failed to recognize the truth then, those caustic words had even more prophetically described him.

In that battle of wills and stubborn pride he'd long fought with King Cronan, he'd both won and lost. Won, in continuing to thwart the king, saving Haversin from being consumed in that insatiable maw of power-hunger and greed. Yet lost, as well, in his renunciation of what had truly, profoundly mattered . . . before he'd fully comprehended how profoundly it *had* mattered.

'Twas a terrible price—this willing, if ignorant, sacrifice—a price he must pay to the end of his days. His pride, his misguided sense of honor, had led him down a path he now deeply regretted taking. 'Twasn't a path, however, Dane reminded himself, releasing Arien at last, an innocent such as this sweet lady must also take. No bonds between a man and a woman should be that strong.

One person's ruin should never bring on another's.

"I-I beg pardon, your grace." His voice unsteady, Dane stepped back, his hands clenching into fists at his sides. " 'Twas crude and impertinent of me to touch you as I did."

"Nay." Smiling through her tears, Arien laid a hand gently on his arm. "If the truth be told, 'twas just as crude and impertinent of me. I found our embrace pleasurable, wanted it to go on forever, until your, er, rising passion finally recalled me to my higher responsibility."

He laughed, but there was nothing joyous in the sound. "Your Moondancer vows, of course. How thoughtless of me to tempt you from them."

"Aye, tempt me you did," Arien acceded gravely, "but the thoughtlessness was mine, not yours. Please accept my deepest apologies, m'lord."

For an instant, Dane wasn't certain if he'd heard correctly. Was it possible? Was Arien admitting to an affection for him?

A savage elation flooded him. Then, inexplicably, anger flared bright and hot, burning away that more tender emotion. Curse her for being so kind, so understanding, so . . . so good, he thought. It only made him want her more.

"Apologies aren't necessary," Dane growled, unable to bear her sweet sincerity a moment longer. "What *is* necessary is that I procure your assistance in escaping Castle Talamontes. To linger here even another day will, I fear, be the end of me."

"And what purpose would escape serve, m'lord? Even if I helped you, where could you go that my sister couldn't soon find you?"

Kathleen Morgan

Curse her for asking, Dane thought. Curse her for putting into words his greatest fear. And curse himself for not at least killing Edana when he could. But what Arien didn't know of his plans, she couldn't be coerced into revealing.

" 'Tis best you not ask, your grace." Try as he might, he couldn't keep weariness and frustration from creeping into his voice. "Suffice it to say, I've a friend with considerable magical talents. He can protect me from your sister if anyone can."

She studied him closely, unspoken questions roiling in the depths of her luminous green eyes. "You speak of King Aidan of Anacreon, don't you, m'lord, once known as the Demon Prince because of his killing eye?" Arien returned his now furious glare. "Well, I cannot say whether his powers are sufficient to defeat a Moondancer, but I can tell you I greatly fear the outcome of such a battle."

"How so?" Dane demanded tautly, now wary of her intent.

"Think on it." She cocked her head at him, sending a long, thick lock of ebony hair tumbling down onto her chest.

For a heady instant, Dane's glance fell to that lush curl, nestled atop a full, pert breast. His fingers twitched with the effort it took to restrain them from reaching up and gently lifting the recalcitrant lock. If he touched her breast, would her pouting little nipple harden with excitement? he wondered. And would she lose control yet again, and press into him, her mouth parting for another of his hot, hungry kisses?

If she came to him, offered up her sweet lips and even sweeter body just one more time, Dane didn't know what he'd do. He yearned for her like a man long starved, like a man who'd risk every-

130

thing—his pride, his honor, even his life—for just one passionate night in her arms.

. . . even his life . . .

Blinding as a bolt of lightning, reality slashed through Dane's mind. In sickening slow motion, he saw his hand lifting to Arien's breast. He saw himself willingly surrendering to the domination of feelings he'd long ago suppressed. He saw the grave danger they both faced if they dared allow their emotions to cloud the far more important issues.

As if seared by a red-hot brand, Dane jerked back his hand. He swallowed hard. By the holy ones, he never should have come here this night.

"I-I must go." He backed away, turning to the door. "I was a fool to come here. There's naught you . . . naught anyone . . . can do."

"Wait."

With a grip surprising for such a small woman, Arien's hand came down on his arm. Her fingers were strong, their warmth radiating through the fine linen of his shirt. Yet still he hesitated, fearing that to turn back to her would be his final undoing.

"Dane . . . mayhap there's yet a chance."

The words were tearful, whispered. For an instant, Dane wasn't certain he hadn't misunderstood. Then the grim reality of his situation surged back, nearly drowning him in a flood tide of despair.

"Nay." He shook his head with savage vehemence. "You spoke true when you warned of the possible consequences of involving my friend in this. Greystone's problems must remain within Greystone, lest we risk the well-being of all."

" 'Twasn't what I meant."

Arien tugged gently on his arm. Reluctantly, Dane turned to face her. She gazed up at him, a fierce resolve burning in her eyes, her expression and stance so much like that of a warrior princess of old that it took his breath away.

"Tell me, then, what 'tis," he said.

"I cannot," was her reply. "You must trust me, and trust that what I do, I do for you and the sake of Greystone. Can you do that? Can you . . . will you . . . trust me in this?"

Trust me. . . .

Did she know what she asked? Dane wondered. Did he dare surrender his fate into her hands? A tiny voice whispered that she might yet be in league with her sister.

Yet, in his heart, Dane refused to believe ill of Arien. Before, he'd admired her solely for what he perceived was her goodness. But now . . . now she was luminous, glowing, lit from within by a fire and determination, a sense of purpose that hadn't been there before. She was a woman filled with courage, with a renewed vision of her true path in life. Somehow, Dane knew it was the same path he must tread.

It was enough they'd travel it together. It was enough to open his heart one time more, and permit hope to enter therein. It was enough to find the forgiveness he so desperately sought, and heal the festering wounds in the soothing balm of her love.

"oAye," he said, his voice rusty. "I trust you."

Soon thereafter, Dane left her. After his departure, Arien spared little time in dreamy contemplation of the wondrous things shared between them before bolting the door. She threw on her cloak, and hurried from the castle through the secret corridor. There wasn't a moment to spare. In that impulsive instant when she'd offered Dane her assistance, everything had changed. Far, far too much depended on this night . . . now that she knew he trusted her.

In deference to Moondancer laws directing that no magic should be used on a night of the full moon, save that performed within a holy circle, Arien had originally planned to forswear all use of her powers. Now, though, time was too quickly passing. Soon the holy assemblage of Moondancers would leave the Glen of Women. With each minute the danger grew.

Capturing an errant moonbeam, Arien used its light to weave a spell of flight. The force of her magic soon caught her up, lifting her high above the trees in a whirling gust that carried her out into the blackened countryside. The wind whipped at her unbound hair, snatching at her cloak with cold, moisture-laden fingers, and the simple peasant's garb offered little protection from the night's chilling temperatures.

Yet the discomfort of her body was nothing compared to the unsettled emotions roiling within her. Though she knew this was a thing she must do, still Arien dreaded the inevitable confrontation. The dwarf was wise, as learned and far-seeing as he was ancient. And he drew his magical strength from a source potentially even more potent than that of the Moondancers—the great Mother Earth. If ever he turned against her, Arien sensed he'd be a formidable enemy.

As the standing stone within its protective grove of trees swiftly came into view, Arien wondered how she would contact the dwarf. He was definitely nowhere outside, she soon realized, scanning the circle of sturdy oaks whose branches were clattering wildly in the violent winds. A bolt of lightning slashed overhead, thunder rumbled menacingly in its wake; then rain began to fall. The first drops were big, and plopped loudly on the ground, but soon the gentle downfall became a torrent.

Muttering a disgusted oath, Arien tugged up her hood and clutched her cloak tightly to her. Apparently only fools were out and about on a night such as this, and the dwarf was no fool. He must be snugly ensconced in his underground den.

She circled the standing stone's hillock with great care, using her magic to ascertain where the dwarf's hidden doorway might be, and found nothing. Try as she might, Arien couldn't discern any sign of an entrance. The admission that his magic appeared more powerful than hers angered Arien.

"You said I'd be back, you arrogant little man," she cried out. "Well, here I am now, all but drowning in this rain. The least you can do is come out and invite me inside."

"And the least *ye* can do is cease yer incessant yammering, afore ye waken the entire countryside," a gravelly voice unexpectedly replied.

Arien swung about. A small wooden door protruded from the side of the hill, a misty yellow light streaming from deep within to meet the driving rain. Garth Dorwen stood there in the diminutive doorway, dressed in a sweat-stained leather jerkin, threadbare hose, and lumpy shoes, his stubby fingers grasping a carved deer-antler door handle. As the rain pelted his shaggy gray hair and coursed down his long beard, a decidedly irritated expression replaced his usual, mildly grumpy look.

"Well, what are ye waiting fer? Dawn, mayhap?" He made a motion for Arien to follow him. Then, without another word, he turned and hobbled back into his den.

Chapter Eight

Arien was still eyeing the diminutive portal, gauging whether the opening was adequate to allow her entry, when the dwarf stomped back up and thrust his shaggy head out the door. "I said come in, didna I?" he demanded, as the muddy rainwater sluicing down the hillock splattered into his eyes and drenched his hair. "The door is magic, silly lass. 'Twill widen to fit the size o' any I bid enter. E'en any daft enough to be out on such a night."

"You knew I'd be back," Arien snapped, then gathered her skirts and ducked low to follow him into the underground dwelling. "You could at least be more hospitable. 'Tis hardly—"

She drew up short, the words dying in her throat. A musty, yet aromatic odor redolent of drying herbs and medicinal flowers pervaded the large, one-room chamber. The floor was strewn with a thick layer of straw that desperately needed freshening. The walls were hard-packed earth, and the furnishings were sparse and coarsely made.

It looked like the nondescript hovel of some peasant, except for the glimmering light bathing the room in a golden luminescence. Glancing about, she initially imagined that the glowing light was emanating from the small forge hewn into the base of the tall standing stone. Seeming to arise from the very heart of the earth, the great stone thrust its way through the dwarf's den to pierce the hillock above. Yet though red coals smoldered within the crater of hard, white rock, and most definitely were the den's source of warmth, the light they shed was dim.

Arien moved farther into the underground room. As the corner hidden by the stout pillar came into view, she at last discovered the true source of the glowing light. It rose from a coarsely woven bag sitting open on the ground before a rickety wooden spinning wheel and a waist-high pile of straw. She removed her hood, cast a quick glance over her shoulder at the dwarf, who appeared momentarily preoccupied with dragging shut the thick wooden door, then hurried over to the glowing bag.

At first, all Arien could see was light. As her vision adjusted to the sparkling radiance, however, she could make out gossamer strands of golden thread. Strange they were in their startling luminescence, like no kind of gold Arien had ever seen. Strange and magical, no doubt, she thought, recalling the tales she'd heard of dwarves and their treasures.

"A mite nosy, aren't ye?" asked the now familiar, gravelly voice from immediately behind her. "Are ye in the habit o' snooping 'round someone's dwelling wi'out e'en a by-yer-leave?"

Arien rolled her eyes. "And are you in the habit of finding fault with everything your guests do?" she asked, turning to face him. "If so, this promises to be a most unpleasant and short-lived visit."

He eyed her for a long moment, then grinned. "Ye're a feisty lass, and no mistake. E'en," he added, his glance taking in her sodden, bedraggled state, "when ye're wet to the bone and the sorriest-looking sorceress I've e'er bid enter my humble abode."

"Well, that can soon be remedied." With a shake of her cloak and a few whispered words, Arien magically willed herself dry.

The dwarf chuckled, then turned and hobbled over to a crudely wrought table. A lumpy little pottery pitcher and two equally lumpy cups sat there. "Have ye a taste fer some freshly pressed cider?" he asked over his shoulder, already pouring himself out a cup.

Though her throat was tight and dry, and a cool swallow of cider would have been most welcome, Arien thought it best not to take anything she didn't absolutely need from the dwarf. She wasn't here to pay some social call, after all.

"Nay." She gave a sharp toss of her head. "I haven't time to spare for such niceties."

He lowered himself to a spindly stool consisting of a thick slice of bark-encrusted tree trunk and three squat, gnarled limbs, and took a deep draft of his cider before replying. "In a hurry, are ye? Well, ye're in my home now, and if ye wish aught from me, ye must slow yer pace to mine. Here"— he motioned to the other of the two stools set beside the table—"leastwise take yer ease. We can jest as well sit and talk, as stand."

Arien shot the stool a sideways glance. Like its mate, it appeared far too flimsy to trust. Once again, she shook her head. "Nay, if you don't mind, I'd rather stand."

"Have it yer way, then." With a final swallow, Garth Dorwen emptied his cup and set it down. "What would ye have o' me, fair princess? 'Tis why ye're here, isn't it? Because ye can find no one else to help ye?"

There was something in the dwarf's infuriatingly accurate assessment that set Arien's teeth on edge. Curse him, she thought. *Already he imagines he has the upper hand and I'm in his debt.*

"In every other circumstance save this one," she said, "I hardly think I'd need your or anyone's help. But this problem with Edana is, er, complicated, and may require skills I'm not trained to use."

"So ye come to me, hoping I'll tread where ye dare not. Is that what ye truly mean to say, fair princess?"

It was little use trying to dissemble with the dwarf, Arien realized, a betraying warmth flushing her cheeks. Not only did he easily and most disconcertingly ascertain her true motives, but he also wasted little time pointing them out.

She exhaled a weary breath. It was also obviously pointless to threaten him with the use of his name. He'd not be swayed. Already, he knew he'd won. " 'Tis quite simple, really," she explained. "You can perform dark, earth magic and I cannot. Unfortunately, this time I fear your kind of magic is the only effective weapon to best my sister."

"So the love o' yer heart is finally worth the risk, is he? To risk yer precious Moondancer vows, I mean?" The dwarf cocked his shaggy head and clucked his tongue. "My, my, how fickle and e'er-changing are the young."

" 'Tisn't just for him that I do this! No matter who the man was, I'd never risk what I risk this night for him alone."

"Nay, ye wouldna," Garth Dorwen agreed solemnly. "And more's the pity. In the end, loving him will teach ye far more o' life and what truly matters than all those holy Moondancer precepts e'er could. How else do ye think ye'll e'er open yer eyes and name the secret? How else will ye find yer way through the frightful morass yer sister and her Ravens have cast us all in?"

"And do you know how weary I am of your cryptic riddles?" Arien's chin lifted in angry affront. "Well, I'll tell you true. It grows increasingly irksome being talked down to by you, as if you hold all the knowledge and power, and I'm some simpleton."

"Ye're no simpleton, my fair, green-eyed princess." He shoved awkwardly to his deformed feet and limped over to her. "But ye are, for all yer wondrous powers, not yet wise in the way o' living. Ye havena seen what I've seen, nor endured or lost what I have lost. It tempers the soul, ye know, such suffering does, and opens yer eyes to a world far different than 'twas before. A world ye see much more clearly, fer what's truly important, and what is not."

He meant well, Arien thought, lowering her guard for a brief moment. There was much truth in his words, too. Wisdom was acquired and honed in the crucible of life, after many years of pain and struggle. It wasn't some right of privilege and power, even if that privilege rested in royal bloodlines and the power lay in magic. She just didn't like, particularly at a time when she needed his help most, feeling inferior in any way to Garth Dorwen.

" 'Tis true enough," Arien reluctantly agreed with a sigh. "I've yet to gain your wealth of years and knowledge. Indeed, 'tis a large part of the reason I came to you this night." She locked gazes with the dwarf. "My sister means to take Lord Haversin as husband. Naught will thwart her intent.

"To make matters worse, my father supports Edana's decision, and our holy high priestess chooses to turn from the terrible consequences of such an act. Yet, despite all their warnings not to involve myself in this, I cannot allow such a thing to happen. I must act, for Dane's s-sake"—for an instant Arien's voice faltered. Then she steeled herself to go on—"and for the sake of Greystone, too."

"All o' which I warned ye about when last we met."

"Aye." She dragged in a steadying breath and nodded. "That you did. But 'twas too hard to face, to accept, then. Indeed, 'tis hardly easier now, but I cannot ignore it any longer."

"Nay, ye cannot."

Garth Dorwen walked over to stand before her, that faint, musty odor she now recognized as a combination of damp earth and dried herbs wafting up from his shabby, threadbare clothes. Gazing down at him, Arien was struck by the kind, concerned, even caring look in his dark eyes. A hope flared deep within. Mayhap, just mayhap, Arien thought, she had an ally at last.

"P-please, I-I need your help."

He stared up at her for what seemed an interminably agonizing time, then nodded. "Aye, ye do indeed need my help. Tell me what ye wish o' me."

For a fleeting instant, Arien's courage failed her. By the Mother, it was so hard to put words to her desires, much less utter such an unholy request. But there was no one she dared discuss this terrible dilemma with, and she could honestly not conceive of any other solution.

"First," Arien finally replied, meeting the dwarf's now intent gaze, "I need to know exactly when and how Edana plans to force Lord Haversin to wed her."

"On the morrow, after the banquet, she intends to cast a moonspell o'er that lord, inflaming his lust fer her." For the space of a breath, Garth Dorwen paused. "And what o' the rest?" he finally asked. "Ye've the answer to yer first question. What more do ye wish o' me?"

Holy Mother, Arien thought in an agony of revulsion for what she must next request. But now, with her worst fears confirmed, she needed the dwarf's help more than ever. "For the morrow and the morrow only"—Arien forced herself to utter the words—"I desire the same abilities as Edana. I desire knowledge of how to cast a dark spell and coerce others to my will."

" 'Tis wise to fight yer sister wi' equal powers. E'en if such powers are no longer sanctioned by yer holy sisterhood."

As he spoke, the dwarf's eyes narrowed, yet deep within them flared a look of triumph, even joy. Arien's heart sank. It was as she feared. She'd played right into his hands.

Yet what other choice had she, save turn from Dane and leave him to his fate? And turn, as well, from the rising threat of the Ravens, a threat even she could no longer ignore. Whether she used earth magic or not, to go against Edana might well mean her doom. Yet at least this way, though Arien risked her soul in the bargain, her self-sacrifice might produce some good for others.

"Well, can you do this for me? Can you teach me how to cast a dark spell to coerce others?" she demanded tautly when the dwarf remained silent. "Or have all your dire predictions and offers of aid been for naught?"

He smiled, but the light never reached his eyes. "Can I help ye? Aye, I can. I'll give ye fair warning, though. Once acquired, 'tisn't a skill easily or willingly discarded. And 'twill cost ye, too."

"I thought as much," Arien muttered. "A dwarf never gives aught away for free."

" 'Tis the tradition o' the Little Men." He shrugged. "Besides, naught o' any value comes wi'out a price. Fer yer sake, though, I pray 'twon't be more than ye can pay."

"For my sake!" Arien gave a disparaging laugh. "As if you'd care one way or another." She clenched her hands. "And pray, dwarf, exactly what is that price? I'll pay most anything. I have to, and well you know it."

Undaunted, the little creature met her gaze. "Aye, well I know it."

"Pray, be done with it then," Arien said, wanting only to put an end to this detestably sordid haggling. "Tell me what 'tis you want."

Instead of answering her, Garth Dorwen turned and hobbled around the great stone pillar to where the spinning wheel and the glowing bag lay. "Come," he beckoned, when Arien remained where she stood. "First, I've something to show ye."

Choking back a frustrated curse, Arien gathered her skirts and followed. "Well, what is it?" she snapped when she finally drew up before him.

He gestured to the spinning wheel. "Do ye know much o' spinning, fair princess?"

"What do you think?" She frowned in exasperation, puzzled by the dwarf's question. "Neither princesses nor Moondancers find much call to spin. Truly, you ask such strange questions."

"Mayhap," the dwarf replied nonchalantly. "Then again, mayhap not. Strange as it now seems to ye, the difference 'atween Moondancer and dwarf magic isna so very wide." He stooped awkwardly and scooped up a handful of straw from the stack piled behind the spindle. "Indeed, 'tis nearly the same as spinning straw into gold."

Garth Dorwen took his seat on a stool set beside the spinning wheel. With a quick flick of one spoke of the wheel, he set it twirling. Then, holding up a few pieces of straw, the dwarf began working them between his fingers until they became pliable and elongated.

"How different are they really, straw and gold, I mean?" he asked. His tone was casual, but Arien sensed that the question was laden with deeper meaning. "Though one is o' inestimable value and the other but fodder fer animals, both are yellow, both are quite useful and precious in their own way, and both can be cleverly fashioned for different purposes."

As he spoke, the dwarf worked the straw until he was able to anchor one end about the bobbin. In the flickering glow from the luminous bag, he then began to spin the straw until it appeared to become a shimmering golden thread.

"May I?" she asked several minutes later when he finally paused. She was not quite sure her eyes weren't playing tricks on her. Hesitantly, she lifted her hand toward the bobbin.

"Aye." The dwarf leaned back to give her room. " 'Tis gold, fair princess. 'Tis what ye're wondering, isna it?"

Ever so tentatively, Arien fingered the glowing strands. "Straw into gold," she murmured.

"Aye. 'Tis nearly the same as earth magic is to white. 'Tis the wielder who makes it what 'tis, who sees beyond the outward appearances to far different possibilities. 'Tis never the substance itself that determines its use, nor the source o' the magic, be it white or dark."

"In the hands of a dwarf, mayhap," Arien said with an unsteady laugh.

"In the hands o' all who dare wield magic, fair princess," the little man corrected her. " 'Tis our sacred calling, to transform the gifts o' nature for the good o' all."

"For the good of *others*, not ourselves," she countered.

"And isna that what ye wish to use my magic fer?" As if in eager anticipation of her reply, he leaned close. "Fer the sake o' Lord Haversin and Greystone?"

"A-aye."

"Then how can what I teach ye this night be evil, or rise from demon-spawned black arts? And why do ye fear it so?"

"I fear it because my Moondancer training has told me to fear it," Arien cried, refusing to be lured into some philosophical debate over the fine points between white and dark magic. "I fear it

145

because naught good can come from something evil. I fear it because, in the using of such powers, I risk entrapping myself in the same pit my sister has fallen into. And because . . . because try as I might, I cannot trust you or your motives."

"But aren't yer powers sufficient to protect ye—from my schemes as well as from yer sister's? Ye're one o' the most adept Moondancers I've e'er encountered in the hundreds o' years o' my living. Surely my meager, if ancient, powers are no match fer yers."

By all that is holy, Arien thought, I hope and pray that it is so. There was no way to be certain, however. Only time would reveal exactly which of the dwarf's words were truth and which might be lies. Only time would make known the rightness of her quest. "Your price," she muttered with stubborn persistence. "Name it now, and be done with it."

"A wee bit weary o' all the talk, are ye?" The dwarf leaned back. "Well, mayhap 'tis past time then that we speak o' the terms. Naught more matters, if ye willna pay my price."

He gave the wheel a spin and then, his foot exerting a slow, smooth rhythm on the treadle, began once again twirling straw into shimmering strands. As the threads wound about the bobbin with a steady, almost hypnotic monotony and the seconds stretched into minutes, Arien felt the tension rise. Curse him for working her as he did, she thought. Working her as skillfully as his gnarled, stubby fingers worked the evolving golden strands.

"If and when I wish it, ye must render me a magical favor in turn," Garth Dorwen said unexpectedly.

Taken aback, Arien stared at him. "A magical favor?" she repeated finally. "That's all you want?"

"Aye." He nodded, his gaze, for a change, clear and guileless.

Relief flooded Arien. Could it truly be that easy, that simple? "Then 'tis agreed. One magical favor for another."

"A moment more, fair princess." The dwarf lifted his hand as if to rein in the eagerness of her acceptance. "Afore ye think the bargain struck, tell me true. Have ye given any thought to the consequences if ye fail to repay my favor wi' one o' yer own?"

"And why should that concern me?" Arien frowned in puzzlement. "I cannot return your favor with evil magic, but I've no fear of meeting your price."

"Ye've no worry on that account. I wouldna e'er ask ye to deal in aught that was evil."

With a gentle touch, Garth Dorwen stilled the whirling spinning wheel. Gold threads sparkled on the bobbin, casting a light both luminous and bright. As luminous and bright as the light emanating from the coarse, homespun sack on the floor.

Straw into gold . . . Arien thought she'd never seen anything more beautiful. Who would have thought such a thing possible?

"You spoke of consequences if I failed to grant your magical favor," Arien said, thinking it best to know the full extent of her bargain with the dwarf. "Exactly what might such a consequence be?"

" 'Tis simple enough. If ye're unable to perform the magical spell I ask, ye must instead grant me yer heart's greatest treasure."

"My heart's greatest treasure?" Confusion filled Arien. The dwarf would indeed have the right and power to enforce her vow, even though she was magically stronger in every other way. That was why wielders of magic gave their oaths but rarely—their own magic would turn on them if they forswore a vow. "I don't understand," she said. "My magic *is* my heart's greatest treasure. Only if I lost my powers would I be unable to grant your wish."

The dwarf arched a shaggy gray brow. "Do ye think so, fair princess? I must cede to ye in yer assessment o' what ye consider yer heart's greatest treasure, but 'tis sad, isna it, ye've so little o' value in yerself to treasure."

"You can say that, you who've naught left *but* your magic?" She gave a disbelieving laugh. "So little of value indeed! I say instead my magic is of the greatest value to me. It has at least bought me the respect of the people. And 'tis because of that magic that my father and sister are unable to force me to go against my Moondancer vows or coerce me to do their will. Lastly, my magic has earned me a high rank in the sisterhood."

"Aye," Garth Dorwen conceded gravely, "yer magic is indeed a treasure. But yer heart's greatest treasure? I wonder."

"Well, wonder all you wish. 'Twill not matter a whit until the time comes. In the meanwhile, I agree to your terms, so let us begin with the lessons. I dare not linger here overlong."

"We've a few hours till sunrise. 'Twill be more than enough time to teach an adept such as ye what ye need to know."

"I need only to learn enough to stop Edana, and no more."

"There's but one sure way, ye know, to thwart yer sister in her intent to wed the young lord." The dwarf's piercing gaze locked with Arien's.

"And that one way?" Arien asked. " 'Tis too late to mince words or couch unpleasantness in honeyed phrases. Tell me what you mean, and be done with it."

"There's but one way to best yer sister in this. One way to end this struggle o'er Lord Haversin and buy, at least fer a time, some peace in which to strengthen yer bonding afore the final battle for Greystone begins."

The dwarf rose unsteadily from his stool. Behind him, the fat skein of golden threads glimmered with a beguiling, yet unsettling beauty. As beguiling yet unsettling, Arien mused, as a man in need who'd come to her earlier this night, who'd held her in his arms and kissed her—then placed his life and trust in her hands.

"Ye must accept the man fate has chosen fer ye," the little creature replied, his dark, ageless eyes never once wavering from hers. "Ye must do as the visions I spun fer ye foretold. Ye, and no other, must take the Lord Dane Haversin fer husband."

Chapter Nine

As Dane strode down the marble steps and across the huge reception area leading to the Great Hall, excitement thrummed in his veins. In but a few minutes, this eve's banquet would begin and he'd see Arien. See her again for the first time since last night's clandestine meeting in her bedchamber.

He'd missed her fiercely since then. However, try as he might, once more she'd managed to thwart all his efforts to find her. It was most likely a bit of Moondancer magic keeping them apart, Dane reasoned, grinning wryly. The lass could be singularly elusive when she wished to be.

But she'd not evade him much longer. Arien had promised to help free him from her sister's ensorcelment. And surely, after she'd had a whole day in which to act further on that promise, he could rightfully expect some explanation of what she planned.

As if summoned from the deepest recesses of his mind, the memory of last night floated lan-

guidly into Dane's thoughts. The memory of
standing close to Arien, of inhaling her fresh,
clean scent. The memory of his surge of joy upon
learning of her desire for him, and his surprisingly immediate arousal when he took her into
his arms and she brushed innocently against him.

Even now, as he recalled how good she'd felt,
Dane's body responded. By all the holy ones, he
inwardly groaned, he was as randy as some
smooth-faced lad mooning after his first lady
love. Yet, though the feelings were intense and
blood-stirring, Dane also recognized that his response was more than the purely sexual one of a
man long without a woman.

Eighteen months ago, he'd finally taken a mistress to ease his more carnal needs. Blond, willowy, beauteous Glenna, the beloved only child of
Haversin's chief armorer, had been inconsolable
when her father had died. Inconsolable, save in
Dane's comforting arms.

Though Dane, still in mourning for Katrine and
his child, heretofore had given little thought to his
physical need for a woman, Glenna, in her sor-
rowing naivete, had clung to him until Dane's
body, if not his heart, had awakened to the nubile
young woman. Their eventual coupling had been
passionate. Afterward, compelled by his fierce
sense of honor, Dane, though he could never le-
galize his union with a peasant girl, had taken her
under his protection as his leman.

The arrangement had suited both well. Dane
found frequent and easy release in the ardent, af-
fectionate Glenna's arms, losing himself, with all
his still unresolved guilt and anguish, for a time,
at least, in her delectable body. And Glenna, now
content and well cared for, was equally satisfied,

not having been forced, in her father's absence, to wed one of the castle's men-at-arms. That she'd borne him a fat, healthy son six months ago only enhanced Dane's satisfaction. Though the lad, named Tynan, could never inherit Haversin, Dane at last was a father.

In that one way, at least, he'd thwarted the Moondancer witch's curse. Though his legitimate line ultimately might die out, some part of him would now live on. It was more than he'd ever dared hope for after the tragic loss of his wife and their unborn son. And it was far more than he deserved.

Yet as physically fulfilling as his couplings always were with Glenna, Dane had not thought he'd ever again experience the kind of relationship or depth of emotion he'd once shared with Katrine. Never, until late last eve in Princess Arien Talamontes's bedchamber . . .

"Dane . . . cousin . . . over here!"

The happy, inebriated voice of Phelan intruded on Dane's self-absorbed musings. Dane halted just inside the arching stone doorway of the Great Hall and scanned the room. Across the span of long trestle tables set with pewter goblets, trenchers of bread, salt cellars, foaming pitchers of ale, and flasks of wine, sat a florid-faced, boisterously drunken Phelan, surrounded by other equally drunken nobles.

Dane frowned. The king and his two daughters were even now entering the Great Hall. The banquet couldn't officially begin without them, yet Phelan and seven other lords—some of Dane's closest allies—had apparently been drinking for several hours now. Out of the corner of his eye, Dane spied Duke Crowell motioning to a servant bearing additional pitchers of ale. As he watched, Crowell directed the servant to take the pitchers to Phelan's table.

A warrior's instinct, honed to an edge as sharp and deadly as a battle sword, warned Dane something secret and deceitful was afoot. Duke Nevyn Crowell never acted on his own volition when he could just as easily hide his murderous tendencies beneath the guise of serving his king. He was Cronan's spokesman in all things politic, as well as his personal advisor. Many whispered he was also the leader of the assassins it was rumored were sent out to punish those who dared criticize the king.

Dane turned, riveting his gaze back on the head table. Perched high upon a wooden dais, the royal banquet table was set with fresh white linens, decorative salt cellars, silver and gold tableware, bowls of fresh fruit, and elegant, swan-necked crystal flagons of finely aged wine. Even then, King Cronan was lowering himself into his tall, carved chair, his daughters waiting, out of respect, to seat themselves once he was comfortably settled. Immediately, Dane dismissed Duke Crowell's manipulation of Phelan and the others—and the motives behind it—from his mind. This night's first priority must lay with Arien, and finding opportunity privately to speak with her.

There was no time to be lost, Dane realized as he strode out once more toward the head table. He must find a way to sit beside Arien.

Edana was first to see him. A self-assured, proprietary smile on her crimson lips, she refused the servant's offer to seat her and turned, expectantly awaiting Dane's arrival. Anger stabbed through him. *Curse the woman. Already she has me all but wed to her.*

The admission Edana was capable of doing those things and more was bitter as gall.

It also terrified him. An honorable death on some battlefield was preferable to what he envisioned his fate to be if he was forced to yield to Edana's evil dominance. To relinquish his freedom, to sacrifice his pride and honor on the altar of another's power-hungry ambition, was a consideration past bearing. He'd kill himself rather than become a pawn in the unholy schemes of a spellcaster gone mad.

"Ah, Lord Haversin," Edana purred as he drew up before her. "You've arrived just in time to join me at table. Pray, assist me with my—"

"By your leave, your grace." He interrupted Edana by rendering her the requisite bow. "A moment more and I'll gladly return and assist you in any way I can."

Ebony brows arched in affronted incredulity, she nodded sharply. "As you wish, but don't tarry overlong, or you'll risk my displeasure."

"But a moment, and no more, your grace," Dane assured her, backing away even as he spoke. He strode around the king's chair to the other side, where Arien had already been seated.

"Your grace?"

Almost reluctantly, it seemed to Dane, Arien lifted her head and met his gaze.

"Aye, m'lord?"

Her acknowledgment of him was guarded. Dane frowned. After last night, he'd begun to think there was some affection between them. But now . . . now Arien seemed distant, troubled.

She didn't look well, either. The translucent skin below her emerald green eyes was smudged with shadows. Her face was pale and washed of color, and she looked as if she'd not slept in a day or two. Concern filled him. What had transpired since they'd parted to disturb her so?

He bowed, then straightened. "Would you do me the honor of dining beside me at table?" Pausing, Dane carefully ascertained that no one was eavesdropping and continued in a low voice. "If I have to endure another meal with only Edana to talk to, I swear I'll go mad. Have pity on me, sweet lady. Sit on my other side so I may, from time to time, find respite in more pleasant company."

Unaccountably, Arien's eyes filled with tears. "I fear I'd be poor company this eve, m'lord."

The sight of her pain was like a knife gutting his insides. Dane leaned close. "What is it, Arien?" he whispered hoarsely. "What troubles you so?"

"N-naught." With a fierce effort, Arien blinked back her tears and rose. "Pray, don't pry further. Already, many here spy on everything we say and do. 'Tis too dangerous to share honest thoughts in such a place."

"Aye, 'tis true enough." Wordlessly, he took her by the elbow and led her back down the table past the king and Edana, to a seat one chair down from his. Though she said naught, Dane could feel Edana's furious gaze boring into his back. Thinking it wisest to avoid confronting the irate woman just then, he instead busied himself seating Arien and taking his own place.

The grand entry just then of the royal cupbearer, and a servant bearing the royal washbasin and a ewer of water spared Dane from having to face Edana. Marching up to stand before the king, the servant who performed the ceremonial hand-washing bowed low, then straightened and proceeded to lay a towel over the king's table setting. Next, he presented the king with a shallow basin.

After an equally low bow, the royal cupbearer accepted an offering of water from the other servant. Once the agate-lined, silver gilt cup was full, the royal cupbearer tasted the water for poison, then kissed the king's towel. Taking that gesture to mean the water was free of poison, Cronan held out his hands. The servant immediately poured warm, scented water over the king's hands.

When the ceremonial niceties were completed, the servant whipped out a fine linen napkin and dried the king's hands, removed the towel covering the royal dishes, then performed the same ritual for Edana, Arien, and, finally, Dane. In the meanwhile, the king's bread was cut and placed before him, while other servants scurried to bring in the first course.

With a resounding fanfare of trumpets, at last a silver tureen was carried in. Shaped in the form of a huge fish, the vessel was an intricately worked piece of craftsmanship, from the gaping mouth to the myriad scales covering the shiny body. The soup, to Dane's great satisfaction, was equally sumptuous. Consisting of ground capon thickened with almond milk and seasoned with onion, saffron, and other spices, the tasty liquid was served with pomegranates and red comfits.

The soup was soon followed by a roast dish of kid, duckling, and well-fatted capons—all presented on the same platter and garnished with fresh herbs—baskets of soft, braided breads with a satiny luster of baked egg white, and bowls of steaming cabbage, leeks, and onions fragrantly scented with mint and parsley. Between the efficient service of the food and Edana's incessant requests to assist her with the cutting of her meat or passing of the salt cellar, Dane found little opportunity to turn to Arien until the initial onslaught of courses began finally to slow.

Not that she'd made any effort to talk with him, either, he thought as he shot her a wry glance from time to time. Indeed, it appeared as if Arien was studiously avoiding any occasion to draw his attention or engage him in conversation. That realization, combined with her tears earlier, only added to Dane's growing unease—and his resolve to probe the reason for Arien's unusual behavior more deeply.

The arrival of the minstrels with an accompanying troupe of acrobats, tumblers, jugglers, and dancers finally provided Dane with a brief excuse to query Arien under pretext of complimenting her on the banquet's superb organization. She blushed, fumbled momentarily with her wine goblet, and then looked up.

"'Twas a simple enough task," Arien murmured, managing a wan smile. "Once I'd arranged all the meals and entertainment for the week, I mean."

Caught up in the slow, tender movement of her delicately molded lips, Dane was slow to reply. Edana, however, moved with lightning speed. Under the cover of the table linens, she surreptitiously slid a hand up his thigh. Only a hairsbreadth from his groin did she stop, to stroke him boldly there.

At her touch, it took all Dane's self-control to keep from leaping from his chair. Instead, he

157

turned back to Edana, reached for her hand, and gently but firmly pulled it from his leg. Then, maintaining a grip on her hand, he smiled. "I seem to have been amiss in my attentions to you, your grace."

Edana glared back at him, a hard, furious light in her eyes. "Have you, m'lord?" she inquired silkily, fingering a long, lustrous lock that had tumbled onto her breast. "Then you must make amends by taking me for a walk in the palace gardens. 'Tis the only honorable solution, wouldn't you say?"

He *wouldn't* say so, if circumstances had permitted him any other choice. But they did not. As greatly as he desired to speak further with Arien, he knew he must postpone their talk yet again.

" 'Tis a pleasant prospect, your grace." Try as he might, Dane knew the proper enthusiasm was lacking in his voice. Who could blame him, though? Edana was already brazen in her seductive advances while in the presence of others. What she might attempt in the relative privacy of the palace gardens staggered the imagination. " 'Twouldn't be courteous, though, to depart without the king's leave. Mayhap later, when the banquet has ended or, better still, on the morrow—"

"My father has already granted us leave, Lord Haversin," she interrupted smoothly. "He well knows of my deep affection for you, and sanctions aught that would permit us additional opportunity to foster our budding relationship."

She held out her hand, the faintest of smiles teasing her crimson mouth. It was a smile of triumph.

In a sickening rush, Dane realized that her plan had, from the start, included taking him to the garden this night, even before the meal was finished. That would gain the greatest notice and add credence to any claims Edana might later make that Dane was as overcome with passion as she.

Rage swelled in Dane. Curse her and her conniving father! The jaws of a trap were closing about him, and there seemed nothing he could do about it. He cast Arien a smoldering, frustrated look.

To his surprise, her chair was empty. A quick scan of the Great Hall found her hurrying past the last of the banquet tables and toward the arched portal leading from the room, oblivious to the curious gazes following her. Stunned by her hasty departure, and the crashing end of his hopes to speak with her, Dane half rose to go after Arien. Then, as some dark power swarmed over him, forcing him downward, he sank back into his chair.

Though he fought it with all his might, there was nothing Dane could do. He looked up, locking gazes with Edana. She arched a brow in challenge. Again, Dane tried to rise . . . and failed.

A pitying look in her eyes, the crown princess extended her hand once more. This time, with a sense of deep and utter despair, Dane took it.

Curse Edana for her endless attempts at seduction, Dane thought bitterly, rising to stand beside the witch who now controlled his body, if not yet his mind. Curse the king who, in his greed and vengefulness, encouraged her to destroy him. But curse Arien most of all, for she'd been the one to dangle hope of salvation before him, then snatch it away.

159

It was the cruelest act of all, Arien's false enchantment, and far, far worse than any her sister could ever conjure.

Arien wrenched open her bedchamber door and staggered inside, slamming shut the stout wooden portal behind her. Her heart hammering, her ears roaring, she leaned against the door to support her quivering limbs, and fought to catch her breath.

From the instant she'd departed the Great Hall, she'd run the entire distance to her bedchamber, scrambling up the slick marble stairs and racing down the long corridors, heedless of the curious looks and pitying shakes of the servants' heads. All that mattered was that she had escaped before it was too late. Before she told Dane everything.

That would have accomplished nothing. Dane was defenseless against Edana's magic. It was all up to her now . . . if she dared use the powers she'd gained from the dwarf.

At the recollection of what Garth Dorwen had revealed to her the night before, Arien shuddered. His spellcasting was very different from hers, for he called on the powers of Mother Earth rather than those of the Moon Goddess. His spells were laden with ancient words and powers long ago forbidden and, because of that, now poorly understood. Words and powers, she realized now, that could easily turn against the user.

With difficulty, she repressed another shudder. Though she but imperfectly understood the reasons behind the Moondancers' overthrow of the dwarves so long ago, she at least finally understood, in a bone-deep way, why her sisters had found the dwarves' spellcasting so unsettling.

There was a power there, hot, dark, and dangerous, seething just below the surface of their magic. A power, though unfamiliar to women, rife with great potential, but also rife with great peril.

Ah, if only she could discern the true source of that peril, Arien thought despairingly. Mayhap then she could better understand the magic, better contain it. Above all else, a Moondancer must be in control of her magic—

With an ungainly thwack against her back, the door was shoved partly open. Arien straightened. "Who goes there?" she demanded. "In whose name do you dare intrude on the royal chambers?"

Onora peeked around the door. " 'Tis only me, m'lady. I've yer fresh linens and the cloak ye bade me wash and return as quickly as possible to ye."

The cloak, Arien thought. The one she'd worn to visit the dwarf last night. The one soaked by rain and splattered with mud. She moved back from the door.

"Come in, Onora." Impatiently, Arien motioned the maidservant in, then shut the door behind her. "I beg pardon for my rudeness. I didn't expect anyone this late."

"And I beg pardon for being so tardy." Onora paused, blushing prettily. "I thank the Mother my marriage is on the morrow. My Tomas can hardly restrain himself anymore. He kept me overlong this eve, speaking of final wedding plans and . . . and whispering sweet words of love."

Arien smiled. She could well imagine how Tomas used his lips to whisper sweet words of love. But who could blame the couple? They were young and deeply in love. That was how it should

161

be . . . how she, too, would have felt if Dane returned her love.

The startling and totally unexpected admission drew Arien up short. *If Dane returned her love . . .*

Almost reflexively, her hand rose to her mouth. Why had she thought such a thing? She didn't love Dane.

Or did she?

Memories flooded Arien. Of Dane, gay and carefree that day she'd first met him three years before. Of her unnerving, emotion-laden response to the magical visions the dwarf had granted her. Of her unbidden yearning to see him, to touch him, to have him hold her in his arms and kiss her. It had all culminated last night, when he'd indeed taken her into his arms and kissed her.

Ah, such bliss, such sweet, sweet sensations. Such a joyous union of heart and soul!

But was any of that proof she loved him?

Ye risk much, fair lady, the dwarf had told her as she'd finally prepared to leave him. *Be certain the purchase price is worth it. Be certain, fer ye might well be asked to pay, and pay dearly, and ye dinna want to regret yer decision. Nay,* he'd said, a grave expression on his ancient face, *ye ne'er want to regret what ye do here this night.*

Was that, then, proof of her love for Dane? Arien wondered. That she was willing to pay any price to save him?

"M'lady? M'lady, are ye all right?"

A gentle touch on her arm and a pair of brown eyes studying her with concern wrenched Arien back to the present moment. "Aye. I'm fine, Onora. Just fine."

She took the linens from her maidservant. "Go back to Tomas. I won't be needing you further this eve."

"But yer gown. Ye may need help with its unfastening, and yer hair will need brushing, and yer bed—"

Arien held up a silencing hand. "All of which I can do myself."

"Well, if ye're quite certain . . ." Onora eyed her doubtfully, edging toward the door even as she spoke.

"Begone." Arien made a shooing motion. "Begone with you before I change my mind."

The maidservant needed no further encouragement. She turned on her heel and bolted for the door, pausing only long enough to grasp the handle, shoot a grateful grin over her shoulder, and hurry from the room.

Arien watched her leave, feeling as if, in sending Onora away, she'd just relinquished the last ties with her old life.

Once again, Arien shivered. She only hoped her newly acquired dark skills were equal to the task she'd set for herself. Once she took on Edana, there was no turning back.

Chapter Ten

After she'd stripped him naked, Edana laid Dane on her bed. Then, as if she needed further opportunity to gloat, she stood there, her dark eyes glittering in satisfaction and rising lust.

"Aye," she whispered huskily, her possessive, hungry gaze raking over him, "you'll suit me well. As I'll suit you," she added, leaning down to lightly stroke his hair-roughened chest. She traced a long-nailed finger consideringly down his tautly muscled abdomen to where his sex lay, flaccid and unresponsive. Edana eyed the organ briefly, then boldly took it up in her hand.

At her touch, Dane shuddered. Edana smiled. "Even in the depths of ensorcelment, you're exquisitely sensitive." Ever so slowly, she ran her cupped hand up and down his shaft. "I'll allow that, your response to me, I mean. In fact, I'll encourage it. How else will we ultimately join, sealing, at long last, our lifelong commitment?"

Though he tried mightily to fight it, Dane's manhood engorged, then hardened. He groaned,

164

frustrated, despairing, but the sound never reached his lips. All he could manage were impotent little jerks, and the furious censure of his gaze, as his mind battled to regain control of his body.

Edana's plan was made evident at last. She meant to couple with him and force him to wed her afterward. But how could she prove they'd lain together this night? There were no witnesses, and witnesses were essential to invoke the ancient law.

From down the long stone corridor, a faint snatch of music caught Dane's ear. It was familiar, a rowdy tavern song he'd sung many times himself before he'd finally wed and put aside such idle pursuits. Occasional drunken shouts punctuated the slurred song, reverberating off the stone walls to produce an eerie, cavernous effect.

Then Dane recognized one particular voice. The horrible implications behind the presence of the obviously inebriated revelers finally struck him. It was Phelan, accompanied most likely by the other lords Dane had seen drinking with his cousin earlier.

Who would be better witnesses to his coupling with Edana than his cousin and their closest friends and supporters? If he dared protest his unwilling liaison with Edana, it would be his word against theirs.

Desperation fueled his anger, and he fought against the ensorcelment even more savagely than before. Sweat broke out on his body. His head arched back, his eyes clenched, his muscles grew rock hard with strain. Nothing, however, could free him from Edana's spell.

"You intrigue me," she breathed, never faltering in her expert stimulation of his hardened shaft until it jutted now, like some iron spike, from his body. "Your pride . . . your indomitable will . . . 'tis most appealing." Hitching up her skirts, Edana climbed onto the bed to straddle Dane's nude body. "When the time comes, I'll tap into some of the most potent magic I've ever experienced. Until that time, though, you'll pleasure me well."

Leaning down until their mouths nearly met, she extended her tongue and, like a serpent savoring its prey before striking, flicked it over his lips. "Aye," Edana breathed, excitement coarsening her voice, "you'll please me very well."

"Not so, sister." Another feminine voice rose unexpectedly from the shadows. "You'll not have him, not now or ever."

With a gasp, Edana wheeled around. Arien stepped from the curtained alcove hiding the entrance to the secret corridor joining all their rooms, and strode over to stand beside the bed. Though close enough to reach out and touch her sister, Arien held back. One more chance. She'd give Edana one more chance.

"Think again, sister," she said softly. " 'Tisn't too late to repent your evil ways and return to the true path. Dorianne will still accept you."

"The true path?" Edana threw back her head and laughed derisively. "Ah, how blind you are, little sister. Neither you nor I are truly on the right path. The old Moondancers, in their overweening pride and arrogance, chose only the easier path, not the true one. 'Twas simpler, safer, to wipe out all they didn't understand, what they felt threatened them. 'Tis the real reason they destroyed the dwarves. But some new nemesis always rises to take the place of the old one, doesn't it?"

"Such as the Ravens?" With sinking heart, Arien edged yet closer. Edana wouldn't be moved, not now or ever, to renounce the Ravens. In some twisted way, she saw a need to punish, even destroy the Moondancers for what she perceived as their grave failings.

"Aye," her sister snapped in reply. "Now, leave us. I've no further time for you. Lord Haversin has need of me."

"Nay, you are wrong, sister." As she spoke, Arien began silently to summon the dwarf's dark powers, readying herself for the conflict to come. "Dane neither wants nor needs you. And you shall not have him."

"Dane, is it now?" Edana's lips curled in a sneer. "Is it possible? Has my chaste little sister finally succumbed to the forbidden lure of the flesh? Then have a care. You venture into realms perilous and new, where your puny powers can ill protect you."

"I do so only because what you attempt here is immoral and wrong. 'Tis you who force me into this."

"Do I now?" Edana chuckled. "Then I triumph doubly this night. I gain power over this man and you, at long last." She turned back to Dane. "You're welcome, though, to try to stop me with your gentle, ineffectual Moondancer magic. But when you've finally admitted defeat, pray have the good grace to leave us.

"Unless," she added with a lascivious smile, "you've an itch to view your first coupling, and see how well Lord Haversin lives up to his impressive promise. Either way, it matters not to me."

For an instant, Arien looked at Dane. He appeared dead save for his eyes. Revealing his thoughts and emotions, they spoke more eloquently than words, beseeching her to help him. Relief, hope, trust burned in those blue orbs. In that instant, Arien was filled with the certitude that whatever purchase price might eventually be asked of her, it was worth it. Whatever the price, she'd never regret what she did here this night.

Wrenching her gaze from Dane, Arien drew in a fortifying breath, marshaled her powers, and melded them with her dwarf-given ones. She reached out, touching her sister on the arm. Golden sparks flew. Edana gave a choking cry, tumbling backward.

Before she hit the floor, however, Arien conjured yet another spell, transporting her sister's now insensate body to the privacy of Arien's bedchamber. No one would disturb Edana there until it was too late for her to interfere. By that time, Arien would have made sure that neither her father nor Edana could ever threaten Dane again.

She turned back to him. Now, without the shield of Edana's clothed body, Dane lay fully exposed, his tall, powerful form sweat-sheened and straining. Her gaze lowered to the tumescent protrusion of his manhood. It was still huge and thick, roused and held by Edana's spell at the peak of excitement.

Arien knew she could disperse her sister's magical influence over Dane with but a simple incantation. But then Dane would immediately seek to leave, refusing to accept what was truly the only option left to him. And it wouldn't be long before Edana wakened from her spell-induced sleep. Then she and their father would set their minds again to concocting another plot to gain control of Dane and his lands.

There was but one way to save Dane and avert what Arien feared might soon become open warfare. She must take Edana's place on the bed and, when her father slipped in with his entourage of noble witnesses, make it appear as if she were Edana. Though Arien intended only to simulate the act of coupling with Dane, all present—Dane included—must believe otherwise. Then her father could do nothing but insist Dane wed her, even if she hadn't been the daughter he'd originally intended to give in marriage.

Only later, when Dane was safe and the issue of Edana and the Ravens had been resolved, would Arien finally reveal the truth. Then Dane would be free to wed whomever he pleased, and she, still a virgin, could return to the life she'd chosen. But never would she stray from Moondancer ways, even as she played out her role as Dane's wife.

Dane would be saved, and her father, sister, and the dwarf thwarted. Dorianne would be displeased, but in time she would surely accept Arien's solution, content in the knowledge that her protégé was still eligible to become high priestess. And Arien, freed of the dwarf's unholy predictions, would be in control of her destiny once more.

Drawing her Moondancer veil to cover the lower half of her face, Arien carefully climbed onto the bed to straddle Dane. As she did, his eyes widened in surprise, then confusion, and, finally, a growing look of horror at the realization of what she intended. His response tore at Arien's heart. Never would she have wished to hurt him in any way, or give him a moment of doubt or fear. Her options, though, were as limited as his.

"I asked you once before to trust me," Arien said, forcing herself to meet Dane's now suspicious gaze. "I told you what I did, I did for you and for the sake of Greystone." She hesitated, then forged on. "Though you may doubt those words just now, I still believe in them as strongly as I did then. Someday, the Mother willing, mayhap you'll believe them again, too, and . . . and find it in your heart to forgive me."

Voices, low and excited, rose from outside the bedchamber door. Booted feet scuffed and shuffled on the stone threshold. Someone lost his balance and slammed into the door.

There was no time left to explain or beg Dane's forgiveness. In another minute or two, the witnesses would rush into the room. A hot flush warming her cheeks, she gathered her gown up past midthigh and scooted more intimately against him. "You must help me," she whispered. "Though Edana might have known how to couple without a man's assistance, I don't. Help me make all believe, m'lord. I command it!"

Even as the last words left her lips, Arien conjured another spell of coercion, granting Dane just enough freedom to use his body to join with hers. His hands lifted, one moving to grasp his stiffly swollen sex. The other clasped Arien's buttocks and pulled her forward, into the hard strength of his groin.

Hot, satiny flesh touched her where no man had ever been. In a maiden's reflexive response, Arien jerked away. Then, gathering her resolve, she made herself arch back toward him, pressing her warm, moist woman's flesh to his flesh.

170

Dane groaned then, a tormented sound that was equal parts desire and despair. As if he were waging one final battle to break free, his eyes clenched shut, his face contorted in agony. Arien's spell, however, was even more powerful than her sister's.

More powerful, she realized with a start of surprise, than even she was able to withstand. As the sparkling strands rose to swirl about, then encircle her in a gentle clasp, panic surged up, swallowed her. For terror-stricken seconds Arien fought back, summoning all her Moondancer magic to temper the seductive pull of the dwarf's spell.

Yet though one part screamed in horror, flailing wildly against the violation of sacred vows and the loss of her long-cherished chastity, another part hurtled headlong toward a union ardently desired and secretly cherished. Pain slashed through Arien. She felt torn, her will lacerated repeatedly until her life's blood spilled forth, and she bled. And, as the last drops of her resolve flowed away, there was naught left but a weak, quivering shell, desperate to be filled anew.

Filled anew . . . by Dane.

His hips arched upward, began a rhythmic, rocking motion. His thick erection pressed against her in the most intimate of ways, pushing, probing as, bit by bit, the undulations of his lower body forced the tip of his sex into her. Passion and arousal darkened his features, strained them.

A curious weakness, a melting warmth, flooded Arien. The golden threads shimmered brightly, blinding her. With a soft moan, Arien closed her eyes.

It was too hard to fight. The spell had gone awry, and she was powerless to resist it. What cruel irony, a part of Arien thought, even as her arousal grew. She was as trapped in the web as was Dane, and must now follow as submissively as he.

Heat . . . hardness . . . fullness . . . As Dane probed ever deeper, Arien's whole world narrowed to those foreign, yet strangely exciting sensations. Waves of pleasure washed over her, setting her thighs, widespread and white, to trembling. Instinctively now, Arien pushed gently downward, meeting Dane's upward thrusts with a firm, steady pressure of her own.

Desperate for something to support her, she leaned forward to brace her hands on either side of Dane's broad shoulders. Her breast brushed against his mouth. For a long, exquisite moment he nuzzled her there, making soft sounds of unfettered pleasure. Then his lips closed about Arien's nipple. Through the thin fabric of her gown, he took it gently in his teeth to tug on and suckle it.

Arien inhaled a shuddering breath and threw back her head. Her hands moved, grasping his massive shoulders, her nails sinking into his smooth, hard flesh. She arched sensually, instinctively offering yet more of her breast to him.

His probing rhythm came faster, deeper now, his huge shaft pounding against the final barrier of her maidenhead. Arien whimpered as he drove ruthlessly against the wall, not knowing if she whimpered in pain or a lust-induced excitement. Her only certainty was that she wanted Dane inside her, thrust to his full, throbbing length. That she wanted him body and soul, wanted, in spite of the barbaric circumstances surrounding this night's coupling, for Dane to find pleasure in it.

Pleasure in it . . . and in her . . .

From somewhere far away, a key slid into a lock. A door scraped open. Randy comments of ale-besotted men filled the room, before fading quickly to shocked silence. Then Arien heard naught more, save Dane's harsh pants as he finally pierced her maidenhead and thrust past. She cried out once, softly in pain, before Dane grasped her head and pulled it down, covering her mouth with his.

His tongue stabbed into her, fierce, hard, utterly uncompromising, brooking no resistance, demanding her total submission. Overcome by a rush of emotion like none she'd ever experienced, Arien trembled violently. Ah, what ecstasy, what exquisite, mind-drugging sensations!

Nothing mattered but Dane. Though compelled to mate with her by a force beyond his control, he conquered even as he was conquered. In every way she dared, Arien returned his power to him—if not power over his own body, then at least over hers.

And the yielding . . . It was beyond her wildest imaginings! She could feel him, every long, delicious, potent inch of him, all his slickness and power! It was a heady invasion, a mystical violation that stretched her to her limits, yet conversely made her desire, *need* even more.

On and on Dane thrust, taking Arien ever higher on a shimmering journey of physical delight, even as he bound her to him with the simple strength of his gaze. Though the responses of his body were magic-induced, his passion was his own, and the equal of hers. His eyes blazed with desire. His breath rasped thickly. His body glistened with sweat.

Then, in a room filled with witnesses, before a father obsessed with his unreasoning need for vengeance, Arien found a release that carried her to a dark, secret place. A place sparkling with gold-spun threads that furled ever upward to surround her, then merged into a resplendent ball of furiously spinning light. It was like the wondrous vision the dwarf had shown her that night they'd first met, Arien realized, yet somehow different—better.

This time, Dane was truly with her, riding the swirling maelstrom of gossamer threads. And, as she cried out her ecstasy in unison with him, far in a distant corner of her memory, Arien heard a voice—the dwarf's voice—whispering.

Ye see how 'tis 'atween ye? The love o' yer heart . . . the man fate has chosen fer ye?

Aye, Arien thought in dreamy reply as she floated gently back to earth. I see now. I only pray the day will come when Dane can forgive me for this night, and return the love I feel for him. Only then will the purchase price of this night have been fully paid. And only then will Dane and I finally be free. Free to live out our destiny—in our own time and way.

"You've seen. You've all seen the results of Lord Haversin's unholy passion for my daughter," King Cronan Talamontes exclaimed in horror a few minutes later. "In his unbridled lust, he has taken her maidenhood. There is no other recourse. He must be made to obey our ancient laws. He must now wed my daughter."

For a long moment, there was dead silence except for the unsteady breathing and scraping of feet as the men accompanying the king shuffled about uncertainly. Then Duke Nevyn Crowell's voice lifted from somewhere in the midst of the men. "Our sovereign speaks true. Lord Haversin has ravished the fair Edana, and must now pay the price."

The words pierced the soft, hazy mist still surrounding Arien in the aftermath of her climax. She struggled upward from that warm, sleepy place, knowing she must. All her plans had revolved around this particular moment, when she must convince all that she and Dane had coupled.

That she and Dane had coupled . . .

Like the waves sucked from the sand by the force of the moon's pull, the sweet, dreamy moment was devoured by a surging swell of horror. The Mother above, Arien thought, fighting back the hysterical need to scream out her dismay, Dane and she *had* coupled. Her worst fears had come to pass. She had lost control of her magic. Nay, Arien immediately corrected herself, she had lost control of the dwarf's magic. And lost, in the bargain, her maidenhood, and her right ever to be Moondancer high priestess.

Such loss, however, was too great to contemplate at a time like this. Betrayal of the magnitude she'd suffered at the hands of the dwarf must be allowed time to seethe and simmer, before the proper response could be determined. In the meanwhile, more pressing matters awaited.

Arien turned, meeting Crowell's outraged glare with an unwavering one of her own. " 'Twasn't ravishment," she said, her voice strong and sure. "Though Lord Haversin was more than equal to

175

the occasion, any fool could see I was hardly un-willing."

The irony of those words was nearly enough to make Arien choke. She climbed off Dane and flipped the edge of the comforter up to cover him. She also released him at last from the spell.

" 'Twas also not the fair Edana who coupled with Lord Haversin." Arien freed her veil, reveal-ing the lower half of her face. " 'Twas I, Princess Arien, who lay with him."

"By the Mother!" The king staggered backward, his face gone white. If not for the solid crush of nobles standing behind him, he might have lost his balance and fallen. "Nay, it cannot be. Not you, lass. 'Twasn't—"

"Mayhap not, m'lord," she replied softly, "but 'tis how it must be. Lord Haversin didn't bed Edana. He bedded me."

"Aye, 'twould seem so." Briefly, Cronan eyed her with misgiving, then turned to Dane. "And what say you, Lord Haversin? Are you truly the man of honor you've always claimed to be? Whether she was willing or not, you have taken her maidenhood. Will you do what is required and honorable, and wed her now?"

His limbs quivering with the aftereffects of the magical spells, Dane leaned unsteadily on his el-bows. All eyes were fixed on him. Everyone, he well knew, awaited his reply.

As if there were any choice left in the matter, Dane thought bitterly. Though many might se-cretly believe his claim that he'd been coerced by witchcraft, none would repeat that in the royal palace or to the king's face. To do so would be to risk a mysterious death sometime later, when no one would be able to attribute it to any specific cause.

There was really no choice left at all. He would either be executed by beheading or he would marry a Moondancer witch. The law was totally on the side of the now defiled woman and her family. Either way the king won; either way he gained legal possession of Haversin lands.

In the midst of the unsettled, uncertain gathering, Phelan gazed dolefully back at him, troubled, confused, but still loyal. Dane scanned the other nobles. Most appeared equally as perturbed as Phelan, but still met Dane's eye, still looked prepared to draw sword to defend him if he asked it. The realization was of some comfort. Though they might not voice their suspicions, in their hearts they all found this night's liaison contrived and suspect.

Dane looked at Arien. She'd half turned to face him. Her mouth was still soft and swollen from his kisses, her eyes huge, dark, and imploring. There was no foul taint of magic hovering about her now.

Once more she appeared the sweet innocent, beguiling him into imagining he was his own man, once more in control. Beguiling him into believing it was solely his choice to determine if they'd wed or not.

The demon take her! Dane cursed inwardly, furious and frustrated. Even now, a part of him still believed in her, still hoped there was some plausible explanation for what she'd done to him. He refused, however, to allow that part of him to influence his decisions regarding her ever again.

"I've always lived my life with honor. I'll not change now, though the dishonor of others has

177

brought me to such unfortunate circumstances," he rasped thickly. Never once did his glance waver from Arien's. To her credit, she refused to recoil from the searing look he sent her, facing him down with all the dignity and demeanor of the royal princess she was.

But then, what had she to fear from him? Hadn't she just overcome her sister and thwarted her father's carefully laid plans? Truly, was anyone in Greystone more powerful than she?

Yet as powerful, as seemingly invincible as she was, fight her he must. The only question remaining was how badly did Arien wish to wed him? And did she marry solely to please her father, or did she please herself as well?

There was but one way to find out, Dane resolved grimly—demand a difficult boon of her, and see how far she'd go to appease him.

"Then your answer is given and heard by all gathered here," the king proclaimed. "You'll wed our daughter, the Princess Arien, the day after the morrow. There's little point in adhering to the ceremony surrounding a normal betrothal. Little point, either, in delaying what is essentially a very simple undertaking."

"You may attempt the wedding on the morrow or in a year from now. It matters not to me. Regardless of the consequences, I'll not wed your daughter until she and I have had time to discuss a few things." Dane met the king's gaze at last. "In private, if you will, your majesty."

Myriad thoughts and reactions flashed in King Cronan's eyes, then were gone. It was audacious and extremely dangerous to speak to the king thusly, but Dane wagered he was too great a prize to risk losing now.

"No harm's done, I suppose," the king agreed, forcing a bland smile, "in permitting young lovers some time alone together. The wedding, mind you, *will* be held the day after the morrow. No purpose is served in releasing all my nobles to their homes now, only to bring them back again later."

"Aye," Dane growled, "I'd wager not. 'Twould foul all your carefully laid plans, wouldn't it, your majesty?"

The king's eyes narrowed. His face reddened. Then Arien stepped forward, laying a hand on her father's arm and gently turning him.

"We won't be long, sire," she murmured, shooting Dane a quelling look over her shoulder. "And I promise, just as soon as we're finished and I return Edana to her bedchamber, I'll come to you. We've much to speak of."

"Aye, that we do, daughter." Cronan nodded, his mouth tight and grim. "That we do."

He left the room then, followed by his now chastened and nearly sobered entourage. Arien waited until the last man passed reluctantly through the door—Dane's cousin, Phelan—then shut it firmly in his face before he could change his mind and reenter.

She'd apologize to him for her rudeness on the morrow. Tonight, she'd far more pressing matters to deal with.

"You surprise me, your grace. I'd not thought, after what transpired between us but a short time ago, you'd be so eager to spend further time alone with me."

Arien swung about, girding herself for the confrontation to come. While she'd been seeing her father and the others out, Dane had risen and slipped on his breeches. He was, even then, beginning to fasten them closed.

Magnificently muscled, strapping and tall, he presented a stirring sight. Arien swallowed hard. "There was no time to explain, or gain your cooperation. I'm sorry for that, m'lord. If there'd been any other way—"

"Spare me your lies, madam!" Furiously, Dane cut her off. His breeches forgotten, he strode across the bedchamber to take her by the arm and jerk her to him. "You've planned this all along. 'Twas why you couldn't face me at the banquet this eve. 'Twas why you were so evasive last night in your bedchamber." He gave her a hard shake. "Admit it. No purpose is served in pretending anymore."

Pressed as closely as she was to Dane's hard, hairy chest, she had all she could do to reply. "Aye, 'twas the only solution," she croaked, trying desperately to put some distance between them. If Dane, in his anger, was oblivious to the heady effect his warm skin and man scent had upon her, Arien wasn't. He refused, however, to free her.

"Solution?" He gave a sardonic laugh. "And exactly whose solution was it? Your own, or your father's?"

"N-neither!" Arien began to struggle in his grasp. "From the start, I only wished to save you, and avoid a bloody war between the Talamontes and Haversins." She tried to pry his fingers from her arm, but they were like iron talons. "Let me go, m'lord," she finally cried. "Naught will be served handling me thusly."

"Indeed?" Dane's mouth twisted in cynical amusement. "But I could've sworn you liked, nay, preferred rough handling. Though my body might not have been truly mine to control while we coupled, my mind and senses were quite functional. And I say you enjoyed every moment, as sordid and foul and sickening as that union was."

Stung, humiliated, she lashed out without thinking, slapping Dane across the face. The act shocked him as much as it did Arien. He released her and stepped back. For several seconds, as the imprint of her hand reddened on Dane's cheek, both stood there, staring at each other.

Arien was the first to recover. At the realization of what she'd just done, her eyes filled with tears. "I-I beg pardon, m'lord," she stammered finally, hastily wiping away the telltale moisture trickling down her face. "I understand how angry you must be. 'Twas doubly unfair and cruel of me to—"

"Unfair? Cruel?" Dane gave a harsh bark of laughter. "Madam, what you did was naught less than *rape*. You forced yourself on me. You gave no thought to my feelings or desires in this. You ground my pride and honor into the dirt this night, leaving naught intact. Naught save the determination that, if 'tis the last thing I do on this earth, I'll not let you or your father win! And if that requires I must stoop so low as to take a Moondancer witch to wife, then I'll do even that!"

" 'Tisn't how any of this was intended," Arien protested softly through her tears. "I-I don't want you to hate me." She swallowed and looked away, her spirit shattered. She should have known this would happen. Curse the dwarf for his false promises!

" 'Twill all work out, I swear it!" Arien cried, closing the distance between them. She laid a hand on his bare arm. Dane looked down at it, and his expression of utter loathing made her jerk her hand away. "Give it some time," she said with a sigh. "Just give me a chance. I'll be a good wife to you. I'll—"

"Oh, aye, indeed you'll be a good wife and not shame me, or I'll-I'll . . ." His voice faded and a look of utter frustration twisted his features. His shoulders slumped.

"By all that is holy," Dane cursed despairingly. "Even in my own castle, I cannot bring you to heel. Though you swear obedience to me on the morrow, what power can any husband have over a witch? Nay"—he shook his head—" 'tis best I choose beheading. That end, at least, is quick, merciful."

"Nay, Dane! You'll have all the power you desire, the power any good wife grants her husband. And 'twill be given willingly, out of affection and respect."

Dane was quiet for a long moment. Then, ever so slowly, he lifted his head. At sight of the cold, calculating light burning in his eyes, Arien suddenly sensed a trap about to be sprung.

"Power I *will* have over you, madam," he ground out with deadly emphasis, "or I swear I'll not take you to wife. Once before I sacrificed all I held dear, rather than permit a Moondancer witch into Castle Haversin. And I'll have a vow from you now, and have it in the most sacred way you witches know, or blood will flow in this palace this very night."

His gaze was rock hard, implacable. Arien knew he meant every word he'd said. Dane Haversin had been pushed to his limits and beyond. If he'd truly rather die than wed her, he'd nothing to lose by rallying the nobles who supported him to attempt the king's overthrow, here, now, within Castle Talamontes.

But if he did, the blood would flow. Not only would the castle guards come to the king's aid, but so also must all Moondancers. Either way, Dane would surely die.

At the realization, pain lanced through Arien. To lose Dane now, when she'd just surrendered her heart and body to him, when she'd sacrificed far more than she'd ever dreamed she would . . .

"The vow, m'lord," Arien whispered, a fierce resolve filling her. As bleak, as totally confusing as it all seemed just now, she'd not submit so easily. "Name your request, and, if 'tis within my power, I swear I'll honor it."

He grinned wolfishly, like some beast closing in on its prey. "Oh, I'd wager 'tis well within your power, if you've a mind to do it. Call it a test of your alleged respect and affection for me, a proof, if you will, of your intent to avert a bloody war."

"And I say again," she repeated, the tension between them stretching as tight as a bowstring, "name your terms. If I can, I'll honor them."

"Give me your vow to renounce magic for the rest of your days." A barely contained fury emanated from every inch of Dane's taut, powerful frame. "Give it now, or I swear by all that is holy I'll not wed you, no matter what you do to me."

Chapter Eleven

"R-renounce my m-magic?" Arien repeated, struggling to hide her rising incredulity. "Truly, Lord Haversin, I don't understand. Save for this one night, and the dark spells I cast, my magic is safe, good, and free of all taint. No purpose is served—"

"*My* purpose is served, and that is purpose enough!"

At that moment, staring up into his stormy, dark blue eyes, Arien didn't particularly like Dane Haversin. She suddenly found him arbitrary, unreasonable, and most distressingly domineering. Did he seriously believe she could turn her back on her magic, expunge it from her life like some troublesome habit or outgrown belonging?

"After what has happened this night, I can understand your repugnance for my magic," Arien said, attempting to temper his anger with soothing words and irrefutable reasoning. "In time, though, you'll see my powers for what they truly are—valuable tools to aid you, priceless protec-

184

tion against other spellcasters, and the only weapon of advantage you hold in the battle with my father."

"Valuable tools? A weapon of advantage against your father?" Dane shook his head, his laugh disparaging. "It seems a bit late to offer that now, after you've all but trussed and sacrificed me on the altar of the king's greed. Indeed, the only protection I need is protection from you and your kind. Not that there's much danger of you turning against your Moondancers anytime soon for my sake."

"I disobeyed my father and the high priestess; I went up against Edana for you!" Arien protested hotly. "And you know my sister well enough to imagine what her feelings will be when she wakens."

He shrugged. "What do I care? It seems to me but a common case of two women fighting over the same man. And you won and she lost."

" 'Tisn't as simple as that, Dane Haversin! As much as I respect and admire you, if it hadn't been for Edana's determination to take you to husband against your will, I'd never have embroiled myself in such a sorry, sordid mess."

It was her turn for a disparaging laugh. "You've an overblown opinion of yourself, if you think I'd have sacrificed my maidenhood and besmirched my Moondancer vows before the leering view of a roomful of witnesses just because I wished to steal you from her!"

"I never asked for any of this," he muttered, flushing. "And if forcing me to couple with you was your idea of help, I fail to see what I've gained in the bargain. Either way, I'm wed against my will to a Moondancer witch, and must now pledge my word of honor to support the king in any and all endeavors."

As if some memory almost too burdensome to bear had suddenly settled over him, Dane's shoulders sagged. "Either way," he whispered despairingly, "the curse lives on, though your father has finally won. To wed a Moondancer witch is surely to condemn the Haversins to extinction."

" 'Twill only be so if you wish it so!" Arien cried, cut to the quick by his needlessly cruel statement.

Dane gave a bitter laugh. "Indeed, if *I* wish it so? And when have my wishes ever been of any consideration?"

He turned and strode to where his boots, linen shirt, and dark blue, heavily embroidered surcoat lay. "Aye, 'tis a fine muddle you've gotten me into, madam," Dane growled, donning his shirt and boots. "But if I've now lost all control over my destiny, I refuse also to lose control in my own castle and over my own wife."

"I repeat, I'll be a good wife to you. That said, I cannot, I will not, give up my magic."

Dane took up his surcoat, slung it over his shoulder, and returned to stand before her. He hadn't bothered to tuck in his shirt, and, with his tousled mane of hair, he looked roguishly handsome. His expression, however, was anything but charming.

"Then, madam, we are at an impasse," he stated coldly. "I cannot abide a Moondancer in House Haversin. Always will I suspect your motives. Always will I think you your father's agent. And always will I fear the next spell you cast, counting the days until you turn your magic on me once more."

Gazing up at him, Arien searched for and found the answers she sought. Answers she dreaded, as well as expected. Dane truly did believe her capable of such evil. No amount of reassurance would assuage his doubts, or heal the terrible wounds this night had wrought. Only time and repeated good deeds would do that. If, Arien thought glumly, it was ever again possible to regain his trust or affection.

Naught o' any value comes wi'out a price.

Was this, then, Arien wondered, the true purchase price Garth Dorwen had spoken of when he'd warned her of the risks inherent in accepting his aid? In saving Dane's life she'd unintentionally fallen prey to her own magic, in the process losing her maidenhood and violating her Moondancer vows. Had she also sacrificed any hope of winning Dane's love?

Briefly, Arien considered agreeing to his terms, then continuing to practice her spells in secret. In her heart of hearts, though, she knew she could never lie to Dane. Yet if she didn't, what recourse was left her?

"I'll not renounce my magic," she finally said, "but I'll forswear practicing it, unless you give me leave. I'll gain permission to set aside my Moondancer ways, and enter your house only as a princess of the realm." Arien paused, dragged in a deep breath, then continued. " 'Tis the best I can do, m'lord. I hope and pray 'twill be enough."

His handsome mouth drew into a ruthless, forbidding line. For a horrible moment, Arien feared Dane would refuse her terms. She'd spoken true, however. She couldn't renounce her magic. She now required that bright, fiery core, that wellspring of enlightenment and strength, to live. Indeed, she was nothing without it. It was truly her heart's greatest treasure.

Her heart's greatest treasure . . . A chill rippled through Arien.

If and when I wish it, the dwarf had warned her when she'd too eagerly accepted his terms, *ye must render me a magical favor . . . and if ye're unable . . . ye must instead grant me yer heart's greatest treasure.*

At the recollection of Garth Dorwen's words, Arien smiled sadly. One aspect, at least, of the dwarf's intent was made clear at last. In teaching her of darker magic, he had sought to assure himself of some of her powers in turn. But Dane now demanded what the dwarf might or might not ever ask repaid. In agreeing to Dane's terms, however, there'd be nothing left to grant the dwarf if ever he did ask it.

It was a fitting comeuppance for the little creature's foul manipulation and betrayal, Arien decided, her anger rising. All her plans—for Dane, for the kingdom, indeed, for herself—had gone tragically awry. Why should she and Dane be the only ones to suffer and lose this night?

"Well, Lord Haversin." Arien lifted her chin in challenge. "Do you accept my terms or not?"

"Aye." He nodded his acquiescence, though it was obvious he did so reluctantly and with great misgiving. " 'Tis the best I dared hope for. I'll have your most sacred vow as a Moondancer, though, before I'll see this matter finished."

"Then have it you shall." Arien walked across the room to unlatch the window shutters. With a great shove, she pushed the heavy, iron-decorated wood open onto a dark, silent night. The moon shone high above, its soft glow bathing the sleeping countryside with a silver radiance.

She paused to look back at him, then riveted her gaze on the bright orb. "I swear to the moon and the all-powerful goddess who rules it," Arien softly intoned, "that all I have spoken here this night is truth. I swear, as well, to abide by the promises I've offered. And if I should fail either in intent or deed, as is her sacred right, may the beloved moon goddess smite me dead. It can be no other way, when a Moondancer gives her vows to the Mother."

Arien's bedchamber door swung open with a resounding bang. Edana, her face flushed, her dark hair awry, rushed in. Making her way across the room, she halted beside her sister. Arien sat before a mirror, Onora dressing her hair for the wedding soon to come.

"How?" Edana demanded, her face livid with fury. "How did you best me? 'Twould've taken powers far darker than what you're capable of to overcome the spells I cast last eve."

Arien turned to face her sister. At the sight of the rumpled banquet gown Edana had slept in for a full day and a half, thanks to the dwarf's surprisingly potent sleep spell, a fleeting pang of guilt shot through Arien. But it was only fleeting. It was Edana's fault, she swiftly reminded herself, that they'd all been brought to such a pass.

"Are you so certain they were dark powers?" she asked. "They were used for good, in preventing your unholy union with an unwilling man. As such, no harm was done, no evil perpetrated."

"Don't play games with me, Arien." Edana, fists clenched at her sides, leaned toward her sister.

"You know as well as I what Moondancers consider dark powers."

She eyed Arien with a predatory intensity. "Who taught you such skills? 'Twasn't any Raven. None would've dared do so and risk incurring my wrath."

"As if I'd ever go to a Raven for help." Arien sighed, shook her head, then turned back to the mirror. " 'Tis indeed a mystery, is it not? One you can ponder till the end of your days, for all I care. 'Tis a fitting punishment for your foolish lust for a power you've no understanding of or ability to control."

"Yet you *do* understand dark magic now, and can control it? You who until a day or two ago were as pure as the driven snow?" Edana laughed shrilly. "There's more involved here than simple Moondancer magic, and you know it! If you think to thwart me, think again, little sister. Even though you'll take him to husband, Dane Haversin is mine, and mine he'll always be. Sooner or later, I'll have him. 'Tis but a matter of time."

"I know Father denied your request to cancel the wedding," Arien replied, refusing to be unnerved or intimidated by her sister's rage. " 'Tis as I suspected. In the end, he doesn't care which daughter takes Lord Haversin to husband, just as long as one of us does. A pleasing consideration, is it not? As favored as you've always imagined yourself to be, ultimately, one daughter will do as well as the other."

"The old fool believes you've finally chosen, and your choice is for him." Edana threw back her head and gave a mocking laugh. "But we both know better than that, don't we, sister dear? In your own self-deluded way, your pride and ambition are as great as mine. The only difference is that I'm wise enough to admit to it. 'Tis my greatest strength, just as 'twill finally be your undoing."

With that, Edana turned and, in a great flurry of rumpled gown and flying hair, stalked from the room. For long minutes, Arien and Onora stared after her. Then, with a great sigh, the maidservant walked over to shut and latch the door.

"She's always been too full o' herself, that one has," Onora muttered, returning to resume the dressing of Arien's hair. " 'Twill be *her* undoing someday, 'twill." She paused to peer at Arien's reflection in the mirror. "Do ye think she'll attempt some trick during yer marriage ceremony? I'd so hate for the happiness o' yer wedding day to be marred by Edana's selfish actions."

The happiness of her wedding day. Arien couldn't help a small grimace at the irony of her friend's well-meant words. Ah, if only Onora knew the full extent of the terrible bargain she'd struck, first with the dwarf and then with her husband-to-be!

Well, it would be revealed soon enough, Arien thought miserably. In her only request of Dane Haversin and her father, she'd asked for permission to take Onora and her new husband, Tomas, with her to Castle Haversin. Perhaps she'd been selfish, dragging Onora and Tomas into such a potentially untenable situation, but Arien knew she lacked the courage to journey far from the only home she'd ever known without someone dear to her nearby.

It had been an easy enough concession to gain from the king, especially after Dane had refused his offer of a generous royal dowry. And, though

Dane had hesitated initially, obviously loath to grant Arien even that small boon, he'd finally relented. One lady-in-waiting would present few additional problems, he'd said. In comparison to her, Arien knew, was what he really meant.

Her maidservant was all she truly wanted, at any rate. Once the real reasons for their marriage were discovered, Arien doubted she'd be welcome in Castle Haversin. To remain there then, without the comfort of Onora, would have surely been more than she could have borne.

The trip to Castle Haversin would take nearly half a day. That was why the wedding was set for midday. Dane wished to depart immediately thereafter. He refused, he'd told her, to remain another minute in Castle Talamontes, once the odious marital requirements were complete.

"Have no fear, Onora," Arien said, forcing herself to answer her maidservant's question. "Edana won't attempt to obstruct the wedding. She knows she cannot best me just now. She'll wait, instead, for a more opportune moment."

"And when would such a moment be, m'lady? When ye're too far from the dwarf for him to help ye?"

Stunned, Arien swung about and stared up at Onora. "What the dwarf and I shared in confidence must remain so," she said. "You've no right to pry."

"Don't I now?" Her maidservant pursed her lips in prim censure. "Yer sister all but accused ye o' stooping to the black arts in yer rescue o' Lord Haversin. Do ye think I can stand by, then, and watch ye risk yer immortal soul, and not say aught about it?"

"What I did, I did of my own free will. That is all you need know."

"Ye schemed with a dwarf, a master o' that dark and sordid earth magic, and ye can truthfully say ye did so freely and with full knowledge o' the consequences?" Onora gave a disbelieving laugh. "Well, I say instead ye stepped a bit too close to the fire this time, m'lady, and have burnt more than even ye've yet to know."

"Mayhap, Onora," Arien admitted. "Mayhap I *have* burned more than I ever care to know. But 'tis too late to turn back now. If you find the path I must now follow not to your liking, then just say so," she added with a defiant lift of her chin, "and I'll not importune you further. I've had my fill of mistrust and censure in the last day or two. I'll not bear it from you, of all people, too."

"Ye're a proud, haughty one, that ye are, to imagine I've suddenly become some stupid, unthinking slave, only to do yer bidding and not care what or why ye bid it!" Onora flung down the brush and the handful of hairpins she'd been holding, and stomped off to stand before the open window. "Truly, ye've changed in the past week," she said in a choked voice, staring outside, "and I cannot say I care for it much."

With a sigh, Arien rose and walked over to stand beside the other woman. She laid a hand on her friend's shoulder and squeezed gently. "Onora," Arien said, " 'tisn't how I meant it. Truly, 'tisn't."

The maidservant refused to look at her, and, for a time, Arien chose not to speak further. A warm breeze, laden with the scent of rich earth, ripening apples, and baking bread, wafted up and into the room. Sounds of happy voices from the enclosed gardens far below rose in the air.

They were scents and sounds both familiar and dear, she realized with a deep pang. As familiar and dear as was Onora, her one true friend.

"You must trust me in this," Arien said softly. Once again, she squeezed Onora's shoulder. "In time I'll tell you more. Indeed, I ache to tell you more, but not now. 'Tis far too dangerous to speak of such things here."

The red-haired woman's face softened and she turned, managing a wan smile. "Aye, ye speak true in that if naught else. I can wait a time, I suppose, to hear the rest o' it."

"Good." Arien glanced about the room. "Have you seen to all the packing then?" she asked, reminded of the need for haste if all was to be in readiness for their impending journey. "You didn't forget my lute, did you? And you saw that my letter to the high priestess was safely sent, didn't you?"

"Aye, yer lute is well wrapped and ready. And I had Tomas take yer letter to old Dorianne, so there was no chance o' it being seen by anyone but her." Her maidservant's eyes narrowed. "Now what o' yer Moondancer gowns, books, and magical aids? Ye never mentioned their packing, yet surely ye must wish—"

"Once I'm Lady Haversin," Arien said, quickly cutting her off, "there'll be no place in my life for such things. Pray, speak no more of it, to me or anyone!"

At the bitter implications of her words, Arien blinked back an unexpected swell of tears. She swallowed hard, overcome with remorse. It was bad enough she must relinquish her magic to please Dane. But now, on top of it all, to have to disappoint Dorianne . . .

It was a coward's way, Arien well knew, to inform the high priestess of her impending marriage in a letter rather than face-to-face. But even if there had been enough time to pay her a visit, Arien lacked the heart for it. Dorianne's hopes for Arien were at an end; she'd have to choose another to follow her as high priestess.

"As ye wish, m'lady. I'll speak no more o' it," Onora said, shooting her a puzzled look. " 'Tis passing strange, though," she murmured. "The haste wi' the wedding, I mean, and then yer betrothed's need to hie it immediately home thereafter," Onora added as she turned and, taking Arien by the arm, led her back to sit before the mirror.

She began tucking white jasmine sprigs into Arien's upswept hair. " 'Tis a shame, 'tis, that ye'll not have a fine wedding feast and all the pomp surrounding it."

"It matters not, Onora. Truly it doesn't. You know as well as I that no love has ever been lost between my father and Lord Haversin. 'Tis best for all that we leave here as soon as possible."

"Aye, mayhap so." She finished placing the last few sweetly scented flowers in Arien's hair, and stepped back. "Well, what do ye think? Are ye not a most pleasing sight, sure to rouse the love and passion o' yer intended?"

To satisfy Onora, Arien granted the image reflected in the mirror a quick if unenthusiastic inspection. Onora had outdone herself. Soft, ebony curls were coiled high atop Arien's head, then carefully coaxed into lush swirls that shone like a gossamer crown about her face. In every spot

195

imaginable, Onora had arranged a sprig of jasmine, providing a stark, fragrant contrast to the glossy abundance of jet black hair.

" 'Twill look most pleasing indeed," Arien murmured, glancing up at her maid, "especially when the wedding veil is added."

"Ah, aye, yer wedding veil." Onora crossed the room to where a delicately wrought lace veil sewn onto a thin, gold tiara lay spread across Arien's bed. Returning, she ever so carefully slid the tiara into the base of curls crowning Arien's head, draping the long, sheer folds of fabric so that they cascaded elegantly over the simple cream-colored silk gown. Over the dress Arien wore a crimson mantle trimmed with gold lace.

"I'd wager ye look just like yer sainted mother in that veil o' hers," Onora said, a slight catch in her voice. "I only pray yer marriage is far happier than hers ever was."

Onora's well-meant words were like a dagger slicing through Arien's heart. Ah, she thought, if only her friend knew, had heard Dane's cruel words the night before. Then Onora would understand the utter hopelessness of her simple wish.

To wed a Moondancer witch is surely to condemn the Haversins to extinction.

As long as Dane believed such a thing, indeed, as long as that curse lay over him, there was no hope of any happiness between them. Arien smiled sadly. *Hope of happiness* . . . When had that become even a remote possibility? she thought.

True, she cared deeply for Dane, perhaps even loved him, but never once had she hoped to use the dwarf's magic to elicit a similar affection from

Dane. It wasn't hers to expect, much less demand. She was a Moondancer, and had given her vows to remain chaste.

But now . . . now she was no longer chaste. Now, in the joining of her body with Dane's, Arien had sealed a new covenant. In that ardent, soul-affirming union she'd made promises far more sacred and binding, promises far more ancient and primal, than any Moondancer precept or magical teaching could ever be. It didn't matter that she'd not intended for a true coupling to occur. What mattered was the bond that had formed between them. For Arien, at least, it was a bond that would last all the days of her life.

Aye, the path ahead lay clear, Arien thought, and a most daunting one it was. Free Dane from his curse, win his love, help him and her father find peace, and solve the dilemma of Edana and the Ravens.

And then there was yet the enigmatic dwarf, Garth Dorwen, and a promise given that could no longer be kept. . . .

With a rustle of silken wedding gown, crisp underskirts, and heavy mantle, Arien rose. She could only take each obstacle as it came. And the first obstacle to be hurdled was this marriage ceremony with a most reluctant bridegroom.

"Come, Onora," Arien said, forcing some semblance of maidenly eagerness into her voice, " 'tis past time we were going. My father and the others await. And 'twouldn't be seemly for the bride to be late to chapel on her wedding day."

Chapter Twelve

The chapel was draped with greenery and silken banners in the Talamontes colors of crimson, cream, and gold, festooned with tall vases overflowing with pale pink roses, blue cornflowers, creamy white and yellow yarrow, and scarlet bee balm. At the high altar, hundreds of tall beeswax candles burned brightly, illuminating the small but elegant castle chapel with a sparkling radiance. The scent of spicy incense smoldered in the censer hanging to the left of the altar, its aromatic smoke wafting lazily from the intricately worked brass container.

All was in readiness, Arien noted from the main doorway, her hand clasped firmly in her father's. The nobles were seated expectantly in their pews; the priest, arrayed in his gilt-encrusted ceremonial robes, stood before the altar with leather-bound prayer book in hand; and even Edana, surprisingly and most piously attired in the traditional Moondancer *luna* and veil, had taken her designated place. Aye, Arien thought in nervous anticipation, all was in readiness, lacking but one final, yet crucial element—the groom.

Then, from a door to the right of the altar, Dane entered, his cousin Phelan at his side. Atop an ivory, high-collared silk shirt and fine, midnight blue breeches tucked into flawlessly shined black leather boots, Dane wore a long burgundy cape, trimmed with wide bands of gold-worked embroidery, fastened at one shoulder by the Haversin talisman, a large golden lion's head. His face grim, he strode to his place to the left of the priest and turned, his gaze sweeping over the heads of all assembled until it met and locked with Arien's.

Anger shimmered in his indigo blue eyes. Fleetingly, Arien recoiled from its onslaught. She looked into the eyes of a stranger, a stranger both frightening and unapproachable, and saw the chasm of her treachery separating them. Saw, as well, the undisguised hatred burning there—burning for her.

Then the musicians launched into a gay, lilting wedding song. To the accompaniment of lute, viol, and flutes, the king stepped out. For an instant Arien hesitated, dragging back on his arm; then she compelled her leaden limbs to move.

Unable to bear the wrath emanating from Dane, she averted her gaze. Fixing it instead on the priest, she forced a resolute smile, and made the difficult journey up to the altar. Save for the muted rasp of her wedding mantle and veil brushing across the stone-paved floor, and the soft notes from the musicians, the chapel was silent, weighted with the same tense, unsettled feeling Arien had felt once before—in the vision the dwarf had granted her.

At the memory, a sense of déjà vu engulfed Arien in a smothering clasp. All was coming to pass as the dwarf had predicted, she realized. Frustration welled at her own helplessness, anger at being manipulated, and overshadowing it all was a deep regret that she'd inadvertently hurt Dane in the bargain.

Both Edana and Onora had been right when they'd accused her of pridefulness, for in her pride she'd ventured where she had no right to go. Good intentions notwithstanding, she had trusted her own abilities too much, presuming a degree of skill that had never truly been hers. That failing, in the end, may have well made her the perfect pawn in the dwarf's game, whatever it was.

Perhaps the Moondancers of old had been wrong to drive the dwarves from the land. Perhaps there *had* been a better answer, some means yet untried to enable them all to live peaceably together. But Arien's one experience with that dark earth magic had graphically, and most regretfully, illustrated why the Moondancers so feared the dwarves.

Dwarf magic was potent, but that same potency made it equally difficult to control. And magic uncontrolled was like riding a wild stallion without saddle or bridle. One could do naught but follow where it led, be it good or bad.

Yet no one had forced her to return to the dwarf, to ask for his assistance. And she'd learned an invaluable lesson in the doing, forging a new respect for dark magic based on a hard-earned, painful experience. That deepened understanding might stand her in good stead in the future, aiding her in the inevitable confrontation with Edana and her Ravens.

She squared her shoulders, lifted her chin, and met Dane Haversin's gaze once more. He'd every right to distrust her, to feel anger toward her. But in taking her to wife, he had gained much. Even if this marriage proved loveless in the end, at least it would not prove barren, or destructive.

Already life stirred in Arien's belly. With the special powers granted a Moondancer of the highest Border, she sensed the presence of the child created when she and Dane had first joined. A child . . . a son and heir for House Haversin.

Despite the man glaring at her from the altar, despite the fury emanating from her sister, despite the unsettled future that lay ahead, joy filled Arien. With this day's marriage, she decided, the curse that Reyene had placed over Dane and his family ended. Though unbeknownst to him, it was her wedding gift to her husband.

They halted at the foot of the altar. Dane walked over to stand before them, bowed low to the king, then extended his hand. "Your majesty," he said softly, "if I may have your daughter's hand? As you said, I am a man of honor, and will fulfill my obligations, however unfairly they were thrust upon me."

Cronan eyed Dane for a long moment, then gestured to the spot on the stone floor directly before him. "Kneel, Lord Haversin, and first render us your oath of allegiance. Swear to serve us above all others, without question, without hesitation. Swear to support us in all our endeavors and come to our aid whenever and wherever we ask it."

Dane went pale. Every muscle in his body grew taut. His chest heaved with the effort it took to control himself; his hands clenched white at his sides. Then, with a shudder, Dane sank to his knees. "I-I swear."

"Nay!" The king took the holy book from the priest, thrusting it in Dane's face. "Swear on the most sacred of all books," he cried, lifting his voice until it reverberated off the chapel's stone walls. "Swear word for word as we have spoken them that, on pain of death, you'll do all this and more!"

Murderous rage burned in the eyes Dane lifted to the king. A dark flush crept up his neck to suffuse his face. Gazing down at him, Arien thought Dane would leap up and throttle her father. The royal guards, skulking in the shadows, must have feared the same thing. They stepped forward, their gauntleted hands gripping their swords.

Their less than subtle actions weren't lost on the assembled nobles. They moved restlessly, and an angry murmur spread through the gathering. Glancing about her, Arien saw the blood lust rise. If Dane should falter, and turn against the king now . . .

She slipped from her father's grip and knelt facing Dane, the holy book between them. "Swear, m'lord," Arien whispered. "Swear. 'Tis the best, the only thing you can do."

"Is it now?" Dane smiled grimly. "For me, or for you?"

"For us both, m'lord," Arien whispered. " 'Tis our destiny, our honor, to join, to fight as one."

"Honor?" A note of mockery resonated in the deep timbre of his voice. "In a Moondancer?"

"Try me. Trust me. Please, m'lord."

A gentle, pleading light gleamed in Arien's eyes. Luminous and mesmerizing, her eyes beckoned him with a hauntingly familiar, compelling intensity. For just an instant, Dane was swept back to that night he'd awakened from his fall to find himself lying in Arien's arms. It was that night that he'd chosen not to kill her.

He'd been a fool then to squander the opportunity to rid Greystone of at least one Moondancer. In that failure he had brought himself to this current, pitiable state of affairs. Yet, kneeling here on the unforgiving stones in public abasement before the king and all the nobles of the realm, Dane found he could no more refuse Arien than he could have found the courage to have killed her that night.

It wasn't a matter of trust. Her presence in House Haversin would remind him of her betrayal for the rest of his days. Nay, 'twasn't trust, Dane thought bitterly. It was but the fact that he was so weary of fighting, of struggling back to his feet after yet another devastating blow.

"I swear," he intoned, his despairing gaze riveted on the leather-bound tome as he laid his hand on it. "I swear to serve your majesty above all others, without question, without hesitation."

As he spoke, Arien placed her hand atop his. "And I swear to serve *you*, m'lord, above all others," she said, looking deep into his eyes when Dane jerked his head about to stare at her, "without question, without hesitation."

"I—I swear to support you in all your endeavors," Dane continued unsteadily, unnerved by Arien's personal rendering of her father's demands, a rendering he knew she meant only for him, "and come to your aid whenever and wherever you ask it."

"As I swear to support *you* in all your endeavors," she repeated softly to him, "and come to your aid whenever and wherever you ask it."

"I swear this on the most sacred of all our books," he rasped, unaccountably moved by the sincere devotion and purpose he saw in Arien's eyes. By the holy ones, Dane thought in an agony of despair. It was too much to bear.

He clenched shut his eyes, and steeled himself for what was yet to come. "I swear it on pain of death," Dane said between gritted teeth, "that I'll do all this and more."

"On pain of death," she echoed. "All this and more."

"One would think you'd just made your wedding vows," the king muttered, pulling the holy book from beneath their hands. He handed the tome to the priest, then took Arien's hand and pulled her to her feet. " 'Tis passing strange, what you just did," he whispered, quite evidently meaning his words for her ears alone, though they also reached Dane's, "but we thank you. You may have just averted a disaster, sweet child."

"Aye, Father, but if I did," Arien replied, " 'twas meant for all, not just one, yet for just one, too, who now *is* my all."

Her glance, as she spoke, slid from her father to lock with Dane's. At her cryptic words, a fierce joy surged within him. Just as fiercely, Dane quashed it.

Curse the witch! he thought, his rage flaming hot and bright. Once more she has bespelled me, in coaxing me to render that odious oath to the king. Now I am surely lost.

Cronan turned from his daughter and stared down at Dane. "Well done, Lord Haversin. 'Twas always how 'twas meant to be, your submission to your overlord. And because your loyalty is hard won, we cherish it now above all, and reward your act of fealty with the gift of one of our precious daughters."

He motioned for Dane to rise. When he did, the king took Dane's hand. Turning it palm up, he placed Arien's hand there. "You asked for our daughter; you said you'd honor your obligations. Do so now, Lord Haversin."

With that, the king stepped away, leaving Dane and Arien to stand alone before the priest. The holy man's eyes widened momentarily. Then, after a moment of throat-clearing and erratic page-turning, the priest intoned the opening words that, ultimately, would bind them this day and for all eternity.

As the sacred phrases flowed from the priest's mouth, weaving an old, familiar web of hallowed promises about them, guilty memories and bittersweet regrets swelled in Dane. Five years ago he'd stood in a chapel such as this, and made these vows to another woman. Vows to love, honor, and protect her. Vows he'd meant to fulfill with every fiber of his being, yet had eventually broken in every way.

How much more difficult would it be to keep the vows spoken this day? he wondered. Sacred vows given to a soulless Moondancer witch, with eyes both haunting and compelling. Holy vows that were inherently lies, lies that ripped and tore at his heart even as he spoke them.

Yet Dane gave them nonetheless, each of his promises echoed by Arien until, at long last, there were no more left to give. The rings of plain gold were blessed and exchanged. Then the priest was closing his book and urging Dane to kiss his bride.

His bride . . . his wife, the Lady Arien Haversin.

As if in a daze, Dane took Arien by both arms and pulled her close. She stumbled, tripping over the hem of her gown, her body brushing inadvertently against his groin. Instantly, he hardened, his desire exploding into fiery, glinting shards that stabbed deep to the core of him. The pain of his hunger was acute.

Suddenly, all he knew was a need to infuse Arien with some of that same painful desire. He slammed his mouth down on hers; he clasped the back of Arien's head, imprisoning her, his tongue thrusting, seeking, punishing.

She fought him for a brief, panic-stricken moment. Then, with a low moan, she relented and stepped closer still. Pressing her softness into his hard form, Arien arched up, yielding her will to his. As she did, something imperceptibly changed between them.

Dane's hold on her eased, became almost caressing, rousing yet again that honey-sweet sense of déjà vu. His mouth softened, gliding warm and hungry over hers. The scent of him, clean manflesh and sandalwood, mingled with the heady spice of incense. His heart thudded and hard muscle flexed, quivering with excitement. Deep in his throat, he groaned.

Caught up in a moment as emotionally intense as their lovemaking had been, Arien forgot everything save the man who held her in his arms. A tormented anguish burned in his eyes. His mouth, even as it slanted feverishly over hers, trembled as if . . . as if he expected pain and punishment as much as passion.

But indeed, Arien asked herself, what else could he expect? She'd asked so much of him, then repaid his trust with treachery.

An ache rose from deep within her, a need to make amends, to ease Dane's pain and fury. How she wanted to pull his head down to cradle it on her breast, to stroke his hair and soothe away the taut furrows of frustration from his forehead and mouth. She'd whisper words of atonement, and seal them with her fervent kisses, then take him to her, all his hot, hard, throbbing length, burying him in the snug depths of her loving body.

As it was always—*always*—meant to be.

A cough sounded from somewhere in the distance, then a nervous titter. Booted feet shuffled. All were harsh, intrusive sounds.

Arien's lids lifted. She stared up into eyes she knew must mirror her own disorientation. Even as she watched, however, Dane's gaze hardened with the cruel return of self-awareness. His fingers gouged into her arms. He shoved her away from him, a look of utter loathing on his face.

She expected it, deserved it, but his rejection, following so closely on the heels of his ardent possession of her, hurt nonetheless. It took all Arien's considerable self-control to plaster a smile on her face and turn to face the expectant gathering. The gloating look she saw then, shining in her sister's eyes, was nearly her undoing.

Dark eyes smoldering with malevolent triumph, Edana sat there, never once averting her gaze. She thinks she has won already, Arien realized. She thinks she has destroyed me through

Dane. She thinks me so weak that his hatred will crush me.

But she doesn't know that Dane is and has always been my destiny. She doesn't know I already carry his child within me. And she can never know what wonders love can work. Indeed, Arien thought with a secret smile, 'tis the finest, the most powerful magic of all. And it was one kind of magic she was free to use, though she'd given her vow not to work her magic again.

The music swelled around them, signaling that it was time to depart the chapel. It would soon be time, Arien knew, to depart Castle Talamontes as well. Yet though earlier today she'd looked upon the journey with fear and trepidation, now she welcomed it eagerly. Her new life had begun. Now all that lay ahead sang with promise.

Promise . . . gold-spun promise . . . of a love ripe and beckoning. A love she now faced with eyes open and heart ready. Just as Garth Dorwen's strange little song had foretold.

Arien took Dane's proffered hand and stepped out, a deep, abiding satisfaction filling her. The dwarf's song had questioned if she'd ever be ready. The dwarf didn't know everything, it seemed.

An hour and a half later, with a great fanfare of trumpets and multicolored banners snapping in the breeze, the Lord and Lady Haversin's party departed Castle Talamontes. The farewells were perfunctory. Edana refused even to lend her presence to the small group of well-wishers clustered at the foot of the castle keep, and the king seemed more concerned with the delivery of last-minute instructions to Arien.

"You're our representative at House Haversin now, you know," he told Arien as they walked from the palace to join Dane, who was busy making final preparations for the journey. "Of course, now that your husband has finally sworn fealty, we've little worry of further treachery from him, but periodic reports on his plans are still of vital interest to us. Likewise," Cronan added softly, "rumors of discontent from any nobles who might visit from time to time."

"I'm fully aware of what you'd like to know, Father," Arien replied tersely, having no intention of carrying out his wishes. "But, as you say, now that Dane has pledged his fealty—"

"True enough,"—the king hurriedly waved aside her objection—"but 'twon't hurt to send Duke Crowell to visit every few months or so. We're sure, locked away in that isolated mountain fastness Haversin calls home, you'll be more than eager for news of the rest of the kingdom by the time Duke Crowell arrives."

"Aye, 'tis certain to be an adjustment," she concurred mildly, well aware her father's concern was for the reports he wished to receive on Dane's activities, not for her welfare as Dane's bride. "I have had little training in being a wife."

"Fear not, daughter. You're like your sainted mother in that," Cronan said with a smile. "You've a kind, loving heart." He took her hand and gave it a squeeze. "You'll take to the role of wife and mother quite naturally."

Arien looked up at her father. This was the first display of affection she'd seen from him in years. Had her imminent departure stirred feelings deeply buried and long denied? There was no way of knowing, and no time to delve further. Dane awaited, impatient to be on his way.

She paused when they drew up before her husband, turned, and gave her father a quick kiss on the cheek. "My thanks for your confidence in me," she said softly. "I'll endeavor to be all you imagine me to be."

"All that you already are, daughter," Cronan corrected her. He hesitated but a moment, then enveloped Arien in an awkward embrace, before stepping back to distance himself once more.

Unaccountably, tears filled her eyes, and all she could do was nod mutely. Why now, Arien wondered, when she must leave him, did her father finally become the father she'd longed for?

"Come, madam." Dane took her by the arms and, without further preamble, lifted Arien bodily to sit sideways atop her horse. He shot her a piercing glance as he handed the reins up to her, but said nothing more.

A few seconds later, Dane swung up onto his warhorse. He wheeled the animal about to face the king. "By your leave, your majesty," he said, " 'tis past time we departed."

"Have a safe journey, m'lord," Cronan cried. "Our best wishes go with you, that you and our beloved daughter live a long and happy life together."

" 'Tis my fondest wish as well," Dane said in reply. Then, turning his horse, he led the way from Castle Talamontes.

Determined not to allow her new husband to shut her out or ignore her, especially not before his men, Arien quickly urged her mount forward until she drew up alongside him. He graced her with a sideways glance and an arch of a dark brow before fixing his gaze back on the road ahead.

"You wished something of me, madam?"

"Naught at the moment, my lord." Arien pretended sudden interest in the rolling expanse of countryside. "I but deemed it more fitting to ride beside you than behind."

He smiled ever so slightly. "By all means, *your grace*. I beg pardon for my poor manners in failing to render you the respect your position as royal princess deserves."

"I care not for such silly customs!" In spite of her best intentions to remain friendly and calm, irritation thrummed through her. Curse him, Arien thought. He refuses to make aught easy. "I spoke of my riding beside you as your wife. It seems the proper thing to do."

"Indeed?" Dane shrugged indifferently. "And who among our party imagines our marriage aught more than it truly is—a union formed solely for the king's convenience? Your efforts at pretense, I'm sorry to say, are wasted on these men."

"I'm your wife, m'lord," Arien hissed, her anger rising. "Marriage of convenience or no, naught is lost in an appearance of mutual respect. 'Tis the very least I intend to give you. Is a like return so difficult?"

"Aye, madam, 'tis." He clenched his teeth, never once looking at her. " 'Tis more than difficult. 'Tis so loathsome even the remotest consideration of what I've done in wedding you makes me physically ill. You ask far too much, in asking for respect in turn."

"Then can I at least expect consideration, and the same courtesy you'd extend to one of your lowliest peasants?"

"Even one of the lowliest of Haversin's peasants is more deserving of my courtesy than you are, madam. Indeed, they have my affection, as they are entrusted to my care. But you . . . you deserve naught. Naught!"

"Then what will you do when we reach Castle Haversin?" Arien knew she shouldn't push him. But no purpose was served in avoiding the realities of their situation, either. "Will you lock me in some lonely tower, feed me bread and water, and visit only when you wish to beat me?"

"I'd never treat a woman, no matter how despicable, in such a manner!"

"Then you'll give me leave to go where I wish, whenever I wish, at Castle Haversin?"

"Aye."

"And what will my role be?"

Dane shot her a puzzled look. "Your role?"

Arien nodded. "In the past, I've filled my days with service to my father and my Moondancer duties. Neither of those are now possible. I am not and never have been, however, a woman given to idleness."

"Well, I've no idea what a royal princess does to keep herself occupied each day. And, to tell you true, I've no intention of concerning myself with it now."

"Your wife . . . you were wed to her for nearly two years, were you not? Surely she was happily occupied with some duties when you were otherwise engaged. What was her role at Castle Haversin?"

He reined in his horse abruptly, and then turned in his saddle. Behind them, in a jumbled chaos of snorting horses, jingling tack, and surprised exclamations, their party halted.

"You delude yourself, madam," Dane enunci- ated slowly and with icy conviction, "if you cher- ish any hope of replacing Katrine in my life or affections. You two are as unlike as day is to night. But, as my current wife, you've free run of Castle Haversin. You have my leave to find what- ever you wish to occupy yourself, as long as it doesn't involve magic, further intrigue, or con- spiracy against me. Content yourself with that. 'Tis more than you deserve."

"And *I* am far, far more than *you* deserve, Dane Haversin," Arien said softly, gripping her reins so hard the leather cut into her palms. "You are the most closed-minded, pigheaded—"

With a snort, Dane's big warhorse reared. Dane, his battle instincts immediately at the ready, turned around in his saddle, his free hand reaching for his sword. "By all that is holy," he growled, as his searching gaze finally discovered the cause of his horse's fright.

An instant later, Arien also made out the ghostly figure in the dappled forest light. 'Twas Dorianne, the Moondancer high priestess, stand- ing a distance away in the middle of the road, her gauzy veil and iridescent *luna* swirling about her. She was alone, and the look on her face boded no good.

Arien turned to Dane. He stared straight ahead, his jaw clamped, his mouth tight, refusing to look at her. Unease coiled and twisted in her gut.

"She wishes to speak with me." Though Arien was loath to ask his permission, especially after his rude speech but a few minutes before, she still felt it the wisest course. It was up to her to dem- onstrate her good intentions. She only hoped he would not refuse her request. She didn't know what she'd do if he did.

"Does she know you've renounced your Moondancer magic?"

His unexpected query took Arien by surprise. "Nay, how could she?" she answered carefully. "I've had no opportunity to speak with her."

"Then best you inform her posthaste." Frigid eyes finally met hers. "I want no unexpected visits from her or her kind at Castle Haversin."

"As you wish, m'lord." When he made no move to dismount and assist her from her horse, Arien nimbly jumped down on her own. "Of course," she muttered under her breath as she walked over and handed him her reins, "a body would have to be daft to wish to visit you, if your home is as cold and unfriendly as you can evidently be."

"What did you say, madam?" Dane leaned toward her to accept the reins, his eyes narrowed.

"Naught, m'lord," Arien replied with a roll of her eyes. She gave him her reins, then, without further comment, turned and set off to meet Dorianne.

The older woman awaited, her gaze inscrutable, her mouth grim. Upon reaching her, Arien sank immediately to one knee. "My lady."

Dorianne stood there, neither offering her ring nor bidding Arien to stand. "And when were you planning to inform me of the reasons for your wedding and sudden departure?" she demanded at last.

Arien rose to her feet. Though she owed Dorianne respect, she refused to make her explanations on her knees. "I was wrong, my lady, not to tell you myself. But everything happened so fast, and there was no time. . . ." She paused to inhale a fortifying breath. "I sent a message. Didn't you receive it?"

"Aye, 'twas delivered." The high priestess's lips pursed in disdain. " 'Twas not acceptable, though, and you know it. You're a Moondancer. How dare you lie with a man, then wed him! I expected far more of you than such despicable, whorish behavior!"

"You'd no difficulty accepting the idea that Edana planned to wed Dane," Arien shot back, stung by the insult.

"I had other plans for you, and well you know they didn't include marriage. But you . . . you purposely disobeyed me. I ordered you to leave this man to Edana. Why, oh, why did you not do so?"

Frustration filled Arien. What could she say to convince Dorianne she'd had no choice? It was as much the high priestess's fault as it was Edana's, her father's, and the dwarf's. Dorianne had refused to face the reality of a rapidly worsening situation. She'd refused to censure or discipline Edana, even when confronted with the truth about her. She would rather have sacrificed an innocent man, and hope the problem was solved.

"I couldn't accept the consequences to Dane if I'd obeyed you, my lady," Arien finally replied. " 'Twasn't right. In my heart, I didn't believe a true Moondancer would permit such a tragedy to occur."

"A true Moondancer obeys her high priestess," Dorianne cried. "A true Moondancer is faithful to her vows."

"Above all, do no harm." Steadily, Arien returned the old woman's gaze. " 'Tis the guiding precept of all Moondancers."

Dorianne's glance grew hard. " 'Tisn't fitting for you to throw our laws back at me. If only you knew how close you stand to being cast out of the Order."

The blood drained from Arien's face. It was one thing to swear not to practice her magic, but entirely another to be banished from the Moondancers!

"I've never wished for such a thing, my lady. The Moondancers are my life, my reason for existence!"

"Then you're back where you were that day you last came to visit me."

Arien frowned, puzzled. "I don't understand."

"The man. You must give him up."

"Give him up? I've lain with him; I carry his child within me; I've wed him! 'Tis too late to give him up."

"Nay, child." The high priestess gave a sad, gentle shake of her head. " 'Tisn't too late. I've powers beyond your imagining. I can turn back time and be with you that night you chose to thwart Edana. I can stop you before you make the most tragic and senseless decision of your life. All it takes is your leave."

All it takes is your leave. . . .

Bitterness welled up in Arien. Aye, she thought, though 'twas a questionable manipulation of Moondancer precepts, if there was no coercion in the act, Dorianne might well be able to do exactly as she claimed, and none of their laws would be violated.

It would solve so many problems in the bargain. She'd regain her maidenhood, not fall prey to the dwarf's evil manipulations, not be forced to renounce her magic or risk endangering her

Moondancer status, and not have to endure Dane's continuing suspicion and disdain. All would be as it once was, and Arien could return to the safe, comfortable life she'd always known.

"The man is doomed, child, one way or another." Dorianne's soft, soothing voice intruded on her anguished musings. "If Edana doesn't destroy him, your father surely will. You risk far more, though, in binding your fate to his. More than the life of one man is at stake here. Far, far more."

A heavy sense of despair settled over Arien. Ah, what was the use? she asked herself dejectedly. Dorianne was wiser than she. Perhaps it *was* best to follow where she led, to trust a far wiser judgment over her own.

"Well, child?" the high priestess prodded, the look in her rheumy old eyes now kind and benevolent. A sense of warm acceptance, of loving favor, filled Arien. Ah, to be free of all the doubts and cares, she thought with a great surge of longing, to relinquish this fearsome, confounding responsibility and go back to the way it was!

"Time is of the essence if I'm to correct this grievous error before 'tis too late," Dorianne continued, opening her arms like a mother welcoming her child back into the fold. "You must decide; you must tell me now. Do you or do you not give me leave?"

Chapter Thirteen

Do you give me leave?

Over and over, the question echoed in Arien's head, hammering at her heart and mind until she thought she'd go mad. It was a simple enough question, with an equally simple answer. Why couldn't she speak the words and be done with it?

She tried, truly she did, opening her mouth to form her reply. Yet, each time, Dane's face rose in her memory. Not his face of late, angry and full of distrust and loathing, but a recollection of his expression when he'd kissed her that night in her room. He'd looked down at her with such longing, such tender affection. For the first time in her life, Arien had known what it was to be wanted, needed, cherished.

And then his wedding kiss. There'd been a passion, strong and sure, beneath his anger. In that moment, his hunger had been hers. She'd seen the heart and soul of him, and knew hope still burned there. Knew he was worth fighting for, worth risking all for—and knew she could never turn from him no matter the cost.

218

Naught o' value comes wi'out a price. The dwarf's words filled her mind yet again. *Fer yer sake, though, I pray 'twon't be more than ye can pay.*

Despair swamped Arien. Holy Mother, hadn't she yet paid enough? Must she now be cast out from the Moondancers as well? And would even that be sufficient, or must she keep on giving and giving until nothing was left of her?

She lifted her gaze and met Dorianne's. "I'm sorry, my lady," Arien whispered, "but I cannot give you my leave. If Dane is doomed, than I surely am, too. I've cast my fate with his. I made my vows to him. I cannot—"

"What of the vows you made when you became a Moondancer?" Dorianne snapped, all pretense of loving benevolence gone. "Were they but convenient until another, better opportunity made itself known? You're thinking with your loins, child, rather than with your head. Don't, I beg you, make this foolish, fatal mistake!"

"The only mistake I risk making, my lady," Arien countered firmly, "is to turn my back on someone in need. 'Twas the first and greatest vow I took as a Moondancer—that the rule of my conscience must override all others, even that of yours and the order. And my conscience tells me that to leave Dane to my father and Edana would be as evil as destroying him myself."

"Yet in squandering everything for this one man," the high priestess cried, "you'll endanger us all!"

"Do you think I haven't agonized over that possibility time and again?" Ah, how could she make Dorianne understand? Arien wondered. No one seemed to understand, no one save the dwarf.

It was a strange, unsettling relationship she'd formed with that little creature. He'd encouraged her and used her, deliberately fostering powers he'd surely known she had little ability to control, then left her to sort out the terrible consequences of what she'd done. Yet still, especially at times like this, Arien thought of him with longing, and wished he were here to help her.

"Obey our laws." Dorianne's voice sliced relentlessly through Arien's wistful musings. "There can be no other recourse, if you wish to remain a Moondancer."

Arien smiled sadly. "I cannot, my lady. At least not in the way you deem best."

Slowly, like a cloud darkening with the oncoming storm, the high priestess's complexion mottled, then turned purple. " 'Twas the dwarf who corrupted you, wasn't it? Curse his devious, destructive soul! He knew he couldn't directly attack me, so instead he used you to undermine me. And what better way than to involve some man already enmeshed in the Talamontes's web of deceit and treachery."

Dorianne shook her head. "I don't like this. Your devotion to this man is too strong, too quick. The dwarf's hand is in that, as well, I'd wager." Dorianne stepped close. She took Arien's chin in her palm, lifting her head to stare into her eyes. " 'Tis indeed too late for you, isn't it? Already you're corrupted beyond salvation, first by the dwarf and then by this man."

"You may see it so, my lady." Quietly, resolutely, she returned the high priestess's searching gaze. "I hope and pray 'tisn't true. I'd never deliberately cause you pain or harm."

"It doesn't matter. Good intentions aren't enough in times such as these." Dorianne's grip tightened on Arien's chin. "I cannot risk allowing one with your powers to defy me in any way, though. You must relinquish your magic, child. Now, or I will take it from you."

"N-nay." Arien struggled to break free of the old woman's clasp, but Dorianne's strength was suddenly like iron. Panic flooded Arien. She couldn't, she must not, lose her magic. Some instinct told her, above all else, she must protect her magic.

Summoning all her abilities, Arien threw up a shield between her and the high priestess. As magic collided with magic, sparks flew in every direction. Thunder exploded around them. Dorianne staggered backward, a look of shock and horror on her face. Arien was thrown to the ground.

"Y-you dare turn your powers against me?" the high priestess stammered, incredulous. "You dare oppose my desires in this?"

Arien got unsteadily to her knees. "Please, my lady. Don't do this. Don't take my magic!"

"You cannot have it all. You knew the consequences, yet in your arrogance and pride you refused to yield to my higher authority. I cannot—I will not—abide that."

"And what of Edana and the Ravens?" Arien cried. "You punish me for what I've done in good conscience to save a man's life, yet you turn a blind eye to the evil they do? If you must punish me, then punish them as well, before they grow too strong and you haven't sufficient power to control them."

"Edana is deluded if she thinks to gain control with her Raven magic. 'Twill never happen. But

221

you . . . you are in league with a dwarf, the Moon-dancers' greatest enemy. And now you've compounded it all by not only lying with, but *loving* a man. If only you knew what dark and dire things you've roused, things we'd safely put to rest long ago."

"Then tell me what to do," Arien pleaded. "Help me understand, so I may find my way through it all. I want no harm to befall Greystone or the Moondancers. I swear it!"

Dorianne sighed and shook her head. "Nay, 'tis too late. You are beyond my influence." She lifted her hands to Arien. "Yield your magic. Now and forevermore."

As she spoke, an eerie, greenish light leaped from her fingertips and arced to Arien. It encompassed her, then closed in, squeezing until Arien felt as if the life was being pressed from her body. She threw up her hands to shove the magical aura aside, struggling with all her might, and still the pressure increased.

She was dying, Arien thought, as the agony became excruciating. Whether she truly intended to or not, Dorianne would surely kill her.

"Release the magic, child," the high priestess urged. "Your resistance is the source of the pain. I wish you no harm, but harm you'll surely do if you continue to fight me. Give it up. Yield. 'Tis your only hope."

Give it up. Yield, Arien thought, her body engulfed in a searing, suffocating heat. But if she did, she could no longer protect Dane. Edana could take him whenever she wished. Take him, and use him for her own savage, sordid ends.

"Dane," she whispered achingly. "Ah, Dane."

"Surrender. Submit. Give me your magic," came the hard, implacable demand yet again.

From somewhere far away, Arien heard a shout, heard her name called. She struggled to stand, to warn whomever was coming not to get any closer. It was too dangerous for an outsider to step between two Moondancers.

Then arms, strong and supportive, encircled her, pulling her to her feet. Arien sagged against a hard-muscled body, knowing in that moment who held her so protectively.

"D-Dane," she breathed. Turning in his arms, Arien gazed up at him. "You came. Wh-why?"

If the truth be told, Dane had no answer. All he knew was that when he'd heard the crack of thunder and seen Arien fall to the ground, something inside him had snapped. As tumultuous and bewildering as his feelings for her were, she was his and no man—or woman—would harm her while he lived.

His grip about her tightened. " 'Tis of no import. Are you all right, lass?"

"Tell her to yield her magic," the high priestess commanded.

Dane glanced up. An old woman with scraggly white hair and wild eyes glared back at him. He looked at Arien. "Why does she want your magic?"

Arien closed her eyes and glanced away. "It doesn't matter. But just as I cannot give up my magic for you, I cannot give it up to her."

"Order her to yield her magic," the old woman cried. "She has sacrificed all to be yours. 'Twill be her death if she refuses, and I've no wish to kill her."

Panic filled Dane. He stood between two Moondancer witches apparently locked in mortal combat, and there seemed nothing he could do to halt them. Yet if he didn't, Arien might die.

For a fleeting, shameful instant, Dane considered stepping aside and letting fate decide the outcome.

She has sacrificed all to be yours.

Unbidden, the high priestess's words rose tauntingly in Dane's mind. What did the old woman mean? he wondered. It was beyond belief that she wasn't involved in Arien's treachery. That was as hard to believe as the idea that Arien wasn't in league with her father.

There was no time, however, to ponder the matter any further. He must make a choice, and make it now, whether to step aside or stand with Arien.

Dane forced a grim smile. "You threaten my wife, madam. I say, think again before you make the gravest error of your life."

With a horrified gasp, Arien twisted free of his clasp. "Nay, Dane," she cried. "You do not know . . . you cannot hope to—"

There was no time to say more. The high priestess threw back her arm. Then, with a harsh exhalation, she flung it forward. Once more an eerie green light arced from her fingertips, but this time it shot straight at Dane.

Transfixed, he watched it come for him, knowing it was his death, yet knowing as well that he was helpless to stop it. Strangely, though, Dane wasn't afraid. Indeed, he felt a relief of sorts. It was an honorable way to die, defending one's wife, however undeserving she might be of such devotion.

"Nay!" Arien screamed. In a blur of swirling cloak and unbound ebony hair, she leaped between him and the oncoming light. She threw up her hands, crossed at the wrists, meeting the magical onslaught full-force.

There was another deafening crack, then a brilliant flash and a powerful gush of air. Dane staggered back, blinded. "By the holy ones!" He threw up his hands to shield his face, and flung himself forward. Arien. He had to get back to Arien.

Somehow, though he knew not how, Dane found her. Immediately, and with a strength surprising for a woman of her size, Arien shoved him behind her. "Stay back," she cried. " 'Tis my fight."

Once again the high priestess let loose another burst of magical fire. Again, Arien countered the attack. Yet, instead of weakening with each blow, she only seemed to grow stronger.

Pressed against Arien's back in support, Dane sensed the power rising within her. In some strange way he felt a part of it, as if the melding of their flesh enhanced Arien's strength.

It was a frightening yet strangely exhilarating realization. Yet even as Dane feared the outcome of such a union, he moved closer. Battle instincts drove him now. Later would be time enough to consider the consequences of what he'd done. Now . . . now all that mattered was survival.

Then, as suddenly as the conflict had begun, it was over. Shaken, deathly pale, Dorianne stumbled back. "How?" she whispered, confusion and fear in her eyes. "How, where, did you gain such powers?"

Arien shuddered, then shook her head. "I-I don't know. The dwarf warned that his magic

225

wasn't a skill easily or willingly discarded. But 'twasn't one I ever wished to foster after that night, so I thought it gone."

"Little fool!" Dorianne hissed. "Did you think such powers would be given without a price? Already, the dwarf has begun your corruption. 'Tis a rot that will surely spread to us all."

"N-nay." Trembling violently, Arien sank back, pressing into Dane. His grip tightened on her arms, and he stood firm against her. " 'Tisn't true," she protested tearfully. "I-I can control it. You'll see."

"And if you can't?" the older woman prodded. "What then?" Once more, she extended her hand. "Give me your magic, child. 'Tis your last chance."

Arien dragged in an unsteady breath. "I cannot. I'm sorry, my lady, but I cannot. Too much is at stake to give away what I may someday need."

Dorianne's shoulders sagged and she became, once again, a frail, failing old woman. "Then we are all doomed, and you will be the one who leads us to our destruction."

"Mayhap, my lady," Arien said softly, "but I do not think so."

"Indeed? Well, we'll soon see, won't we?" Her countenance changed, became austere, ruthless. "In the meanwhile, there's still the issue of your place in the Order. A place you are no longer worthy to hold." She motioned to several Moondancers, who, Arien now realized, had been watching all along from the trees.

As they stepped up to stand beside her, Dorianne brought both palms together, lifting them high above her head. It was a gesture Arien had seen only once before—in a ceremony of rejection of a professed Moondancer. Anguish engulfed her.

"Nay," she whispered, shaking her head. "Please . . . don't."

"As the Goddess clasps you to her on the night you are first joined with her," Dorianne intoned, "she can turn her gaze and cast you away. Cast you away as I do now, Princess Arien Talamontes. No longer may you call yourself Moondancer, or invoke the Goddess to bless your spells. You are exiled, pariah, she-who-will-be-nameless. We know you no more."

With that, the high priestess went limp, sagging into the arms of her sisters. Half leading, half carrying her, the other Moondancers walked off, soon disappearing into the depths of the shimmering, sun-dappled forest.

Her heart thudding painfully in her chest, Arien watched in stunned disbelief until the women disappeared into the forest. Then Dane released her and stepped back. She turned, shaken and drained, to meet his gaze.

For long minutes he stared down at her, myriad emotions flaring then fading in his expressive eyes. Finally, a hard, shuttered look settled over his features.

"I'm not certain I fully understand all that has transpired here," Dane muttered. "It changes naught, however."

Already, Arien thought despairingly, Dane retreats into the fortress of his suspicion and mistrust. Is there naught, then, I can do—or sacrifice—to convince him of my love and loyalty? "What do you mean, m'lord?" she forced herself to ask.

"The bargain we struck, of course. Though you refused to give up your magic even to your high priestess, I still expect you to keep your promise to me."

Holy Mother! Arien thought in exasperation, quashing her surge of anger before it formed into words she might later regret. "And exactly which promise, of all the many I've made," she demanded tautly, "are you holding me to now?"

He fixed her with a smoldering look. "Which do you think? The most important one of all—that I'll have no magic in Castle Haversin. Do you understand me, madam?"

"Aye, m'lord," Arien said, so frustrated and disheartened it was all she could do to reply. "I understand."

It was dusk before they arrived at Castle Haversin. The party's speed had slowed as the altitude increased, until they were riding through foothills into increasingly mountainous terrain. The views were gorgeous, lush, flower-strewn meadows slowly giving way to scattered forests of pine and birch, then thicker stands of pine interspersed with massive granite boulders. Sparkling streams rushed past them, some gentle courses of water wending their way down with little noise or disruption, others raging torrents that foamed over moss-slick rocks.

There was ample opportunity for Arien to observe the changing country. Since their encounter with Dorianne, Dane had all but ignored her. 'Twas for the best, she thought. She wasn't in the most amiable of moods herself.

Yet despite Arien's growing misgivings, the sight of Castle Haversin in the setting sun was welcome nonetheless. It was an imposing fortress, set upon an immense outcropping of earth and rock. Surrounded on three sides by Rothbury, a quaint little town of half-timbered houses that sprawled on either side of the winding road leading up to the castle, Haversin perched on the edge of a cliff overlooking a wide river valley.

Long and high, the castle's battlemented walls were connected by several towers, both square and cylindrical. From high atop those towers, pennants of midnight blue, emblazoned with the golden Haversin lion, snapped briskly in the early evening breeze. In colorful contrast, the castle, formed from stones carved from the mountains in which it lay, varied in hue from gray limestone to yellow and dark red sandstone.

It was an ancient fortress with several periods of construction, Arien thought, gazing at the differing layers of rock. The Haversins were an old family, their roots dating back as far as those of the Talamontes. Indeed, thanks to episodic intermarriage between the two houses, she and Dane were distantly related.

At sight of their party, a shout went up from the castle walls. Soon men were scurrying along the parapets and out the huge, iron-studded wooden gate to join women and children in forming a welcoming line wending down through the town. From soldiers to craftsmen to peasants who had followed the party from the small crofts scattered outside the town, they composed a joyous jumble of bodies and happy, healthy faces, all cheering and waving in greeting. A far cry, Arien realized, from the dour, silent receptions her father usually received.

As Dane led the way past his people, their quite evident and honest pleasure at his return began to affect even him. His weary, troubled expression faded. A smile lifted his lips. He waved, shouting back greetings to the crowd.

It was good to see him happy, once more the man she'd first known and admired. She was equally glad he was the sort of leader who inspired respect and affection in his people. It renewed her hope—for their future as well as for the kingdom.

That brief moment of pleasure, however, quickly faded when Dane drew up before his imposing keep. He swung down from his warhorse and stalked over to her. "Come down, madam," he said tersely, once more stern as he lifted his arms to her. "The night draws on and I've much to attend to before I can take my rest."

She bit back a tart retort that she was sorry to add to his burden, and instead slid off her horse. For a fleeting instant, as their bodies touched, Arien thought she felt him shudder in response. Then he released her and offered her his arm.

"If you will, madam." Turning, Dane led her up the steps to the main door, where a smiling, elderly couple stood. "Allow me to introduce you to John Bidwell, my steward, and his wife, Willa. She serves as my chatelaine."

He then turned to the Bidwells. "John and Willa, this is my new wife, the Princess Arien Talamontes."

The old couple bowed low, but not before Arien discerned a look of curiosity mixed with guarded surprise in their eyes. Who could blame them? she thought. Her father's heavy-handed, unpopular rule had reached even as far as this mountain fortress and its lands. And Dane Haversin, she wagered, had never been one to hide his true feelings about any form of injustice.

She extended her hand, first to the steward, then his wife. "I'm pleased finally to make your acquaintance, and look forward to learning all you can teach me of this beautiful place."

Willa, a fine-looking woman with gray hair and rosy cheeks, stepped up and took Arien's hand, enveloping it in her own soft, wrinkled one. She patted it and smiled. "We're equally pleased to have ye here, m'lady. Aren't we, John?" she prodded when her tall, balding husband just stood there, eyeing Arien.

"What? Oh, aye," he muttered, when his wife was finally forced to deliver a swift backward kick to his shin to gain his attention. "We're glad to have ye, m'lady. Most especially my wife." He shot her a wry, slanting look. "Willie has been harping at m'lord for some time now to find himself a new lady to help with the castle duties. Seems she claims she's getting a mite too old to do it all herself these days.

"Not that she yet lacks the energy to keep me in my place," John added slyly, "be it in or out o' bed."

"Oh, get on wi' ye, John Bidwell," his wife scolded, flushing like some young girl. "Lady Haversin doesn't care a whit about our private matters. Just now, I'd wager all she can think o' is a good meal, a hot bath, and a soft bed."

"Aye, I'm certain all those things are foremost in m'lady's mind," Dane cut in before Arien could answer. He smiled at Willa Bidwell. "Would you escort her and her maidservant up to my bedchamber, then see to their needs? In the meanwhile, I must meet with your husband."

"I'd be honored to assist yer lady in any way she wishes, m'lord," the old woman said. "Fair warning, though. I'll not allow ye to keep my John up till all hours talking o' things as easily discussed on the morrow. He's not as young as he used to be, and needs his rest."

Dane chuckled. "Aye, and 'tis easy to imagine what kind of 'rest' he envisions, too. I'll not keep him long, though. An hour or two and no more, Willa. I promise."

"See that ye remember that promise afore I do, m'lord." She turned to Arien. "By yer leave, m'lady?"

Arien smiled and nodded. "But a moment more, and I'll be pleased to accompany you wherever you lead." She looked up at Dane. "Could I first have a private word with you, m'lord?"

With considerable effort, Arien noted, Dane controlled his irritation. With a jerk of his head, he indicated a small, curtained alcove to the right and just inside the main door. "As you wish, m'lady."

Silently, she followed him to the little alcove. As Dane pulled the heavy wool curtains closed, Arien took a seat on the wooden bench inset in the outer stone wall.

"Well, what is it now?" Dane growled, turning to her as soon as the curtains were closed. "I give you fair warning—I'm bone weary and my patience is thin. So I'd strongly advise—"

"I've but one question," Arien interrupted, lifting a hand to silence him. "You told Willa to take me up to your bedchamber. I assumed, as in the usual way, I'd have private quarters of my own."

Dane rolled his eyes and sighed. "The Haversins, who until of late have always wed for love, don't follow the 'usual way' of the lord and lady sleeping in separate bedchambers. Though I must admit," he added sardonically, "that custom suddenly has a definite appeal."

"Aye, that it does," Arien muttered, sick to death of his snide, insulting remarks. "Surely, in a castle this large, there are extra rooms that can quickly and easily be prepared for me."

"Are you trying to tell me you refuse to render a wife's conjugal duties?"

Taken aback by the bluntness of Dane's question, she did not respond at once. "Nay, I'm not saying that," she finally replied. "But after what has transpired between us in the past few days, I must confess I assumed you had no further wish to couple with me."

Dane gave a mocking laugh. "I intend to obtain everything I can from this farce of a marriage, as little as 'twill most likely be." He moved forward until his legs nearly touched Arien's gown.

Ever so slowly, Arien let her glance travel up his tall, strapping body until she locked gazes with him. Dane's face was set in wary determination. A muscle twitched violently in his beard-shadowed jaw.

He looks like some wild mountain cat ready to strike, she thought. Ready to lash out if threatened in any way.

At the realization, a deep sadness filled her. Even before he'd encountered her, Dane had evidently been too badly hurt to trust easily again. And, though she was already weary of fighting with him, the road back to trust and friendship boded to be a long, upward trek. Arien, however, had barely enough strength left to get through this night.

She sighed in resignation. "What do you wish of me, then, m'lord? I only thought to spare us unnecessary interaction, and imagined your private chambers were the last place you wished to share with me."

"Oh, but you're wrong, madam." The timbre of Dane's voice changed suddenly, going deep and husky. "I'm committed to using that nubile young body of yours to fulfill our marital vows. For all you've gained in wedding me, both for yourself and your father, surely 'tis only fair that you grant me the one thing I want above all else."

"And that one thing is, m'lord?" Arien asked, even as the hot, dark implications of his words sent a delicious shiver rippling through her.

"What else, madam?" Dane's blue eyes gleamed with a suddenly savage, sensual light. "In the past few days I've had time to ponder many things. And surely one witch can counterbalance another witch's curse, and assure that I once again produce heirs? That's where you, my young, healthy, and presumedly fertile wife, come in. Surely 'tis in your power to give me those heirs. Heirs to carry on the Haversin line. Heirs to inherit this castle and its lands, and keep them from your father's greedy grasp.

"To that end"—he went down on one knee before her and took her by the arms—"until you present unmistakable proof you carry my child, you'll sleep in my chambers and couple with me whenever I wish."

Chapter Fourteen

Dane was so close his warm breath caressed her face, and his powerful form radiated an animal magnetism that roused an answering fire deep within her. Arien didn't know whether to laugh in relief or slap him for his arrogance. So, she must sleep in his chambers and couple with him whenever he wished until he got her with child, must she?

Well, Dane Haversin need trouble himself no further. Already she carried his child. Already it was past time he gave her private chambers.

Yet when Arien opened her mouth to inform Dane of precisely that fact, something made her stop and reconsider. Perhaps the wisest course *wasn't* to aid him in his ultimate intent to shut her out of his life. Above all else she'd ever desired, Arien desired to regain her husband's friendship, then win his love. To that end, the more time they spent together, the greater the chance they might eventually work through their differences.

First, though, she must win his trust anew, before she could ever hope to win his heart. And what better place to begin than in the privacy of Dane's chambers, in the safe haven of his bed? Isolated from the rest of the world and its distractions, surely there he would feel strong, in control once more. Surely there she could prove her devotion and affection, in the unselfish giving of her body.

Nay, Arien decided, no purpose was served by informing Dane he was already to be a father. The babe growing within her belly would reveal the truth soon enough.

Arien feigned an unconcerned shrug. "If that is your wish, m'lord, then I'll be happy to share your bedchamber and couple with you. 'Tis my conjugal duty, as you so aptly put it."

Dane eyed her closely, then gave a snort of disgust and rose. "Your ardent response warms my heart, madam."

"As does yours for me, m'lord."

Surprise flickered momentarily in his eyes. "Play no games with me, wife," he snarled. "I don't need your pretense at passion to couple with you. You're comely enough to stir any man's desires, whether he cares for you or not."

"And you, husband," Arien replied softly, "can at times be crude enough to squelch any gentler affections in a woman's heart."

Ever so slowly, a dark flush suffused Dane's striking, rough-hewn features. He averted his gaze, apparently choosing to stare at something over her right shoulder. "Mayhap I *am* being overly crude," Dane said finally, a husky note in his voice. "For that I beg pardon. 'Tis no excuse, I well know, but you stir an unreasoning anger in me."

Arien stood. "Then mayhap a truce is in order."

"A truce?" he asked warily.

"Aye. Let us strive at least to avoid insulting one another. 'Twill not change the difficulties that lie between us, but at least it may ease the tension a bit." A smile lifted her lips. " 'Tis possible to be enemies without the insults, is it not? Civil enemies, but still enemies?"

Dane looked as if he didn't know whether to laugh or be angry again. "Civil enemies?" He cocked his head. " 'Tis a novel consideration. One I'll ponder further on the morrow."

He turned, swept open the curtains, then took her by the arm. "In the meanwhile, we've others awaiting us. 'Tis past time we returned to them."

"Aye, lord husband," Arien replied, feeling in her heart that she'd won a victory at last. A small one, to be sure, but progress nonetheless. And that was accomplishment enough for one day, she thought, following him from the alcove.

His threats to the contrary, Dane didn't come up to bed until late; then he shed his clothes quietly in the darkened room, climbed into bed, and promptly turned on his side away from Arien and went to sleep. He was gone before she awoke just after dawn. She didn't see him again until the supper meal in the Great Hall.

Despite his conspicuous absence, Arien's first day in Castle Haversin was a full one. After rising and quickly washing in a basin of cold water, Arien donned a simple gown of light green wool and a sleeveless surcoat of darker green. Next, Onora braided her hair into a long plait, and helped Arien slip on a pair of soft leather shoes. Then they shared a light breakfast of fresh-baked brown bread and a cup of watered wine.

Soon thereafter, Willa Bidwell arrived with the servants bearing the rest of their baggage. The remainder of the morning was spent unpacking and setting out Arien's belongings among Dane's. Her husband, she noted, lived as simply as he dressed and traveled. Besides the huge, four-poster wooden bed with its dark blue bed hangings that could be drawn to keep out drafts in winter, the room boasted a red sandstone hearth with two tall, padded wooden chairs set before it, a stout, low chest below the single, large, leaded-glass window, and a taller chest of inlaid wood standing near the bed.

There was little other decoration, except several leather-bound books piled on a small table beside the hearthside chairs, and an ancient tapestry depicting a golden lion rampant with crimson claws and tongue against a midnight blue background hanging over the hearth. The low chest was locked. Dane had few personal items in the tall chest, however, so Arien, at Willa's urging, placed all her clothes there. Her own small, silver jewel chest she placed atop the tall chest, then propped her lute beside one of the hearth chairs.

It still looked like a man's chamber, Arien mused as she glanced around when all the unpacking was done. It wasn't her right, however, to attempt drastic changes in Haversin or Dane's life just yet. Better to make small, subtle inroads until he looked around one day, and discovered she was as integral to his life and happiness as these hallowed old stones.

Dinner was served at noon. Because a fine banquet was to be given in Arien's honor that night, the meal was a far simpler affair than usual. Dane sent his regrets, claiming he was still in conference with his council and wouldn't be joining her, so Arien chose to eat in the privacy of their bedchamber. Afterward, she decided on a tour of the castle, with Onora and Willa as her attendants.

They toured the kitchen, with its great, round central hearth where a pig intended for the banquet was already roasting on a spit, then the pantry and buttery, before heading outside to the bailey and the castle gardens. Peach, apple, pear, and plum trees grew on one side, with plots for herbs and flowers on the other. Just outside the half-walled garden lay the fish pond, stocked with trout and pike.

The Great Hall was visited next, then the upper rooms. The tour finished with a brisk stroll along the parapet walk enclosing the entire fortress. All her life Arien had heard Castle Haversin's praises extolled, but until this day she had never actually seen it. The tales, she decided, didn't do the fine old castle justice.

"The Haversin family must indeed be wealthy," she observed as she walked along, Willa at her side, Onora following closely behind, "to have maintained this fortress all these years."

The older woman beamed. "Aye, that it is. Ye're a fortunate girl, to have won the love o' such a fine man."

Onora, walking close behind them, made a noise that sounded suspiciously like an indignant snort. After giving a warning glance over her shoulder, Arien turned back to see if Willa had noticed her maidservant's response. She hadn't. The old woman had stopped abruptly and, hands clenched about one of the stone merlons, was gazing down into the outer bailey.

Curious, Arien and Onora joined her. It was then that the sound of soft sobbing first reached them. Far below, John Bidwell was half leading, half dragging a young, blond-haired woman carrying a baby, across the bailey toward the main gate. Behind them came a guard, his arms loaded with two large cloth bundles.

Alternately, the slender young woman cried, then pleaded with John, all apparently to no avail. The steward continued to make his stoic way toward the main gate, pulling the woman and her child with him. A few servants going about their business paused to stare after them, then shook their heads and continued on their way.

Arien turned to Willa. "Poor lass. What has she done to merit expulsion from the castle?"

Haversin's chatelaine sighed. "Suffice it to say her services are no longer needed, m'lady. She'll be well cared for, though. Have no fear o' that."

"I'm pleased to hear it." Arien glanced at Onora, whose lips were pursed and brows drawn together as if whatever she considered was decidedly distasteful. Bemused, Arien turned back to Willa. "Mayhap the lass could be trained as a lady-in-waiting? I brought only Onora with me. In time, surely I could find some use for another personal servant."

The blood drained from the old woman's face. "Nay, m'lady." Firmly, she shook her head. "The lass wouldn't suit. Ye've my word on it."

"As you wish." Arien shrugged. "I'm certain your judgment on these kinds of things is best. 'Twas just a thought."

"And a most kind one 'twas, m'lady," Willa hastened to assure her. "Meantime, I'll keep an eye out for a suitable lass for ye. 'Twill not be too difficult to find one, once word gets out o' m'lord's fine new wife."

Arien managed a wan smile. "To be sure." She glanced up at the sun, just beginning to dip slowly toward the west. "I must confess to a need for a short rest. It has been a most informative but tiring day so far, and I'd like to be at my best for this eve's banquet."

"As ye wish, m'lady. Shall I escort ye back to yer room, or can ye find it well enough yerself by now?"

"Castle Haversin is large," Arien said with a chuckle, "but m'lord's bedchamber is easy enough to find." She motioned to Onora. "Come, my friend. I'll need your help in readying for my nap."

Her maidservant joined her and, with a nod of farewell to Willa, Arien and Onora walked back toward the Great Hall. They walked for a time in silence, finally drawing up before Dane's bedchamber door. Once inside, Onora helped Arien out of her surcoat and gown, then tucked her into bed.

"By yer leave, m'lady," Onora finally said. "I'd like to use the time while ye're resting to see to a few personal matters."

"You've my leave." Arien paused, staring thoughtfully up at the blue canopy overhead. She almost envied her friend. Already, Onora had other matters to attend to, not to mention a loving, attentive husband. All Arien had, now that she'd sworn not to practice her magic, was a castle that hardly needed her services and a husband who so far chose to avoid her.

"Onora?"

"Aye, m'lady?"

"You know as well as I that Dane wed me under duress, and bears no affection for me. Nonetheless, I still wish to be a good and true wife to him."

"Aye, m'lady."

"Will you be my eyes and ears here in Castle Haversin?" Arien leaned on one elbow and stared imploringly at her friend. "Whatever is of use to Dane, I wish to know. 'Tis as Willa said: I *am* fortunate to have wed him."

"He's equally fortunate to have wed a woman as fine as ye," her friend muttered. " 'Tis past time he began to realize it."

Arien smiled, revealing all the hope and love in her heart. "He will, Onora. He will . . . in time."

"The banquet went well, wouldn't ye say, m'lady?"

"Hmmm?" Arien looked up from the dressing table where Onora stood, brushing her hair. Just then a servant entered the bedchamber, carrying a bucket of steaming water, which she emptied into the wooden tub set near the roaring hearth fire.

Arien waited until the woman left before answering. "The banquet? Oh, aye, I suppose so. Willa's an excellent chatelaine. Everything was perfect, from the exquisite table settings to the delicious food."

"Does it concern ye, that Willa's so skilled, I mean?" As she spoke, Onora ran the brush through Arien's hair, using long, soothing strokes that eased the tension of the day. "That ye may never measure up to such efficiency?"

Arien's lids grew heavy and closed, her muscles slowly relaxing under her maidservant's ministrations. "Nay, comparisons with Willa don't overly concern me," she said, smiling. "She seems willing to teach me what I'm lacking, and, as large and grand a castle as Haversin is, my own home was larger and grander still. Besides, those two Triennials prepared me in ways that will stand me in good stead here."

" 'Tis yer marital relationship that's the problem then."

"Aye." Reluctantly, Arien opened her eyes. The face staring back from the mirror was troubled and sad. "I fear I may have irrevocably destroyed our friendship."

Tears suddenly blurred her vision. Angrily, Arien blinked them away. "I fear I've made a frightful mess of it all. Not only with Dane, but with the Moondancers and my magic. And then, atop it all, there's that promise I made to the dwarf—"

Abruptly, the brushstrokes ceased, and Onora's face, wide eyed and pale, appeared above Arien's in the mirror. "Ye made a promise to the dwarf? By all that is holy, whatever did ye vow? And why, m'lady? Whatever could be worth putting yerself in thrall to that horrid little creature?"

With a creak of ancient hinges, the bedchamber door swung open. Yet another servant walked in with a bucket of hot water. Both women lapsed into silence until the servant finished her task and departed.

"I never finished telling you the whole story, did I?" Arien asked softly as the door closed once more. "I went to the dwarf to gain the dark powers I felt I needed to save Dane from Edana. Powers I'd intended to use solely to trick everyone into thinking Dane and I had coupled so he'd feel compelled to wed me. Those powers were more than I could manage, however. They controlled me, rather than the other way around."

"And what happened?"

"All my careful plans went awry. I coupled with Dane, lost my maidenhood, violated my Moon-dancer vows, and inflicted grievous insult on an innocent man. Then Dorianne demanded I give up my magic—which I would not do—and now she has cast me from the Moondancers."

Arien gave a self-deprecating laugh. "So, thanks to my self-indulgent conceit, I've sacrificed every-thing that truly mattered to me, and have little to show for the loss."

"What o' yer promise to the dwarf?"

She shrugged. " 'Twas a strange vow, to render him a magical favor if and when he asked it, or give him my heart's greatest treasure." Arien drew in a despairing breath. "But now that I've sworn to Dane never to practice my magic, which *is* my heart's greatest treasure, I've naught to give the dwarf if he should ask. Truly, could anyone be in a worse muddle?"

"Well, though ye've angered yer husband, there's still hope ye can win his heart back to ye in time," Onora offered consideringly, "and though ye cannot use it just now, ye still have yer magic. As far as that dwarf goes . . ."

She paused to pull back Arien's hair and twist it into a loose coil that she anchored to the top of her mistress's head with a few pins. "Well, I'd say *he's* the least o' yer problems," Onora said. "He cannot expect to obtain what ye're no longer free to give. Besides, 'tis all his fault ye're in such a muddle. He knew what his magic could do, and still he dabbled where he shouldn't have dabbled."

"That's the same conclusion I came to," Arien said, "yet I still wonder, and worry. I made him a vow. I am honor-bound to fulfill it if ever he should ask. Yet I also made Dane a vow."

" 'Tis indeed a dilemma. But I'm more o' a mind to wonder if yer husband will bed ye this night."

At the bluntness of her friend's question, heat flooded Arien's face. "I don't know. He didn't touch me last night, and was gone before I awoke this morn. But he did tell me he intends to get me with child, that he wants an heir."

"And how do ye feel about that?"

An impulse to tell Onora she already carried Dane's child filled Arien, but something kept her from revealing that precious secret. Perhaps she wished Dane to be the first to know. Perhaps it was still too fresh, too special, to put words to. For whatever reason, Arien said nothing.

"How do I feel about bearing Dane's children?" she repeated instead. "I'm his wife. 'Tis my duty."

"But a duty isn't necessarily a joy. Especially if ye don't love yer husband, and never wished to bear children."

Arien turned and looked up at her. "I think motherhood will bring me great happiness. I also think I was always meant to wed Dane. And as far as loving him—" She smiled. "I've loved Dane Haversin since the first moment I met him. Why else would I risk what I've risked, sacrificing my magic and home and even the hope of winning his love?"

"Why else, indeed?" Onora murmured.

Once again, tears filled Arien's eyes. Not wishing her friend to see them, she rose and walked over to stare out the window. The black vault of the heavens looked closer up here in the mountains, the stars brighter, sharper, clearer. It was a compelling, majestic place, this land of craggy peaks and windswept valleys, of deep, dark pine forests and mercurial weather. She could grow to love it all, become one with this land.

But did she dare? A single tear escaped to trickle down her cheek. Already, the pain of loving Dane tore at her heart, and the guilt at what she'd done to him was a burden she could barely carry. To open herself to this land and its people seemed too great a risk atop all the rest. And she didn't dare ponder what would happen when she bore the Haversin heir.

Yet how could she stop herself from feeling, from reaching out to all she saw and experienced? It was both her curse and her blessing, this instinctive, impetuous, almost insatiable yearning to have it all. Perhaps that was why she'd created more problems than she'd solved when she came to Dane's aid.

"Come, m'lady." Onora's voice rose from behind her. "I've scattered the dried lavender and herbs in yer water. 'Tis time for yer bath before it cools."

With a sigh, Arien turned. "Aye, a hot bath will suit me well. This has been a busy day, full of new things to learn and acquaintances to make. Time now, though, to put all that aside."

She followed Onora to the tub. After removing her bed robe, Arien stepped gingerly into the water. As she lowered herself into the steaming, fragrantly scented bath, Onora left her side momentarily to retrieve a large, folded bath towel and drape it over a nearby chair. Ever so carefully, Arien settled herself, drawing up her knees in the oval-shaped tub until she had sufficient room to hunker down so the water nearly covered her shoulders. Soon the water's warmth began to seep into her body, easing the last vestiges of tension from her muscles.

"Ye've been through much in the past week." Onora lathered one of Arien's arms and began to wash it. "Ye must never give up hope, though, that all will turn out well. Happiness is yer destiny as surely as 'tis—"

Once again the bedchamber door creaked open. Muttering under her breath, Onora turned. "Can ye not knock? We've enough water for m'lady's bath and ye can—"

At sight of the newest intruder, her voice faded. She gave a startled gasp. "M-m'lord! I didn't realize 'twas you. Pray, forgive my impertinence."

Her hands instinctively rising to cover herself, Arien turned toward the door. There, his tall form backlit by the torches burning in their iron wall brackets, stood Dane. For a long moment, no one spoke. Then Dane gestured toward Onora.

"Leave us. Now."

The maidservant swallowed convulsively, then looked at Arien. "M'lady?"

Arien knew Onora's first loyalty was to her. If she'd asked it, the maidservant would have defied even Haversin's lord. But there was no point in angering Dane. He was, after all, her husband, and this was his castle and bedchamber.

"Do as he asks." Arien forced an encouraging smile. "I'll be fine."

Onora nodded slowly. Then, with lips indignantly pursed, she gathered her skirts, flounced past Dane with only the most cursory of curtsies, and hurried out the door.

Dane closed and bolted the door behind her. "She's a haughty one." He turned back to Arien. "If she continues in such a fashion, she'll not do well at Haversin."

"Onora knows her place, m'lord." Dane's piercing regard made Arien feel decidedly uncomfortable. She turned her back to him and sank lower, until the water lapped gently at her chin. "She was worried about me."

"Worried, was she? About what, a husband entering his own bedchamber?" He strode over to stand beside the tub, facing her. "About a husband who has every right to be alone with his wife, even as she bathes?"

He squatted, so close his body pressed into the tub's wooden sides, and the steam misted his face. "Or is it really you who is worried?" Dane demanded huskily.

He dipped his hand into the water and began making swirling patterns with his fingers, languidly working his way ever nearer to where Arien's breasts were hidden beneath the herb-strewn water. "Does it offend you that I found you in your bath?"

She watched his fingers move ever closer, her heart beating a staccato rhythm in her chest, and wondered how it would feel, and what she'd do, if he touched her. Arien shuddered involuntarily. Indeed, it was too arousing, too unsettling to imagine.

"Has your bath cooled already?" Not awaiting a reply, Dane rose and moved to where Onora had draped a bath sheet over a chair. Picking it up, he unfurled it and held it open. "Come then. Let me wipe you dry, then warm you in another way."

A shard of pure sensual excitement stabbed through Arien, lodging deep in her woman's core. There was no mistaking his meaning or intent, not with that hot, hungry light burning in his eyes. But to rise from the water and stand naked before a man for the first time in her life . . .

What if he found her lacking? Arien's cheeks flamed hot. What if he regretted his decision to couple with her? What if he turned and left the room?

"Come, madam." There was a note of impatience, of strain in his voice now. "You knew I'd come to you this night. Why else did you time this bath to coincide with my arrival, knowing 'twould stir my passions like naught else?"

"T-truly, I didn't know when you'd finally leave the banquet," Arien stammered, all but undone by his admission of lust. "Indeed, you made your way to bed so late last night—"

"Will you come out now," Dane savagely cut in, "or must I drag you from there? 'Twill go poorly for you, I swear, if you force me to do so."

"N-nay."

Dropping the hands she still clasped over her breasts to the sides of the tub, Arien gripped the wooden boards and shoved herself to her feet. Water sluiced down her body, coursing around soft, ripened curves and through gentle valleys, its sensuous passage drawing the eye ever downward. Her nipples tightened, a flush warmed her cheeks, and her hands clenched into fists at her sides, but she stood there, totally exposed, exquisitely vulnerable.

Stood there, and gave Dane what he'd demanded.

Chapter Fifteen

Gazing at Arien's naked, water-slick body, Dane thought he'd go mad with the sudden explosion of his desire. He was grateful for the shield of the bath sheet he still held before him. His sex was so engorged it thrust lewdly now against his breeches. Thrust . . . throbbed . . . heavy with blood, swollen with need.

For a crazed instant his mind swam with a hot, brutal fantasy of walking over, hauling Arien into his arms, and carrying her to the bed and throwing her on it. Not bothering to undress, he'd pause just long enough to free his jutting organ, wrench apart her legs, then plunge himself into her. Despite Arien's protests and cries of distress, he'd drive into her soft, yielding body with ever increasing force until, in a shattering, exquisitely satisfying release, he'd spill his seed deep within her.

It was only what she deserved, Dane struggled to convince himself, even as he battled his compunction at contemplating such a beastly act. It was only fair recompense for her rape of him. Only this time his strength would overcome hers. This time, *he'd* take what *she* didn't wish to give.

Then Arien shivered, gooseflesh tightening her fair skin. Reflexively, Dane reached out, offering her the bath sheet. "Come, lass," he rasped, his throat suddenly raw with the bitter upwelling of his remorse. "You're cold. Come and let me dry you."

She hesitated, then climbed carefully from the tub and, with head held high, walked over to him. Her dignity, naked as she was, filled Dane with shame. Though Arien had given her word to honor her marriage vows and bed him, he'd never been half so honorable. All he'd promised her in return was that he'd use her to get himself an heir, implying she was nothing more to him than a receptacle for his seed.

That was all he dared let her be. To open his heart again would be worse than foolhardy. It could be fatal.

Whether he lived or died, Dane knew the king would be well served. Only cold, calculating actions held any hope of thwarting Cronan's plans. And if it was the last thing he ever did, Dane intended to best the king.

Arien might well be a pawn in her father's greedy schemes, an unwitting innocent manipulated for another's evil ends. Even now, after all she'd done to him, a tiny part of Dane still refused to believe her capable of such premeditated exploitation. It was a tiny part, though, one he dared not heed. If Arien insisted on coming between him and her father, then she'd suffer the same consequences as her sire.

She moved to stand within the span of the bath sheet and turned. For an instant, Dane glimpsed the sensuous undulations of her back, the lushness of hips and buttocks. But only for an instant. Indeed, he could bear no more.

Bringing the cloth together, Dane encircled Arien in the protective haven of his arms. At his touch, her hair, loosely caught with a few pins atop her head, fell free, tumbling down her shoulders and back.

The scent of lavender rose in the air. Dane inhaled deeply, savoring the heady, sense-stirring aroma. The dampness and warmth of her body penetrated the bath sheet. Instinctively, like one long starved, he pressed close until the ample swell of his manhood nestled against her.

His hands moved, his fingers splaying wide on Arien's shoulders in hungry possession. Hot blood shot through Dane's loins. He groaned, deep in his throat, and lowered his head to nuzzle her neck.

At the touch of his lips, Arien threw back her head, granting him greater access to her throat. It was his undoing. Dane clasped her head, turned it to him, slanting his mouth over hers. His fingers then slid down to grasp her jaw, forcing her lips to part in a deep, languorous kiss.

And, as before, Arien met him with passionate abandon, her tongue rising tentatively to touch his, then retreat, then dance back again into intimate contact. Almost of its own accord, Dane's other hand snaked down to her breast, cupping its soft, enticing fullness. Beneath his questing fingers, her nipple tightened in ardent response.

"Little she-demon." He growled deep in his throat, pulling back from the hot, honeyed delight of her mouth. "Do you disobey already, and turn to your magic to drive me wild with desire?"

"N-nay," Arien answered unsteadily, " 'tis no magic save the natural one arising between a man and a woman. I swear it, m'lord."

"And what value is your word to me?" Taking her by the shoulders, Dane wheeled her around, then swung her up into his arms. In a few quick strides, he reached the bed and laid Arien upon it. A few quick movements more, and she lay there naked, the bath sheet flipped back to expose her once again.

As the cool air washed over her, Arien shivered. Her rosy nipples puckered, pouting prettily for Dane's perusal. She tried to cover herself, but he was too quick, capturing both hands to imprison them above her head, then kneeing her legs wide apart.

"If the truth be told," he said, his voice little more than a harsh, husky rasp in the stone-silent chamber, "at this moment I care little whether 'tis natural or unnatural magic that rouses me so. All I know is my sex is rock hard and aches to join with you. All I desire is to find my release. In the end, naught else truly matters if my seed finds fertile ground, and your body nourishes my child to fruition."

His breath came raggedly now, his chest heaving, as Dane struggled with the burgeoning lust threatening to drive out all thought, all reason, and make him, once again, a helpless slave to her enchantress's body. He clenched shut his eyes to block out the sight of Arien, of her full breasts rising and falling, trembling with her excitement. Of her narrow waist and flat stomach, her woman's hips and succulent white thighs. Of that dark, dense thatch of ebony hair, guardian to a complex skein of feminine mysteries yet to be untangled or probed.

"Ah, by all that is holy!" Dane moaned. His head arched back, the cords of his neck straining with the effort to slow the fires of his passion. "I hurt. I'm near to bursting. Yet I fear . . . I fear—"

"Put aside your fears," Arien whispered, slipping her hands free of his now loose clasp. She reached down, undid his breeches, and slid them from Dane's hips. His thick, turgid shaft strained toward her. Boldly, Arien took it in her hand, squeezing gently at first, then more firmly as she began to run her encircled fingers up and down its massive length.

"You are the master here this night, the magic-wielder," she purred, her words caressing him as erotically as her hand did his sex. "I yield all to you—my body, my will, yea, even my heart. In return, I ask naught save you grant me the same fierce, sweet pleasure we shared that first time. That same fierce, sweet pleasure"—Arien pulled him down toward the pink flesh spread so invitingly before him—"I'll grant to you in turn."

Dane straddled Arien's body, fitting himself against her moist little cleft. The heat of her, pressing so intimately against the stiffness jutting from his groin, sent a delicious shudder vibrating through him. "Ah," Dane groaned in despair, "I can't . . . I need—"

At that moment, Arien arched toward him. His sex, slick with his own excitement, slipped down, wedging at the entrance of her woman's sheath. With a harsh gasp, Dane thrust into her, plunging so deep and hard he touched the tip of Arien's womb.

Startled, confused, she jerked back, but it was too late. Gripping her hips with both hands, Dane lifted Arien by the buttocks and drove into her again and again. Gradually, as she seemed to overcome her fear of his aggressive assault, she began an instinctive, rhythmic motion that met and duplicated his. The world around Dane narrowed to the carnal ecstasy of her tight, hot sheath, of her soft moans, and her wildly bucking hips.

Together, savagely, they slammed into each other, writhing, twisting, drenched with sweat, their passion escalating to exquisite, torturous heights. Dane felt his release begin, and shook violently in an effort to restrain the inevitable. To no avail. In total thrall to the rhythmic spasms that shuddered through him, Dane shot his seed into Arien, his body gone rigid, curving back like some tautly strung bow. He cried out, shouting his pleasure in a voice both tortured and joyous.

Beneath him, Arien gave a cry of her own, her body trembling, shaking, as she impaled herself on him again and again. Then, as suddenly and savagely as it had all begun, the fierce, sweet ecstasy was over. A sense of soaring happiness, of profound peace, encompassed Dane. He lowered himself to lie at her side, clasping Arien in his arms until, at long last, exhaustion claimed him.

With a rhythmic pounding of massive, iron-shod hooves that heralded their approach long before they came into sight, powerful warhorses galloped up the winding dirt road leading to the town. Arien, from the vantage of a window high up in one of the castle towers, leaned forward on the stone sill and squinted, trying to make out who and how many men were approaching. As they drew up before the town gate, she was finally able to ascertain that it was a party of twenty men, three garbed as befitted nobles, the others in the more common clothes and light armor of guards. All wore swords and helmets; all carried shields.

Arien frowned. For the most part, times were peaceful. Few traveled with such large armed escorts anymore. She stepped back from the window, turning to where Onora sat, flute in hand, expectantly awaiting her mistress.

"Well, have we time to practice this ballad once more before ye see to yer unexpected guests?" the maidservant asked. "I know ye wanted to play for yer lord husband this night after the supper meal but, truly, I don't feel ready to perform without a few more practices. Especially," she added with a wry twist of her lips, "if we're now to have additional guests at our performance."

"Mayhap you're right," Arien murmured, her mind still preoccupied with questions and concerns regarding the new arrivals. "I'd wished to play and sing for Dane's pleasure, not to entertain a crowd of strangers. The perfecting of our ballad has taken us nearly two weeks. It can wait a bit longer."

Onora eyed her friend. "This eve won't be as ye first planned, will it, m'lady?"

Arien arched a slender brow. "Oh, and how is that?"

"What else but how it has been every night for the past month since yer arrival at Haversin? First a quiet, intimate supper, then a moonlit walk along the castle parapets, and finally an indecently early departure to bed."

By the Mother, Arien thought, her cheeks flaming hot. At times Onora was far too plainspoken for comfort. "Indecent?" she managed to reply with a shaky laugh. "For a newly wedded woman, you're a fine one to talk!"

"Well, I'm not the only one taking note o' the Lord and Lady Haversin's bedchamber antics." The maidservant pursed her lips and shook her head. "Ye two rut as often as some peasant lad and lass. 'Tisn't seemly for nobles to act in such a way, even newlyweds in love."

Even newlyweds in love. For an instant, Arien was beset with a sharp stab of pain and longing. Then she quashed the fruitless desires. Dane's amorous attentions were intended solely to ease his way into her bed. As hard as that was to admit, it was reality and she must accept it.

"As I've told you before, Lord Haversin has a great desire for an heir," Arien hastened to offer when Onora arched a quizzical brow. "To that end and that end only, we 'rut'—as you so delicately put it—nearly every night."

"He seems quite attentive and tender for a man intent solely on fathering a child. And he's yer husband. By right he can have ye anytime he wants, without any effort at wooing ye."

"I know only what Dane has told me," Arien persisted stubbornly. "He wouldn't even touch me if 'twasn't to get me with child."

"Are ye both blind and daft? Haven't ye ever caught him unawares watching ye?" Onora sighed and rolled her eyes like a girl smitten. "The looks he gives ye, why 'tis enough to melt the heart o' a saint."

In spite of her effort to contain it, Arien flushed again. "Onora, you're a hopeless romantic. The best that can be said for our relationship is that Dane, out of respect for his name and my royal position, tolerates me. And even that, considering all I've done to him, is more than I deserve."

"Pish!" Onora gave a snort of disgust. "I'd say, rather, ye're a pair o' lackbrains, and deserve each other. He tolerates ye. Ye deserve a lifetime o' punishment." Shaking her head, she rose, flute in hand. "A pair o' lackbrains, to be sure," she muttered, walking from the room and down the stairs.

Arien watched her go. Then, with a weary sigh, she ambled over to pick up her lute.

Lackbrains indeed, she thought, her mouth twisting into a crooked smile. As unflattering as Onora's assessment of them had been, Arien suspected her maidservant's description hadn't fallen far from the mark. The challenge lay in finding a cure for such a woeful malady. Unfortunately, Arien wasn't all that sure such a remedy existed.

"Curse that fickle-hearted changeling!" Phelan cried as he paced the library from window to door. "He's naught more than a viperous worm, a degenerate bastard, a baseborn liar!"

"You're speaking of the king, I presume?" Dane asked dryly, watching his cousin stalk to and fro, his usually well groomed blond hair askew, his eyes wild, his fair skin a mottled red. "Pray, what has he done now?"

Shoulders stiff with outrage, Phelan halted beside one of the floor-to-ceiling bookcases and wheeled to confront Dane. "Why, naught more than demand the annual taxes on Dunbarton lands a full eight months early! And with that blight of lowland locusts that descended on us this summer, you know as well as I that raising the money in a year would be a near miracle, much less in four months' time."

He threw up his hands in despair. "I'm ruined, Dane. Cronan has beaten me at last."

As his voice faded, Phelan's head lowered and his shoulders sagged. Anger swelled in Dane. Degenerate bastard and baseborn liar indeed! If it was the last thing he did, the lord of Haversin vowed, he'd not let the king prevail!

"Am I to assume Cronan has demanded early payment of taxes from us all," he asked with deadly calm, "or has he suddenly developed a special dislike of you?"

His cousin heaved a great sigh. "Once again, we're all in this together," he muttered morosely. "So unless you've suddenly discovered a gold mine, 'twill be all you can manage to pay your own taxes, much less Dunbarton's. The king will finally seize my castle and lands. I'll be penniless, an outcast."

"Come, come," Dane said. " 'Tisn't as bad as all that."

"Ah, but 'tis. Surely forfeiture of one's lands is the worst calamity that can befall a man!" Phelan walked over and flung himself in a chair. "A landless lord is little better than roastmeat for worms. Where will I live? What will I eat? Why, I'll be fortunate to survive the winter!"

Though the situation was indeed grave, Dane still couldn't help a tiny twist of his lips in amusement. Phelan's gifts were many, but Dane had to admit his cousin had a tendency to dramatize things a bit.

"You know you always have a home at Haversin." Dane moved to the sideboard, where a flask of wine and several cups were laid out. He poured two cups, then turned and held one out to his cousin.

·Phelan eyed the cup wryly. "Getting me drunk won't help this time. In the morn, the same problem will remain."

"A cup or two won't harm either of us." Dane walked over and offered the wine again. " 'Twill but relax us and clear our minds for the work ahead."

"And what work would that be?" Phelan frowned, eyeing Dane with misgiving, but accepted the proffered cup at last. "You speak as if there's still some chance of thwarting the king."

" 'Twill take a miracle. A miracle from a most unexpected quarter." Dane paused to lift his cup in toast, then took a deep draft. "But then, my lands are rich in minerals and ore. Indeed, richer than even I had imagined."

A spark of hope flared in Phelan's eyes. "You've discovered some new mineral vein then? One that will prove quickly profitable?" He finally took a swallow of his wine.

Dane feigned a nonchalant shrug. "It should, if we can mine the gold fast enough."

"G-gold?" the younger man sputtered, having, in his surprise, inhaled some of his drink. "Y-you've found g-gold in these mountains?"

"Aye." Dane smiled grimly. "It only remains to be seen how much and how long 'twill take to extract it. From initial estimates of the size of the vein, though, I'd say there's enough gold to pay the king's exorbitant taxes for years to come."

Phelan gave a whoop of joy. "Cousin, you're astounding! No matter the obstacles placed in

your path, you find some way to overcome them."
He shook his head in admiration. "Truly, Cronan
has met his match in you."

"Mayhap . . . and mayhap not," Dane muttered,
suddenly awash in memories of Arien, delight-
fully naked, dewy, and replete after their coupling. Though he fought mightily against it, the
past month with her had only made his resolve to
remain distant increasingly difficult. Yet if she
truly was the spy for her father Dane feared her
to be, his plans to best the king might still be in
grave jeopardy.

"Your wife . . . the Princess Arien," Phelan ventured carefully, accurately assessing the reason
for Dane's abrupt change of mood. "How does it
go with you and her?"

"Uneventful enough, considering the situation." Though their nights together could hardly
be called uneventful, Dane wasn't ready to discuss
that most intimate and unsettling aspect of their
relationship with anyone just yet. "She is still the
king's daughter. We must take care she doesn't
suspect what we plan and alert her father."

" 'Twill be difficult to keep the truth from her."
Phelan's brow furrowed in thought. "The discovery of a rich vein of gold isn't a secret long or
easily kept."

Dane emptied his cup, then set it back on the
side table. "Aye, 'tis a problem we must conspire
to solve. 'Tis best for all if it appears that your
taxes are paid from Dunbarton funds. No good is
served if the king discovers my part in covering
your debts. He might construe it as proof I've broken my oath of fealty to him."

Phelan froze in the act of lifting his cup to his
lips. "True enough," he said finally. "As his son-

in-law, your first loyalty must now always be to him. Aiding me in this could be just the excuse he needs to ruin you."

Two days later, Arien watched Phelan and his escort ride away, headed back to the lush lowlands. Then, just a few hours later, she bade a tearful farewell to her husband. Though Dane was singularly closemouthed about his purpose and destination, Arien knew he ventured higher into the mountains, and that his mission involved mining activities of some sort. The warm clothes and packhorses laden with shovels, pickaxes, iron lanterns, stout ropes, and other excavation equipment were too hard to ignore.

It was equally obvious, however, that Dane didn't wish her to know more. Despite all they'd shared in the privacy of their bedchamber each night, Dane had yet to trust her. He still feared she'd betray him to her father.

That painful admission, more than anything else, was the cause of Arien's tears as she bid him a tender farewell. "How long, m'lord?" she asked, gazing up at him, tall and proud astride his big warhorse. "Have you any idea how long you'll be away?"

His face an inscrutable mask, Dane shook his head. "Nay. 'Twill depend on many things. It could be a month or two, even three. If all goes well, though, I'll return before winter."

Winter in this big castle without Dane. At the thought, Arien shuddered. Though the servants were quite efficient, thanks to Willa's capable governance, and the living quarters comfortable and well maintained, Haversin would be a lonely place without her husband. Indeed, the days would be long and dreary enough, but the nights . . . the nights would be cold and desolate without Dane to hold her, warm her.

Suddenly hungry for the feel of him, Arien laid her hand on his leg. At her touch, his thigh muscle quivered, then went rock hard. The warmth of his body radiated into her fingers, down her arm, coursing through her like molten gold. Ah, Arien thought, would she ever cease to respond to him with such excitement and ardent need?

"How will I find you," she persisted, wanting to prolong this moment as much as she needed an answer, "if 'tis necessary to get a message to you, or some problem should arise?"

"John and Willa know how to contact me." Dane paused, studying her intently. "You're not to attempt to pry the truth of my whereabouts from them, though. Their first loyalty must always be to me, and I'll not have you compromising it. Do you understand me, madam?"

"Aye, I understand, m'lord," Arien replied stiffly, stung by his mistrust. "I'm not without proper breeding or courtesy, and, despite your suspicions to the contrary, I'd never do aught to cause you harm. 'Tis enough I know how to go about contacting you, if and when the need should arise."

She removed her hand and stepped back. "Farewell, husband." Once again, Arien's eyes filled with tears. It didn't matter, though, if Dane saw them, she thought defiantly. Let him stew over their meaning in the days and weeks of their separation. It certainly could do no harm, and perhaps he might finally come to realize what lay behind those tears.

Stranger things had come to pass, and Arien felt long overdue for a miracle.

"Farewell . . . wife," Dane growled in reply. Then, his expression as dark and turbulent as a thundercloud, he urged his horse forward—and rode away, never once looking back.

Chapter Sixteen

Onora found Arien in her bedchamber, sewing the tiny bed gowns she hid carefully away from prying eyes. "The duke, m'lady," she announced breathlessly, having taken the stairs two at a time. "Duke Crowell is here and awaits ye even now in the library."

Arien gave a gasp of dismay, hurriedly stuffed her needlework into a small cedar chest, and locked it. Then, laying the chest aside, she rose, smoothing the wrinkles from her brown wool gown. "Crowell here," she murmured distractedly. "By the Mother, what a time to pay a visit, with Dane away on some secret undertaking. That fawning viper will soon suspect something strange is afoot, and nose about until he has his explanation—an explanation he'll lose no time carrying back to the king."

"I've already sent a servant to fetch Willa." Onora returned from the tall chest with a bright crimson gown and embroidered overtunic of fine black wool. "Yer husband must be informed and return posthaste, if he's to have any hope o' restraining that odious wretch." She laid the fresh clothing on the bed, then motioned to Arien. "Now, permit me to assist ye in donning a gown more appropriate to receive the king's emissary in. Ye don't want to be shaming yer husband by wearing that plain garb, when Crowell's expecting an elegant reception, do ye?"

Arien turned and allowed her maidservant to unlace the back of her gown. "Nay, I'd never wish to embarrass my husband in any way. Not that he appears overly concerned with my welfare or conduct of late," she added on a wistful note. "Dane's been gone over three months now, with not a word from him except to say he received the king's letter that I had Willa send to him shortly after he first departed. And all I received in return was a terse thank-you for my promptness in passing it on."

" 'Tis most peculiar," Onora agreed, as she slipped Arien's gown off her shoulders and pulled it down her body. "Several o' the other servants have commented on his extended absence, and for every one o' those who dares speak such thoughts to my face, ye can be certain five more are talking about it behind their hands."

"I'm well aware what the servants think." Arien stepped out of her gown and faced Onora. "I've noticed their pitying looks and whispered comments. 'Twill only worsen when the babe begins to swell my belly for all to see." She sighed and shook her head. "Mayhap I erred in not writing Dane and informing him he'll be a father in late spring, but I so wanted to tell him to his face. Such news is special, and meant to be shared together."

"Aye." Onora shook out the crimson gown and dropped it over Arien's arms and head. "His absence o' late hasn't made it possible for ye to tell him." She turned Arien around to lace up the back. "Surely he'll come back now, though, what with the duke nosing about Haversin."

"One would think so." A pensive little smile lifted Arien's lips. " 'Twould've been preferable if he'd returned because he'd missed me, but I suppose, at least for the time being, I'll take my husband under any circumstances."

"Don't lose heart, m'lady." Her maidservant paused to clasp a gold-and ruby-encrusted belt around Arien's hips, then slip the overtunic over her head. "Ye'll win his heart yet. Ye're as good as ye are beautiful. A blind imbecile would realize that, and yer husband is neither blind nor an imbecile."

Arien chuckled softly. "Dane will be flattered to discover how high he has risen in your opinion. Especially considering where he began."

Onora gave a snort of disgust. "He's a proud, stubborn man, that one is, and he has never given ye a fair chance." She motioned to the dressing table. "Now, no more o' yer lovestruck blatherings. The duke awaits, and I've still to dress yer hair."

Obediently, Arien made her way to the dressing table. Onora was right. It was never wise to leave Nevyn Crowell with too much free time on his hands. He had an irritating ability to ingratiate himself with the servants, and wheedle information from them before they even realized what they'd revealed. Until Dane's arrival sometime in the next few days, it would take all her efforts to keep the duke occupied, and minimize the success of his information-gathering mission.

"Ah, there you are, my dear," Duke Nevyn Crowell exclaimed in pleasure as Arien swept into the library ten minutes later. "I was beginning to think my unexpected arrival inconvenienced you to the point of anger." He made an airy wave of his hand. "But then, you know your father's will when he sets his mind on something. And he wants me to be his eyes and ears at Haversin."

Arien settled herself in one of the two chairs set by the large, leaded-glass window. Watery winter sunbeams poured into the room, washing the stone floor with a wavering, distorted pattern of light. A huge log blazed in the hearth, and, on a small table near Arien, the rich scent of cinnamon and other spices rose from a steaming jug of mulled wine.

It would have been a cozy little haven in which to curl up and read, Arien thought with a small pang of longing, save for the odious presence of Duke Crowell. Surreptitiously, as she pretended sudden interest in arranging her belt, she watched him approach out of the corner of her eye. Thank the Mother Willa had agreed Dane was needed here, and had immediately left to commandeer some trusted servant or soldier to ride out and summon the lord of Haversin home. The duke must be very sure of himself and his mission so boldly to admit he'd come to spy.

"His eyes and ears, m'lord?" Arien asked finally. "Is my father mayhap concerned with my health and happiness, and sent you to ascertain in person that all is well?"

He took a seat across from her. "But of course, your grace. 'Twas one of the king's primary requests of me." Crowell paused to eye her assessingly. "The mountain air must agree with you. You've a becoming flush to your cheeks, and have added curves where you never had them before."

When his gaze lingered overlong on her breasts, it was all Arien could do not to slap the lascivious look off the duke's face. He was a brazen-faced lecher. He overstepped himself, however, in daring to leer at her.

"My husband will be pleased to hear of your favorable assessment of my body," Arien said silkily, smiling sweetly all the time. "As will my father, I'm sure."

Immediately, Crowell jerked his glance back to Arien's face. "Aye, the king will indeed be pleased." He made a great show of looking around. "And your lord husband? What of him? Is he also about in Haversin, or are the rumors true that he's been away for several months now, on some mysterious task?"

Though she knew not Crowell's source of information, Arien easily discerned the man's intent. Despite Dane's oath of fealty, it was apparent the king still didn't trust him. Not that Dane had gone out of his way to reassure her father of his loyalty, she admitted ruefully. Indeed, as much as she'd tried to ignore the gnawing doubts and questions, the fact that Dane had refused to share his plans or whereabouts with her only reinforced Arien's conviction he plotted something against the king.

It galled her that his mistrust was truly unfounded. Ultimately, that very mistrust might well be used against him, jeopardizing all his plans.

Frustration—and not a small amount of anger that her husband had forced her into such an untenable position—filled her. No good was served, though, railing against what couldn't be changed. The best of all options was to play along with the duke, and buy time in which to allow Dane to return home.

"M'lord is indeed engaged elsewhere, but I've sent a messenger to fetch him." As her guest arched a brow and opened his mouth to pounce on that bit of information, Arien quickly forged on. " 'Tis best you hear his explanations from his own lips. In the meanwhile, tell me of my father and sister. Are they both happy and well? And what news do you have of Greystone, and the Moondancers?"

For a long moment, Crowell studied her speculatively. Arien's pulse pounded in dread. She knew that if, as the king's emissary, he demanded to hear more, she must tell him all she knew. To do less, to refuse, would be tantamount to treason against the king.

Ah, curse Dane for placing me in such a position, she thought. Yet, even as her anger welled up, Arien faced the reality of her situation. If this terrible feud continued much longer, sooner or later she'd be forced to choose sides.

Blessedly, Duke Crowell spared her the agony of making that choice just then. "The king is well," he ventured at last. "He worries over your plight, here high in the mountains, wed to a man who, until of late, went out of his way to harry and antagonize him. Are you happy, your grace? 'Twas your father's particular desire to know that above all."

"Lord Haversin's kind and good. I'm proud to be his wife."

" 'Twas your father's fondest wish to join the Talamontes with the Haversins." The duke nodded his approval. "And who's to say that you, in the end, are not the better of the two daughters to wed Lord Haversin? The Princess Edana will suit just as well as the Moondancer high priestess, and 'twill not be long now before she takes that position."

Arien leaned forward in alarm, her hands clenching in her lap. "Is Dorianne ill again? And is Edana the only candidate for her position?"

" 'Twould seem so." Crowell shrugged. "As far as Dorianne goes, aye, she's very ill. Even with her magic to sustain her, talk is she'll not live out another year. Princess Edana shouldn't have to wait much longer."

She shouldn't care what happened to the Moondancers, Arien told herself. Any responsibility for their welfare had ceased when Dorianne cast her from the Order. Indeed, any interference on her part now would be poorly received. For all intents and purposes, she was a renegade sorceress, hovering on the edges of respectability, her magic tainted, her motives suspect.

Yet she did care. Edana and her Ravens were still a threat to them all. And once her sister gained the position of high priestess, her power would grow still greater, even as her influence in the realm rose to equal that of the king. The only question remaining would be who else must fall to clear the way for the Ravens' total rule of the land.

The dwarf had said she'd be part of that final battle for Greystone. But then he'd also said she must first strengthen her bonding with Dane, that he was the man fate had chosen for her.

If everything hinged on her and Dane finding true love, then it was unlikely anything the dwarf had predicted would come to pass. Edana would never become high priestess. The Ravens would cease to be a threat to Greystone.

"If you will," she forced herself to reply, "pray give my regards to Dorianne, and tell her I wish her good health and happiness in the year to come. And as for my sister"—Arien paused, choosing her next words with care—"give her my regards as well, and convey my desire that she find peace and happiness in all her endeavors, as she strives always to follow the true and holy precepts of the Moondancers."

"Well said, your grace." Crowell smiled thinly. "Now, if you've no further messages for me to deliver, I'd greatly appreciate being shown to my chambers. Since I've private words from the king for your husband's ears alone, 'tis apparent I'll be here a few days at the very least." The duke paused, and cocked his head. "Refresh my memory, your grace. Exactly when did you say the Lord Haversin would arrive, and from whence?"

"I didn't say, m'lord." If Crowell hoped to trick secret information from her, Arien thought, he'd have to be more cunning than that. " 'Twill all depend on how soon he leaves and how rapidly he travels. As for the rest"—she rose, tacitly putting an end to the subject and visit—"as I said before, 'tis best you hear the explanations from his lips."

Duke Crowell climbed to his feet, fidgeted a moment smoothing his tunic of fine gray wool and silver bullion, then met her gaze. "You're a loyal, dutiful wife, your grace. Your father will be pleased to hear that."

"As I am his loyal, dutiful daughter," Arien replied. Whether he intended it or not, Arien thought, Dane Haversin had already begun to undermine her relationship with her father. And, whether he wished it or not, she intended that there be a reckoning between them when he returned. Time was fast running out for them and, with Dorianne's approaching death, for Greystone as well.

" 'Tis kind of you to arrange a hunt in my honor, your grace," Duke Crowell said the next day as Arien and a party of attendants accompanied him through the town, intent on a late-morning test of the falcons in Haversin's mews. " 'Twill make the time pass faster, wouldn't you agree, until your husband's return?"

Arien, momentarily distracted by a gathering of women arguing at the town well, jerked her attention back to the man riding beside her. "Oh, aye. 'Tis a beautiful day. From the number of birds passing overhead, the hawking should prove fruitful."

"Your husband's peregrine is a fine bird. Remind me to thank him for its use, when he—"

As they neared the well, the rising agitation of the women standing there escalated to shrieks. Several began cuffing a young, blond-haired woman. The young woman fought back as best she could, but finally broke away and ran, some of her assailants following close behind.

"Slut, whore!" they screamed. "Ye're no better than the rest o' us, no matter how high-placed the man ye spread yer—"

Just then Arien and her party rode by. The distraught young woman, her hair in disarray from her recent fight, must not have seen the hunting party's approach. She darted directly into the path of Duke Crowell's horse. Only with the quickest of reactions did he halt his animal in time.

With a terrified cry, she skidded into the horse. Crowell leaned down, grabbed her by the arm, and pulled her to his side. "Are you daft, wench?" he snarled, giving her a shake. "In your thoughtless flight, you nearly endangered the Lady Haversin. I've a mind to send you up to the castle for a proper whipping. 'Twould sear a bit of sense into your—"

The girl flipped her wild tangle of hair from her face. The duke's voice faded. His eyes widened in admiration. Then, as Arien, who'd drawn up beside him, watched, a look of lust replaced Crowell's earlier expression.

His thin lips lifted in a feral smile. He pulled the young woman close. "They called you a whore and a slut," he said softly. "But a lass of your looks and quality must have a better name than that. Pray, pretty one, what are you called?"

The woman hesitated, licked her lips, and shot Arien an uncertain glance before replying. "M-my name is Glenna, m'lord."

Glenna, Arien thought. Though the name meant nothing to her, there was something nonetheless familiar about the young woman. A beauteous young woman, willowy but well shaped. A woman whose face and form would tempt even a saint.

Sainthood, however, had never been one of Duke Crowell's life aspirations. He leaned down, until his face was only inches from Glenna's. "I find favor in you," he breathed huskily. "Come to the castle this eve. You won't regret it, I assure you."

"N-nay, m'lord." Glenna shook her head and tried to break free, but the duke's grip was too strong. "I-I couldn't. . . . Please, m'lord, I'm not that kind of woman. I've a babe who needs me. Find another to—"

With a savage growl, Crowell jerked her back to him. "Do you know who you refuse, harlot?" he hissed. "I'm Duke Crowell, the king's emissary. Though you live long enough for your beauty to wither, you'll never again have the chance to lie with a man of my position or wealth. Who is your husband? I'd wager he'll sell you to me for one night, if the price is handsome enough."

"I have no husband, m'lord."

"Are you widowed, then?"

Once again, the young woman's gaze brushed Arien's uncertainly. "N-nay. My son . . . he's all I have in the world now, as I am to him." Tears sparkled in her striking blue eyes. "Please, I beg you. Let me go back to my son."

"Aye, let her go, m'lord," Arien interjected with quiet emphasis. "It sickens me to watch you terrorize one of Haversin's people. She told you she has no desire to bed you. Let that suffice."

Not relinquishing his hold on Glenna, the duke twisted in his saddle to glance over at Arien. "From her own mouth, she has admitted she's unwed. Yet she has borne a child. That makes her a woman of loose morals, and fair game for any man who desires her. You know the law as well as I do, your grace."

"I also know a noblewoman's personal servants are exempt from that law," Arien countered, increasingly determined Crowell wouldn't best her in this. Though she verged on the telling of a lie, she didn't care. The duke was disgusting to use such an ancient, barbaric law to satisfy his sordid lusts. No man of honor stooped to such depths.

"And what has that to do with this winsome little vixen?" The duke pulled Glenna close, until she pressed awkwardly against his thigh.

"Glenna is to begin service as my handmaiden on the morrow. Suffice it to say, I don't want her fat and lazy with another child in nine months' time." Arien smiled, but there was a steely edge to her voice and words. "Surely you, of all people, know how tedious a belly-swollen, lumbering maidservant can be? After all the servant girls at Castle Talamontes you've fathered children on, I mean?"

Duke Crowell went red, but whether it was from anger or embarrassment Arien couldn't tell. Nonetheless the remark had its desired effect. As if he'd been holding something slimy and disgusting, the duke released Glenna with a jerk.

"I beg pardon for presuming to desire some strumpet you've apparently taken a liking to, your grace. As comely and nubile as she is, she's not worth risking your disfavor. There are other women who'll do me just as well."

"Aye," Arien muttered under her breath, "anything with two breasts and a womb would do you, I'd wager." More loudly, she then said, " 'Tis truly gratifying to learn of the high esteem in which you hold my favor, m'lord. My father will be pleased."

He shot her a venomous look. "Aye, indeed he will, your grace. Indeed he will."

She'd made a dire enemy, Arien realized, in forbidding him the woman. Duke Crowell had never liked being refused. But it was past regretting. What was done was done. Not that she would have done otherwise.

"Shall we continue our little expedition, m'lord?" Arien inquired. " 'Twill be midday now before we reach the best hunting area, and the food we've brought along for our picnic after the hawking won't keep forever."

"Aye," he snapped in reply. "Let us be gone from here."

As Crowell urged his horse to step out, it was all Glenna could do to avoid being trampled. She ran past Arien, paused to curtsy, then hurried on.

"Oh, Glenna," Arien called after her, "don't forget. Come to the castle first thing on the morrow. I'll be expecting you."

The young woman's steps faltered. She turned, shot Arien a puzzled look, then slowly nodded her acquiescence. Satisfied she'd made her point to Crowell, Arien signaled her horse forward, and thought no more of Glenna or the incident.

The morning sun glinted off the crisp, newly fallen snow, reflecting points of light so intensely bright they dazzled the eye. The air was cold, bracing, redolent with the scent of pine and, occasionally, woodsmoke rising from a solitary stone croft. From time to time eagles shrieked and soared, and a lone mountain cat screamed. Yet, save for those few, sporadic sounds, all was quiet, muted by the snow, rocks, and trees.

It was a beautiful morning to be out in the mountains, Dane thought. A beautiful morning, save for the fact that he must use all haste in returning to Haversin, there to deal with that puling fool, Duke Crowell. Arien's letter had been brief and to the point. Hie himself home, she'd said, before his precious secret in the mountains was made known to the king.

Even if she'd not been quite so blunt-spoken, Dane could have well imagined why the duke had come. The king's letter that Arien had sent him shortly after he'd first left for the mines had merely confirmed what he'd already known. Haversin's taxes were due in four months' time, as were those of all the other nobles.

That, in itself, was of little import. The mining had gone well, if a bit slower than expected, and a full month remained before the taxes were due. In another three weeks at the latest, there should be enough gold to pay his and Phelan's taxes.

Not that Cronan needed to tax him into submission anymore, Dane thought grimly. The king, through his and Arien's marriage, now had legal access to Haversin's wealth and allegiance.

Now was the time, with Dane legally constrained from actively inciting protest and sedition, for the king to complete the destruction of the coalition of nobles formed against him. And what better way, Dane thought bitterly, than to destroy Phelan, the only other person in direct line, after the king's daughters and himself, to inherit the throne?

Ah, curse Cronan's foul, conniving, unfeeling heart! Already, the oath he'd rendered the king hung like some burdensome weight about his neck. Now, more than ever before, there were countless ways Cronan could implicate him. The possibility that Arien, his own wife, could easily incriminate him sent a ripple of dread through Dane.

Though she knew not what he'd done high in the mountains for the past three months, Arien could hardly be called a stupid woman. She might already have betrayed him to the duke. Perhaps this frantic summons was but a trap, with a speedy trial and predetermined execution awaiting him.

That thought wasn't comforting. Not at all comforting after innumerable sleepless nights spent thinking of his pretty young wife. He'd thought time and distance would gradually ease the yearning, the hot desires the memories of their couplings always stirred. He'd hoped the pain of illusions shattered, of bonds fragile as spun gold that had ruthlessly been severed, would find surcease.

But they hadn't.

So Dane rode home, to face anew the living symbol of all he'd once sacrificed and lost. Was this, then, his ultimate punishment? he wondered. To love what he dared not have, yet would hunger for to his dying day? Eternally to seek a forgiveness for an act unforgivable? And did his only hope for redemption truly lie in unselfish service to his people?

His spirit heavy, Dane looked to the mountains. Always before, he'd found answers in their regal splendor. The answers were there now, too, if only he opened his heart as he had so long ago. If only he listened to the ancient voices whistling down from the towering peaks, whipping through

279

the swaying pines, and whispering amongst the winter-dried grass.

But once you'd lost someone dear, he realized with a sudden, piercing clarity, everything changed. What used to be truth, now made no sense at all. What before had appeared noble, was now little more than pretense for actions shallow and self-serving. What had always been of the utmost importance now shimmered with faint glory.

And where pride had mattered more than life itself, only a gaping wound filled with futile regrets remained.

Chapter Seventeen

"M'lady? May I have a word with ye?"

Arien turned from her survey of the Great Hall, where servants were industriously engaged in laying fresh rushes on the floor and sprinkling them with aromatic herbs. Willa Bidwell stood in the doorway, a worried look in her eyes.

"What is it, Willa?" Arien lifted her skirts and hurried over. "Has aught gone awry in the kitchen? Or has some word come from Dane?"

"Nay," the older woman said with a shake of her head, "the kitchen is fine, and I'd wager we'll see yer husband ride through Haversin's gate before we receive some message." She stepped close and took Arien by the arm. "If ye will, I'd like a private word with ye."

After months of working in close association with Willa Bidwell, Arien knew the woman never voiced a concern unless it was well grounded. "The library is near. We can talk there."

Willa waited until the doors were firmly closed, and both women were seated before the hearth fire. Though the day was sunny, there was a sharp bite to the air, and the fire's warmth was welcome. Arien waited patiently while Willa chafed her hands before the fire, knowing the chatelaine's joints ached miserably when the weather turned cold.

At last, though, Willa turned to Arien. " 'Tis about Glenna," she stated bluntly. "Why have ye brought her to Haversin?"

Taken aback by the question, Arien took a moment to reply. "Is she here then?"

The old woman nodded. "Aye. I have her cooling her heels in the curtained alcove inside the main door. She said ye commanded her to come today, and that she's to be yer new serving maid. Onora, I'm sure, will be devastated to hear she's been replaced."

"Oh, I'd never replace Onora," Arien said, laughing. " 'Tis all a ruse, albeit a temporary one, to safeguard Glenna until that lecherous Duke Crowell departs. He took a liking to her yesterday and I had to tell him she was my new serving maid to keep him from bedding her. I'd forgotten about my request until you just reminded me. I'll speak to Onora. She'll find something for Glenna to do to keep up appearances for the next few days."

The chatelaine pursed her lips in disapproval. "Yer intentions are kind, m'lady, but I'd advise against letting Glenna remain here. No good will come of it if she stays."

Puzzled, Arien leaned forward, her elbows on her legs, her hands clasped before her. "She seems pleasant enough. And if she tends toward laziness, well, 'tis of small consequence for a few days or so. Though," she added with a grin, "if she is working under your or Onora's supervision, I doubt that will be much of a problem."

" 'Tisn't that, m'lady."

Arien frowned. "Then what? Does she steal, or gossip incorrigibly?"

"Nay." Willa hesitated. " 'Tis . . . well, she's quite comely."

"Aye," Arien answered carefully. "Then are you trying to say Glenna is a woman of loose morals? That she'll cause problems with the men of the household, and make the women jealous?"

"I wouldn't say Glenna is a loose woman. Though she has borne a child out of wedlock, I've no reason to believe she has slept with any man but the babe's father."

Exasperation rose in Arien. "Then what are your reasons for sending Glenna back into town, and placing her once again at Duke Crowell's mercy? He'll know soon enough, I promise you. Indeed, the lass will bear close watching even in Haversin. Crowell doesn't like being thwarted, and will likely attempt to seduce her right beneath our noses. But at least within these walls, someone might see and hear, and go to her aid."

Willa opened her mouth to reply, then snapped it shut. She sighed, averting her gaze. " 'Tisn't my place to say, m'lady. But I beg ye, send her from Haversin as soon as ye can." She looked up. "Have I yer leave to return to my duties now? There's still much to be done to put all in readiness for yer husband's return."

As far as Willa was concerned, Arien realized, the discussion about Glenna was at an end. There was something not quite right here, though. The chatelaine had never been the sort to mince words or circle about the truth. Her refusal to elaborate on her reasons for her dislike of Glenna was most disturbing.

Exactly who *was* the father of Glenna's babe? Some instinct told Arien to take Willa's advice and send Glenna away. Some instinct warned it was better not to know the answer.

But there were already enough secrets in Haversin. If she was ever to find any peace and happiness here, Arien needed to understand the unique undercurrents moving through and influencing life at Haversin.

She rose and met Willa's inquiring gaze. "Aye, you've my leave to return to your duties. One of which," she added with a firm resolve and a tone of authority she rarely used with the loyal, ever industrious chatelaine, "is to assign Glenna to Onora's supervision and tutelage. Since you've given me no specific reason to do otherwise, Glenna will remain in Haversin—at least until Duke Crowell departs."

Bone-weary and sore, Dane swung off his warhorse and handed the reins to John Bidwell. "See to my mount's care, and have additional servants called out to aid the men who accompanied me. We've ridden for nearly twenty-four hours without rest and with little food. Have hot baths and food prepared for all."

"As ye wish, m'lord." The steward stepped close. "Shall I announce yer arrival to the duke, or do ye wish to delay that particular encounter until the morrow?"

Noting the light of conspiracy in the other man's eyes, Dane managed a weak grin. "If he even notices enough to ask, tell him I was exhausted and beg his understanding in postponing our meeting until the morrow." He paused. "The Lady Haversin. Has she been informed of my arrival?"

"Aye, but only just when the sentries called out the first greeting. I sent my Willie to wake her posthaste. Seeing how 'tis but an hour or so short of midnight, the lass was most likely fast asleep. She hasn't been one for late-night reveling since yer departure, m'lord."

There was something strangely comforting in learning that Arien had led the sedate, respectable life of a married woman while he was away. Yet, as muddled as his feelings were for her, Dane would have been surprised if she'd acted any other way. The extreme disparity between what he sensed was Arien's true nature, and what circumstances had forced him to accept, however, created a constant source of unrest and bafflement within him.

"I thank you for your diligence," Dane replied gruffly. "We'll talk more on the morrow." With that, he strode off toward the keep, not halting until he'd climbed the broad stone steps, entered the building, and begun to ascend the stairs leading to the bedchambers.

Arien, breathless and flushed, her ebony tresses hurriedly brushed back and tied with a crimson ribbon, her equally crimson gown and forest green overtunic donned with apparently similar haste, met him at the head of the stairs. If the stray locks straggling about her piquant face and down the back of her neck, as well as the overtunic worn slightly askew, weren't ample evidence of the speed with which she'd dressed, the bare feet peeking out beneath the hem of her gown were. To Dane's mind, at that moment his young wife seemed the most beguiling and endearing sight he'd ever seen.

They stared at each other for long, emotion-laden seconds, their eyes revealing what lips as yet lacked the courage to say. Finally, Arien broke the silence.

"Welcome home, m'lord. Even now the water is being heated for your bath and, while that is prepared, I've had a cold supper from this eve's meal readied." She hesitated, as sudden doubt seemed to assail her. "Unless, of course, you wish a hot meal cooked. I thought, with the lateness of the hour, lighter fare of bread and butter, cheese, and sliced pork, freshly roasted this very day, might be more—"

Chuckling, Dane held up a silencing hand. " 'Tis quite sufficient, I'm sure. The cold meal, I mean." He climbed the rest of the stairs until he stood at her side. "You look well, wife," he said, studying her closely.

"As do you, husband." Arien returned his bold appraisal with an equally bold one of her own, then held out her hand. "Shall we retire to our bedchamber? Your supper awaits you there."

Dane eyed her proffered hand. It was small, delicately boned, the fingers slender and tapering. It would look well clasped in the darker, larger expanse of his own hand. Just as she would look well beside him, her soft curves fitted close to his harder angles, when they lay naked in bed . . .

The hot, erotic images—and his body's almost instantaneous response—were enough to wrench Dane back to reality. Shaken and unnerved, he took Arien's hand automatically, gripping it tightly. "Aye, let us be gone from here," he muttered. "I've no wish to serve as this night's entertainment for any nosy servants lurking about."

Her only reply, before leading him down the hall, was a slight arch of a brow and a glimmer of a smile. As Dane entered his bedchamber, the scent of woodsmoke and mulled wine greeted him. Like a man long starved, he scanned the room. It was cozy and warm, lit by the fire and several beeswax candles set on the mantel over the hearth, and on the small table beside the bed.

The huge four-poster showed signs of a recent occupant; one pillow was mussed and the coverlet thrown back in apparent haste. Positioned near the fire, the wooden bathing tub already stood in readiness. Nearby, a large, soft bath sheet was draped over the top of one chair; the scented sandalwood soap he favored and a fat sea sponge were nestled together in a large pottery bowl resting on the padded seat.

She'd seen to every detail, Dane realized, from the bath preparations to the cloth-covered tray of food and the steaming pitcher of mulled wine placed on a small table before the other hearthside chair. It was a warm welcome home, indeed, and, considering his purposeful neglect of Arien these past months, a welcome most undeserved.

"My thanks," Dane said, feeling decidedly uncomfortable. "Even at such a late hour and with scant notice, 'tis apparent you've seen to my every need."

" 'Tis no more than any wife would do, husband."

"Mayhap." Too embarrassed to say more, Dane strode over to the table of food and flung himself into the chair. He flipped over the covering cloth and was about to grab a slice of fresh, brown bread when Arien halted him.

"A moment, m'lord." She hurried to the low wooden chest, picked up a pitcher, basin, and hand cloth, and swiftly returned to his side. "Here"—she placed the basin on the table before him and slung the hand cloth over her forearm— "permit me to assist you in washing your hands. After riding all day, surely you've a need to cleanse them before touching food."

"Aye." Dane flushed, beginning to feel as foolish as a schoolboy. " 'Twould be wise, would it not?" Obediently, he held his hands over the bowl and allowed Arien to pour water on them.

As he ate, servants entered with bucket after bucket of scalding water, soon followed by a few more buckets of cold water to even the bath's temperature. Dane, having eaten lightly on the trail, found he was famished and quickly wolfed down everything provided. The servants, their task of filling the bathing tub completed, finally exited with the now empty supper tray, leaving Dane and Arien alone.

Back turned, she busied herself with some task in the clothes chest as Dane undressed and stepped into the tub. He sank into the bracingly hot water, rested his hands on the wooden sides and his head on the tub's back, and heaved a sigh of satisfaction.

Arien walked over and knelt beside him. "Sit up a bit, and I'll soap your back for you."

Ever so slowly, not even certain he should allow her hands upon him, Dane sat up. Arien took the sponge, dipped it in the water, then began rubbing the sandalwood soap across it until the sponge foamed with a rich lather. Mesmerized by the water's soothing heat and her languorous actions, Dane watched, entranced.

Then, as Arien touched the sponge to his back and began to wash him with slow, rhythmic strokes, a wave of pure pleasure encompassed him. He sighed again, dipped his head, and closed his eyes, yielding himself up to the sensual delight of Arien's hands.

It had been so long . . . too long . . . Dane thought. He hadn't realized until this moment how intensely he'd missed her. It had been hard to leave Arien when he'd ridden out for the mines. It would be doubly hard, he feared, leaving her again. But he must—he was so close now to completing the mining of the necessary gold. And Phelan depended on him. Phelan, after all, was his cousin and his friend.

Arien, on the other hand, was the daughter of the king who'd forced him into increasingly difficult and dangerous circumstances. Arien was the woman who'd magically seduced him, whose motives were ultimately suspect. Beautiful, enigmatic Arien, with whom Dane feared he was falling in love, even knowing such a foolish, irrational act might well mean his doom.

With all his remaining strength, Dane fought his way free of the web Arien's sensuous ministrations had spun about him. He lifted his head, squared his shoulders, and straightened. She was clever, he told himself. She knew what he needed, and was willing to do whatever it took to lure him back to her bidding—and bed.

That was why he'd stayed away so long. Though his heart cried out for Arien, his mind warned that her magic could be manipulating his emotions. Though she'd given her word not to wield her magic in Haversin, how could he truly be certain she'd honor that vow?

"Duke Crowell," he said, his voice gruff with anger. "Why has he come? And what have you told him?"

Arien's hands stilled in the process of rinsing his back. "My father sent him to spy on you, of course," she finally replied. "But I told Crowell naught, save that you were away and 'twas best he hold his questions until your return."

An edge of hurt vibrated in her voice. Dane immediately regretted his tactless query. "Aye, 'tis a given Crowell spies for the king," he said more gently this time. "But did he have some specific purpose in coming here?"

"He mentioned rumors that you'd been away for several months on some mysterious task." Sponge in hand, Arien scooted around until she could look Dane full in the face. "Truly, husband, you must share more of your plans with me. I cannot aid you with people like Crowell if I must work in total ignorance."

Dane went stiff, all his defenses rising again to the forefront. "You cannot inadvertently reveal what you do not know, can you, wife?"

High color swept across her fair face, and a pained look darkened her eyes. "True enough," she admitted softly. "But my father will suspect you and your actions just as quickly because you refuse to tell me aught, thinking you must have something to hide that you don't trust me to know."

Anger swelled anew in Dane. "So either way I lose," he growled. "I must share my secrets with you and risk your revealing them to my enemies, or be equally suspect because I don't."

" 'Twould seem so." Arien sighed. "Ah, by the Mother, why must you force me to choose one side or another? You're my husband, but he is my father!"

Her words were heartfelt, anguished, but Dane hardened himself to them. "And when has your marriage to me ever come in conflict with your loyalty to your father?" he demanded coldly. "You knew from the start what the stakes were. I was the only fool in this sordid, shameful game, blinded by the image of what I once thought, hoped, you to be. But now my eyes are open. I see you for what you really are. So play no more games with me, wife, and pretend not that this battle between your father and me places you in an untenable position."

She gave a choking laugh. "So, 'tis all some game to you, is it? Save for one night when I forced you to do what you'd no wish to do, to safeguard not only your life but your immortal soul, when have I ever done aught that was deceitful or hurtful to you? When have I treated you with less than kindness and concern?"

Tears welled in her eyes. " 'Twill never be better between us, will it?" Arien whispered despairingly. "Though I forswore practicing my magic, though I promised to render obedience and loyalty to you alone, though I've tried so hard to be a good wife, you'll never forgive me, will you?"

Her hand slipped to her belly, her fingers spreading as if to cover it protectively. "I'm with child, Dane."

Stunned by the unexpected news, Dane sat there, speechless and staring. Finally, though, he forced words past his now dry, constricted throat. "Wh-when?" he ground out, his voice little more than a hoarse croak. "How long . . . until the babe is born?"

The tears spilled over and coursed down Arien's cheeks. "I am four months along already, for you fathered it that night I took you against your will. Yet in all honesty, I must confess that, though the thought of bearing your child gives me great joy, it also fills me with dread."

"Why?" Dane lashed out. "Because you loathe the fact the child must call me father, that Haversin blood will run in its veins to sully the purity of your own?"

"Nay!" Anger blazed forth from Arien's eyes. "Ah, what a braying ass you are, to utter such nonsense! If you could only see how your unforgiving, suspicious nature has begun to twist and misshape you, you'd understand the true reason for my dread."

She stood, the sponge clenched so tightly in one hand that water from it dripped onto the floor. "How can any child have hope of thriving, much less growing into a good and decent person, with a man such as you as father?" A note of rising indignation entered her voice. "You, a father who hates the mother, a man eaten alive by his bitterness, and shame, and regrets."

"I've no shame or regret over you, madam," Dane gritted. "After what you did to me, I'd no desire ever to wed you."

"I spoke not of your shame and regret over me," Arien said quietly, her look turning piercingly intent. "I meant, rather, your unresolved shame and regret over the loss of your first wife and child. 'Tis that above all, I think, that eats at you, that drives your growing obsession with besting my father.

"Yet, though much fault lies with my father in causing your loss," she relentlessly persisted, "much fault also lies with you. 'Tis that festering wound threatening to rot your very soul that worries me, even more than the stubborn, prideful grudge you hold against me. 'Tis that I dread, most of all, for what it might do to our child."

He glared up at Arien, so furious the words would barely come. "You know naught of what happened, and you dare lay blame at *my* feet? Accuse me of evil acts and motives, when I've always been the innocent party in your father's vicious, unreasoning vendetta against House Haversin? You dare question *my* fitness to be a father?"

"Aye, that I do," she replied steadfastly. "In wars such as you and my father wage, just as in the war between the Moondancers and the dwarves, there are never any truly innocent participants. It takes two to wage a battle, husband, and where one may have been guilty of beginning it, the other bears blame in continuing it."

"He gives me no choice," Dane raged. "Would you have me surrender, or turn tail and run like some milk-livered coward?"

"Nay, but I'd not have you consumed by this terrible need for vengeance, either."

Like rocks slung from a catapult, Arien's words pounded at him, finally beating down the walls he'd built to protect his heart. Frustration and despair filled him, twisting his gut into a tight, painful knot. "Truly, wife," Dane said at last, his shoulders sagging in defeat, "I don't know what else to do. My honor, my pride, will permit naught less."

"And that, husband, is the first honest insight I'd wager you've had in a long while." She smiled sadly. " 'Tisn't the solution, but at least 'tis the first step *toward* the solution. There's pride and honor in that, if naught else."

Dane's gaze lowered in exhaustion. Though he was loath to admit it, there was truth in her words. He just didn't feel particularly heroic or noble at the moment. He was too tired, too confused, too troubled.

"I'll tell you true," he forced himself to say. "I'm past weary of watching my life be manipulated by others to my detriment. I'm tired of never having any choice in the matter. And I'm not so sure I even care anymore, or possess the strength or courage to keep on trying."

"Nor do I, husband," Arien admitted gravely. "Yet, in the end, what has strength or courage to do with it? Sometimes, the best solution is the direct opposite of what we'd choose to do, *if* we had a choice. But therein lies the rub—we never had a choice. 'Tis what we are that permits us to do naught less than our very best."

"Is there aught more you'd like of me, m'lady?"

Arien glanced from the bedchamber window, where she'd been staring pensively out on a frigid, snow-encrusted night. A sliver of ivory-hued moon embellished the darkness, its dim light casting muted shadows over the peaks and dense forests. All was quiet, outside Haversin as well as within. It was time for the land and people to take their rest.

"Nay, Glenna. I need naught more." With a shiver, Arien closed the window, pulled her bed robe more tightly to her, and turned. "You've served me well this day. My thanks."

The maidservant managed a stiff curtsy. "Then have I yer leave to return to my house? My babe is ill, and needs me."

Arien nodded. "Oh, aye. I'd almost forgotten." She hurried to the hearth and plucked a small, cloth-wrapped parcel from the mantel, then walked up to Glenna and offered it to her. "Here. 'Tis some dried meadowsweet and a flask of oil of mint for your babe. Steep the meadowsweet in a small bowl of boiling water, then add eight drops of the mint oil. Once the concoction is cooled, 'twill make a soothing infusion for his poor little stomach and bowels."

Hesitantly, Glenna accepted the parcel. "My thanks, m'lady. Ye're too kind to me, first in protecting me from the duke, and now in thinking o' my babe. I can see now why Dane—I mean the Lord Haversin," she corrected herself quickly, "chose to take ye as wife. Ye're as good as ye are beautiful."

Her face flooding with heat at the unexpected compliment, Arien managed an embarrassed laugh. "And you are kind to speak so favorably of me." She made a shooing motion of her hand. "Now, begone with you. You've a sick babe who needs you. On the morrow, you can let me know if the meadowsweet and mint helped. If not, I'll come personally to examine the babe and devise another herbal mix more suited to his illness."

" 'Twould be most welcome," Glenna said, backing toward the door. "Yer aid in healing my babe, I mean." She turned then and hurried from the room, shutting the door firmly behind her.

Arien smiled. Glenna was a sweet, if simple girl. For the life of her, she couldn't understand Willa's hostility toward her.

Walking to the hearth, Arien took up the book she'd been reading. Then, snuggling in one of the chairs there, she curled her legs beneath her.

Dane should soon be finishing his final meeting with his steward and coming up to bed. She'd had no more than a few minutes to talk with him this day, between his extended private visit with Duke Crowell, then another hawking expedition, and finally more meetings with John Bidwell and several other of the castle staff. Indeed, she'd been forced to spend yet another tension-fraught supper alone with Crowell, Dane having sent word to have his meal delivered while he worked.

She fingered the fine lawn bed gown she wore beneath her robe. It was the most seductive sleeping garment Arien owned. She hoped Dane would find her pleasing in it. After last night, when he had fallen promptly to sleep, she wondered if he would ever make love to her again.

But then, his behavior last night was to be expected, Arien reassured herself. Dane had been weary and quite evidently upset after their conversation.

Tonight . . . tonight, though, Arien hoped and prayed he'd come to her. Only in the ardent intensity of their joining did the barriers between them ever seem to melt away. Only then did she sense a renewed openness in him, a joyous giving, and a return, if only for a short while, of the man she'd come to love.

Indeed, it was their couplings that sustained and strengthened her. Only there, in the dark, sweet haven of their bed, did Arien's hope that she might someday regain Dane's trust and affection flare anew.

A faint sound, metallic and discordant, teased the edges of her consciousness. Arien laid down the book she'd yet to open and cocked her head, straining to discern what the strange noise was.

It became rhythmic, the unusual clangor rising and falling in intensity as if . . . as if it moved about, back and forth.

Arien rose and hurried to the bedchamber door, tying her bed robe closed as she did. Even as she opened the door, the sound grew immediately louder and more distinguishable. It was the clanging of swords . . . striking against each other as if in battle.

She flung the door wide and rushed out. Her heart hammering, Arien bolted down the corridor to where it overlooked the reception hall. There below, Dane, his face livid with rage, battled with Duke Crowell.

Glancing frantically around at the scene beneath her, Arien found John Bidwell with his wife clinging fearfully to him. Several servants, their faces white, huddled together at the foot of the stairs. But the sight of Glenna, her cheek bruised, her hair in disarray, clutching closed the torn front of her simple woolen gown, told the tale.

Crowell must have seen her as she was leaving for the night and decided that, since no one was about, he'd take the liberties he'd heretofore been denied. Glenna, from her disheveled appearance, must have fought him, making enough noise to summon Dane. Dane's utter loathing and long-standing enmity with the king's emissary, combined with Crowell's attempted rape of Glenna within Haversin's very walls, would result in just such a battle.

Yet as much as Nevyn Crowell needed to learn a lesson for his baseborn knavery, the murder of the king's emissary was an act punishable by death. Apparently no one downstairs was of a

mind to put an end to the battle, however. For
Dane's sake, she must do so.

Arien inhaled a deep breath and hurried down
the stairs. The servants standing at the foot of the
steps were so mesmerized by the battle that it was
all Arien could do to shove them aside. Then she
was out on the wide expanse of stone floor, running toward the two combatants.

"M'lady, nay!" John Bidwell cried, having seen
her at last. "Give way. Don't come between them!"

With a shake of her head and a hand raised in
warning, Arien moved on. Wild plans to end this
fight swirled through her head. It would have
been so simple to use her magic to stop them, but
that would require her breaking her vow to Dane.
If there was any other way . . .

As she passed the curtained alcove just inside
the main door, a small footstool caught Arien's
eye. She darted inside, grabbed the footstool, and
darted back out. Then, nearing the two battling
men, she eyed them both, unsure which one she
should accost.

If she managed to trip Dane, Crowell would
most likely seize the opportunity to strike. But if
she tripped Crowell, Dane, in his rage, might do
the same. Arien decided it would be easier to stop
Crowell than her husband in his current state of
mind.

She circled about the two men, awaiting her
chance. Already, Dane was rapidly wearing Crowell down, slashing and thrusting with deadly intent. There wasn't much time left for the terrified,
weakening duke.

Then Dane, his back turned, stepped before
her. Arien crouched low, gripped one of the
stool's legs tightly, and swung back her arm.

Then, a fervent prayer on her lips, she flung the stool, striking Dane hard at the back of his knees.

With a grunt of pain, the lord of Haversin's feet flew out from beneath him. He plummeted to the floor. His sword hand made contact first, striking hard on the unyielding stones. The sword flew from his grip, skidding away. Next, the impact of Dane's body knocked the wind from him. He remained where he fell, dazed.

Crowell staggered backward in surprise. Then, as the realization of his sudden advantage struck him, he gave a great yell and lunged forward, his sword raised for the killing blow. This was what Arien had feared might happen, but she was ready.

She stepped over Dane, straddling his body, and faced the oncoming Crowell. For an instant, he didn't seem to see her and charged onward. Then confusion flared in his eyes. He slowed, hesitated, halted. The upraised sword fell to his side.

"Step away from him, your grace," the duke growled. "No man attacks the king's emissary and lives."

"You're as much at fault as he, m'lord," Arien countered firmly. "*More* at fault, if the truth be told. You disobeyed my express wish that you not touch Glenna. And when you did, you had the audacity to do so within Haversin. In the doing, you defied the king's daughter, and insulted a lord of the realm in his own house."

"The king will punish his insult to me nonetheless," Crowell muttered. "Step aside, I say, and allow me to save us all the embarrassment of a trial and summary execution."

"And if I refuse to step aside, m'lord?" Behind her, Arien heard Dane stir. "Will you kill me, too?"

Crowell looked nervously around. Even more servants now had gathered to watch the spectacle. Arien could see the thoughts flash through his mind. Too many witnesses. Though he might succeed in justifying his murder of Dane, he'd be hard-pressed to explain why it was necessary to kill her, too.

With a disgusted snort, Duke Crowell re-sheathed his sword. "Kill you?" he asked loudly, then gave an unsteady laugh. "You're still a witch, if no longer a holy Moondancer. What chance would I have against you?"

"None, m'lord," Arien replied softly, wishing he hadn't been churlish enough to remind all present of her otherworldly powers. Some were already making furtive warding signs against her.

This night, Arien realized glumly, though she'd saved her husband's life twice over, she'd also lost much of the ground she'd so laboriously gained with Haversin's people in the past months. "I'd suggest you depart for Castle Talamontes on the morrow. No purpose is served by lingering here any longer. My husband tolerates dishonorable guests and potential rapists poorly."

"Does he now?" Crowell's face twisted in a sneer. "And how much better is he than I? At least I am unwed, and chose to take an unwed woman of questionable morals to bed. 'Tis far more honorable than what he has done, in violating his marriage vows."

"That's enough, Crowell," Dane ordered, climbing to his feet to stand beside Arien. "You know not of what you speak. Best you hold your tongue before you provoke yet another fight."

"And why is that, m'lord?" the duke taunted, but wisely took a few steps away from Dane. "Are you afraid for your wife to know the truth? But why should that matter? 'Tis no crime for a married man to keep a leman. And most wives, in time, come to accept their failure to satisfy all the needs of a lusty man."

"Crowell," Dane snarled, "say one more word and you're—"

"Nay, husband," Arien interrupted, glancing at Dane as she spoke. "Let the duke finish." She turned back to Crowell. "Exactly of what are you accusing my husband, m'lord?"

A feral, triumphant smile lifted the man's lips. "That little whore," he said, pointing at Glenna. "Whose child do you think she bore? Who do you think the father is?"

Arien lifted her chin and boldly stared him down, even as the sickening realization of what he implied struck her. "I don't know, m'lord. But somehow I think you're determined to tell me."

"Indeed I am, your grace. That man you took to husband," he said, pointing now at Dane, who'd suddenly gone silent and still beside her, "that man is an adulterer. Glenna, wanton strumpet that she is, is his leman. And the babe she has borne is his son. A bastard son who can never inherit Haversin, but his son nonetheless.

"So now you know, your grace," Crowell taunted with vicious glee. "Now you know. And I ask, who is truly the more honorable man here? Your husband . . . or me?"

Chapter Eighteen

Dane . . . Glenna . . . their babe. The names roiled in Arien's head until she thought she'd go mad. In an effort to still the cacophony reverberating through her skull, she took to pacing the bed-chamber. Back and forth . . . back and forth . . . back and forth.

The hours passed. A wind swept down from the mountains, bringing snow to swirl and billow in the air. With a melancholy wail the fierce blasts shook the leaded glass windows, seeping through chinks in the walls to whistle down the icy corridors.

She turned toward the door, willing Dane to appear. It had been over two hours now since the battle in the reception hall. Why didn't he come? Did he think he owed her no explanation for Glenna? Or didn't he even care?

True, it had been she who had run from him after Crowell's shocking revelation. It had been she who had bolted their bedchamber door and refused both Onora and Willa entrance. But she wouldn't have kept out Dane, if he'd even cared to come.

But he didn't care. The admission tore at her heart, until Arien felt as if her chest was a gaping wound. Dane didn't care. She wrapped her arms around herself, sank to her knees before the hearth, and wept.

After a time, the sound of someone knocking softly at the door penetrated her weeping. Arien muffled her sobs, hoping whoever it was would give up and go away. The knocking, however, persisted, grew louder.

"Arien? Open the door. 'Tis Dane."

Panic engulfed her. Before, she'd wanted him so badly his absence was a physical pain. But for Dane to catch her crying . . .

It was too shameful. It would lay bare too much of her true feelings. Feelings he'd belittle, in his stubborn conviction that she used him to serve her father.

Yet to refuse Dane was just as revealing. Arien climbed to her feet. Best to hide her tears, pretend indifference, and hear him out. It was up to Dane to make amends if he so desired. If he didn't, well, she would be no worse off than she'd been before.

Hastily wiping away the telltale moisture, Arien made her way to the door. For a moment, she rested her head against the rough wood and took several deep breaths, willing her heartbeat to slow. Then, squaring her shoulders, Arien slid back the bolt and opened the door.

Dane stood there, his face thrown into shadow by the flickering light of the wall torches. He still wore the same clothes he'd fought in, the white woolen shirt and black breeches now sweat-stained and soiled. No bloody slashes, though, marred his apparel. Dane was an unparalleled swordsman..

"May I come in?" he asked quietly, when she made no move to offer him entry.

"As you wish." Immediately, Arien stepped aside. " 'Tis your room, your castle."

Dane walked in, not stopping until he came to the middle of the bedchamber and turned to face her. Arien closed the door, bolted it shut once more, then swung about. He stood there, gazing back at her, his expression one of anguished remorse.

"I'm sorry you had to learn about Glenna like that."

"Did you ever plan to tell me about her . . . and the babe?" Arien choked out the question.

He sighed. "Mayhap. I don't know. It didn't concern you, at any rate. I ceased to bed her after we wed."

"Oh, aye, and you expect me to believe that?" She gave a disparaging laugh. "You, who loathes the fact that I am your wife?"

"How I feel about you has naught to do with it!" Dane strode over to stand before her, anger flashing in his eyes. "I can honor my marriage vows without necessarily honoring the marital partner."

"Save for the humiliation you cause me, I can't say I care if you keep a leman." Hurt, angry, Arien lashed out in any way she could. "But now my father and sister, not to mention the entire Court, will know. I'll be the laughingstock of Greystone."

"Why? 'Tis evident from the babe's age that Glenna and I were lovers long before you and I wed. She was good to me when I needed comforting after Katrine's death."

So, Arien thought, Dane took Glenna as mistress after his first wife's death. Despite Crowell's claims, there was no adultery in that. But now that Dane was once more wed . . .

She forced out the question tormenting her since she'd first heard the devastating news. "Did you . . . do you . . . love her?"

"We cared, and still care for each other," Dane replied, an aching tenderness in his compelling eyes. "But, nay, I never loved her . . . at least not the way I loved Katrine. We both knew there was no future for us, that if that witch hadn't cursed me and mine I would someday have wed another noblewoman. And then Glenna bore me a son.

"All that notwithstanding," he hurried to add, "I spared no time in putting her away when I wed you. And, until you ordered Glenna into Haversin to protect her from Crowell, she lived in town and never once set foot back in the castle."

"Who told you . . . what I did for her?"

"Glenna. After the fight with Crowell, I personally escorted her back to her house, and placed an armed guard there—a guard who will remain until Crowell is once more far from Haversin's lands."

"Do you intend to visit her again?"

"Nay. I told Glenna to send word if she or the babe need aught from me. John Bidwell, though, will always be our intermediary until my son is old enough to visit by himself." Dane paused, eyeing Arien closely. "What does it matter if I *did* see her from time to time? As long as I'm discreet, 'twill not humiliate you further. And if you truly are with child, you'll soon be free of my disgusting presence in your bed. I would think you'd much prefer that I find my pleasure elsewhere."

"Contrary to what you might choose to believe, husband," Arien said with quiet dignity, "I've never found your presence in bed disgusting. And I'd much prefer you found your pleasure with me, rather than elsewhere."

"Indeed?" Dane lifted a dark brow in exaggerated disbelief. "And all along I imagined you gave yourself to me out of duty."

He was mocking her, Arien thought. Ah, curse the fate that had forced her to trade Dane's trust for his life!

"Imagine what you wish," she snapped. "You made up your mind about me long ago, and naught I have done since then can change it. It does seem ironic, though, that you expect me to take your word on whatever you tell me, yet all that I say and do is still suspect."

"I've never betrayed you, madam," Dane replied tautly. "Not even with Glenna. Therein lies the difference."

"So you say!"

He went rigid, and glowered down at her. "Do you now, after everything else, dare to impugn my word?"

"Aye, and why not?" Arien fired back, exhausted from the strain of the last few days. "You gave your word to my father, swore an oath of fealty, no less, yet you and I both know you never had any intention of honoring that word!"

Dane opened his mouth to reply, then clamped it shut again. He turned on his heel and stalked over to the hearth. Gripping the mantel with both hands, he stared into the fire, a murderous rage radiating from every inch of his taut, powerful frame.

Watching him, Arien knew she shouldn't goad him further. She'd never pushed Dane past his limits, and didn't think she ever wanted to. Yet somehow, some way, Dane must be made to see how unreasonably and unfairly he was treating her.

She walked over, halting just a few feet behind him. "Well, husband? How is it you bear one standard for yourself, yet expect an entirely different one of me?"

With a furious growl, Dane swung about, taking her by the arms and jerking her to him. "How is that?" he repeated with savage ferocity. "Well, I'll tell you. The standards are different because I know my own heart, and know what I do is for the good of all. You, on the other hand . . ."

"Aye," Arien prodded when he said no more. "What of me?"

Dane shuddered. He clamped shut his eyes for a moment, then opened them. What Arien saw there took her breath away.

Terrible anguish and fearful despair burned in his deep blue eyes. Regret swamped Arien. Holy Mother, she thought. I never meant to rouse such pain in him!

"What of you?" Dane's voice, when he finally answered, was raw with emotion. "I don't know you. I once thought I did, and the woman I knew was a woman I thought I could love. But that night you ensorceled me was the night that wonderful woman died. Now I'm forced to mourn her for the rest of my days, while I struggle to accept the true reality of what she always was."

Sick to the marrow of her bones, Arien took a step toward him. Her hands lifted in supplication, then dropped to her sides. "Dane . . . please. I-I can't bear this enmity between us. Can't you find it in your heart to forgive me, to give me another chance? I'm your wife. I'm carrying your child. For his sake if for naught else, can't we start over?"

"Nay," he whispered brokenly. His head lowered and all the fight, all the power and vitality that made him the man he was, drained from him. "There's no forgiveness, no starting over, at least not for me. I'd hoped, for a time, I could, but I see now 'tis impossible. My mistakes, my failings, have created insurmountable obstacles between us."

He looked up and, with a sad smile, reached out to stroke Arien's cheek. "So don't, I pray, place such a high value on my forgiveness. As I'm not worthy to love or be loved ever again, I'm also not capable of forgiveness."

Tears welled, spilling down Arien's cheeks. "Nay, husband," she whispered. " 'Tisn't true. Your ability to forgive depends on your ability to love. And if you love much, you can forgive much—even in yourself."

"Little fool!" Dane gave a despairing laugh and backed toward the door. "I was doomed long before you met me. There's naught you can do to save me. Naught!"

With that, he staggered from the room, leaving Arien to weep again, this time for her husband— and for all those like him, souls so pain-racked and heart-crippled they didn't dare risk paying the price that love—and loving—would always demand.

That night, Dane never returned to their bedchamber. Early the next morning, before Arien had even risen, he departed. He left no message, save that he must go back to the mines, but if all went well, he'd return in three weeks' time.

It wasn't what she'd wanted to hear, Arien thought as she left John Bidwell's office, but at least this time Dane had shared his plans to return. It seemed, though, that her husband was expending more effort running from her than in any attempt to work out their problems. Ah, if only she understood him better, she thought, perhaps then she'd find the right words to ease their marital discord!

By late morning, Glenna had yet to arrive. Concerned that her son had failed to recover, Arien ate a quick dinner, then donned her warmest wool cloak and set out for town, a basket of dried herbs and potions hanging from her arm. Though she wasn't exactly sure in which house Glenna lived, a few questions soon directed her to the young woman's door, where a soldier stood guard nearby.

Glenna blanched when she saw Arien. "M-m'lady," she stammered after a long moment. She made a hurried curtsy. "Why . . . why have you come?"

As Arien had made her way through town, she'd wondered what her initial reaction would be to seeing Dane's mistress again. Curiously, though, there were no feelings of jealousy, anger, or even pain. Concern, as Glenna's color failed to return, and Arien feared she might faint at any moment, but nothing else.

She forced a wan smile and held up her basket. "I was worried about your sick babe, and brought additional herbs in case the ones I gave you yestereve didn't work." When still no reply was forthcoming, Arien took a step forward. " 'Tis cold standing out here. Won't you invite me inside?"

The other woman's eyes widened. Then, in her haste, she stumbled back, motioning Arien in. "Oh, of course, m'lady. Pray, excuse my rudeness. I just never thought you'd be wishing ever again to see the likes of me."

Entering the house, Arien made a great show of looking around rather than formulating some reply to that awkwardly couched statement. The dwelling appeared to consist of one large room that served as kitchen, living, and dining area. From the open door of what seemed the only other room in the house, Arien spied a large, comfortable bed.

That was where Dane slept, she thought fleetingly before she quashed that painful realization. If he did sleep here anymore.

The babe's crib sat near the hearth. If this was the usual temperature of the house, Arien thought as a shiver rippled through her, she could easily see why the babe slept beside the fire. Aside from the coolness, though, Glenna looked well provided for, from the sturdy oak table and chairs, to the many cook pots, pottery dishes, and well-stocked cupboard.

"My husband provides well, does he not?" she asked, turning to Glenna. "You could use more wood for your fire, though. 'Tis not good to keep a young babe in such cold quarters."

"Aye, m'lady." Glenna flushed and looked away. "M'lord's steward is a good man, but he sometimes forgets how much wood it takes to heat a house in winter."

"Then tell him, and make no bones about it," Arien admonished. "John's no different from most men, who don't thrive on subtlety."

"True enough." She sighed. "But 'tis difficult. I don't fancy being seen as a grasping, greedy shrew."

"Then ask for the babe's sake. He's Dane's son, after all. In the end, 'tis your lord you must answer to, not John Bidwell." Arien's glance caught on a pile of wood stacked near the hearth. "Lay more logs on the fire. Let's warm this room."

"That's all the wood I have until the day after the morrow, m'lady," Glenna said, looking decidedly uncomfortable. "Every week, a guard brings me a fresh supply then."

"I'll have more sent down this very day." Arien motioned to the wood. "Now, no more of it. 'Tis as inhospitable to freeze your guests as 'tis to mistreat your babe in such a way."

Glenna hurried to do as she was bid. The fire soon flared hot and bright. She hung a heavy iron pot of water over it. "Would ye like a cup of tea, m'lady?"

"Aye." Arien nodded. " 'Twould be welcome on such a cold day." She walked to the table, placed her basket on it, then pulled out a chair and sat. "Once the room is warm, I'll examine your babe. I fear to unwrap him in the cold."

"Aye, m'lady." The blond woman carried over two pottery mugs, spoons, and a bowl of tea leaves. "I've some clover honey, as well," she offered, "if ye like yer tea sweet."

"Plain tea, as long as 'tis hot, will suit me well." Arien hesitated, debating whether she should tell Glenna the truth, and decided it would be best. She pulled out the other chair. "Pray, sit, Glenna. I confess I came here for another reason besides the welfare of your babe."

Slowly, reluctantly, Glenna lowered herself into the chair. "And how may I be of assistance, m'lady?"

"You didn't come to Haversin today. Yet I haven't given you leave to stay away. Who told you not to come?"

The other woman lowered her head. "Yer husband, m'lady. Last night, after he escorted me home, he told me to stay away."

"And why did Dane tell you that?"

"He said my presence in Haversin might unduly upset ye."

Arien sighed and shook her head. " 'Tis kind of him to consider my feelings, if that truly was his motive."

Glenna's head jerked up. " 'Twas his intent. I swear it!"

"Well, be that as it may, I want you to know I bear you no ill will, and will do naught to cause you or your babe harm." Arien inhaled a deep breath, then forged on. "Dane assured me he hasn't bedded you since we wed."

"Oh, 'tis true, m'lady," Glenna hastened to reply. "He's been faithful to ye, and ye alone."

Ah, if only it were true, Arien thought longingly. "My husband is a good man," she continued, choosing her words with care, "but he's tormented by terrible guilt, so much so I fear for his well-being."

Glenna nodded her solemn agreement.

"He told me, though, that you were good to him when he needed comforting." Tears prickled in Arien's eyes, but she fought to keep them at bay. " 'Tis more than I've been able to do for him, no matter how hard I've tried. So I come here to ask you to do what you can for Dane, even . . . even if you must take him back to your bed."

Mouth open, the blond woman stared at Arien.

"I d-don't know how to help him, Glenna," Arien quavered. "I want to with all my heart, but, try as I might, I only seem to make things worse. So I ask you to help him, if you will. If not"—in spite of her best efforts to contain them, the tears finally coursed down her cheeks—"if not, I-I don't know what will become of him."

"M'lady, m'lady," Glenna exclaimed in distress. She reached out, took Arien's hand. "Don't cry, don't lose heart, I beg ye. Dane loves ye. I can see it in his eyes, and hear it in his voice when he speaks of ye. Indeed, ye're his only hope."

" 'Tis kind of you to say that," Arien whispered through her tears. "If the truth be told, though, my husband despises me."

"Nay, nay, m'lady." Glenna smiled and squeezed her hand. "He may fear to love ye, and fights mightily against his feelings, but he doesn't despise ye." She paused, and eyed Arien speculatively. "Have ye ever told him ye love him?"

Arien's cheeks grew warm. "Nay. Is it that obvious then?"

Glenna released her hand and sat back. "And what sort of wife would hand back her husband to his former mistress?" she asked with a laugh. "To my way of thinking, 'twould be either a wife who loathes her husband's touch, or one who loves him with all her heart."

The beginnings of a smile trembled on Arien's lips. "And what woman alive would loathe the touch of a man like Dane Haversin?"

"Indeed," Glenna agreed with an emphatic nod. "But though I once was honored to take him as lover, I am now as honored to have him as friend.

You, on the other hand," she said, leaning forward, a conspiratorial gleam in her eyes, "are the woman he loves. Listen closely, and I'll tell ye what must yet be done. . . ."

Four months later

Unexpectedly, the labor pains woke Arien in the middle of the night. She lay there for a time, hoping and praying they'd cease. It was too soon, she thought, fighting to contain a sense of panic. The babe wasn't due for another month yet.

Dane. Dane must be informed. He'd been working like a madman in the mines for the past three months. The gold he'd amassed before had been stolen in a vicious, surprise attack when he and his men had finally brought down the nuggets from his mountain mines to the lowlands of Greystone. Though Dane had nearly lost his life, all that mattered to him was the harsh reality that the king's taxes were gone, and he must labor anew to acquire more gold.

In the darkness of the sleeping castle, Arien made a silent entreaty. Holy Mother, she prayed, he has suffered so much. Don't take this babe from him, too.

An hour passed, then two. Finally, when it became evident the pains would not relent, Arien rose. Awkwardly making her way to the little sleeping closet off the bedchamber's anteroom, she woke the page she'd set to wait on her in these last weeks of her pregnancy. "Go fetch Onora and Willa," Arien ordered tautly. The young, towheaded boy rubbed the sleep from his eyes, nodded solemnly, and set off on his mission.

As she closed her bedchamber door, the cramping suddenly worsened. Fluid began to trickle, then gush down her legs. Arien clutched her belly and staggered to the nearest chair.

It seemed hours before Willa, followed closely by Onora, arrived. "M'lady?" The chatelaine hurried to her side. "Whatever is the matter?"

"My babe." Arien gasped, caught in the grip of a painful contraction. "Ah, Willa, it comes too soon!"

The old woman turned to Onora. "Light candles, then help me get m'lady to bed."

"My water. 'Tis broken," Arien cried. "Help me first to change to a clean bed gown."

Willa ran to the large chest, and returned with some drying cloths and a fresh bed gown. By the time Onora had the candles lit and the room glowing with light, Willa had Arien stripped of her soggy sleeping garment, dried off, and redressed. Together, the two women helped Arien back to bed. Onora then left to waken several servants, and have them gather the birthing supplies.

While she was gone, the chatelaine checked Arien, confirming what Arien already knew. She was in active labor. "Will my babe live born this early?" she cried, grabbing Willa's hand.

" 'Twould be best if it waited another two weeks, but I've seen a few babes born this early survive. 'Twill depend on its strength and how long ye labor." Suddenly, as if remembering some horrific thought, Willa's eyes widened in fear.

"What is it? What's wrong?" Arien's grip tightened. "Tell me, Willa."

" 'Tis naught." Emphatically, she shook her head. "Naught."

Arien leaned on one elbow. "Tell me nevertheless. I command it."

"I-I can't, m'lady. 'Twill only make things worse."

"Well, if *she* can't find the heart, I can." Onora came up to stand beside the bed. "The Lady Katrine died in childbed in exactly such a way. Her babe came a month early, was trapped sideways, and, after two days' labor, both died. 'Twas that Raven's curse that killed them. And now it seems the same curse has befallen ye."

"Nay," Arien moaned, another contraction rippling through her. "My m-magic's stronger than the curse. It c-cannot be!"

"And when, in these many months since ye wed," Onora hissed, "have ye practiced yer magic, or set a spell o' protection about ye and yer babe? Ye've yer blunt-witted husband to thank for that, making ye promise ne'er to use yer magic in Haversin. Now ye may well die because o' that." Her face twisted in anguish. "Ah, curse him, he who isn't even here when ye need him most!"

"S-send for Dane." Arien panted. "I gave him my word, swore it before the moon. Only he can grant me leave to break it, or the moon goddess will smite me dead. Send for Dane before 'tis too late!"

"Aye, send for him we will," her maidservant muttered. "I only hope he'll make it back in time." She turned to the ashen-faced chatelaine, who'd been listening in speechless disbelief, and led her a short way from the bed. "Go, Willa. Send out a rider on the swiftest horse in Haversin's stables. And then," Onora added grimly, "lift up yer most fervent prayers to the Mother above. Unless some miracle happens, the Lord Dane will surely never make it back in time."

Chapter Nineteen

Someone coughed, a raw, deep reverberation that grated on the ears and set the nerves on edge. Booted feet sloughed through the mud and melting snow, the sound coming to an abrupt end as the newest visitor halted outside Dane's tent. A throat cleared nervously. With a weary sigh, the lord of Haversin laid down his pen and waited for the inevitable query.

"M'lord? May I have a word wi' ye?"

For an instant, Dane closed his eyes, then shook his head and forced a welcoming smile. It wasn't his men's fault they'd all had to labor in the mines through early spring. The least he could do was listen to their concerns and support them in any way he could.

He was just so tired of the cold and wet and deprivation. He longed as much as any of them to return home. Arien was but a month from bearing their child, and, in all the time since he'd first learned of her pregnancy, he'd been with her little more than a month. He'd be a fortunate man if, when all was over, she ever stopped hating him for his neglect.

There was nothing, however, to be done for it. Both he and Phelan were now delinquent on their taxes. The king had graciously extended the payment deadline. He'd been forced, however, to charge them interest.

Now, as the new deadline neared, Dane faced the inevitable at last. They'd only been able to mine enough gold to pay Haversin's taxes and the exorbitant amount of interest. And, though he'd sent a small contingent of workers to reopen his copper and lead mines, Dane knew it would do little good. There wasn't enough time left to make up for the gold's devastating loss.

Phelan was in dire trouble. The king seemed intent on confiscating the young lord's lands, and Phelan seemed equally determined not to give them up. Even as Dane labored alongside his men in a frantic attempt to mine enough gold, he knew the day of reckoning wasn't far away. It only remained to be seen what part the king would ask him to play—and what part, if any, he could stomach to carry out.

The rasping cough came again, wrenching Dane back from his morose thoughts. "Er, aye," he called, "come in, come in."

Martin Prestwich, the soldier standing guard at the mine entrance, walked in. Dane leaned back in his chair and gazed up at him expectantly. "Aye, Martin?" he finally prompted when no further speech was forthcoming from the burly, bearded man.

"There's strange goings-on in the mine, m'lord." Martin looked decidedly uncomfortable. "*Magical* goings on, m'lord."

Dane straightened with a jerk. "What did you say?" he prodded softly.

"I heard singing and the sound o' a pickax being used against stone inside the mine. An eerie light gleamed from there, too. Yet when I went in to investigate, I saw naught. As soon as I left, though, the sounds and light began again." Martin shuddered. " 'Twas very strange, and set my skin to crawling."

"Have you told anyone else of this?"

"Nay, m'lord." Martin shook his head vehemently. "I came straightaway to ye. The men are miserable and tired enough, wi'out setting their imaginations running wild in the bargain."

"You did well." Dane rose, grabbed his sword and scabbard, and fastened it about his hips. Next he took up his heavy wool cloak and flung it over his shoulders, hiding the sword. "I'll walk back with you to the mine and have a look inside, myself."

"As ye wish, m'lord. I'd say my strange visions came from imbibing too much ale, but we've been out o' ale for the past week, so I cannot lay the blame there."

Dane grinned. "Well, if 'tis any consolation, I've sent for more ale, and it should arrive any day now." He lifted the tent flap. "Come, let us return to the mine."

"Aye, m'lord."

The night was cold and frost gave a bite to the air. Spring in the mountains, even in late April, was always an unpredictable mix of balmy days and frigid nights, interspersed with occasional snowfalls. At least the ground would soon freeze, Dane consoled himself, and the mud would harden. He was weary of wet boots and cold feet.

As they neared the mine entrance, a faint, dancing light emanated from the tunnel. A song, sung by a low, gravelly voice, rose on the night air, a song bittersweet, haunting, yet strangely compelling. The melody plucked at Dane's heart, rousing emotions he'd thought long ago buried.

Angrily, he shook aside the painful feelings. 'Twas indeed magic, Dane thought. At all costs, he must maintain his defenses, lest the foul spells ensorcel him.

He halted at the entrance and turned to Martin. "Stand guard and allow no one to enter. I won't be long."

The big man eyed him with misgiving. "Are ye certain 'tis wise fer ye to go in alone, m'lord?"

"If you hear sounds of fighting, you're more than welcome to come to my aid," Dane said. "And if 'tis truly some sorcerer within, 'twill hardly matter if one man or many go up against him. Either way, one man is more than enough for the present."

"Aye, 'twould seem so, m'lord."

Martin wasn't at all convinced, Dane well knew, as he turned and entered the mine. If the truth be told, he wasn't all that pleased himself about confronting the sorcerer. But he must discover who the intruder was. All he needed now was someone stealing the rest of the gold.

Following the singing, Dane took first one tunnel and then another. Gradually, the words of the song became clearer, until Dane began to make out phrases, then whole verses.

"Love at long last beckons,
Ripe wi' goldspun promise,

320

Yet still her eyes are closed.
Will she e'er be ready?

Too late, too late,
Fer her, fer us all,
Unless she names the secret
O' her shame—and her glory."

As the song ended, Dane rounded a corner,
coming face-to-face with a gray-bearded dwarf
dressed in a ragged brown homespun tunic tied
at the waist with a stout rope, darned hose, and
threadbare, misshapen boots. In his stubby fingers, he clenched a pickax, which he even then
raised to strike the rock wall.

Momentarily, Dane stared in surprise, then
found his voice. "This is Haversin land and Haversin gold. You've no right—"

"Yer claim's to the land's surface," the dwarf
remarked with surprising calmness. "What lies
deep in Mother Earth is dwarf holdings. Content
yerself we're generous, and share what's rightly
all ours."

"I might agree, if times weren't what they
were." Dane eyed the pickax, gauging a safe distance between him and the little creature. "However I need all the gold we mine, though it still
won't be enough. So I must ask you to leave. Your
presence here wouldn't be well tolerated, if my
men were to discover a dwarf was about."

"And when has any o' yer kind acted hospitably
to one o' the Little Men?" The graybeard gave a
mocking laugh. "E'en yer wife, the holy ones bless
and protect her, has ne'er known whether to trust
or doubt me."

Dane's features hardened with cynical incredulity. " 'Tis difficult to believe my wife, with her Moondancer upbringing, would ever associate with the likes of you."

"Aye, 'tis true enough," the dwarf agreed amiably. "But she was desperate fer a way to thwart her sister's plan to seduce and wed ye. The Princess Arien knew, wi' only her Moondancer magic, she could ne'er hope to best that foul hag o' hell. So she came to me, and I taught her what she needed."

Memories assailed Dane. Of Arien, trying to explain there had been no other way to save him, that except for that one night and the dark spells she'd cast, her magic was good and free of taint. He recalled her attempts to convince him she was a loyal wife, her pleas for forgiveness—a forgiveness he'd refused to grant.

"I warned her afore I taught her the dark magic that, though ye were indeed her destiny, naught o' any value comes wi'out a price. Do ye know what the princess told me?"

"Nay." Dane shook his head, his emotions roiling. "Why don't you tell me?"

"The princess said she'd pay most anything." His sharp little eyes bored into Dane. "Yet e'en she had no way o' knowing the terrible price you'd demand, o'er and o'er and o'er again."

Dane's jaw went taut with rage. "Yet I'm her destiny," he muttered, so disgusted with himself he could barely speak. His eyes slid shut in abject misery.

"Aye, that ye are."

Suddenly, Dane's nearly unendurable anger swung to the dwarf. "And why should you stand there and pretend to care what happens to Arien?" he said with a snarl. "You're a dwarf, and she, until not long ago, was a Moondancer. I wonder at your motives for involving yourself with her, especially for the likes of me."

The dwarf grinned, revealing several rotted teeth. "Ah, and aren't ye as suspicious as yer wife? But no matter. The terrible divisions that have been wrought will take time to mend." He propped the pickax against the stone wall, and motioned to where several boulders sat. "My tale will take a time in the telling. Ye may as well rest yerself as ye listen."

Dane followed the dark little creature to the rocks and sat, taking care to continue to hide his sword amid the folds of his cloak. Not that it would do him much good, he thought wryly, against one as magically superior as a dwarf.

"Ye ask why one o' the few remaining Little Men in Greystone would help a Moondancer," the dwarf said, picking up the thread of their conversation. "Well, if ye havena noticed, the Ravens are swiftly rising to power. Already, they've mastered some o' the skills o' the ancient Moondancers—skills that will eventually make them the most dangerously adept sorcerers in the realm. But, in order to do so, they've had to enlist the aid o' the demon himself. The consequences o' such an act will destroy us all. There's little time left if we're e'er to defeat them."

"Aye, 'tis a concern I've had for some time now," Dane agreed grudgingly. "But why this particular interest in Arien? You've a reason for involving yourself with her, haven't you?"

The dwarf nodded. "She's the most naturally adept sorceress I've seen in all my years. She's also kind, good, and brave. 'Twas why Dorianne chose the princess to succeed her, why I also chose her."

Dane's eyes narrowed. "Chose Arien for what?"

"Yer wife, my fine young lord"—the little creature leaned toward Dane with a fierce intensity—"is the one and only hope fer Greystone, and fer the long-awaited and desired reconciliation 'atween Moondancers and dwarves."

"Indeed?" Dane gave a disparaging laugh. "And exactly how is she to acquire the kind of powers she'd need for that particular endeavor? She may have used your services once, but I hardly think Arien cares to dabble in dark magic. Eventually, 'twould corrupt her as it has corrupted Edana."

The dwarf rolled his eyes in exasperation. "Nay, nay. As I told her, I'll tell ye. 'Tisn't the magic but the wielder who makes it good or evil. If the intended use is fer good, then the magic is good. And if the intent is fer evil . . ."

"Then there's no white and dark magic? Only what the wielder makes it?"

"Aye. Yer wife, though, needed to enhance her abilities if e'er she was to defeat the Ravens' demon-spawned powers." A wry smile quirked the dwarf's lips. "That's where ye came in."

Dane frowned. "I don't understand."

" 'Tis an ancient, long-forgotten Moondancer tradition. The priestess who mated wi' the best man in the realm gained the greatest powers, and so became the next high priestess. 'Twas why Edana wished to take ye to her bed. She discovered the old tradition, and then determined 'twas ye who was that 'best man.' "

" 'Twas a sad day when *I* was determined the best man." Dane sighed ruefully. "It all makes sense, though. Edana aspires to become the next

Moondancer high priestess. I was but a stepping stone in her climb to that power."

"But now yer fair wife has gained that power instead." The little creature cocked a shaggy brow. "It grows in her whenever ye couple, and because o' the babe ye placed in her womb."

"Then I've served my purpose and am no longer needed." Bitter disappointment filled Dane. "In the end, Arien has used me just as Edana intended."

"And have ye gained naught in the bargain?"

Puzzled, Dane stared at the dwarf. "I cannot see how I'm any better off than I was before. Indeed, wed to the king's daughter, my options now are even more limited."

"Ye've a loving, devoted wife. Ye've a son and heir about to be born. Ye're equally called and as vitally important in this quest to save Greystone as is yer lady." The dwarf gave a shake of his unkempt head. "Truly, rather than calling yer life limited, yer purpose served, I'd say ye're standing on the edge o' a wondrously happy existence, if only ye've the courage to face yer failings and look past them to what truly matters."

"You sound a lot like Arien." Dane smiled sadly. " 'Tis too late for me, though."

The dwarf snorted in disgust. "Mayhap, if ye see things so dismally. 'Tis fer the best then, that yer wife die afore the great cataclysm befalls Greystone. She'll ne'er succeed, at any rate, wi' a mate like ye at her side."

A chill of foreboding gripped Dane. "Die? What do you mean, 'tis best Arien die? She's innocent in all this. Why must she, too, suffer for my transgressions?"

"Why? Because her destiny is so tightly interwoven wi' yers," the dwarf said. "E'en now, she lies in childbed, endangered by the same curse that killed yer first wife. A curse, I might add, that ye and ye alone brought down on yer house."

Disbelief clawed at Dane, raking him with talons of dread. " 'T-tisn't possible. The babe isn't due for another month."

"Didna yer beloved Katrine die in exactly such a way?"

"Aye." Dane groaned. He buried his face in his hands. "By all that is holy, what am I to do? *What am I to do?*"

"Ye must go to her, aid her in her battle to o'ercome the curse and safely deliver yer son. 'Tis the only way she can best this—wi' ye at her side."

"N-nay." Dane shook his head. "She doesn't want me, doesn't need me. I'd only drag her down."

"If ye love her, how can ye drag her down? Ye do love her, dinna ye?"

Ever so slowly, Dane lifted his head. "Do you know everything then? Even the secrets of a man's heart?"

"Nay, I dinna know everything. But I've only to look at ye to see the truth written all o'er your face." The dwarf hopped down from his rocky seat. "Now, no more o' this pointless blathering. Do ye wish to go to yer wife or no'?"

"Aye." Dane jumped off his rock. " 'Twill take a good twenty-four hours of hard travel, though, to reach Haversin. Can I make it in time?"

"Not if ye intend to use horseback."

"What mode of travel did you have in mind?" Dane asked suspiciously.

The dwarf shrugged and grinned. "What else? Magic will serve us nicely, if ye've the courage to put yerself in my hands."

"And if I refuse?"

"Ye know the answer as well as I."

By all that was holy, Dane thought with a shudder. Must he now place his trust in a power he'd always found so vile and despicable? The mere idea of surrendering himself to magic filled him with horror. Yet if he didn't, Arien and their babe might well die. And that was a horror beyond any other.

Summoning the tattered remnants of his resolve, Dane nodded his assent. It was past time he risk his precious pride and honor in a cause transcending his own petty needs and concerns. It was past time he risk all for the woman he loved.

"Let us be off, then," he said. "Now, before I lose what little courage is left in me. Now, before 'tis too late."

"Wasn't it possible to get us a bit closer to the castle?" Dane asked with ill-disguised irritation four hours later, as he gazed up the long, winding expanse of road still to be traversed. In the graying darkness before sunrise, lights already flickered in a few windows. "From all the tales, I never expected we'd arrive over five miles off course."

"And would ye have preferred if I'd risked a miscalculation and set us down inside that rocky cliff ye built yer castle upon? Or mayhap smack dab in the depths o' that great lake o'er there?" The dwarf gave a disgusted snort. "Magical flight isna a precise art, like alchemy or herbal manipulations can be. I do my best, in the safest way I know. In the bargain, I shaved twenty hours from yer journey. So stop yer scolding, afore I take ye back to yer mines and let ye start out all o'er again."

"Fine," Dane muttered. "I'm just worried about Arien and wish to be with her as soon as I can. But you're right. Another five miles is naught in comparison to what my journey could've been. I beg pardon for my ingratitude."

"And well ye should, my fine lord," the dwarf grumbled, scuffing his misshapen boots in the dirt and refusing to meet Dane's eye. "By the Mother Earth, I've yet to find one o' yer kind who cannot find fault wi' something a dwarf does fer them!"

Remorse flooded Dane. "Truly, I am sorry. I took out my foul temper on you, and that was unpardonable. I'd gladly repay you for your service. I'm short of money just now, but I could write out a voucher and as soon as I—"

"I dinna want yer money." The little creature held up a silencing hand. "I've all I want and need. There's a favor I'd ask o' ye, though."

Dane's instincts warned him it was chancy promising anything to the dwarf, but he didn't care what the price might be. If Arien and his child lived, the dwarf deserved whatever he wished. "Name it and 'tis yours."

"Well, I've a small token fer ye." He jammed his stubby fingers into the pocket of his tunic, finally extracting a small, cloth-wrapped package. He handed it to Dane. "Here. 'Tis fer ye and the fair princess."

Gingerly, Dane unwrapped the dingy piece of homespun. In the center of the worn cloth lay two gold rings of exquisite workmanship—tiny gold lions alternating with silver dragons clasping a crescent moon in one front claw. The family crests of the Haversins and Talamontes.

" 'Tis a pair o' wedding rings, one fer ye and one fer the princess," the dwarf explained, his swarthy complexion deepening with what Dane guessed was an embarrassed blush. " 'Tis said wedding rings made by one o' the Little Men confer the promise o' a happy, fruitful marriage on the rings' wearers."

"Aye, I know what the legends say." Ever so carefully, Dane rewrapped the small parcel and tucked it in a secure pocket within his cloak. "We'll be honored, both Arien and I, to wear these as our wedding rings. Truly, these will be cherished far more than the hastily made rings given us at our marriage."

"Er, aye." Once more the dwarf looked down and scuffed his feet. "See that ye do. They were no' easy to craft, wi' all the fine detail o' the creatures."

"It seems unfair to accept such a splendid gift, when instead 'tis I who should be gifting you. Will you at least accompany me to the castle, where I can have a feast prepared in your honor?"

The dwarf turned his gaze eastward. The faintest tint of rose painted the predawn sky. "Nay," he said with a sigh, turning back to Dane. " 'Twill be light soon, and I must be hidden deep in the earth or risk turning to stone. 'Tis past time I left ye to yer wife."

"But what if she needs more help than I can give her?" Dane made a move to halt the dwarf, then drew back. Lord that he was, with a battle sword at his side, and all the impressive power of his name and holdings to back him, he was no match for the dwarf's magic. "Couldn't you stay in Haversin for a time, just in case we need you? The dungeons are deep within the earth, and dark. Surely 'twould be safe—"

The dwarf chuckled softly. "Nay, though I must admit the offer o' yer fine dungeons is most attractive. Go to yer wife. Ye're all she needs." He turned and began to walk away.

"Wait. A moment more," Dane called after him.

"Aye?" The dwarf halted.

"Will we ever see you again? Arien . . . I'm certain she'll wish personally to thank you."

Once more, the dwarf chuckled. "Oh, she'll be seeing me again, and no mistake. We're not finished, she and I. Nay, by no means are we yet finished."

Dane's unexpected arrival at Haversin created quite a stir. Fortunately, it was well past sunrise before he gained the castle gate, and the sentry easily identified him. As he strode across the outer, then the inner bailey in his journey to the keep, servants stopped and stared. John Bidwell, Dane's eternally unflappable steward, all but dropped his jaw onto his chest when he first saw his liege enter the main building.

"M-m'lord," the old man stammered as he rushed to his side. "We just sent a rider off to fetch ye four hours ago. How could ye have returned so quickly? How could ye have known—"

"That the Lady Haversin is in the throes of childbirth?" Dane smiled grimly. " 'Twas magic, John. *Good* magic."

He left his steward staring in surprise. Taking the steps to the upper level two at a time, Dane hurriedly made his way to his bedchamber. The door was unlatched. He shoved it open.

"Ahhh," Arien groaned, writhing in pain on their bed. "I hurt. I hurt so badly. When will it stop? When?"

Onora clasped one of Arien's hands, Willa, the other. "Soon, m'lady," the maidservant crooned. " 'Twill all be over soon, and ye'll have yer sweet babe."

"D-Dane." Arien began to sob. "I n-need Dane. But he won't come. He doesn't care. He doesn't care!"

"Curse him for his pride," Onora said in a hiss. " 'Twill be the death o' you, and yer babe. I vow I'll throttle him with my bare hands if he fails ye this time!"

Dane stood rooted to the floor, suddenly terrified, swamped with a sense of total inadequacy and utter helplessness. What could he really do to help Arien, to save her life? Why, he couldn't even love her as she deserved!

His head lowered in despair. He couldn't love *anyone* as they deserved. That pathetic fact had been brought forcefully home with Katrine's death. He couldn't love, because he couldn't forgive himself for what he'd done, and had failed to do.

Yet why was the concept of self-forgiveness so abhorrent? Dane wondered. Did it mayhap lie in the realization only a humbled man, a man who cast aside his pride and faced his frailties, could ever truly forgive? He shuddered in revulsion. All his life he'd striven to be strong, certain in his thoughts and deeds, never doubting what he did was right and good. Even in his soul-eating, unceasing remorse over Katrine's death, Dane had been convinced it was a just and fitting punishment.

Nay, husband. Unbidden, Arien's sweet voice filled his mind. *'Tisn't true. Your ability to forgive depends on your ability to love. And if you love much, you can forgive much—even in yourself.*

If you love much . . . you can forgive much. . . .

He lifted his head, and looked straight into Arien's eyes. Eyes as tear-filled as his. Eyes awash with love, with forgiveness, with need.

"Dane," she whispered and reached out to him.

With startled gasps, Onora and Willa turned. He hardly noticed them. His world had narrowed to the ebony-haired woman lying in his bed, the woman bearing his child, the woman who loved him.

Staggering to her, Dane fell to his knees and took Arien's hands. After kissing each one fervently, he clasped them to his chest. His heart thundered. Words rose, then were choked off in the sudden constriction of his throat.

Groaning out his despair, Dane tried again, fighting past his pride, his self-doubts, his nameless fears. "Arien, I-I love you," he rasped. "Forgive me."

"First," she said, smiling through her pain and tears, "forgive yourself."

Dane looked deep into Arien's eyes, eyes gloriously luminous, brimming with love. Though he'd always be unworthy of such devotion, he desperately needed and finally meant to accept what she offered. With that admission, Dane's burden of guilt lifted, burned away like the mists of morn.

"I do," he said, and meant it with all his heart.

Chapter Twenty

Sunlight streamed through the open window, bright, coruscated beams that gilded the floor with a glorious radiance. Arien carried her son to the center of the shimmering rays, and immersed him in their soothing warmth. "Ah, how beautiful you are," she crooned. "My lovely, golden child, my precious Oren."

She cradled him to her, reveling in his smooth skin, clean smell, and downy soft black hair. Oren moved against her neck, nuzzling it tentatively, then, with gentle smacking sounds, attempted to nurse. Arien laughed and pulled him back into the crook of her arm.

Dark eyes of some yet-to-be-determined shade gazed solemnly back at her. As if in reprimand for the meal now denied, a tiny fist waved in the air. Moist, rosebud pink lips opened in a huge yawn.

" 'Tisn't time for your next nursing, sweet one," Arien chided lovingly. "Indeed, Willa has warned me that, for a wee lad of six weeks, you're already as plump as a piglet."

"So, now you're calling our son a piglet, are you?"

With a soft cry of delight, Arien spun around. "Dane! When did you return from the mine?"

"Just a scant five minutes ago." He grinned. "If I hadn't been momentarily waylaid by John, I'd have been up to see the two of you four minutes ago."

Arien smiled. Though, these four weeks past, Dane had been forced to return to the mine and complete the final preparations for the transport of the gold to Castle Talamontes, the first two weeks after Oren's birth he'd remained at Haversin. Those weeks had wrought an amazing transformation in him. At long last, her husband trusted her again. At long last, he was the man she'd known before she'd ensorceled him.

Aye, Arien thought contentedly, Dane was that man and more. The haunted look in his eyes was gone. He seemed more relaxed, at peace. And, with the safe delivery of his son and her survival of childbirth, he was supremely happy. The curse was dispelled. A curse that they, in the combined ardor of their love, had finally overcome.

Or rather, Arien corrected herself as her new wedding ring caught her eye, it had been their love, a bit of her magic, and the timely intervention of a certain dwarf. Though she was grateful for his getting Dane swiftly to her side, a lingering unease twined about her heart. The dwarf still wasn't finished with her, it seemed.

"What is it, lass?" Dane asked, his deep voice husky with concern. "What troubles you?"

Arien looked up, into eyes as dark and blue as a storm-tossed sea. She shook her head and sighed. " 'Tis of no import. I just wondered why the dwarf had told you he'd be seeing me again, that we weren't finished. Truly, if I had my way, I'd wish never to see him again."

Dane stepped close, wrapping his arm about her. "I can understand your sense of betrayal, after the magic he taught you turned on you. But 'twas all for the best in the end. And he did help you when your life was endangered. 'Tis the act of a friend, albeit a strange one."

"Mayhap," Arien admitted grudgingly. "Yet still I wonder. . . ."

Her husband leaned over to kiss her tenderly on the nose, then bent and bestowed a kiss on his son. "If the truth be told," Dane said, his tone mildly admonishing, "I didn't ride all day and night to waste time discussing a dwarf. All I care about is how my wife and son are doing. And, from your earlier comments, I gather Oren is thriving nicely."

At Dane's mention of their son, all thought of the dwarf faded in Arien's motherly swell of pride. "Aye, Oren's doing splendidly. He sleeps through the night now, nurses well, and hardly makes a sound save when 'tis time for his feedings."

"And you, wife?" His gaze swept down her body, a decidedly sensual tone roughening his voice. "How are *you* faring?"

A wild hope filled her. Was it possible? Arien wondered. Did Dane wish already to bed her, and resume his marital rights?

"I fare well, husband." Afraid her rising excitement might betray her, she found sudden interest in her drowsing babe. "I've been out riding frequently in the past few weeks. 'Tis safe to say my strength and energy have returned to normal."

"So, you're healed in every way?"

She lifted laughing eyes to him. "In *every* way, husband."

Dane smiled. "Our son sleeps. Will he awaken soon?"

Arien shrugged. "I last nursed him an hour ago. He should hold for at least another hour."

"Then best you return him to his cradle." His gaze went hot, hungry. "What I've in mind precludes the presence of a babe."

"Indeed?" Arien's lips lifted in an impish grin. "So 'tis time for you to begin sowing your seed in me again, is it? That *is* the reason you lie with me, is it not? To make more heirs?"

Dane had the good grace to blush. "Aye, more heirs would be deeply appreciated. But not too soon. I'm content to enjoy Oren for a time . . . and you." Sudden doubt clouded his features. "Do I offend you, desiring to bed you so soon after our son's birth? I can wait a time longer, I assure you, if the thought of coupling is still abhorrent or—"

"Hush, my love." Arien placed a silencing finger to his lips. "I'd wager I desire to bed you as much as you do me. And I've never, ever, found the thought of coupling with you abhorrent. On the contrary, I can think of naught—"

Someone knocked on the bedchamber door, the sound forceful, urgent. Dane hesitated, then, with a sigh of resignation, released Arien. " 'Tis John. Only he would presume to intrude at a time like this, and only for the most dire of reasons."

"Go see to his needs," Arien urged, smiling in understanding. "I'll put Oren to bed."

" 'Twill not take long, I promise," Dane said, backing toward the door even as he spoke.

She laughed. "Oh, and well do I know it." Her glance dropped to his cloth-covered groin and the swollen evidence of his need. "Aye," she reiterated throatily, "and well do I know it."

Dane rolled his eyes and chuckled, then turned and hurried to the door. He slid back the bolt and opened the door to find, as he'd expected, his steward standing there. A look of deep concern burned in the older man's eyes.

"Aye, what is it, John?" Dane asked, taking care to shield the lower half of his body behind the door. "Unless the castle's under attack, or the packhorses have escaped with all the gold, surely this can wait?"

The steward handed Dane a small, wax-sealed scroll. "A rider from Dunbarton just delivered this. He said 'twas most urgent ye read it and send back a reply. Even now, he awaits yer return missive."

Dane frowned. " 'Tis obviously from Phelan." He unrolled the document and quickly scanned the script, his horror growing with each word he read. Finally, Dane looked up. "Have the messenger come down from his horse and partake of a hot meal. While he eats, have a fresh horse saddled for him."

"And what shall I tell him is yer reply, m'lord?"

"Tell him naught for the moment," Dane said with a growl. "I'll prepare my answer and have it waiting when he's ready to depart."

John Bidwell nodded. "As ye wish, m'lord."

Dane watched his steward walk away, then quietly shut the door.

"What is it, husband?" Arien drew up behind him.

He gave a scornful laugh, then turned to face her. "What else? Your father plots and preys again."

337

The color drained from Arien's face. "By the Mother, what has he done now?"

"Phelan—" Dane dragged in a shuddering breath. "Since he does not have the excuse of a newborn babe to justify yet another extension, his overdue taxes were to be delivered two weeks ago."

"Aye?" Puzzlement tightened her voice. "And what of it?"

"He never had the money to begin with," Dane rasped. "*I* was to subsidize Phelan's taxes. And I could have, if the first supply of gold hadn't been stolen. But not a second time. Not at least without several more months of work in the mines."

Tendrils of rising horror crept in to twine about Arien's heart. "And my father—" She swallowed hard. "He has now taken some action against your cousin, hasn't he?"

"Aye, that he has." A savage fury burned in Dane's eyes. "The king has decided 'tis past time to confiscate Phelan's holdings in lieu of his overdue taxes. And Phelan, refusing to surrender his ancestral lands, has sent out a call for help, begging me to come to his aid against the king."

They set out the next day for Castle Talamontes and an audience with the king. Though Dane was dubious any good would come of the meeting, Arien still insisted they try convincing her father not to confiscate Phelan's lands. It was worth any amount of trying, she'd said, to avert an all-out war—a war in which she'd be forced to take sides against her father.

As they broached the final hill separating them from sight of the royal castle, a dark shroud passed before Arien's eyes. The vision of a dying woman, crying out her name, rose before Arien. Her lids closed in presentiment and dread. "Dorianne," she whispered, shaking her head. "Nay, not now. Not now."

Dane turned in his saddle. "What's wrong, lass?"

Though Arien was loath to add to his already heavy burden of concerns, she knew he'd hear soon enough that the Moondancer high priestess was dying. Tightly clutching Oren, who slept contentedly in a sling she'd tied about her neck and shoulders, Arien met her husband's worried gaze. "Dorianne . . . Even now she lies on her deathbed. I-I must go to her."

"Why?" A pair of penetrating blue eyes leveled on her. "She tried to kill you the last time you met. She cast you from the Moondancers when you refused to renounce your magic. Indeed, who knows what she or her underlings might do if you now presume to enter their holy sanctum. Nay"— Dane shook his head in grim determination— " 'tis too dangerous."

"Dane, I must." Holy Mother, Arien thought. How could she convince him of the grave import of this deathbed visit? She could hardly articulate it herself; she just knew she must go. "Dorianne, for all her failings, has given me so much. I owe her this small courtesy, at the very least. Besides," she added, managing a wan smile, "she may not wish to see me; I could be turned away. But at least then I will have tried. I have to try."

"And what of Oren?" An edge of desperation crept into Dane's voice. "He's still a nursling. He needs his mother. Think of your son, if you care not what becomes of me!"

Ah, it was so good to know how much Dane loved her. Arien had yearned for that love for so long, it now seemed doubly precious just because she'd not won it easily. And her darling Oren—he was a treasure beyond compare.

"No harm will come to me, my love," Arien assured him. "My powers have grown greatly since I wed you. I didn't discover how strong I was until you gave me leave to use my gifts to destroy Reyene's curse that night I delivered Oren. None of my sister Moondancers can best me, and Dorianne is dying. Though," she added softly, "I wonder if even she could best me now."

"Have a care, wife, that your confidence doesn't outdistance your abilities," Dane cautioned. " 'Tis the surest path to ruin."

"The night he first taught me of his dark magic, the dwarf warned me that, once acquired, 'twasn't a skill easily or willingly discarded." A troubled look clouded her eyes. "Naive fool that I was, I paid him little heed. But now I fully understand what he tried to tell me. The dark magic is with me still. 'Tis with me, but I do not glory in it. Nay, on the contrary, I fear these new powers, and won't use them save in dire need. In such need, however, they far surpass aught a true Moondancer can command."

"You cannot know that for certain," he said with a growl. "And you spoke of 'true Moondancers.' What of Edana and her Ravens?"

"Aye," Arien admitted, "Edana and her ilk are hardly true Moondancers. And I cannot say how my powers will measure up to theirs. Only of late have I come into the darker side of magic, while they've been privy to it for years." She couldn't restrain a small shiver. "Edana, of course, is the most powerful of them all. I greatly fear what might happen if I went up against her. 'Tis why, at all costs, I mean to avoid such a confrontation."

"Yet aligning yourself with the Moondancers once again might force just such a confrontation."

"Possibly. I hope and pray 'twill not be so, though."

For a moment, Dane looked ready to say more. Then, with an anguished glance, he reined his horse down the road leading to the Moondancer monastery. " 'Tis apparent there's no swaying you," he muttered, "so let us begone to your holy house. Now, before I withdraw my consent, or question my sanity in risking, yet again, a dearly bought happiness."

Like some huge coverlet of deep gray-blue tinged at the edges with fading tones of crimson and copper, twilight settled softly, comfortingly over the land. The Haversin party soon drew up at the monastery. From the distance across the lush lawn and gardens, the marble-faced buildings with their pillared porches gleamed a ghostly white.

Arien dismounted, then handed Oren up to Dane. "It might take a while," she said, a smile tenderly curving her lips. "Why not ride on to Castle Talamontes and take your ease? 'Twill be safe enough for me to make my way there when I'm finished."

"Nay," he repeated obstinately. "We'll wait for you. You needed me once before when you went up against your high priestess. You may need me again."

"As you wish then." She turned and walked away.

"Arien," Dane called after her.

With a sigh, she halted, glancing over her shoulder. "Aye?"

"No matter how they beg, how persuasive they become, promise them naught without talking first to me. Give me your vow on that, wife."

He feared the Moondancers and their magic still, Arien realized. Feared he might yet lose her to them. But that would never be. Her husband and son were what mattered now, more than her magic ever could. Indeed, in the past months, she'd hardly noticed the lack of magic in her life. And she had missed it not a whit.

"I give you my vow, husband," Arien replied softly, still marveling over the startling revelation. Then, with a final wave, she turned and continued on her way.

Ursla awaited her at the door. Her eyes were red, her expression grief-stricken, but her lips, as her gaze met Arien's, lifted in a tremulous smile. "Ah, thank the Mother," she exclaimed in relief and welcome, "you've come. Our high priestess began asking for you but a short time ago. We were even now deciding among us who should go for you."

"How is she?"

"Our high priestess is fading." Ursla's eyes welled with fresh tears. "I'd wager she'll not last more than another few days." She grabbed Arien's hand, pulling her inside and shutting the huge door. "I-I beg pardon for my rudeness and disrespect to you all these months, m'lady," Ursla then hurried to say. "Can you ever forgive me?"

" 'Twasn't of your making alone, dear sister."
Arien gave Ursla's hand a quick squeeze. "I was
too preoccupied with myself, and my magic, and
not always the most pleasant person to be
around."

"Well, none of that matters anymore. What
matters is that you, though Dorianne cast you
from our midst, came back when she needed you
most."

"Then she'll see me?"

Ursla nodded vigorously. "Aye. Come. I'll take
you."

Together, they crossed the smooth, polished
marble floor of the sparsely furnished reception
room, entered another door, and traversed the
length of the great moon temple. The huge, cavernous chamber was empty at this time of day,
but tall stone vases of fresh, springtide flowers
adorned the long altar and pleasantly scented the
air. An elegant array of fine beeswax candles
added not only light but also their own delicate
scent.

Everything was as she'd remembered, as she'd
last left it, Arien thought. Mysterious . . . beautiful . . . familiar. Yet though the sisterhood had
been taken from her, in all truth, she couldn't say
she wished it back. Not that, or her magic, either.

At long last, Sister Ursla opened one final door
to the right of the altar and motioned Arien
through. It was the high priestess's living quarters, she well knew, her stomach churning in nervous anticipation and inexplicable dread.

She found Dorianne, her long white hair unbound and spread across her pillow, lying on her
bed. The old woman truly did look as if she lingered on the threshold between life and death.

Her fair skin was gray, withered. Her eyes were sunken, circled with shadow, and held no sign of their former luster or fire. Long, skeletal fingers plucked aimlessly at the coverlet, but, aside from that, Dorianne lay there, limp and motionless.

Six priestesses—all members of the elite Assembly of Elders—stood around her, varying expressions of grief, worry, and anguished concern on their faces. Arien's steps faltered, then ceased. What was she to say or do, now that she was no longer considered a Moondancer?

Dorianne made the decision for her. "Come, child," she croaked, extending her hand. "Thank the Mother. You've arrived . . . before 'tis too late."

The sound of that old, familiar voice snapped the last of Arien's control. With a joyous cry, she rushed over. Kneeling beside the bed, she took up the old woman's hand and clasped it to her breast. "I thank the Mother, as well," Arien whispered, "that you're willing to see me."

" 'Twas pride," the high priestess quavered. "I'd had such plans for you . . . then you wed that man . . . without even conferring with me. But now . . . now there's no time left for bruised feelings . . . imagined insults."

"No time left," she agreed with fervent conviction, "save for what truly matters." Arien lifted Dorianne's hand and kissed it. "I love you like a mother. In truth, I've known you longer than I ever did my own."

"Aye . . . your mother . . ." A faraway look misted the high priestess's eyes. "She was a good girl, though quite headstrong and rebellious . . . when first she came to Castle Talamontes as your father's bride."

Dorianne coughed, then began to wheeze and choke. It was several minutes more before she could catch her breath. "Ursla." She motioned for the priestess to come close. "Tell . . . tell her the rest."

Ursla nodded, then turned to Arien. "She didn't love your father when first she wed him." The woman emotionlessly picked up the thread of the story. "That came later . . . much later. 'Twas the reason her firstborn was sired by a different man—a dashing young stable hand in her father's castle."

Arien reared back, stunned. "Nay, 'tisn't possible! I-I can't believe—" She shook her head fiercely. "Surely you're mistaken. 'Twould make Edana—"

" 'Twould make Edana illegitimate, and you the true heir to the throne," Ursla finished for her. To give additional credence to the tale, the high priestess nodded her agreement. "Our lady didn't know for a long time," Ursla then continued, glancing at Dorianne, "until your sister, at two and ten, wished to become a Moondancer. Even then 'twas evident Edana wouldn't suit. Dorianne refused her entrance. 'Twas then your mother came to our lady, telling her of Edana's great desire to enter the sisterhood, and that, in the end, 'twould be all the position and power she could ever hope to achieve. 'Twas then, after swearing our lady to secrecy, she told her about Edana's true father."

"So," Arien concluded, so shaken her hands trembled, "Edana was accepted into the Moondancers only to please my mother."

"She was never suited . . . isn't to this day. Her powers, despite intensive training, were always of

345

the most limited kind, until"—Ursla made a warding sign—"until she made her pact with the demon."

The color drained from Arien's face. "Ah, by the Mother!" she whispered in an agonized voice. "I'd always wondered . . . suspected . . . but hoped against hope 'twasn't true."

"Do you see now why she can never become high priestess?" Dorianne cupped Arien's chin and directed her gaze back to her own. "Do you see now why I called you to me, before . . . before 'twas too late?"

" 'Tis best I know the truth. Does my father know?"

"He only learned of it . . . on your mother's deathbed." Once again Dorianne resumed the telling of the story. "It did him no good, though. Edana immediately cast a spell . . . about him, stealing his memory of what your mother had told him. And, with the success of that first spell, it encouraged her . . . to try another, then another and another, until she finally had your father . . . totally at her bidding."

"I've always wondered if she'd ensorceled him. But I could find no trace of a spell."

" 'Tis the way of the demon's magic," Ursla interjected hotly. "It leaves no sign."

"Ah, where will it all end with Edana?" Arien moaned, clenching her eyes shut in despair. "She must be stopped."

"Child?"

Arien opened her eyes and leaned close.

"You . . . you must . . . stop her." Dorianne inhaled an unsteady breath. "I name you . . . name you . . . my successor."

Once again, Arien reared back in shock. "It cannot be, my lady," she cried, when she finally found her voice to speak. "I'm no longer even a Moondancer. I cannot be high priestess."

"As I took, I can give again," Dorianne rasped. She reached up and touched Arien's forehead with her thumb, tracing the sign of the moon on it. "You are reinstated, sister."

"Nay." Arien stared down at the old woman in dismay. Didn't Dorianne understand? She didn't want to be high priestess. In her heart of hearts, Arien knew now she'd never wanted to be high priestess. She'd only pretended to want it for Dorianne's sake. Now all that truly mattered was bringing peace to Greystone, then returning home to Haversin. All that mattered was being a good mother to Oren and wife to Dane.

Dane . . . Her heart ached for him. He deserved a time of happiness. Indeed, *she* deserved a time of happiness. Yet it seemed now that fate had contrived never to let that be.

"Choose someone else." Arien forced herself to meet Dorianne's gaze. "You said yourself a wedded Moondancer could never be high priestess, that Moondancer law forbade it. And I'll never renounce my marriage. Never."

Dorianne glanced up at Ursla. "Tell her. Tell her . . . all."

"The law forbidding a wedded Moondancer from becoming high priestess," Ursla explained, "was devised after the dwarves were driven from the land. 'Twasn't just the powers of the Little Men that were feared. 'Twas also the greater powers of any wedded Moondancer. Because they mated with men, they were always privy to the darker abilities gained from that masculine side

347

of magic. No virgin Moondancer, no matter how considerable her natural abilities, could ever hope to compete."

"Because of that, no virgin Moondancer," Arien supplied, beginning to see where Ursla's tale was leading, "could ever hope to become high priestess. So, under the pretense of banning all dark powers after the dwarves were defeated, the requirements for high priestess were also changed."

"Aye," the other woman agreed. " 'Twas wrong, though, to make such a law. 'Twas most definitely unwise, considering our current dire straits."

"Because Edana and the Ravens have seized on those old ways, and threaten to become even more powerful than the rest of you?"

" 'Twas never . . . the correct solution . . . to the problem, child," Dorianne croaked. "The decision . . . to ban wedded Moondancers from becoming high priestess . . . arose from jealousy and fear, rather than from sound reasoning. In the process, we turned our good laws . . . against us."

"And, in the doing," Arien added fervently, recalling the words she'd once spoken to Dane, "evil finally found the secret to overcoming good."

"There's still hope, though, if you accept the honor of leading us, m'lady," Ursla offered, an eager, trusting light shining in her eyes.

Fiercely, Arien shook her head. "Nay, I'm not worthy."

"You have always been the most worthy . . . the chosen one." With a superhuman effort, Dorianne struggled to her elbows. "There is none better suited, none with more powers to fight . . . and defeat Edana and her Ravens."

"Powers far too difficult to control," Arien countered hotly, her frustration rising anew.

"Powers that teeter as much on the edge of evil as good."

" 'Tis a grave responsibility, to be sure. But 'tis one you accepted long ago . . . when you first took your vows."

And what of your responsibility? Arien wanted desperately to fling back at her. *So many of our current problems could have been prevented if only you'd had the wisdom, the courage to use your magic as 'twas intended.*

But instead of voicing what was truly in her heart, Arien recalled her promise to Dane and just shook her head. "Nay. I cannot. I will not!"

"Then we are doomed . . . the Moondancers . . . the people . . . Greystone."

"I cannot, my lady!" Arien cried, leaping to her feet. "I owe my husband and child some loyalty, too."

The high priestess's eyes narrowed, her expression calculating, almost sly. "They have become everything to you, then? You treasure them above all else . . . even your magic, your sacred obligations to the sisterhood?"

"A-aye." Proudly, Arien faced her. "They are everything to me . . . my heart's greatest treasure."

" 'Tis as I always thought," a gravelly voice intruded unexpectedly, as some new visitor came up behind her. "Ne'er did I believe yer claim that yer magic was yer greatest treasure."

With a gasp, Arien turned, and came face-to-face with the dwarf. "You . . . what are you doing here?"

"Amongst a dwarf's greatest enemies, ye mean?" Grinning, he cocked his shaggy head. "Desperate times demand desperate alliances,

349

wouldn't ye say? And yer priestesses have finally come to realize that, in so many ways, the threat was always greatest amongst their own kind."

Arien eyed him suspiciously. "Your timing is most opportune. Or do you visit here regularly now?"

Garth Dorwen gave a bark of laughter. "Ah, ye havena changed much, fair princess. After all I've done fer ye, ye still dinna trust me, do ye?"

" 'Tis my growing indebtedness to you that gives me reason to fear. As I said before, a dwarf never gives aught away for free."

"Aye, 'tis true enough." He scratched his bearded chin. "There *was* something about a magical favor, if I do recall correctly. One ye vowed to render me if and when I wished it."

"I . . . I warned you, did I not, child?" Dorianne quavered from her bed. "I warned you . . . and now you will pay the price for your disobedience."

"Ah, dinna be so hard on the lass." The dwarf hobbled over to stand beside the old woman. "E'en ye didna know the full extent o' the danger at the time. If the truth be told, ye didna care to know, either."

Arien jerked her gaze from the high priestess back to Garth Dorwen. "Tell me, then. Tell me what you wish from me," she said, wanting to be done with this increasingly untenable situation. Dorianne and the dwarf now in league against her! By the Mother, would the impediments thrown in her path, the injustice of it all, never cease?

The dwarf glanced briefly at the dying woman, then back to Arien. "I'll make it easy on ye, fair princess. Give her what she asks, and yer debt to me is paid."

Arien's eyes slid shut in disbelief. "She asks me to follow her as high priestess," she finally said, riveting her gaze on the dwarf. "She wants me to fight Edana and her Ravens. A strange return of a magical favor, I'd say, especially one demanded by a dwarf."

"And do ye think I dinna gain in the bargain?" Garth Dorwen chuckled softly. "The Ravens seek total power, and dwarves are as great a threat to them as are Moondancers. Indeed, aside from ye, yer sister counts us as the greatest threat o' all."

"Why? You are the only dwarf remaining in the land."

"The only dwarf remaining who e'er comes out above ground fair princess," he corrected her. " 'Twas part o' the bargain my ancestors made wi' yers. But e'en relegated to the depths o' Mother Earth, the Little Men are always near. And if e'er some Moondancer high priestess should find it in her heart to free them . . ."

"Ah, at last I begin to understand." So this was the reason for all the convoluted machinations, she thought. "It benefits you greatly for a high priestess friendly to you and your kind to follow Dorianne."

" 'Tis essential fer the survival o' the Little Men, fair princess."

Arien sensed a trap about to be sprung on her. Once more, she looked from Garth Dorwen to Dorianne. Both stared back at her, their gazes resolute, their resolve steadfast. They'd not be swayed, she realized, with pleas to choose another candidate, or by protestations that she was now a wife and mother.

What they failed to understand, though, was that their hope in her was misplaced. Thanks to her rash dealings with the dwarf, Arien's magic had become unstable. It was unpredictable now, with as much potential to do harm as good. Perhaps in time she'd learn to control it, but by then it could well be too late.

"Choose another," she replied. "No matter what the two of you may have hoped, I won't be forced into wielding powers I cannot control. My magic could be more fearful, more destructive, than Edana's ever could."

"Ye refuse for cowardly, selfish reasons!" Hands on his hips, stubby legs wide, Garth Dorwen glared up at her.

"Cowardly? Selfish?" Stunned and hurt, Arien met his reproachful gaze. "How can you say that, you, who above everyone else, know why I did what I did, and what I sacrificed? 'Tis the magic, *your* magic, that I fear, and naught else!"

"The magic isna the true source o' yer fear, and ne'er has been! Do ye recall what I told ye about spinning straw into gold? Do ye?"

"Aye," Arien snapped, glaring back at him. "What of it?"

" 'Tis the wielder who makes the magic what 'tis, who sees beyond the outward appearances to far different possibilities. 'Tis ne'er the substance itself that determines its use, nor the source o' the magic—"

"Easy for you to say! You won't have to live with the consequences if I fail."

"Nay, I willna. I'll be dead, destroyed by yer sister. But then what will become o' yer people, yer beloved husband and child? Do ye think Edana will let them live?" He paused, stroking his beard in consideration. "But then again, she might keep yer man alive fer a time. He can still serve to feed

352

her evil powers, till she finally drains him o' his life essence."

"You say these things to frighten me into doing your will!" Arien cried, her hands clenching at her sides. "Well, I won't be frightened or manipulated again. Not by you, not by anyone!"

Garth Dorwen shrugged. "Then have it yer way. But if ye refuse to repay what ye promised me, ye must instead grant me yer heart's greatest treasure—a treasure ye admit is no longer yer magic."

Her shock reached out and grabbed Arien by the throat, squeezing the breath from her. The room dimmed, whirled crazily. She went hot, then cold.

"Ye canna refuse me." Ruthlessly, relentlessly, the dwarf hammered his point home. "E'en if ye tried, I'd still have the right, the power to take what ye promised. And take them I will, both yer husband and yer child."

"N-nay," Arien whispered piteously, knowing he spoke true. "Please . . . I'll give you aught else you ask. Gold, jewels, a fine castle and servants—"

"I dinna want any o' that." His long, thin nose wrinkled in disgust. "I want peace in the land, the Ravens destroyed, and the Little Men free once more to live as they wish. Can ye give me any o' that, wi'out doing as I ask? Can ye?"

Her head dropped, her shoulders slumped. "You know I can't."

"Then do as I ask."

"I-I must have time to think on this . . . speak with my husband."

"Suit yerself," the dwarf said with a shrug. " 'Twill change naught, though. I'll return in three days fer yer answer. Three days and no more. If ye havena decided by then, 'twill be all the same to me. Ye canna escape the coming battle unscathed, no matter how great yer wondrous powers."

Tears coursed down Arien's cheeks. "And what have my wondrous powers ever done for me, save hang as a millstone about my neck?" she asked with a sob. "I don't want them anymore. All I want is Dane, and Oren!"

"What ye want is o' no import. Ye're as much a part o' the land and its people, as ye're the source o' magic that weaves all o' it together. Do ye begin to see it at last? Do ye? 'Tis yer destiny, fair princess, and a glorious one 'tis, if only ye can name the secret o' yer shame and yer glory."

"I-I don't care!" Arien lifted a furious, anguish-racked face. "Do you hear me? I don't care!"

"Ye dinna care?" Garth Dorwen's expression went black with pain. "Then 'tis indeed too late," he said softly, sadly, "fer ye and fer us all."

Chapter Twenty-one

"Tact, husband. Above all else, you must remember tact," Arien whispered the next morning, as she and Dane walked down the stairs, then across the reception area to where the king awaited them in the great hall. "All effort must be made to assure my father of your utmost loyalty."

" 'Twill do no good, Arien," Dane said in reply. "Too long has Cronan awaited this day to relinquish the victory so easily. With Phelan's downfall, he'll have finally crushed the alliance."

"You can't know that for certain. They still look to you—"

"They'll look to me no more," he said in a snarl, "if I stand by and watch my own cousin humiliated, stripped of his ancestral lands. How could any of them trust me then, or be certain I wouldn't turn from them when they needed me most?"

"Yet if you defy my father, you'll give him the excuse he's always sought to destroy you." Quashing a swell of freshened fear, Arien gripped Dane's arm and tugged him to a halt. "Then where will any of us be who look to you for leadership? In the midst of the confusion and chaos, you must stand above it all. You must maintain a clear head, or we are all lost."

He jerked free of her hold. "I know my responsibilities. I'm just not sure how much more I can compromise."

"We've all had to compromise." Arien gave an unsteady laugh. "When the time is right, though—"

"And have you never considered, wife, that *my* time might not be yours? That mayhap it might just require the sacrifice of my life to arouse the nobles into the long-dreamed-of rebellion?"

The blood drained from Arien's face. "N-nay," she quavered. "I haven't . . . I won't consider such a horrible solution. I won't give you up now, no matter what my father, or Dorianne, or the—"

"Or the what?" Dane's gaze sharpened. "You've yet fully to explain what happened last night. And now you've not the excuse of exhaustion to hide behind."

"True enough." Though she agreed with him, Arien had no plans to tell Dane about that meeting anytime soon. He had enough to stew over without adding Garth Dorwen's hard-hearted demands. Besides, the dwarf had given her three days. Three days to think, to sort through all that had transpired at the Moondancer monastery, and to find an honorable, yet bloodless solution to it all. A solution that wouldn't require she become high priestess, yet would still fulfill her promise to the dwarf.

"This isn't the time, though," Arien continued, "to discuss such matters. We've an important meeting." She motioned that they should continue on their way. "Mayhap later, once we've come to some agreement with the king . . ."

"Aye," Dane muttered, stepping out once more, "when and *if* we come to any agreement."

They strode into the Great Hall, passing servants scurrying about their chores, and clusters of nobles and ladies talking and laughing, and walked up to the ornately draped dais, where the king sat upon his throne. The royal seneschal worked at a small table off to one side, industriously scribing all the king's commands. Nearby, Edana and Duke Nevyn Crowell stood together, speaking in low tones.

At Arien and Dane's approach, however, the pair fell silent. Crowell's lip curled into a sneer as he locked gazes with Dane, and Edana riveted her attention on her sister. Pretending to ignore the malicious aura emanating from Edana, Arien halted before the king and curtsied. Beside her, Dane drew up and bowed low.

"Come to deliver your share of the overdue taxes, m'lord?" Cronan inquired mildly.

"Aye, sire." Dane straightened. "And also to present your grandson, the young Lord Oren Haversin."

"Where is the lad?" the king asked, glancing around. "Is he ill, that you've not brought him to this audience? We heard of his early birth and prayed all would go well."

"All is well, sire," Arien replied. "Oren's fine. I thought 'twas better for us to talk before I sent for him."

"And what is there to talk about?" Edana asked, leaving Crowell's side to climb the dais and stand beside the king. "You have brought along the taxes, haven't you? 'Twould be impossible to grant yet another extension. Indeed, 'twould be unfair even of you to ask."

Outraged at her sister's audacity in speaking for the king, Arien opened her mouth to reply. Dane, however, quickly grasped her hand and gave it a warning squeeze. "The money, all of it, is here, delivered last eve to the royal treasury." He shot the seneschal a sharp look. "Obviously, your man here is remiss in reporting his receipt of the Haversin gold."

Cronan looked at the little man. "And pray, why is that?"

The seneschal's eyes widened. He swallowed convulsively. "The Pr-Princess Edana t-told me—"

"I told him," she smoothly interrupted, "first to have all the gold weighed and tested to ascertain its true worth. Only then can we be certain the full value of the taxes has been paid."

" 'Tis all there and more," Dane growled, his jaw clenching tightly. "Have no fear of that."

Edana smiled thinly. "Oh, I'm quite certain of that, m'lord. 'Twas merely a formality before official acceptance by the king."

"Unfortunately, the same cannot be said for Phelan Guilford," Cronan muttered, shaking his head. "That young lord, 'tis sad to say, is far in arrears. Did you know he had the effrontery to lock the gates of Dunbarton Castle to the men we sent to confiscate it?"

"I'd heard rumors, sire." Dane stepped forward until he stood at the bottom of the dais. " 'Twas yet another reason for our visit. Give Phelan more time to pay his taxes, I pray you. He is young and inexperienced, but means well. And he's fiercely devoted to his ancestral lands. To take Dunbarton from him would kill him."

The king sighed. "Well we know of Lord Phelan's devotion to his home. 'Twas why we gave him the extension. But to grant him more time would stir discontent among the other nobles who met the deadline. We cannot be found to be showing excessive favoritism to our closest relatives, can we?"

Dane looked at Arien, and the expression of weary resignation in his eyes told her all she needed to know. He'd feared this would be the king's answer, and had swallowed his pride and asked only because she'd begged him to.

Despair welled in her. Would her father never budge from his rigid stance? One glance at Edana's slyly triumphant smile answered Arien's question. It also stirred an anger that roused her to action.

"Aye, in this case you can—and should—Father." She moved to stand with her husband. " 'Twill be a gesture of good faith to the nobles, an assurance you wish to begin a new reign of tolerance and cooperation."

"And when did we make such a decision?" A frown formed between the king's bushy gray brows. He looked over his shoulder at Edana. "Do you recall our saying something to that effect? If we did, then 'twill be as Arien suggests, but we—"

"You've said no such thing, not now or ever," Edana snapped, glaring at Arien. "Suddenly, my sister imagines herself more highly placed than she is, to presume now to serve as your adviser. But *I* am the crown princess, not she."

Aye, you're crown princess, Arien thought, returning her sister's stare with an unwavering one of her own, but in name only, not by true right of birth. Those very words formed in her throat, hovered on her lips, but she refused to voice them. The time wasn't right. Indeed, if there were any way to avoid it, Arien would never reveal Edana's—and their mother's—shameful secret.

"The greater issue, to my mind, sire," Duke Crowell interjected, stepping forward to draw the king's attention, "is not what you will do to win the loyalty of your nobles, but what Lord Haversin is willing to do to prove his loyalty to you."

Out of the corner of her eye, Arien saw Dane clench his hands at his sides. "Sire," she hastened to say, knowing her opportunity to influence her father was fast fading, "for once in your life, I beg you, listen to someone other than the duke or Edana. They've advised you poorly all these years, and are—"

The king held up a silencing hand. "You do Duke Crowell and your sister a grave disservice. We'll hear no more." He turned to Crowell. "Your suggestion intrigues us, m'lord. Exactly what did you have in mind?"

"The Lord Phelan has offered you challenge in turning away your emissaries. 'Tis only fitting the Lord Haversin, as his cousin and your son-in-law, be the one to take his cousin to task for his insult to your royal personage. 'Twould also send a strong message to the other nobles, would it not, sire?"

"And seal, as well," Edana added softly, "the vow of fealty Lord Haversin made to you on his wedding day."

The king appeared to consider the suggestion, then nodded. "Aye, 'tis a fine idea, and a true test of the Lord Haversin's intentions."

"And I, sire, disagree," Dane warned with a deadly calm Arien knew presaged the explosion to come. " 'Twould test naught save my honor to ask me to discharge such a contemptible duty. Rather than question my loyalty, I'd suggest you examine the loyalty and motivations of the two who challenged it."

"Duke Crowell's loyalty to us is unrivaled!"

"Is it now, sire?" Dane leveled a piercing look at the duke. "Then he's shared all the gold he stole from me, has he?"

The king gave a start of surprise, then turned to Crowell. "You told us brigands attacked and robbed Lord Haversin. Have a care, m'lord, if his accusations prove—"

"The Lord Haversin attempts to divert your attention from the issue of *his* loyalty, by casting aspersions on mine, m'lord," Duke Crowell replied smoothly. " 'Tis an old ruse, one I'm certain you were about to recognize."

"Aye, Father," Edana said. " 'Tis apparent what game Lord Haversin plays. 'Tis also past time you put the question to him and demand an answer. Will he or won't he confiscate Lord Phelan's lands in your name?"

For an instant, the king appeared to waver, torn between Edana's demands and the doubts raised by Dane's accusations against Duke Crowell. Then the old hard, impenetrable expression returned, shuttering his true emotions. 'Twas too late, Arien realized. Edana had their father too deeply entrapped in her magical spells. He could barely make a decision anymore without her advisement.

" 'Tis a question well put." Once more, the king riveted his gaze on Dane. "What is your answer, m'lord?"

Dane turned to Arien. His haunted, yet resolute look seared straight to her heart. He'll sacrifice himself as he threatened he might, she thought. He sees no other recourse.

"Nay," she whispered, tears filling her eyes. "Nay. There's no purpose to this, no honor won or saved."

" 'Twas you who once warned I'd be as consumed by this terrible conflict as your father, if I continued to fight," he said softly. "That 'twould eventually rot my very soul."

"But I never meant for you to give up, to sacrifice your life!"

"And I pray 'twill not come to that." Dane smiled, a sad, loving look in his eyes. "But I refuse to destroy even one more life in this battle to best the king. There must be some other way, or we are all lost."

"Your answer, Lord Haversin," King Cronan boomed. "We'll have your answer, lest we're forced to accept the crown princess's and Duke Crowell's accusations against you."

"You'll believe what your daughter and that spineless toady want, no matter what I or anyone of integrity ever says to the contrary," Dane rasped, turning back to the king. " 'Tis your greatest failing, and 'twill be your downfall in the end. But I'll not be a part of your treachery, nor knowingly do harm to aid you in your vile plans."

"So, m'lord," Edana prodded, "you refuse the king his rightful request for your aid? You forswear the vow of fealty you made on our holiest of books?"

Dane stood tall and proud, never once wavering in his resolve. "Aye, that I do."

"There is naught else to be done then, sire," she said. "With his own words, Lord Haversin has condemned himself. He is guilty of the highest treason and must be executed."

"Aye, 'twould seem so," the king agreed reluctantly. He hesitated a moment more, then signaled to his guards. "Take the Lord Haversin to the dungeons," he ordered when five well-armed soldiers halted before him. "Chain him to the wall and post a company of men to assure he cannot escape, until the day of his execution."

Dane let the guards take him. He refused, however, to go quietly. " 'Twill do no good to kill me," he shouted as they led him away. "Another will rise to take my place, until you're finally defeated, or Greystone lies in ruins. Either way you'll have lost; either way you'll cease to rule. This battle can have no other outcome, for naught good can arise from evil. Naught!"

"Sister, I must speak with you."

Edana paused as she departed the Great Hall after Dane was led away, and turned to Arien. Her glance raked her sister. " 'Twill do you no good to ask me to beg Father for clemency. Your husband has been a thorn in Father's side for many years now. His punishment is long overdue."

Arien bit back a scathing retort. Though Edana despised weakness, she'd not tolerate a shouting match, either, and a matter of far greater import than her own pride was at stake here. "This isn't the place to discuss such matters," she forced herself to say quietly. "Pray, come with me to my bedchamber."

Her sister eyed her speculatively, then shrugged. "As you wish."

363

They uttered not another word as they walked along, though their passage drew raised brows and whispered comments from the servants. Onora, who'd stayed to watch Oren, was quickly dismissed, and the bedchamber door locked behind her. As Arien turned, however, she found her sister standing over her son's cradle.

Tamping down a frisson of fear, Arien hurried to stand beside her. Edana's expression, as she stared down at Oren, was a curious mixture of envy and anger. It was best, Arien decided, to divert attention from Oren posthaste.

"Despite all that has come between us," she began, "we are still sisters. Though you claim you'll not help me win Dane's freedom, surely there's something I can do to change your mind."

With a faint smile and the arch of an ebony brow, Edana turned at last from her avid contemplation of Oren. "I heard you lost no time visiting Dorianne last eve, before you arrived here," she replied unexpectedly. "I also heard, though Dorianne had cast you out, she quickly forgave all. Not only were you immediately reinstated into the Order, but she named you her successor. And then there was some mention of a dwarf present at the meeting, and that he threatened to claim your husband and son in repayment for some favor you owed him, if you didn't agree to become high priestess."

"I see there are Ravens masquerading as Moon-dancers in our midst."

"And I see at long last how you were able to best me that night," Edana countered smoothly, "and steal the Lord Haversin from me. You had that vile little dwarf teach you the dark powers."

"You left me no choice, sister."

Edana smiled. "As you leave me no choice in destroying your husband, unless . . ."

Arien went very still. Her eyes narrowed. "Unless what?"

" 'Tis said you claimed you had no wish to be high priestess, that all you desired was to return home to your husband and son." Edana paused and again glanced down at Oren, fingering his little hand-embroidered coverlet consideringly. "I could mayhap be persuaded to have Father spare your husband, if you were to reject Dorianne's demand to make you high priestess. He listens to me, Father does, and follows most everything I suggest."

"Aye," Arien muttered, "I imagine he does. I suppose you had no choice but to ensorcel him once Mother told him the truth?"

The fleeting look of surprise in Edana's eyes faded beneath the rapid onslaught of her rage. "So you know that, too, do you? Did you also know I killed Mother," she taunted, "when the bitch discovered I'd joined with the demon in my quest to become a Moondancer?"

The shock and intense horror Arien felt must have shown on her face. Edana smirked triumphantly. " 'Twas a fitting punishment for our slutish mother. Not only did she spread her legs where it gained her naught, but, in the doing, she destroyed all opportunities, both magical and royal, for her firstborn. You knew, of course, that the magic you wield so effortlessly came from Father's family, not Mother's?"

"Nay," Arien whispered, sickened now to the marrow of her bones, "I didn't know."

"Well, be that as it may, it must have filled you with the deepest satisfaction to discover you've been the true heir all along."

Arien gave an emphatic shake of her head. "Nay, sister. It didn't. I've never wished to rule, either as queen or high priestess. And I've no wish to do so now."

"Then you'll give it all up to me?"

"Aye, if you'll promise to renounce the Ravens and their evil deeds, and rule both Greystone and the Moondancers with fairness and love."

Edana gave an incredulous laugh. "Have you gone totally daft in your romantic dreaming? Such choices are no longer within my power, even if I wished them to be. The demon rules my every thought and action now."

Frustration filled Arien. Frustration and a deep, aching sadness. By the Mother, she didn't want to fight Edana and risk killing her, or be killed herself. But it seemed her sister was controlled now by an evil that refused to let go. "Then how can you expect me to surrender the position of high priestess to you?" she asked. "Indeed, how can I allow the illegitimacy of your birth to remain secret any longer?"

"And how can you not, sister dear? Unless, of course, you wish to risk losing your husband and, mayhap, even your child?" As if an immensely pleasurable thought had suddenly struck her, Edana chuckled softly. "It has just occurred to me that, whether you become high priestess or not, you'll still lose. 'Tis a sorry impasse, to be sure. A sorry impasse," she added, a malicious light gleaming in her dark eyes, "brought on by your pride and ambition, just as I warned you that day of your wedding."

As if the meeting with Edana wasn't enough, that eve Arien learned Dane's execution was set for three days hence. Duke Crowell had advised that three days would allow just enough time for the other nobles to arrive for the beheading, but not enough to make adequate plans for battle or to raise sufficient troops. The king, it seemed, had every avenue of escape covered. Dane's fate was sealed.

Harking back to her sister's smug assessment earlier that day, Arien realized there truly was no hope for her husband. Too many wished for, or stood to gain by, his death. And now, whether she wished it or not, she was as deeply embroiled as he.

Even if she became high priestess to honor Dorianne and please the dwarf, there was no guarantee she could defeat Edana before her sister turned on Dane. Indeed, there was no guarantee she could defeat her sister.

As the hours passed, she turned all the possible outcomes over and over in her mind, and still could see no way to save Dane. That admission mired her in the depths of despair. For a full day, Arien closeted herself in her room, refusing food or visitors. Then came the news that Dorianne had died.

"You must accept or decline, m'lady," Sister Ursla informed her on the eve of the second day of the dwarf's deadline. "The Assembly of Elders cannot await your answer indefinitely."

"How long?" Arien asked, barely able to lift her head to meet the other woman's gaze. "How long do I have?"

"The full moon rises on the morrow. The law requires that the next high priestess be named and invested on the night of the full moon following the last high priestess's death." Ursla sighed.

"I wish 'twere longer, but the timing of Dorianne's death . . ."

" 'Tis an unfortunate time for us all," Arien murmured. She forced herself to meet Ursla's troubled gaze. "Inform the Assembly, if you will, that they'll have my answer by then."

"I pray 'twill be the answer we all hope 'twill be." Ursla leaned forward and laid her hand atop Arien's. "We need you, m'lady, desperately so. The Moondancers *and* Greystone."

With that, the older woman rose and walked from the bedchamber, leaving Arien to the deepening shadows, the scents of flowering trees wafting in from the open window, and her anguished thoughts. It was too much to consider, to bear alone, the realization reverberated repeatedly through her. Once before she'd tried singlehandedly making a decision involving others—and one man in particular—and had barely escaped destroying her and Dane's budding relationship. "It was hardly different now, save that the same man seemed doomed no matter what decision was made. Nonetheless, Arien resolved, she owed Dane the courtesy of allowing him to decide the course of his own destiny.

After nursing Oren and dressing him in his sleeping shirt, she tucked her now sated, drowsy son into his cradle. Onora, apprised of her mistress's plans, agreed to remain with Oren until Arien's return. With a few magical words, Arien whisked herself from her room to the castle dungeons. A few words more, and the guards at their posts were asleep, and Dane's door was unlocked.

In the heavy gloom dimly illuminated by a single, smoky torch, Dane sat on his threadbare, wooden bed, chained to the wall. As the thick oak door creaked open on rust-stiffened hinges, he slowly, wearily lifted his head. After two days without much light, the sudden glare of the guardroom was too much for his eyes. They watered, burned, and, for a long moment, he couldn't see.

"Who's there?" he rasped, his voice almost as rusty as the door hinges.

" 'Tis I, Dane. Arien."

He blinked back his tears of pain, and rubbed his face on his grimy sleeve. "Arien?" Dane squinted, trying to make out her face. "Why have you come? Have I lost count of the days? Is my beheading already at hand?"

"Ah, nay, husband," she cried, running to him then and throwing herself down to kneel at his feet. "I came but to see you, talk with you."

The thick chains clanked and clattered as he reached out and stroked her ebony hair. By all that was holy, Dane thought, she felt so good. He cupped her chin in his palm, lifting her face to his searching gaze. " 'Tisn't Oren, is it? He's not ill, is he?"

"Nay, nay," Arien crooned. "Our son is fine, and growing fatter every day." She turned her face into his hand, her soft lips nuzzling, then kissing him. "Ah, my love. I've missed you so."

"As I have you, sweet wife." Dane chuckled. "How did you manage to convince your father to allow the condemned man one last visit?"

" 'Twas simple," she replied, a smile lifting her lips. "I didn't ask. And the guards were most docile once I ensorceled them."

He frowned. "I thought I had your promise not to practice magic anymore."

"And if *I* recall correctly, that promise applied only to Haversin." She pulled back and gazed up at him, her eyes filled with an earnest concern. "You're not angry with me, are you? Truly, I didn't think you'd take offense—"

"Hush, my love." Dane laid a callused finger to her lips. "I took no offense, nor imagined you broke your vow. 'Twas always wrong of me to have asked such a sacrifice. I release you of that onerous promise here and now."

Arien sighed. " 'Tis best you do. I've come to free you and need my magic to do so. 'Tis too dangerous for you or Oren to remain in Greystone any longer."

"Indeed? And where do you imagine we'd be safe? Once before you warned me Edana would seek me out wherever I went. What has transpired in the meanwhile to change that?"

"There's hope your friend, the king of Anacreon, could protect you. 'Twould be only for a short while," she hurried to add, "until I find some way to best Edana. Then you and Oren could return."

"And what of you?" A chill finger of apprehension ran down Dane's spine. He caught Arien by the arms. "What would become of you while we were gone?"

"You know as well as I what must happen. Edana and the Ravens must be stopped."

"Well, 'tisn't my way to turn tail and run while my wife stays behind to do battle."

"You don't understand." There was an edge of desperation in her voice. "Edana has made it clear she wants to be high priestess. If I accept the position instead, she vows to kill you. Yet if I don't, the dwarf vows to take both you and Oren from me."

Dane's grip tightened on Arien's arms. "Edana wanting me dead I can understand. But why would the dwarf do such a thing? He's our friend."

"As much a friend as a creature looking out for his own kind can be," she said with a sniff. "I'll tell you true, Dane. He wants me to become high priestess as fiercely as Edana fears it. Which places you in a very vulnerable position."

Tenderness filled him. "Ah, sweet wife, 'tisn't so much I who am vulnerable, but the love you bear me that makes you vulnerable. 'Tis even, I'd wager, the true source of your distress."

She stifled a sob. "Naught is easy or simple as once 'twas. Either way, it seems certain I'll lose you. Do you understand now why you must take Oren and flee Greystone this very night?" She touched his shackles, first his right wrist, then his left. With a spray of sparks and a crackle, the metal bands fell away. "Come away now," Arien urged, tugging him to his feet. "Now, before 'tis too late."

Dane pulled Arien to him, cradling her head upon his breast. " 'Tis already too late, wife, and well you know it. Neither Edana nor the dwarf would permit you to send me away. To do so would be to relinquish their greatest leverage over you. And, in the battle to keep me here, Oren might well be endangered."

He paused to kiss her slowly, gently, savoring the taste and feel of her. Indeed, Dane thought, this moment might be all he'd ever have with Arien again. Her cheeks were wet with tears. Ever so carefully, he wiped them away. "In the end,

Oren is what matters, not I," he then whispered hoarsely. "He is Haversin's hope for the future."

"Don't talk like that." Arien wept. "You matter, too. I want, I need, my husband as well as my son."

"And I want to live, for you and our son." Dane gazed down into her eyes. "But as I once was forced to make a choice between my people and my family, now so must you."

"But I don't want to choose. I haven't your strength or courage. All I want is to be your wife, and Oren's mother!"

"And what has strength or courage to do with it, sweet lady?" Dane asked, overcome with a poignant remembrance of similar words she'd once spoken to him. Words that had come full circle to test and torment her, in the bittersweet destiny that was now their lives. " 'Tis what we are that permits us to do naught less than our very best," he said softly, achingly, "though 'tis the antithesis of what we'd choose to do . . . if we had a choice."

Chapter Twenty-two

As Arien left Castle Talamontes, a warm rain began to fall. It was barely dusk and, though she'd once before needed the moonlight to perform the more difficult forms of magic such as flight, Arien now also possessed the powers of the Earth. These she now harnessed to do her bidding.

The force of her magic lifted her high above the trees, carrying her into the twilight-shadowed countryside. To cover her passing, Arien added a spell of invisibility. She did not want Edana to discover her clandestine visit to the dwarf.

It was the eve of the third day, the deadline he'd given her to decide if she'd assume the office of high priestess. It was also the night of the full moon, when she must render the Assembly of Elders her answer. First, though, Arien meant to seek out the dwarf.

There was but one hope, dishonorable as it might be, still left her. *'Tis the power to subdue if not totally destroy a dwarf's magical abilities*—the words threaded through her mind. And then

Garth Dorwen had told her his name.

Perhaps that knowledge could at last be used to her advantage. Arien fervently hoped so. Why did everything have to depend on her? Why wasn't the dwarf's dark magic equal to Edana's? And why couldn't some other Moondancer be high priestess? There were still so many questions yet unexplained, Arien thought as she alighted finally at the base of the standing stone. Questions she would have answered this night, or know the reasons why not.

The rain continued, settling gently onto freshly budded leaves and tender shoots of grass. The fragrance of rich, damp earth rose on a faint eddy of air, chasing before it a haunting perfume of wood violets. Arien paused to inhale the soul-stirring scents, willing them to fortify her for the battle to come. Then, shoulders squared, she circled the mound until she reached the spot where she knew the dwarf's magical door to be.

"Come forth," Arien cried. "Now, before I break down your door!"

"And what purpose would that serve?" an irritated, gravelly voice demanded from behind her. "A little taken wi' yerself these days, aren't ye, to be issuing such toplofty commands?"

Arien swung around. "How . . . how did you get out without my knowing it?" She glanced about uneasily. "I sensed no magic wrought, yet here . . . here you are."

"Did ye think I'd only one way in or out?" Garth Dorwen gave a snort of disgust. "Truly, fair princess, ye depend far too much on magic." His stubby hands fisted on his hips. "Well, what is it? What do ye wish, to disturb me so rudely at supper?"

"What do you think I wish?" she snapped. " 'Tis the third day. You said you wanted my answer by the end of the third day."

He arched a shaggy brow and cocked his head. "Aye, so I did. Well, what's it to be then? My supper grows cold e'en as we stand about and yammer."

Irritation flooded Arien. "You'd like that, wouldn't you? To see me rushing to do your will, so you can then get back to your supper. Well, 'twill not be." Angrily, Arien gestured to the sky. "The least you can do is to stop the rain before we sink ankle-deep into the mud."

"Ankle-deep," the dwarf muttered. "The grass is hardly wet. And if ye're so set on the rain stopping, do it yerself."

Arien sucked in a startled breath. "I can't stop rain . . . can I?"

"Ye havena a clue, have ye, as to the full extent o' yer powers." He rolled his eyes, then lifted his gaze to the heavens. "And this is the best ye can do, is it?" he then seemed to ask the Mother above.

"Don't play games with me, dwarf!" Arien made an angry swipe toward the sky. Immediately, the rain stopped. Startled, she shot a glance upward. Then, with a disbelieving snort, Arien forged doggedly on. "I want answers. I'm weary of everyone else, save me, knowing what's going on. And, vow or no, you'll get naught more from me until I get those answers!"

The dwarf eyed her narrowly. "And if I don't? What will ye do then?"

So he thought to call her bluff, did he? "Have you forgotten what power you gave me in telling me your name?"

The color drained from the dwarf's face. His swarthy complexion turned a sallow gray. "Ye wouldna do such a thing. 'Tis . . . 'tis dishonorable."

"And what would you call your hard-hearted manipulation of me all these months?" Arien countered, her temper rising. " 'Tis past dishonorable, I'd say. 'Tis despicable!"

"Well, be that as it may, ye said ye wanted answers. So what would ye know from me?" He scowled, his mouth twisting in annoyance. "I told ye afore, my supper grows cold and I—"

"Ah, cease your peevish prattle!" Arien burst out irritably. She made another swipe in the air. "There, that cursed meal of yours is back in the cook pot. 'Twill stay warm for hours now."

The dwarf's eyes widened. "Yer magic's strong, to penetrate the protective circle about my den. Stronger than I dared e'en hope." He paused to eye her consideringly. "Ye didna burn my supper, did ye?"

She dragged in an exasperated breath. "Nay, but if you don't stop your yammering about it, I'll burn more than that."

Surprisingly, Garth Dorwen grinned. "A bit feisty, aren't ye? Marriage and motherhood have set well wi' ye, I can see."

Arien glared back at him.

He sighed. "Fine, fine. What do ye wish to know?"

"Why can't *you* go up against Edana? Why must it be me? And why must *I* be high priestess?"

"When ye dinna get yer questions answered, they've a tendency to build up, dinna they?" the dwarf observed with a smirk. "But I'll answer them and gladly," he hurried to add when anger flashed once again in Arien's eyes "if ye'll jest give me a moment. Firstly, 'tis forbidden for a dwarf to lift a hand agin' a Moondancer, e'er since we made a pact wi' yer kind so long ago. If we did, 'twould be the end to our magic once and fer all. And e'en a rebel Moondancer is still a Moondancer.

"As far as why must it be ye, well, I told ye once afore, ye are one o' the most adept o' yer kind. Ye were born wi' powers greater than most, powers Dorianne recognized and fostered."

"Powers you then decided to manipulate to your own purpose."

Garth Dorwen chuckled. "If the truth be told, I did little, save aid ye a bit in pointing ye down the road to yer destiny. Ye were always meant to join wi' the Lord Dane. I but e'ened the odds when yer sister chose to step 'atween ye and the love o' yer heart."

"And what of my dark powers?" Arien demanded. "Will you also claim not to have had any involvement in that?"

"I but opened the door to those deeper, darker skills. 'Twas ye who flung it wide, each time ye joined wi' yer man. Besides, 'twas past time the Moondancers had another high priestess of the highest powers—and that could only be one who'd coupled wi' a man. Edana knew that, and cold-bloodedly set out to achieve that aim. Ye were also destined to travel the same path."

He spoke true, Arien realized, looking back on the tortuous journey her life had taken. She'd always loved and wanted Dane, even as a young girl, even as she fiercely quashed the emotions and turned anew to her Moondancer vows. Yet she couldn't deny him forever. When Dane became Edana's unwitting pawn, she had found it impossible to remain aloof or uninvolved any longer.

But had she truly, as the dwarf claimed, flung wide the doors to her destiny, a destiny that had always led to this moment? If so, she'd freely chosen the path she'd walked—princess, Moondancer, wife and lover, mother. But high priestess and lifelong wielder of magic? For some reason, Arien still found it difficult to embrace that role as wholeheartedly as she'd embraced all the rest.

"I can't be high priestess," she whispered. "I don't want it. I never did."

"Ye fight what ye shouldna, fair princess," the dwarf chided softly. " 'Tis yer destiny, as much as 'tis yer destiny to love yer man and child."

Arien shook her head. "I'm too afraid. Please . . . choose another."

"Aye, ye're afraid. 'Tis the reason ye fight it so. But ye must accept the moonstone o' office and all it entails, or we are all lost. Ye're the only one who can stop yer sister. Ye're our last and only hope."

"And what if, in the doing, this magic of mine corrupts me?" she cried, fiercely blinking back her tears. "What if, in the victory, I lose all I hold dear?"

The dwarf smiled sadly, and shrugged. " 'Tis a dilemma, is it not? A riddle still to be solved. I only pray ye discover its answer afore 'tis too late."

A painful lump of desolation swelled in her throat. "Aye, as do I. As do I." With a final, anguished look, Arien turned and began to walk away.

"What will ye do, fair princess?" Garth Dorwen called after her. "Ye've yet to give me yer answer."

"I go to accept the office of high priestess," Arien replied, not even pausing to glance back. " 'Tis the antithesis of what I'd choose, if I truly had a choice. But I don't. You know that, have always known. And now I know it, too."

The ceremony of the full moon would be held in the Glen of Women at moonrise. Arien was to meet with the Assembly of Elders there and give them her answer. It wouldn't be long now, she thought, glancing at the ivory disk already beginning its majestic ascent into the ebony canopy of the sky. First, though, she meant to return to Castle Talamontes and Dane. After the dwarf, he must be the first to know all she planned. He must be protected, as must Oren, before she sought out her sister.

It would be wisest to weave a spell of protection about her husband and child. Not only would the spell keep them safe from Edana, but, if she failed to return from her meeting with her sister, the spell would also protect them from her father. Protect Dane, the love of her heart, and her precious babe, Oren.

As she made her way down the dungeon stairs, a fetid odor wafted up from the cavernous depths. A frigid gust of air swirled around her, lifting her skirts and chilling Arien to the bone. She moved as if through a thick mist, her actions slow, awkward, heavy.

Then she saw the guards sprawled everywhere, lifeless, eyes staring, and the door to Dane's cell flung open. Terror engulfed her. Edana had been here. The taint of her magic was unmistakable.

Somehow, she'd discerned Arien's intent to become high priestess. And, true to her word, she'd taken Dane.

With a lift of her arm and a swirl of her hand, Arien cast a spell of flight that took her through the castle's thick walls and sent her winging her way into the black night. There were many places Edana could have taken Dane, but Arien ventured a guess he was now deep in the bowels of the earth, hidden away in the Ravens' ceremonial cave.

There was no time to be lost. Even now, Dane could be in the gravest danger, hanging to life by the slenderest of threads—if not already dead. Arien cursed herself for not seeing to Dane's protection sooner. Instead, she'd been confused, overwrought, grasping for anything that would give her the answers she needed.

Before, Arien had always found solutions to any dilemma placed before her. As long as she trusted in her intelligence, her magic, there had been nothing she couldn't ultimately do. But if Dane should now die because of her negligence . . .

The possibility filled Arien with terror. Before she had wed Dane, she'd lived her life complacently, and with a certain smug certitude that she was in control of all she did. Indeed, it had been easy, as emotionally isolated as she'd been from others. She'd never known her mother and, though she'd tried mightily to love her father, it had always been a detached sort of love. He'd hurt her too many times to risk more. All she had truly loved, until she'd met Dane, was her magic.

That was why she'd been so afraid to relinquish it. It had been her pride, her ultimate means of control over her life.

But magic was a poor replacement for human intimacy and love. A poor replacement threatening to lead her down a dark, dangerous path if it was practiced in isolation. Magic, to be used well, must be tempered with wisdom, insight, and love. All of which, Arien realized belatedly, could only be learned in contact with, and understanding of, others.

Aye, there was much risked and possibly lost this night, she admitted, alighting at last at the well-hidden mouth of the cave she'd long known to be the Ravens' ceremonial gathering place. Using her magical night vision, Arien probed the cave until she at last discerned a faint light. Someone was within. A sixth sense whispered that it was Edana.

As Arien made her swift passage down the tortuous tunnel of stone, a feminine voice, rife with savage satisfaction, reached her ears. It was Edana, talking to someone. What Arien heard filled her with fury.

"She was a fool to imagine I'd let you live," Edana was saying, "whether she surrendered the role of high priestess to me or not. In her love for you, and yours for her, you were an endless source of power to her. Because of that, high priestess or not, Arien would have always been a potential threat. I dare not let you live."

On a murmur of air, Arien halted just inside the opening to the main cavern. Illuminated by hundreds of magically fed torches, the huge chamber was a maze of stalactites and stalagmites formed by the minerals seeping from the earth. Slick and shiny, the stone walls oozed moisture that reflected the torches' eerily flickering light. Only the very center of the cavern appeared dry, and there the Ravens had placed their sacrificial altar.

That was where Arien found Edana, standing over Dane. Spread-eagled to the four corners of the massive stone altar, he lay there unmoving, the front of his tunic ripped apart to expose his sweat-sheened chest. With all his might he struggled against the spell Edana had cast over him, his blue eyes blazing with defiance.

" 'Twill do you no good, my handsome lord," Edana purred, stroking the tip of the long, sacrificial knife down the middle of his chest. "Indeed, you should wish to die now rather than live to see me destroy your wife. 'Twill be ugly, and horrible to behold."

As she spoke, Edana began to press the knife downward. Yet even as she did, her hand froze. She frowned, pushed harder. Still, nothing happened.

"Arien!" she shrieked in outrage. With the knife still gripped in her hand, she swung about.

"Did you think I wouldn't know you'd taken my husband?" Arien asked, halting but a few feet from her. "Your days of subterfuge and evil deeds are at an end, sister. You'll cease now, once and forever, or 'twill go very badly for you."

Edana gave a shrill, derisive laugh. "It has always gone badly for me, from the day you were born. 'Tis an inequity that won't be remedied until the day you die."

"My existence was never the source of your life-long torment," Arien shot back. " 'Twas your inability to forgive Mother and Father."

"They were both weak and stupid," her sister spat, "and more than aught else, I despise weakness and stupidity."

"Then you don't understand how high a heart can still soar, though it once groveled in the dust. 'Tis the secret to forgiveness, both for others and yourself."

"Father was a fool!" Edana's lips curled in disgust. "He should have suspected Mother's infidelity long before she told him."

"Have you never considered that mayhap he did know?" Arien countered softly. "But that, in his love for Mother, for you, he chose to ignore it? If no one knew, no one could ever question the legitimacy of your birth, or your claim to the throne."

Edana blanched. She staggered back, the knife plummeting to the ground. "F-father never loved me," she croaked out in disbelief. "At least not once he discovered I wasn't his."

"How do you know that, Edana?" Arien stepped closer, until she stood at Dane's head. "You never gave him a chance. 'Twas soon thereafter you began your ensorcelment of him, was it not?"

For a fleeting moment, doubt and confusion seemed to flare in Edana's eyes. "I-I couldn't risk his disinheriting me. 'Twas all I had . . . my power . . . my position." Then, as if the demon's influence took hold once more, her features hardened into a mask of cold determination. " 'Tis too late," she muttered. "Father will remain bespelled until I need him no more. In the meanwhile, you and your precious husband must die."

"And you know I cannot let this travesty continue." Arien dragged in an unsteady breath. "Time and again I've asked, even begged you to renounce the Ravens and return to the holy path. Now I ask you no more. Renounce the Ravens, sister, or renounce your magic. It can be no other way."

Edana chuckled maliciously. "If you think to best my demon-spawned powers, sister, you're an even greater fool than our father. See for yourself if I'm still the inept apprentice." Lifting her hand, she flung a bolt of blazing green light at Arien.

With only the quickest of reflexes, Arien defended herself. The intensity of the blast, however, sent her staggering backward against the stone altar. She straightened, regained her composure, and smiled grimly. "You are indeed powerful. Shall I take that reply, then, to mean you refuse to renounce the Ravens?"

"Fool!" Once more, Edana sent forth a fiery green light. And, once more, the ferocity of the impact knocked Arien backward. She gasped in surprise, momentarily encompassed by a power so malevolent it turned her blood to ice and set her heart to pounding painfully. A shard of terror, of doubt as to her abilities to withstand such demon-strengthened powers, stabbed through her.

This time, however, as she gripped the altar to support herself, a large, callused hand clasped hers. Startled, Arien turned and met Dane's glittering gaze. In the measureless depths of his eyes, she found a fierce resolve, an ardent love, and the strength to do what must be done.

. . . *Loving him will teach ye far more o' life and what truly matters than all those holy Moondancer precepts e'er could*, the dwarf had once assured her. *How else do ye think ye'll e'er open yer eyes and name the secret? How else will ye find yer way through the frightful morass yer sister and her Ravens have cast us all in?*

The secret . . . Was that the final piece to the puzzle? Arien wondered. She'd learned so much in the past months of loving Dane. She'd learned much, as well, in the cauldron of pain and sacrifice that love had demanded of her. If, after all she'd endured, she still wasn't ready—as the dwarf's ancient song had bemoaned—then she never would be. With Dane at her side to strengthen and encourage her, what else was necessary?

The secret of her shame and glory . . . Suddenly, the answer flooded Arien with a brilliant, blinding clarity. It was the cause of the Moondancers' and dwarves' tragic downfall, and the tragedy of her own past life as well.

Nothing in itself, in isolation from life and people, was good or well used. Yet the Moondancers and dwarves had worshiped their magic beyond its true value, placing it above considerations of conscience and honor, of human love and kindness, of just plain fairness and common sense. Now, the only glory left them was to name that terrible failing, to forgive themselves and learn from it in all humility. And then never, ever, to allow such a tragedy to occur again.

"Nay, Edana," Arien said softly, achingly, " 'tis you and your mentor who are the fools. But not me, not ever again, and not the Moondancers, nor the dwarves, nor all of Greystone."

With that revelation, a strength such as Arien had never known before filled her. It seemed to emanate from the earth on which she stood, yet flowed as well through the stones overhead, as if it poured from the heavens above. Moon goddess and Mother Earth, she thought with a fierce elation, joined once more in battle against the demon. Joined in her . . . the source of the magic that wove it all together.

Do ye begin to see it at last? Do ye? 'Tis yer destiny, fair princess, and a glorious one 'tis. . . .

Clasping Dane's hand tightly, Arien lifted her other hand and released a long, concentrated blast of green light. As the light struck her, Edana gave a choking cry, lurched back, then stood rooted there, shuddering helplessly. Her mouth moved in soundless horror; her gaze was piteous, pleading, as all her magic unraveled, like the threads of some huge tapestry.

At long last, Arien freed her sister. As Edana slumped weakly to the ground, Arien wove a spell that sent her back to the castle and the haven of her bedchamber. Then Arien turned to Dane. The spell holding him in thrall dissipated before the force of her magic, and she helped him rise.

Wordlessly, they clung to each other, still not quite certain they understood all that had just transpired, almost afraid to believe the terrible days were behind them at last. Finally, though, Dane released her and stepped back. " 'Tis the end, then? Edana will never be a threat again?"

"Aye, 'tis the end." Arien took in her husband's disheveled appearance, from his torn, sweat-stained tunic to his wild mane of hair, and smiled. It was indeed over, she thought, relief flooding her until she felt almost giddy. Their lives and destinies were once more firmly in their hands, as they had always been meant to be. "Mayhap I'll finally have the chance now to get to know the woman Edana was always meant to be. Mayhap we can finally and truly be sisters."

Dane grinned down at her. "And when will you have time to spare for that, what with your new duties as Moondancer high priestess, mother to a growing boy, and wife to a man who intends to make long and frequent amends for his former pigheaded and unfair treatment of you?"

"Long and frequent amends, eh?" Arien asked with a giggle as she turned and, arm in arm, walked with Dane from the cavern. "Oh, have no fear, my ardent mate. I'll find the time and more. Like a starving man long denied, I come to the banquet with greedy anticipation. And I intend to sample all the delights of the table, beginning most assuredly"—she paused to lift on tiptoe and kiss him thoroughly and deeply—"with you."

Epilogue

A spring-kissed breeze, warmed by the late-morning sun and redolent of budding flowers and dark, damp earth, wafted through the castle garden. Blossoming cherry trees quivered and shook, blanketing the tender, emerging blades of grass with their pale pink petals. Overhead, high in a towering elm, a mother bird, a fat worm dangling from her beak, hopped through the gently swaying limbs until she at last reached her ravenous nestling. With one efficient dip of her head, she deposited the delectable morsel in her offspring's gaping mouth. Then, with a flutter of sapphire blue wings, she soared back into the heavens.

From his vantage on the sprawling stone balcony, Dane briefly followed the bird's flight, then turned to the tall, sable-haired man standing beside him. "Life is rich, good," he murmured consideringly. "Mayhap even more so now, because I was once bereft and despairing."

"Aye," Aidan, king of the neighboring realm of Anacreon, agreed. "Those long-starved appreciate the banquet far more than those never deprived. They have learned never to take aught for granted. Not now, or ever."

Feminine laughter mingled with childish squeals of delight. Both men turned and gazed in eager anticipation across the expanse of flowers and shrubs to where the huge, stone dragon fountain stood, spewing forth its watery version of fire. Two young women, one ebony-haired, the other golden, paused there, watching their sons splashing in the turbulent pool. In the golden-haired woman's arms slept a babe. In the ripely rounding belly of the ebony-haired woman grew another.

"Aye," Aidan reiterated softly, huskily, "life is indeed good."

Dane nodded. " 'Tis what makes our separations all the harder, when I must needs return to Haversin and Arien must remain here. Her father's unexpected death six months ago left much in turmoil. We hope, though, in time, to set things aright, and leave more of the day-to-day matters of ruling the kingdom to a council of dwarves and Moondancers. 'Tis our fondest dream, you can be sure."

" 'Tis a dream I'm certain you'll attain." Watching his wife and son splashing happily in the dragon fountain, Aidan felt himself warm with affection. "It takes a strong, fearless, determined woman to love men such as us, my friend. And such women will never be overcome by aught that keeps them from the men they love."

"Yet, in the end, what has strength or courage to do with it? They could do no less," Dane observed, engulfed with a poignantly sweet recollection. "Not, at least, without going against everything that makes them who they are."

"Just as we would not be who we are if we stopped loving them."

Dane smiled in agreement, his soul tranquil, his heart at peace. As he stood there, pondering it all, the sun disappeared behind an errant cloud. Then, in a blaze of light, its rays pierced through, gilding the land in luminous glory.

Strands of gold the sunbeams were, precious and rare, Dane thought in sudden, joyous remembrance. As precious and rare as true love . . . as forgiveness of oneself and others. It only remained to discover this, like one must someday unravel the twisted strands of one's destiny, and name the secret at last. Discover the rightful, and only, source of all pride and honor.

Dear Reader,

Well, in case you didn't recognize my cleverly disguised fairy tale, it was based on Rumpelstiltskin. Yeah, I know, the ending didn't turn out quite the same. The dwarf didn't lose and fall through the floor in a fit of anger after finally being thwarted by the heroine. But then, I never particularly liked that ending. Though old Rumple wasn't right to demand her child, she *did* give her word and should have found some way to honor it. He did, after all, give her what she asked, and saved her from the greedy king in the bargain. And then the heroine married this king and lived happily ever after with him? Well, I guess that's definitely a case of "to each his own." Kind of makes you almost feel sympathetic to old Rumple.

At any rate, I hope you enjoyed *Strands of Gold*. For those of you who've already read *Demon Prince* and know all about Aidan and Breanne's story, I hope the tiny peek into their lives in the epilogue was satisfying. And for those of you yet to discover that Waldenbooks bestseller and Romance Writers of America RITA finalist for Best Paranormal Romance of 1994, it's still available from Love Spell. For an excerpted flyer of *Strands of Gold* with a list of my past and upcoming books, please write to me at P.O. Box 62365, Colorado Springs, CO 80962. A self-addressed, stamped, business-size envelope is appreciated.

Happy reading!
Kathleen Morgan

Futuristic Romance

KATHLEEN MORGAN

Demon Prince. Breanne has heard the legends about the Demon Prince, but the man who saves her from certain death is as gentle and kind as he is reckless and virile. Breanne vows to uncover Aidan's secrets and to quench the fires he has ignited in her innocent heart.

___52237-3 $5.50 US/$6.50 CAN

Firestar. Sheltered and innocent, Meriel is loath to mate with the virile alien captive her mother has chosen. But during a night of lovemaking their souls touch, and when devious forces threaten to separate them, Gage and Meriel set out across the universe and back to save their love.

___52218-7 $5.50 US/$6.50 CAN

Dorchester Publishing Co., Inc.
P.O. Box 6640
Wayne, PA 19087-8640

Please add $1.75 for shipping and handling for the first book and $.50 for each book thereafter. NY, NYC, and PA residents, please add appropriate sales tax. No cash, stamps, or C.O.D.s. All orders shipped within 6 weeks via postal service book rate. Canadian orders require $2.00 extra postage and must be paid in U.S. dollars through a U.S. banking facility.

Name_____
Address_____
City_____ State_____ Zip_____
I have enclosed $_____ in payment for the checked book(s).
Payment <u>must</u> accompany all orders. ❑ Please send a free catalog

Futuristic Romance

CRYSTAL FIRE
KATHLEEN MORGAN

"A unique and magical tale!"
—Janelle Taylor

The message is explicit—no other man will do but the virile
warrior. Determined that Brace must join her quest, Marissa
rescues him from unjust imprisonment, then nurses him back
to strength. She never tells the arrogant male that he is just
a pawn to exchange for her sister's freedom. But during the
long, cold nights Marissa finds herself irresistibly drawn to
the hard warrior's body, and as the danger-filled days fly
by, she knows her desperate mission is doomed to failure.
For how can she save her sister by betraying the only man
she can ever love?

_52065-6 $5.50 US/$7.50 CAN

**Three captivating stories of love in another time,
another place.**

MADELINE BAKER
"Heart of the Hunter"

A Lakota warrior must defy the boundaries of life itself to claim the spirited beauty he has sought through time.

ANNE AVERY
"Dream Seeker"

On faraway planets, a pilot and a dreamer learn that passion can bridge the heavens, no matter how vast the distance from one heart to another.

KATHLEEN MORGAN
"The Last Gatekeeper"

To save her world, a dazzling temptress must use her powers of enchantment to open a stellar portal—and the heart of a virile but reluctant warrior.

__51974-7 *Enchanted Crossings* (three unforgettable love stories in one volume) $4.99 US/
$5.99 CAN

Dorchester Publishing Co., Inc.
P.O. Box 6640
Wayne, PA 19087-8640

Please add $1.75 for shipping and handling for the first book and $.50 for each book thereafter. NY, NYC, and PA residents, please add appropriate sales tax. No cash, stamps, or C.O.D.s. All orders shipped within 6 weeks via postal service book rate. Canadian orders require $2.00 extra postage and must be paid in U.S. dollars through a U.S. banking facility.

Name_____
Address_____
City_____State_____Zip_____
I have enclosed $_____ in payment for the checked book(s).
Payment <u>must</u> accompany all orders. ❑ Please send a free catalog

A Faerie Tale Romance

Prince of Kisses

COLLEEN SHANNON

Daughter of wealth and privilege, lovely Charlaine Kimball is known to Victorian society as the Ice Princess. But when a brash intruder dares to take a king's ransom in jewels from her private safe, indignation burns away her usual cool reserve. And when the handsome rogue presumes to steal a kiss from her untouched lips, forbidden longing sets her soul ablaze.

Illegitimate son of a penniless Frenchwoman, Devlin Rhodes is nothing but a lowly bounder to the British aristocrats who snub him. But his leapfrogging ambition engages him in a dangerous game. Now he will have to win Charlaine's hand in marriage—and have her begging for the kiss that will awaken his heart and transform him into the man he was always meant to be.

—52200-4 $5.99 US/$6.99 CAN

Dorchester Publishing Co., Inc.
P.O. Box 6640
Wayne, PA 19087-8640

GIVE YOUR HEART TO THE GENTLE BEAST
AND FOREVER SHARE LOVE'S SWEET FEAST

Raised amid a milieu of bountiful wealth and enlightened ideas, Callista Raleigh is more than a match for the radicals, rakes, and reprobates who rail against England's King George III. Then a sudden reversal of fortune brings into her life a veritable brute who craves revenge against her family almost as much as he hungers for her kiss. And even though her passionate foe conceals his face behind a hideous mask, Callista believes that he is merely a man, with a man's strengths and appetites. But when the love-starved stranger sweeps her away to his secret lair, Callista realizes that wits and reason aren't enough to conquer him—she'll need a desire both satisfying and true if beauty is to tame the beast.

_52143-1 $5.99 US/$6.99 CAN

Dorchester Publishing Co., Inc.
P.O. Box 6640
Wayne, PA 19087-8640

Please add $1.75 for shipping and handling for the first book and $.50 for each book thereafter. NY, NYC, and PA residents, please add appropriate sales tax. No cash, stamps, or C.O.D.s. All orders shipped within 6 weeks via postal service book rate. Canadian orders require $2.00 extra postage and must be paid in U.S. dollars through a U.S. banking facility.

Name_____
Address_____
City_____ State_____ Zip_____
   have enclosed $_____ in payment for the checked book(s).
Payment <u>must</u> accompany all orders. ☐ Please send a free catalog.

Someone's Been Sleeping In My Bed

A Faerie Tale Romance

LINDA JONES

**WHO'S BEEN EATING FROM MY BOWL?
IS SHE A BEAUTY IN BOTH HEART AND
SOUL?
WHO'S BEEN SITTING IN MY CHAIR?
IS SHE PRETTY OF FACE AND FAIR OF
HAIR?
WHO'S BEEN SLEEPING IN MY BED?
IS SHE THE DAMSEL I WILL WED?**

The golden-haired woman barely escapes from a stagecoach robbery before she gets lost in the Wyoming mountains. Hungry, harried, and out of hope, she stumbles on a rude cabin, the home of three brothers, great bears of men who nearly frighten her out of her wits. But Maddalyn Kelly is no Goldilocks; she is a feisty beauty who can fend for herself. Still, how can she ever guess that the Barrett boys will bare their souls to her—or that one of them will share with her an ecstasy so exquisite it is almost unbearable?

_52094-X $5.99 US/$6.99 CAN

**Dorchester Publishing Co., Inc.
P.O. Box 6640
Wayne, PA 19087-8640**

Please add $1.75 for shipping and handling for the first book an $.50 for each book thereafter. NY, NYC, and PA residents please add appropriate sales tax. No cash, stamps, or C.O.D.s. A orders shipped within 6 weeks via postal service book rate. Canadian orders require $2.00 extra postage and must be paid in U.S. dollars through a U.S. banking facility.

Name_____
Address_____
City_____ State_____ Zip_____
I have enclosed $_____ in payment for the checked book(s
Payment <u>must</u> accompany all orders. ❏ Please send a free catalo:

A Faerie Tale Romance

Big Bad Wolf by Linda Jones. Big and wide and strong, Wolf Trevelyan's shoulders are just right for his powerful physique—and Molly Kincaid wonders what his arms would feel like wrapped tightly around her. Molly knows she should be scared of the dark stranger. She's been warned of Wolf's questionable past. But there's something compelling in his gaze, something tantalizing in his touch—something about Wolf that leaves Molly willing to throw caution, and her grandmother's concerns, to the wind to see if love won't find the best way home.

___52179-2 $5.50 US/$6.50 CAN

The Emperor's New Clothes by Victoria Alexander. Cardsharp Ophelia Kendrake is mistaken for the Countess of Bridgewater and plans to strip Dead End, Wyoming, of its fortunes before escaping into the sunset. But the free-spirited beauty almost swallows her script when she meets Tyler Matthews, the town's virile young mayor. Tyler simply wants to settle down and enjoy the simplicity of ranching. But his aunt and uncle are set on making a silk purse out of Dead End, and Tyler is going to be the new mayor. It's a job he accepts with little relish—until he catches a glimpse of the village's newest visitor.

___52159-8 $5.50 US/$6.50 CAN

Dorchester Publishing Co., Inc.
P.O. Box 6640
Wayne, PA 19087-8640

Please add $1.75 for shipping and handling for the first book and $.50 for each book thereafter. NY, NYC, and PA residents, please add appropriate sales tax. No cash, stamps, or C.O.D.s. All orders shipped within 6 weeks via postal service book rate. Canadian orders require $2.00 extra postage and must be paid in U.S. dollars through a U.S. banking facility.

Name_____
Address_____
City_____ State_____ Zip_____
I have enclosed $_____ in payment for the checked book(s).
Payment <u>must</u> accompany all orders. ❏ Please send a free catalog.